Dreams From the Edge of Reality

27 Frightening, Funny, and Fantastic Tales

Phil Giunta

This is a work of fiction. All the characters and events portrayed in this book are fictitious, and any resemblance to real people or events is purely coincidental.

Paperback ISBN: 979-8-9876328-4-0

eBook ISBN: 979-8-9876328-5-7

June 2026

Cover Art by Elena Schweitzer (egal) via iStock

Cover Design by Christopher D. Ochs

Find more books by Phil Giunta at:

https://www.philgiunta.com

"Phil Giunta weaves a tapestry of real magic with these tales of darkness, hope, fear, and wonder. *Dreams from the Edge of Reality* takes us from the shadows of the heart to the farthest reaches of nightmare!"

— Jonathan Maberry, New York Times bestselling author of *Red Empire* and *Ghosts of the Void* and five-time Bram Stoker Award winner

"Lots of people write scary stories. It takes a writer like Phil Giunta to find the humanity in them. You'll never look at a ghost the same way again."

— Michael Jan Friedman, New York Times bestselling author

"*Dreams from the Edge of Reality* presents twenty-seven "What if...?" tales spawned by the prolific imagination of Phil Giunta. Ranging from mysterious to macabre, fantastical to funny, this collection should entertain any reader with the fortitude to follow that fogbound road deep into *Twilight Zone* territory."

— Howard Weinstein, New York Times bestseller and author of *Galloway's Gamble*, winner of the Western Fictioneers Peacemaker Award

All that we see or seem is but a dream within a dream.

— Edgar Allan Poe

Contents

Introduction

In 1993, when I was young lad of—*ahem*—years old, I attended my first Shore Leave and Farpoint science fiction conventions in Hunt Valley, Maryland. In addition to the celebrity guests, I had the honor of meeting several writers whose work I admired.

I stood in line with my stack of *Star Trek* novels and comic books to be signed by such august wordsmiths as Peter David, Michael Jan Friedman, Robert Greenberger, Howard Weinstein, Steven H. Wilson, and others. While I was at it, I asked a lot of questions about writing and publishing and most of these fine gentlemen were all too happy to answer.

At the time, I'd been churning out fan fiction as a training exercise to see if I had the chops to craft engaging stories. While those early efforts were far from perfect, people who read my work were impressed enough to publish it in various fanzines. As much as I enjoyed playing in the sandboxes of *Star Trek, Star Wars, Indiana Jones*, and other popular franchises, the goal was to graduate from fan fic someday and create my own worlds, populated with original characters and their adventures.

That someday happened in 2007 when I was halfway through writing would become my first published novel, a paranormal mystery called *Testing the Prisoner.* By that time, self-publishing and small presses were beginning to flourish and Steven H. Wilson had self-published his first novel based on characters from his award-winning science fiction podcast series, *The Arbiter Chronicles.* At Farpoint that same year, I gave Steve an elevator pitch for *Testing the Prisoner* and he agreed to read it for potential publication through his new imprint, Firebringer Press.

That novel was launched at Farpoint in 2010 along with my part-time writing career. Shore Leave brought me in as an author guest a few months later and I've had the honor of attending both cons, and many others, in that capacity ever since. Fast forward fifteen years and I started scribbling this introduction at Shore Leave 45 in Lancaster, Pennsylvania.

At one of those early cons, Howard Weinstein said to me, "Once you hit twenty-five, time starts flying by." How right you were, Howie. Decades pass. Memories accumulate. People come and go. At my age, they're mostly going. Too many have already gone. As of this writing, it's been six weeks since the brilliant and prolific Peter David left this world, a fact that even now is difficult for me to process.

While I only have three published novels under my belt (a fourth is in progress), I've penned nearly three dozen short stories across multiple genres (with more on the way) and edited several anthologies for various publishers.

This book is a compilation of most of those short stories. Why not all of them? Well, my first two were part of a shared world anthology series called *ReDeus* by Crazy 8 Press and are owned by that publisher in perpetuity, so I did not include them here. It should be noted that Crazy 8 Press was formed by Peter David, Michael Jan Friedman, Robert Greenberger, Aaron Rosenberg, Howard Weinstein, and Glenn Hauman.

They've grown over the years and have added more writers to their stable.

What if all of the ancient gods from every pantheon around the world returned in the 21st century? That was the premise of *ReDeus,* created by Bob Greenberger, Aaron Rosenberg, and Paul Kupperberg, all long established writers of media tie-in books, comics, and original works. I had a blast contributing to that series and am as grateful to Bob, Aaron, and Paul as I am to Steve Wilson for giving me my start in this wild and wacky business.

I've also penned several science fiction and space opera stories that have been published in various anthologies and magazines over the years. Although I didn't plan it this way, they ended up being set in the same distant (and fictionalized) region of our galaxy. Thus, I intend to release them in a separate collection in the near future.

So those stories ain't in this book, but let me tell you about the ones that are.

This collection is comprised mostly of reprints, with two exceptions. "Man to Man" and my Sherlock Holmes tale, "The Five-Day Killer," are presented here for the first time.

I live on the East Coast of the United States and as an aspiring beach bum, I long ago developed an affinity for the Delaware coast. The stretch from Lewes to Fenwick Island is a local paradise to me and as it happens, there was a small niche publisher there called Cat & Mouse Press. They specialized in novels and anthologies set along the Delaware, Maryland, and Virginia (Delmarva) coasts. Four of the five beach stories in this collection were published in Cat & Mouse anthologies between 2016 and 2021 including "Tower Sixteen," "Tapestry," "The Celestials," and "Where Do I Begin?"

"Tower Sixteen" was published in *Beach Nights* and won second place in the 2016 Rehoboth Beach Reads contest sponsored by Cat & Mouse and one of the best indie bookshops around, Browseabout Books.

My fifth Delaware beach story, “Pearl of Great Price,” was published in 2023 by Hawkshaw Press in their detective noir anthology, *Hard-Boiled and Loaded with Sin* (a title I had hoped to use for my autobiography, but I digress).

One of the many features that captivates me about the Delaware coast is the system of WWII fire control towers that are featured in “Tower Sixteen” and “Pearl of Great Price.” The first one that opened to the public was Tower #7 near Fort Miles in Cape Henlopen State Park. Thanks to donations, Sussex County legislators, and the efforts of the Delaware Seashore Preservation Foundation, Tower #3 was restored and opened to the public in April 2023.

I can’t visit “slower, lower Delaware” without climbing the spiral steps of both towers to take in the gorgeous views of the ocean and bay. The Delaware coast is a magical place that never fails to ease my stress and bring me peace, so I jumped at the chance to write stories set there.

As a member of the Greater Lehigh Valley Writers Group in Pennsylvania, I'm honored to be part of the team that produces our biennial anthology every odd year. Our most recent volume, *Writing a Wrong*, was published in March 2025 and includes my paranormal mystery “Give Them Peace” starring psychic-medium Miranda Lorensen from my award-winning novels, *Testing the Prisoner* and *By Your Side*.

That story, plus “Help Me Rise,” “Once More with Feeling,” and “Memory Lane Ain't What it Used to Be,” are all in this collection. I recently volunteered to spearhead the group's 2027 anthology.

Ever since I was a kid, I've had a fondness for old-fashioned ghost stories and there is no shortage of them among these pages. In addition to the aforementioned “Tower Sixteen” and “Give Them Peace,” I've included “Bottom of the Hour” about a haunted car, "So Hungry..." about a haunted mesa in New Mexico, and "Burn After Writing," dedicated to my one of my literary heroes, Harlan Ellison.

But wait! There's more. You'll also get two tales about haunted pictures. "Photos from the Attic" deals with a box of cursed photographs while "Before She's Gone Forever" goes digital. The latter was nominated for a Pushcart Prize.

"Where Halloween Never Ends" offers a unique twist on the haunted corn mazes that are so popular during the spooky season and "Don't Go Fussin' Over Me" could be considered a ghost story depending on the reliability of the protagonist's point of view. I'll leave that up to you to decide.

What happens when a fugitive, a priest, and a possessed teenager walk into a church? You get one of the darkest stories I ever wrote, "Break and Enter."

My one and only time travel yarn to date, "A Thorne in Time," came about when editor and writer pal, Ann Stolinsky of Celestial Echo Press, invited me to contribute to *Ruth and Ann's Guide to Time Travel* in early 2024. Ann and her partner in crime, Ruth Littner, received enough solid submissions for two volumes. My story appears in volume one.

The timing of Ann's invitation was impeccable. I'd been struggling with a bout of depression and anxiety for well over a year. During that time, I took a hiatus from writing new material to re-edit and self-publish a second edition of *Testing the Prisoner* and was starting to do the same for *By Your Side*. I had never written time travel before, but I don't like to shy away from a challenge.

Besides, when Celestial Echo Press started in 2019, I was busy with other projects and couldn't make time to submit to their first two anthologies. Thus, I didn't want to let this third opportunity pass and disappoint Ann who was kind enough to invite me and six other writers as the headliners. So, I buckled down and ended up producing one of the best short stories of my career. "A Thorne in Time" went on to win first place in the 2025 Pennsylvania Press Club Communications Contest.

Every October, I attend a writers retreat outside the small town of Ligonier, Pennsylvania nestled in the Laurel Highlands region of the Allegheny Mountains. I mentioned earlier that the Delaware coast is a magical place that brings me peace. Ligonier is another. The Mindful Writers Retreat is a small group of about 20 or so who gather at a lodge to spend a quiet five days immersed in writing, sharing meals, and hiking the trails. The autumn colors are glorious.

The year before I joined in 2018, the group decided to produce an anthology of stories called *Into the Woods*. Since then, we've published five more, each with a unique theme and each supporting a different charity. I have stories in four out of those five books and included three of them in this collection—"Limited Time Offer," "Where It's Needed Most," and "There's A Certain Magic About This Place."

The fourth is a science fiction comedy called "See You Around the Cosmos, Sweet Cheeks!" and might end up in the SF collection I plan to publish later. Haven't decided yet. Recently, the Mindful Writers announced a Halloween theme for our 2026 anthology and I'm already conjuring up a ghost story for it.

The centerpiece to this book, "The Forest for the Trees," is a mythology novelette set in 17th century Finland. It started life as one of three story ideas I pitched for *Beyond Borders*, the second installment in the aforementioned *ReDeus* series. The other two were a medical drama set in Ireland and a comedy that begins in the USA and travels to Luxembourg and France. The editors chose the comedy, which was the least developed idea, but turned out to be one my best stories. To be honest, I'm glad they didn't take "The Forest for the Trees" because it works much better set in 1697 than in modern day.

Later, I had occasion to write the Irish medical drama for an anthology called *Elsewhere in the Middle of Eternity* and after two or three working titles, I settled on the apropos "Life and Limb." You'll see why when you read it.

Rounding out this collection are "My New Shiny," a comedic urban fantasy about a warlock and a homeless man, and "Take a Cue from the Canine." This story about a boy and his dog remains close to my heart six years after it was published and still chokes me up at the end.

Thanks for letting me take you on this brief reminiscence. Here's hoping for 15 more years of fun, frightening, and fantastic tales and maybe a second volume of this collection. I appreciate your support for small press and independent writers.

Phil Giunta
August 2025

Tower Sixteen

Rehoboth Beach,
Delaware - Summer 2006

From atop the fire control towers, you could see forever. At least, that's the way it had seemed to 23-year-old Reggie Prell during the Second World War. Back then, Corporal Prell had been assigned to Fort Miles, where the Army had constructed a series of observation towers to protect the Delaware Bay from incursion by German vessels.

"Grandpa, is a battleship the same as a U-boat?"

More than sixty years had passed since those days. Now, Reggie stared out through the horizontal slit in the tower wall alongside his son, Craig, and eight-year-old granddaughter, Hannah. Outside, densely packed evergreens, awash in August sunlight, eventually gave way to the calm blue waters of the bay in the distance.

"No, a U-boat is a German submarine. The *U* stands for *Unterseeboot*, which means 'undersea boat.' Now, you see that other tower way over there?" Reggie pointed to the left and Hannah nodded. "These towers were built in pairs so we could triangulate the position of a ship out in the water and radio the coordinates back to base."

"You ever sink any ships, Grandpa?"

Reggie chuckled. "No, they never made it this far. You want a better view? Let's go to the top."

Craig lowered Hannah to the metal landing. "Are you sure you're up to it in this heat, Dad?"

"I'm eighty-four, boy. I'm not dead. Don't need you henpeckin' me. Got enough of that from your mother, God rest her soul. Now, fall in and forward *march.*"

THE TOP LEVEL of Observation Tower Seven in Cape Henlopen State Park allowed for a 360-degree view of the park and surrounding water. To their right, the white buildings and massive guns of Fort Miles were visible seventy-five feet below.

Hannah waved down at her mother, Candace, before gripping the chain-link fence with both hands. "I wish Mommy could see this."

"You know Mommy's scared of heights," Craig said.

Hannah pointed to the other tower they had seen earlier. "How many towers are there, Grandpa?"

"There were fifteen along the Delaware coast and four in Jersey," Reggie replied. "They tore down two in the Wildwoods years ago and there are only eleven left here."

"Thirteen," Craig said. "Unlucky number."

"They were built to last, at most, twenty years, and here we are, sixty-one years later. Pretty damn lucky, I'd say."

"How many soldiers were in each tower, Grandpa?"

Reggie shrugged. "About eight, give or take. Back in the day, there were no spiral steps. We had to climb a ladder all the way up and there was a wooden floor at every level. All those little windows near the bottom had glass in them." He sighed. "About the only thing left now is the concrete." *Just a shell of their former selves.*

Reggie looked at Hannah. “You know how long it took to build each tower?”

She shook her head.

Reggie held up a bent, gnarled finger. “One week, start to finish. They’d pour all the concrete in a day and...” Reggie trailed off, staring down at Fort Miles. All of the buildings were gone, and in their places stood olive drab tents. Several men in World War II army uniforms hurried about. Still others were inspecting the guns.

“Dad, are you OK?”

Reggie frowned. “Must be some reenactment.”

“What are you talking about?”

Reggie nodded toward the fort. “All those men in uniforms down there, and those tents are like the ones that were there before the buildings.”

Craig followed Reggie’s gaze. “I only see a bunch of tourists taking pictures. Are you feeling all right? Maybe we should go back down. I think the heat and the walk up here might’ve been too much for you.”

“I’m fine.” Reggie removed his sunglasses and rubbed his eyes. When he looked again, the buildings were back and the soldiers were gone, replaced by the usual strolling sightseers. “I know what I saw...”

Although Reggie would never admit it, life had been lonely since Beverly died. They’d made a lot of friends after retiring to Rehoboth Beach, finally living in the house on Hickman Street that they’d rented out every summer for decades.

Still, everyone else had heard all of Reggie’s army stories more than once. Certainly, his son and daughter-in-law were sick of them by now. His granddaughter, on the other hand, was a fresh audience and her enthusiasm helped fill the void left by the loss of his wife—the grandmother that Hannah never met.

Of course, Reggie would never admit that, either. He had a cantankerous image to maintain.

The sight of Hannah and Candace approaching from the shoreline snapped Reggie out of his reverie. With drenched bathing suits and matted hair, each was carrying a bucket filled with water. Hannah dropped to her knees in the sand just beyond the shadow of Reggie's umbrella and emptied her bucket.

Candace set hers down and reached for a towel from one of the empty beach chairs. "Making a castle?"

Hannah shook her head. "A tower like the one we were in today with Grandpa."

With a smile, Craig looked over at his father. "See what you started?"

Reggie grunted a brief acknowledgement but had become distracted by a young man sporting the khaki shirt and matching trousers of a World War II army summer service uniform. The soldier strode purposefully across the beach, and as he drew near, Reggie was able to attach a name to the face. *That's impossible.*

"Zeke?" Reggie struggled to his feet, keeping his gaze fixed on the soldier, noting the rank insignia of technician fifth grade on the upper sleeve of his shirt. "It *is* you."

The soldier didn't weave around the horde of sunbathers and beach chairs in his way—he simply passed *through* them. Yet no one seemed to notice him, except for Reggie. The soldier disappeared behind a group of young people crowded under a canopy. Reggie waited, but the soldier never emerged.

Craig raised an eyebrow. "What are you looking at, Dad? Cute little honey catch your eye?"

Sidestepping Hannah's pile of wet sand, Reggie started off

across the beach. Craig shot up out of his chair and caught up with him easily. "Dad, where are you going?"

Reggie didn't reply. There was no time to explain and doing so would only cause Craig more concern about the state of his old man's mind. Finally, they reached the canopy, but the soldier was nowhere to be found. A petite young blonde in a blue-and-white bikini stepped away from her friends and smiled as she looked from Reggie to Craig.

"Hi! Lose something?"

Possibly my sanity. Reggie looked right and left. "He was just here."

"Who?"

Craig gently took Reggie by the arm. "No one, ma'am. I'm sorry to bother you. My father is just... having a moment."

"Gotcha. No worries. Have a good one, guys!"

"Come on, Dad. Let's head back to the house and get cleaned up for dinner."

This time, Reggie didn't protest. Perhaps Craig had cause to be concerned.

~

"Ever since Mom died, I've been worried about him," Craig said. "I knew letting him live here alone was a bad idea. Seems like he's declining fast."

"Maybe it's time to consider a nursing home—one that's closer to us."

"He won't leave Rehoboth without a fight."

"Well, then, I'm sure we can find something for him around here."

In the hallway just outside his spare bedroom, Reggie leaned against the wall, listening to the exchange between his son and daughter-in-law. The door was ajar, allowing him to remain out of sight. It hadn't been his intention to eavesdrop, but damn it, this was his home! No one had a right to conspire behind his back and make decisions about his life. *There's only one way I'm leavin' this house—*

"Grandpa, what are you doing?"

Reggie spun to see Hannah standing behind him. "Don't scare an old man like that," he whispered. "I was just... heading downstairs."

"Can you tell me more stories about the army?"

After a brief pause, Reggie smiled. "I can do better than that. I can *show* you."

Reggie found his old photo album and he and Hannah sat down at the dining room table. Hannah pointed to a picture of one soldier saluting another. "Is that you? You were skinny."

"Yep, that's me as a corporal saluting one of my superior officers, Captain Trusten D. Lee."

Hannah raised her right hand to her forehead in a mock salute.

"No, no. That looks like you're shading your eyes from the sun. Let me show you a proper salute. Stand up and face me."

Reggie and Hannah rose from their seats and stood about four feet apart.

"Straighten up, soldier. Shoulders back. Posture is critical to a proper salute. Start with your right arm straight at your side, hand flat, all fingers together. Now, raise your hand quickly to your brow like this." Reggie snapped his hand up at a slant, index finger gently touching his eyebrow.

Hannah mimicked the movement, albeit clumsily.

"Your upper arm should be parallel to the ground and your forearm at a forty-five-degree angle, just like mine."

Hannah adjusted her arm accordingly.

"Now, turn your hand so that neither the palm nor the back are visible."

Hannah twisted her hand back and forth a few times until she decided it was correct.

"Better. Now drop your arm quickly to your side like this." Reggie lowered his arm in one swift chopping motion.

Hannah did likewise.

"Very good. Might make a soldier out of you yet."

"Not if I have anything to say about it."

Reggie turned to find Candace standing in the doorway. "Time for bed, Hannah, if you want to be rested up for Jungle Jim's tomorrow."

"After Jungle Jim's can we go see some more towers, Grandpa?"

Reggie shrugged. "Sure, if your parents are OK with it. We can't go inside the other ones, but we can see 'em. Maybe even walk up to a few of 'em."

Everyone was fast asleep by the time Reggie crept out of the house for his usual midnight stroll along the boardwalk. There were still plenty of night owls milling about, but as Reggie passed Rehoboth Avenue, their numbers dwindled. By the time he reached Olive Avenue, there was no sign of life at all. Even Obie's outdoor patio was devoid of the usual party crowd.

Reggie glanced over his shoulder and stopped, incredulous at the sight of a boardwalk utterly deserted. *Where the hell did everyone go?*

Shivering against an unseasonably cool ocean breeze, he gazed up at the Edgewater House and over at the Boardwalk Plaza. The balconies were all empty. *Lights are on, but no one's home.*

Further north, from the direction of the Henlopen Hotel,

the sound of heavy footfalls gave Reggie hope that he wasn't entirely alone in the night.

Under the boardwalk lights, a group of men jogged toward him. They formed two lines, leaving a gap between them. Even at this distance, it was clear they weren't dressed for summer—but rather for a war that ended sixty years ago.

He recognized the combat uniforms and M1 rifles slung over their shoulders. While Reggie's mind screamed at him to get out of their way, his legs refused to budge.

Four soldiers passed him on either side without so much as a nod.

Reggie recognized the last man on the right as the same one from the beach. "Zeke? Zeke, it's me, Reggie!"

He reached out to grab Zeke's arm, only to grip thin air. Reggie stared as the unit continued on—all but Zeke, who fell out of formation just long enough to give Reggie a casual salute before catching up with the others. Reggie felt another tremor in his chest, but there was no sea breeze this time.

The men turned and vanished down Rehoboth Avenue. Reggie knew it would be useless to follow.

"Grandpa?"

Reggie's frozen legs nearly buckled. "Hannah!"

All around them, life returned to Rehoboth. Obie's came alive with music and laughter. People chatted on balconies.

"Hannah, it's after midnight. What are you doing out here?"

"I followed you."

"Where are your parents?"

"Asleep."

Reggie rubbed his forehead. "I need to sit down a moment."

He led Hannah to one of the white benches and they sat facing the beach. Reggie reached into the pocket of his cargo shorts. After looking around, he pulled out a metal flask and downed a quick snort.

"What's that?"

"Scotch. Don't tell your parents you saw me drinking this. They're looking for any excuse to put me away."

"I won't say a word. Why are you out so late, Grandpa?"

"Oh, I sometimes take walks late at night when the air is cooler and the stars are out. We really should start heading back. If your parents find out you're out here with me, we'll both be in for it. On the way, I'll tell you another story about the towers."

Reggie took her hand as they strolled along the boardwalk. "Do you remember how many were built here in Delaware?"

"You said fifteen."

"Right, and the four in Jersey were numbered twenty-three through twenty-six."

"What happened to the numbers in between?"

"Funny you should ask. Some of us in the battery used to joke that when we died someday, we'd all go to the big tower in the sky. From there, we would look out for the rest of our brothers-in-arms, keep them safe. After a while, we started calling that Tower Sixteen. It became sort of a code.

"Over the past decade or so, many of the guys have... passed away. We ain't getting any younger. The rest of us would see each other at the funerals and we'd say that Ben, or Dwight, or Paul, or... anyway, we'd say they went to Tower Sixteen and we'd all know what that meant.

"I got a letter in the mail last week from a lady whose father served with me at Fort Miles. Zeke Watkins. He and I often worked the same shift in the tower. Anyway, Zeke died a month ago. His daughter even wrote in the letter that he went to Tower Sixteen."

Hannah squeezed his hand as they turned off the boardwalk onto Hickman Street. "I don't want you to go away, Grandpa. Not to a nursing home or Tower Sixteen."

Reggie smiled. "Me neither."

They continued in silence until they neared the house.

Reggie opened the storm door slowly, letting Hannah enter first. "All right let's be quiet now. Don't want to wake your parents." He took one last glance toward the boardwalk but couldn't see beyond the silhouettes of the eight soldiers standing shoulder-to-shoulder across the intersection.

THE FOLLOWING EVENING, after returning from dinner at Grotto Pizza, Candace ushered Hannah out to the backyard, leaving the men alone in the living room. Reggie knew immediately that something was amiss. His suspicions were confirmed when Craig motioned toward Reggie's favorite easy chair.

"Dad, do you have a minute to chat?"

Reggie shrugged. "Where else am I going?" He lowered himself into the chair and settled in for what would undoubtedly be an uncomfortable conversation.

"We've been concerned about you lately."

"So I noticed." Reggie leaned forward. "Why don't we get to the point, boy? You want to put me in a home because you think I'm losing my mind, especially after my behavior over the last few days. Well, I don't blame you."

Craig stared at him for a moment. "I'm... glad you're being reasonable about this. I've been worried about you living here by yourself these past nine years."

"And yet I've managed pretty damn well on my own. I have a lot of friends here in Rehoboth and we look after each other."

"But they can't be with you twenty-four seven." Craig

waved toward the stairs to the second floor. "What if you fall down these steps—or worse, the basement steps—and crack your head open on the concrete floor?"

Reggie held up his hands. "I'm not arguing, Craig. Every man should know his limits. Tell you what, how about I sleep on it tonight and we'll discuss it again tomorrow—I promise."

~

Once again, Hannah waited until Grandpa reached the corner of Hickman and King Charles before setting off after him. This time, she wore sneakers instead of flip-flops and made sure to stay far back so he wouldn't hear her.

By the time she caught up with him, Grandpa was standing at the top of the closest ramp that led down to the beach. Hannah approached slowly, wondering what he was staring at.

"Grandpa?"

He turned, slowly this time, as if expecting her. That's when she saw the concrete tower at the end of the beach looming above the crashing waves.

Hannah stood beside him. "How did that get there?"

"It's the real reason I've been taking these late-night strolls. I've been waiting for it since I learned about Zeke, and now it's finally come for me."

Hannah's head snapped up to look at him with wide eyes. "Is that—?"

Grandpa nodded. "Maybe from there, I'll find your grandma again."

"No!" Hannah shook her head and threw her arms around his waist. "You can't go. I don't want you to go!"

"It's OK, Hannah."

"No, it isn't!" Tears clouded her eyes, but she didn't care. All that mattered was keeping Grandpa here with her.

He lowered himself to one knee and reached under his collar. He lifted a beaded chain over his head and held up two small metal plates. "These are my dog tags. I won't need them where I'm going." He slipped them over Hannah's head. "Now, you tuck these under your shirt and keep me close to your heart and I'll keep you close to mine. Always know that I'm looking out for you no matter where I am."

With that, Grandpa leaned forward and kissed her on the forehead before making his way down the ramp to the beach. Tears welled up in Hannah's eyes as she ran after him, but the sight of the tower, something that once excited her, now filled her with dread. She stopped and watched as he walked toward it, then disappeared inside.

BACK AT GRANDPA'S HOUSE, Hannah found her mom standing outside. Tears streaked her face. "Hannah Prell, where have you been? We looked all over the place for you!"

Hannah was nearly out of breath from running. "I was with... Grandpa on the beach. The tower... came for him."

Her mother shook her head and took Hannah into her arms. "Tower? No, sweetie, that's impossible. You couldn't have been with Grandpa. Your father went to check on him earlier and... God, I don't know how to tell you this. Grandpa died in his sleep."

Hannah pulled back and shook her head. "No. Grandpa went into the tower with the other soldiers."

Her dad emerged from the house. "Girl, where have you—?"

"I'll show you. The tower's out there on the beach. Come on!" Hannah broke free of her mother's grasp and ran back toward the boardwalk at full tilt.

~

Hannah's parents caught up with her at the end of the ramp. They peered in awe at the tower along the shoreline just as a group of soldiers filed out. As they lined up on either side of the door, Hannah counted eight of them. Then, a skinny young man with short brown hair stepped out of the tower. He wore an old-style army uniform, just like in Grandpa's pictures.

Hannah wiped her eyes and looked at his face. He wasn't just one of the men from Grandpa's pictures, he was—

"Grandpa?"

Craig stepped onto the sand. "Dad?" He began running, with Hannah keeping pace beside him.

"Grandpa!" Hannah stumbled as she neared the tower, falling to her knees in the sand.

Grandpa stood over her. "On your feet, soldier. Straighten up. Shoulders back." He raised his right hand sharply to his eyebrow. Hannah picked herself up and returned the salute, just like Grandpa had taught her. Then, he turned to his son. "I'm afraid a nursing home just ain't for me, boy."

It was now Craig's turn to cry. "Dad, wait..."

"I'll be sure to give your mother your love." With one last smile, Corporal Reggie Prell turned and stepped into the tower.

The other soldiers followed.

The door closed.

And, as Hannah saluted one final time, Tower Sixteen faded into the night.

~

This story first appeared in *Beach Nights* (Cat & Mouse Press, October 2016).

A Thorne in Time

Captain Garrett McNally straightened his tie as he marched along the concrete walkway that led from the driveway to the front of the sprawling Thorne Mansion. The weed-infested gardens and overgrown lawn clashed with his memory of the last time he stepped foot on this property twelve years ago. Every inch of the place had been immaculate then—a paradise at the edge of the city.

Its luster had since faded and McNally couldn't help but wonder if that began the moment he informed Robert and Emily Thorne that their daughter, Tanya, had been the latest victim of a serial killer at the tender age of twenty-two. Robert suffered a fatal stroke a few days later and Emily lost her battle with cancer six years after that. As far as McNally knew, Tanya's twin sister Noreen still lived here, alone.

He jogged up the steps to the portico where two dead plants in mold-covered cement pots flanked a weathered mahogany door in dire need of a cleaning and new finish. He rang the camera doorbell. A few seconds later, a form undulated in the frosted privacy glass before the door swung open. McNally had expected to be greeted by a woman in her mid-thirties, but Noreen's salt and pepper hair, tired eyes, and drawn complexion lent her the appearance of someone much older.

"Ms. Thorne. It's been a long time."

"So long in fact that it's *Doctor* Thorne now. Nice to see you again, Captain. Please, come in. I appreciate you driving all the way out here so soon after I called. Can I get you anything? Water, coffee...?"

"No, thank you. I'm good. When you said you had new information regarding the Westside Slasher case, I cleared the rest of my day."

"Well, I hope to make it worth your time." She closed the door behind him. "Let's go to my office. So, how's your daughter these days?"

"Darla's doing well. Joined a new law firm not too far from here. Still misses Tanya. Talks about her once in a while."

"They were closer than anyone realized back then."

She led him down a short hallway to a room with four large monitors mounted in a square formation above a cluttered desk. They were connected to a single laptop by a tangle of cables and adapters.

Thorne tapped the space bar. Every screen lit up, each with a video file ready to play. "I must ask you to indulge me, Captain. Twelve years ago, the first victim of the Westside Slasher was Sarah Peretti. Do you recall his sixth and final victim?"

"Of course." McNally cocked his head. "It was your sister."

"Are you sure about that?" She grabbed the mouse and clicked the play button on the first screen. An anchorman with Channel 14 News shifted in his seat. "The sixth victim of the Westside Slasher has been identified as twenty-eight-year-old Mae Kaplan of Roycetown. Kaplan worked for MacHale

Medical Center, just three blocks from where she was attacked and stabbed seven times. Police are—"

Thorne stopped the video.

"That's not right." McNally frowned. "I don't recognize that name and as the detective on the case, I remember every victim."

"What about this one?" Thorne launched the video on the second monitor.

"The sixth victim of the Westside Slasher has been identified as twenty-one-year-old Hailey Mahlberg of Bartlett Village," the same anchorman reported. "Mahlberg was a senior at Declan University—"

"Hailey Mahlberg was the third victim not the last one," McNally said. "What is this?"

"As I said, Captain, indulge me." Thorne slid the mouse to the third screen and clicked play.

"The sixth victim of the Westside Slasher has been identified as thirty-year-old Deb Webb, a mother of three and math teacher at Upper Carlton Middle School. Police are—"

"Are these deepfakes? Did you use AI to fabricate them?"

"I don't have access to that kind of technology." Thorne folded her arms and leaned against the desk. "Even if I did, I wouldn't use it to disrespect these women, especially since my sister was one of them. What you watched are three videos from three different timelines."

"Come again?"

"I don't have the tools to make deepfakes, Captain, but what if I had something that could help you stop the Westside Slasher before he claimed his first victim?"

McNally snickered. "Like what, a time machine?"

~

"A more accurate term would be time portal. Beautiful, isn't it?"

In the center of Thorne's sub-basement lab, McNally gaped at the gray metal arch that stood floor to ceiling. Several pairs of colored cables wrapped around its thick metal framework, terminating in scattered sockets where small green and amber lights pulsed and flashed. A shimmering, translucent field of pale blue filled the span beneath the arch. Across the room, four monitors were mounted on the wall above a long white counter, reminiscent of the office upstairs.

McNally paced around the arch, examining every detail, before shooting a sidelong glance at Thorne. "You gotta be kiddin' me."

"It's no joke, Captain. Those videos I showed you were the result of my three failed attempts to save Tanya's life in the past, which spawned three alternate timelines. Originally, she was the slasher's second victim. Each time I traveled back, I managed to steer her out of harm's way only for her to be murdered somewhere else a few days later. In the process, the list of victims always changed."

McNally rubbed his forehead as the reality of Thorne's words set in. "So every move you made had a kind of butterfly effect."

"Right, but where you and everyone else remembers only the final sequence of murders—the *current* timeline—I remember all four timelines, perhaps because I was tethered to the time portal. The computers in the house are all connected to the arch, which allowed me to save the videos I showed you from each timeline."

"How long did it take you to build this?"

"It was my father's invention. He spent two decades designing it and working out the math before constructing the arch. All he wanted to do was explore history, but he died before the portal was finished. So, I dedicated the past twelve years to learning the science behind it and making a few upgrades."

"How does it work?"

"I could show you fifty-five pages of equations." From the pocket of her cardigan, Thorne produced a small device with a screen displaying several rows of icons, similar to a phone. Its edges glowed with the same blue light as the arch. "Or we could just take a trip."

"You control your time travels with that?"

"Correct again. I leave through the arch and when I need to return, this handheld controller generates a portal back to it. I have two of these devices, should you decide to help me."

"I'm listening."

"Regardless of the changes in the timelines, a few things remained the same. The first victim was always Sarah Peretti, you were the detective assigned to the case, the murders stopped after six, and the killer was never caught. Now we have the perfect opportunity to stop this bastard before he even gets started."

"You want me to go with you twelve years into the past and catch the Westside Slasher before he becomes the Westside Slasher?"

"That about sums it up."

McNally laughed. "This is insane."

"Captain, when you came here twelve years ago to tell us that my sister had been murdered, I peppered you with questions about whether you had any suspects or witnesses or any leads at all. Do you remember what you told me?"

"I couldn't say much. It was an open investigation. Technically, it still is. But I believe I said I wouldn't give up until I found the killer."

"I'm offering you that chance now, Captain. Please help me save my sister."

Dried leaves crunched underfoot as McNally and Thorne emerged from the arch into darkness. A short distance ahead, through a cluster of pine trees, lampposts illuminated a paved trail lined with the occasional park bench.

McNally whirled in time to watch the arch and the lab fade into the night as if they had been nothing more than a mirage. He flexed his hands and shook his arms until the tingling subsided.

"Sorry. Should've warned you about that," Thorne said. "I got used to it by the third trip."

"Where are we... or should I say *when*?"

"Cannon Park. October 11, 2012." Thorne glanced at the controller. "It's 9:03 p.m. Sarah Peretti will be killed nearby in about ten minutes. Let's get to the trail. She should be here soon."

When they reached the edge of the tree line, McNally held up a hand. He waved Thorne back into the shadows as four chatty teens sauntered by. No sooner were they out of sight than Sarah hurried into view from the opposite direction. Once she passed, Thorne started after her.

"Wait." McNally gripped her hand. "Slow down. We're a couple on an evening stroll."

After looking both ways, they crept onto the trail unseen and maintained a casual pace behind Sarah. The distant cacophony of city traffic, car horns, and street music meant that the park's entrance was about a quarter mile around the next bend.

"This is surreal," McNally whispered. "Seeing her alive."

"Tell me about it. Stay sharp. Should be any second now."

McNally slid a hand inside his jacket, fingertips brushing the grip of his gun. Minutes passed as they rounded the bend. The park entrance was now in sight. Sarah quickened her pace and jogged up the short flight of steps to the street where she joined a group of people waiting at the corner bus stop. Thorne and McNally ambled out of the park and turned left.

"Let's hang out here and make sure she gets on the bus," McNally said.

"Do you think we scared the killer off by following her?"

Thorne's question was answered by a scream from the park.

"Stay here." McNally dashed back to the entrance and down the steps. He rounded the bend to find three people standing over a woman lying prone on the trail. Two others knelt beside her, hands pressing a jacket against her abdomen.

"What's going on here?" he called.

"Some guy came out of the woods and jumped her." A middle-aged man pointed toward the same tree line from which McNally and Thorne had emerged earlier. "Stabbed her a few times then took off that way. We called for an ambulance."

McNally reached for his badge, but hesitated. "Did you get a good look at him?"

"Skinny dude, about six foot. Couldn't see his face. He was wearing a dark hoodie."

"Goddammit! OK. I'll meet the ambulance crew at the entrance and direct them this way. Keep pressure on her wounds."

Thorne met him at the bottom of the steps. "Sarah got on the bus. What happened?"

"I think you were right. We scared him off long enough to save Sarah's life, so he waited for the next lone woman to come along. Some people are helping her now. Ambulance is on the way. Her name is Kelly something... Kelly... Mueller. Shit. I see what you mean about parallel memories. Now, I recall both Sarah *and* Kelly as his first victims. The good news is that Kelly will survive, but nobody saw the guy's face."

Thorne dropped onto a park bench. "I changed history again."

"No, *we* changed history. Question is, what do we do now?"

"In the current timeline, his second victim was Abby LaRuthe."

"Right. She'll be killed three days from now in the Harrison Street parking garage around 10:30 pm."

"Then that's where we go next."

On the third level of the Harrison Street garage, Abby LaRuthe backed her SUV out of a parking space and turned out of sight down the exit ramp.

McNally searched the area but found no hooded figures lurking between the cars or watching from the stairwell. "We didn't scare him off this time, because he ain't here."

"By saving Sarah, we altered the timeline," Thorne said. "And his choice of victims is changing again. Abby was spared, but who's next?"

On the street below, whooping sirens and blaring horns drew near, echoing through the garage. Flashing red and blue lights reflected off darkened windows of nearby buildings. McNally and Thorne hurried to the edge of the parking deck as three police cars and an ambulance pushed through traffic.

"Looks like they're stopping near Declan University." McNally nodded toward the exit. "Let's get down there and see what's happening."

No sooner had they emerged from the stairwell onto the street than McNally gasped. "Darla..."

"Oh no, Captain. Your daughter—"

"She's dead. He killed her instead of Abby. I remember now. Darla's his new second victim!"

He bolted down the street toward the campus. Thorne caught up with him weaving his way through a throng of onlookers gathered along the fence outside Declan's administration building. In the adjacent parking lot, two men unloaded a gurney from an ambulance and rolled it up the walkway.

"God, no. Please." McNally turned away and slumped against the wrought iron fence. "Not my little girl. She's all I have."

Thorne squeezed in beside him and spoke in a low voice. "Captain, listen to me. There's nothing you can do for her here, but—"

"She was walking back from the gym to meet your sister. I remember her lying up there on top of the hill covered in blood after being stabbed seven times just like Abby LaRuthe in the parking garage before we changed history."

"I know, but if we could save Sarah, we can do the same for Darla."

McNally slammed the heel of his hand against the wrought iron picket. "Every time you try to save one, another dies." He leaned toward her, his voice simmering. "All you've done with that damn time portal is leave a trail of bodies in your wake and now my daughter's one of them."

"I never meant for that to happen and among your new memories you'll note that my sister will be murdered two days from now, but we can stop all of this." Thorne produced the handheld controller from her pocket. "The past isn't written in stone."

McNally sighed. "I'd love to tell you where to shove that fuckin' thing, but I don't have a choice now. What's your plan this time?"

"We travel back a few hours. You call Darla and tell her whatever you can think of to keep her from leaving the gym. We'll give this asshole a different target."

"Who?"

Thorne cocked her head.

"Hell no. I can't let you do that. You're a civilian." McNally fixed his gaze on an unmarked sedan pulling into the parking lot. "I have a better idea. We go back and call in an anonymous tip that there's a guy on campus with a knife, stalking women, but we're gonna need backup, and I know just the guy who can help."

A moment later, Lieutenant Garrett McNally climbed out of the driver's seat of the sedan and approached two uniformed cops chatting beside the ambulance. After a brief conversation, he charged off toward the administration building with the officers in tow.

"Captain, we should minimize contact with our younger selves. That could lead to severe complications."

"Look, you might have figured out time travel, but when it comes to police work, we do things my way. You called me for help, so trust me to do my job—in the present *and* the past."

IN THE WOMEN'S locker room, Darla McNally pulled her buzzing phone from the side pocket of her gym bag and pressed the speaker button. "What's up, Dad?"

"So good to hear your voice, kiddo. Where are you now?"

She finished buttoning her shirt and slipped on her jacket. "Heading out of the gym to meet Tanya. You OK, Dad? You sound upset."

"I need you to stay there. Do not leave the building."

"What's going on?"

"We're putting the campus on lockdown. I'll explain later. Just hang tight until you hear from me, okay?"

"Will do. Be careful, Dad. Love you."

"Always. Love you, too."

Darla ended the call and started another. "Hey, babe. I'm gonna be late. My dad just called. The campus is going on lockdown. There's some kind of security problem over here and I'm stuck in the gym until it's over. So wherever you are, you might want to stay there for now."

"I'm walking across campus on my way to you," Tanya said. "The closest building is Student Services. I'll duck in there until—"

"Tanya, you broke up. Can you hear me? Tanya?"

The only response was a muffled scream.

IN THE SECURITY office at Declan University, Lieutenant McNally addressed four campus guards and six plainclothes officers. The latter looked young enough to pass as students.

"We got an anonymous tip about a guy armed with a knife stalking women on campus," McNally began. "From the description, we believe it's the same guy who stabbed a woman multiple times in Cannon Park last week. Tall, thin, wearing a dark hoodie. That's all we have to go on. We have some uniformed officers on the way to help with the search—excuse me."

He reached into his coat pocket and pulled out his buzzing phone. "Darla, you OK?"

"Dad, I was just speaking with Tanya. She was walking across campus to meet me. I told her about the lockdown. She was going to wait it out in Student Services but then she screamed and the call cut off."

"We're on our way there."

"That scream came from back here." With Thorne by his side, Captain McNally charged around the corner of the Student Services Building. He leveled his gun at a hooded figure kneeling over a woman lying prone on the grass. The beam from Thorne's flashlight glinted off the blade in the man's raised hand.

"Don't do it!" McNally inched closer. "Toss the knife and put your hands on your head."

"Just another fuckin' bitch that thinks she's too good to talk to me."

"I don't care. Toss the knife or I will put you down. You're wanted on one count of attempted murder. Don't make it two."

"The fuck you talkin' about?"

"We know you attacked a woman in Cannon Park last week."

"Fuck you both." With that, the man leapt to his feet and bolted around the opposite corner of the building.

"He's getting away again!" Thorne started forward.

McNally gripped her arm. "No, he isn't. Eddie Merko, drug addict and psychopath, is about to collide with eight cops led by a young and dashing Lieutenant McNally. Wait for it... Wait for it."

"Stop!" A familiar voice shouted. "Drop the knife and get on your knees!"

"It's finally over." McNally opened his jacket and tucked his gun back into its holster before turning his attention to the woman who was now curled up on her side, clutching her stomach. "Ma'am, are you OK? We'll have an ambulance here soon."

Thorne knelt beside her, holding the flashlight at an angle that allowed her to see the woman's face without blinding her. "Tanya! Oh my God. Are you—"

"I'm fine. Just... got the wind knocked out of me when he... slammed me to the ground." She sat up with help from McNally. "Noreen? You look... different. What are you doing here?"

"That's a complicated story for another time." She slipped an arm around her sister. "I'm just glad you're alive."

"You and me both. That was the creep who tried to chat up Darla and me at the bar down the street a few nights ago. He got pissed when we asked him to leave us alone. Never imagined he'd stalk me here." Tanya glanced up at McNally. "Do we know each other?"

"Not yet, but we will soon." He pulled the handheld controller from his jacket pocket. "Doctor, I shouldn't be here when those cops show up, but I imagine you want to stay with your sister for a while?"

"I'll meet you back at the lab."

"What lab?" Tanya asked. "And when did you become a doctor?"

"Which of these icons do I tap to get back to the arch?"

"I locked your controller so only the blue button works," Noreen said. "You'll get back one hour after we left."

"Got it. I'm goin' down the street to grab a beer first. See you two later." No sooner had Captain McNally trudged off into the darkness than Lieutenant McNally arrived from the opposite direction with four cops in tow. "Are you ladies OK?"

"Wait, you were just..." Tanya gaped at her sister. "Would someone please tell me what the hell is happening?"

ONE MONTH Later

With a bouquet of flowers in one hand and a gift bag in the other, McNally rang the doorbell at Thorne Mansion. On either side of the polished mahogany door, potted tiger lilies leaned toward the sun's rays stretching across the portico. Surrounding the home, pristine gardens and a sprawling, manicured lawn completed the image of an estate restored to its former glory. A paradise at the edge of the city.

McNally smiled at the sound of light music and laughter. Darla and Tanya's fifth anniversary party was in full swing.

Noreen Thorne stood in the open doorway, wine glass in hand. "About time you got here."

"Was that supposed to be a pun?" He held up the flowers. "These are for you."

"Thank you, Captain. They're lovely. Come in and join the festivities. Would you like a beer?"

"Just what the doctor ordered."

"Follow me, *mon capitain*."

"After what we've been through, you can call me Garrett."

"Only if you call me Noreen."

"Done. So, I'm curious." Garrett lowered his voice as they stepped into the kitchen. Outside on the patio, Tanya and Darla sat with their backs to the house holding hands and chatting with friends. "Now that you saved your sister, what are your plans for the time portal?"

"Not sure yet." Noreen retrieved a bottle of beer from the fridge and handed it to him. "I'll probably explore some interesting points in history. Why, you have something in mind?"

"As it happens, I've been considering retirement," McNally said. "But I ain't one for sitting around. You and I make a good team, and there are plenty of other past murders we could prevent in this town, including several unsolved cases."

"So many lives to save." Noreen tapped her wine glass against his bottle. "So *much* time."

~

THIS STORY first appeared in *Ruth and Ann's Guide to Time Travel* (Celestial Echo Press, August 2024).

Help Me Rise

"Damn it!" Ryleigh Noble cranked the steering wheel as a flash of lightning revealed yet another sharp bend in the secluded country road. "If I'd known we'd be driving home in a monsoon, I'd have canceled. No party is worth this. I can't see a friggin' thing out here."

Reclining in the passenger seat, her husband peered at his phone. "According to the forecast, it's just a pop-up storm. Should be over soon. Besides, when Molly Okan invites you to her house, you go. And look what happened. She asked you to open for her on her next tour."

"She was drunk, Dylan."

"But you weren't, despite the constant temptations." He straightened his seat and gave her thigh a gentle squeeze. "I'm proud of you."

"I wanted every drop."

"I know. Just take it slow. Want me to drive?"

"I'm not getting out of the car in this. I'll manage."

Dylan switched on the radio and began scrolling through XM stations. After a moment, he turned up the volume. "Ah, here's a classic."

"*When I'm drownin' in that unquenchable thirst of addiction...*"

Ryleigh rolled her eyes. "How can you not be sick of hearing that?"

"*...and I'm cruisin' blindly down the road to self-destruction...*"

"Your first top forty hit? Which, may I remind you, we wrote together?"

"Sorry, babe. I'm just trying to focus on—damn it!"

Through the downpour, headlights drifted into their lane on a direct collision course. Ryleigh stomped the brakes and punched the horn. The other car swerved out of view. Blinded by its high beams, she lost sight of the road. The ground dropped out from beneath them, sending the SUV careening down a steep embankment directly into a cluster of gnarled, broken trees.

A moment later, Ryleigh lifted her head from the deflating airbag and winced against the stabbing pain that flared through the base of her skull. Once her vision cleared, her gaze locked onto the bole of a tree that had smashed through the windshield on the passenger side. Where it had impacted the top of the seat, only a bloody mass remained. "Dylan... Oh, God, no..."

"*Help me rise above the darkness and carry me to the light.*"

Ryleigh's trembling hands unbuckled her seatbelt and threw open her door. She stumbled out of the crumpled SUV and collapsed into a patch of mud. Oblivious to the lashing downpour, she pushed herself to her knees and vomited. In her peripheral vision, headlights slowed to a halt at the top of the hill. As the rain washed away the former contents of her stomach, Ryleigh sat with her back against the side of the vehicle.

"*Help me rise to be worthy of the love I've been denied.*"

She wanted to reach in and shut off the goddamn radio

but couldn't bear to see her husband's crushed form again. Instead, Ryleigh crawled toward the back of the vehicle, every inch of her soaked party dress clinging to her skin. A man scrambled down the hill toward her. He shouted something about calling 9-1-1 and asked if everyone was okay.

"Help me rise above the reach of the demons in my mind."

"Shut up!" Sobbing now, Ryleigh pounded on the SUV. "Shut up! Dylan, no, please... Damn it... Damn it..."

Two Years Later

FROM INSIDE THE FARTHEST STALL, Ryleigh heard the women's muffled voices even before the ladies' room door squealed open.

"—so many people accused her of driving drunk and killing her husband, she had to shut down her social media accounts while she went back to rehab."

The other woman raised her voice over the hiss of running water. "Did she get arrested for DUI?"

"No, Dylan kept her sober. She went back to the bottle *after* he died."

"Well, some people just can't control their demons. She sounded great tonight, though."

"We'll see how long that lasts. Remember Amy Winehouse? Anyway, I'm good. You?"

"Yeah, let's go. You see that creepy guy in the back checking us out—"

Ryleigh waited until the women were out of earshot before flushing the toilet. *Perfect metaphor for my life...*

Five minutes later, she ambled out of the ladies' room, head bowed. She slipped behind the bar and hefted her guitar bag. "I'm in the wind, Henry."

"Hold on a sec, Rye." The bartender placed two bottles in front of a clingy couple on the opposite end of the bar and limped toward her. "Zack's got your money. Hey, those new songs were fantastic. Really got the customers excited. Every one of em's gonna be a hit. I know it."

Ryleigh slung the guitar bag over her shoulder. "Thanks, Henry. From your lips to God's ears. See you in two weeks?"

"You bet, hot stuff." He snapped his fingers and pointed at her. "Unless you rocket to stardom again before then."

She smiled and returned the gesture. *Again... because I crashed and burned the first time.*

Ryleigh found her manager scrolling through his phone in the last booth. As she approached, he slid an envelope across the table. "Already took my cut. You were great tonight, as always."

Ryleigh tucked the envelope inside her jacket. "I feel a 'but' coming—"

He slid out of the booth. "You could've at least opened with it."

"—as in you're a pain in my butt. Look, Zack, you've been my manager for three months and you're amazing. You work hard to get me gigs, you're letting me use your private studio to record my new album, and I appreciate that, but I told you when we started working together that I've cut 'Help Me Rise' from my set. I'm trying to put that life behind me and move on with the new stuff I wrote while I was... recovering."

"It's just one song, Rye."

"Exactly, so what's the problem?"

Zack's broad shoulders slumped.

"Hey, I'm not trying to be difficult." Ryleigh placed a gentle hand on his arm. Truth be told, she was attracted to him. More so that she'd ever admit—at least right now. "My reasons are personal. Someday, I'll explain it, I promise. Until then, I'm asking you to trust me."

"Personal, she says. Trust me, she says." Zack's expression softened. "Well, how can I not trust that face?" He held up his phone. "Good news. I just booked you for Musikfest in August."

"No friggin' way!" Ryleigh threw her arms around him and kissed him on the cheek.

"Yes friggin' way, and there's more. Hypatia is looking for a new lead singer. You know their songs, they know yours, and they've been anxious to work with you ever since I took you on."

Ryleigh pulled back. "Seriously? I'm in."

"Good. We'll work up a setlist of your stuff and theirs, but like it or not, when you start playing larger venues again, people will expect to hear 'Help Me Rise.' It's the song that put you on the charts."

"I know and I'll deal with that when the time comes. Trust me."

The excitement of the evening's gig and the news about Musikfest had long faded by the time Ryleigh showered and changed into sweatpants and a T-shirt. She collapsed onto her tattered sofa, propped her bare feet up on the coffee table, and sipped a glass of ginger ale. *Needs scotch, or bourbon, or tequila...*

Chiding herself for the thought, Ryleigh set the glass atop the end table beside her and exchanged it for a framed photo. Drawing a slow, deep breath, she rubbed her eyes and stared at the smiling faces of two newlyweds seated at an outdoor café in the Italian countryside of Vinci. While their waiter had barely understood English, he knew love when he saw it and volunteered to snap the picture.

While the memory replayed in her mind, Ryleigh let her

other hand drift to the ivory handle of a snub nose revolver on the cushion beside her. She closed her eyes and laid her head back. "Dylan... I don't know if I can do this again without you."

"Of course you can." At the opposite end of the sofa, Dylan turned to face her. "And I'm still here by the way. Always will be. Remember our motto? You didn't come this far—"

"Only to come this far," Ryleigh finished.

"You were on your way to the top, babe."

"Because of you."

"All I did was book the gigs and manage the money. You're the talent."

Ryleigh tightened her grip on the revolver. "You wrote my first hit song with me. You got me off the bottle... kept me sober. You gave me love and support when everyone else wrote me off. I don't know if I can make my way back alone."

"You're not alone. Depression and anxiety isolate you. You have friends."

"*Had* friends." Ryleigh slid the gun onto her lap. "Most of them were sycophants. They didn't care about me, only what they could take from me when I was... on the charts." She pressed the barrel behind her chin. "Just like you were taken from me."

Dylan leaned toward her. "Listen to me, Rye. The car accident wasn't your fault. You know that. If you loved me at all, please don't throw away everything we built together."

Relenting to tears that would not be stopped, Ryleigh let the gun slip from her grasp and clatter to the floor.

"Thank you." Dylan slid across the sofa and cupped his hand over hers. "You're a star, Rye. You have everything you need to make your way back to the top. Zack is a solid manager and a good man. He'll take you far, if you let him, but you need to control your demons. No one else will do it for you."

Ryleigh forced a smile. "I know."

"It would mean a lot to me if you would sing 'Help Me Rise' again."

"You of all people know why I can't."

"Because it was playing on the radio when I was killed," Dylan said. "Rye, losing someone you love is a part of life no one can avoid. If you keep clinging to what happened that night, you'll never find closure, and I'll never find peace. Your grief has become a crutch. Just another addiction. Until you face it, neither of us can move on. 'Help Me Rise' is the song that brought us together."

Ryleigh opened her eyes to an empty room. "Then I guess I'm stuck with my demons."

Musikfest—Bethlehem, PA. Seven months later.

Thirty minutes and six songs into their set, Ryleigh's bandmates took a bow and exited the stage, leaving her alone. She tugged at her shirt, peeling it away from her damp skin, and took a sip of water as two roadies hurried onto the stage. One of them handed her an acoustic guitar while the other positioned a high-backed chair front and center. She thanked them as she slipped the guitar strap over her head and climbed onto the seat. "Giving the band a break. Let them cool off. You still having a good time out there? Everyone keepin' hydrated?"

Her question was answered with vigorous applause. Ryleigh kicked off her flip flops and put her feet up on the chair's metal foot ring, inspiring a few catcalls and whistles.

"Sorry, guys. Hot as it is, that's all I'm takin' off. So, these next few songs are from my new acoustic alb—"

"You suck! Go back to rehab!"

Ryleigh held up a hand to shade her eyes from the setting sun. "Wow, and here I thought I'd lost all of my fans."

A plastic cup half-filled with beer splattered across the stage beside her chair. "Drunk bitch killed her husband! Lock her up!"

There was a commotion in the front left section of the audience. Ryleigh craned her neck to see two men being led away by security. "There they go. The last of my adoring public. Thanks for coming, fellas."

"We love you, Ryleigh!" a woman's voice cried out.

Repeated shouts of "Help Me Rise" grew until it became a chant accompanied by pumping fists.

Ryleigh's chest quivered. A hand squeezed her shoulder and she peered up at a face only she could see. *I can't do this.*

Yes, you can. Dylan smiled. *You didn't come this far...*

Ryleigh gazed out at the audience... *only to come this far.*

She drew a sharp breath and leaned forward toward the microphone. "Thank you." She waited until the cacophony faded before continuing. "Maybe I'll save the acoustic set until later. If my bandmates would be so kind?"

To boisterous applause, the musicians returned to the stage. "Ladies and gentlemen, on the bass guitar, Brie McCarrick. On the drums, Oni Ilu... and Darla Baasi on keyboards. Please give some love to the ladies of Hypatia."

After the crowd simmered down, Ryleigh continued. "I wrote this song with my husband, Dylan, who helped me rise above my addictions through love, courage, and hell of a lot more patience than I deserved. I've been avoiding this song since I lost him, but as Dylan made me understand, you can't let your demons control you. This is for you, babe."

Ryleigh moved her pick over the strings of the guitar, joined by Darla on the piano.

"When I was drownin' in that unquenchable thirst of addiction,

"And I was cruisin' blindly down the road to self-destruction,

"You helped me rise above the darkness and carry me to the light.

"You helped me rise to be worthy of the love I've been denied.

"You helped me rise above the reach of the demons in my mind..."

The last of the sun's vermilion rays had long faded and while the stars were not yet visible, a panoply of lights from phones and flashlights swayed with the rhythm of the music. Although her tears flowed and her voice faltered more than once, Ryleigh finished the song to a standing ovation.

Now, rise to be the star you were meant to be. She glanced around for Dylan but found only Zack smiling and applauding off stage as her bandmates took their places beside her. Holding hands, the four women bowed in unison.

And for the first time in two years, Ryleigh Noble's demons faded away.

THIS STORY first appeared in *Writes of Passage* (Greater Lehigh Valley Writers Group, March 2021).

So Hungry...

After scaling a treacherous length of the steep mountain trail, Edwin Santiago turned to extend a helping hand to his wife. Without a word, Prudence waved it away and bounded up through a notch in the cliff wall to stand beside him. As she caught her breath, they turned to admire the view from the northwest face of New Mexico's Starvation Peak. Beige and tan earth—dusted with rouge and mottled with deep green pines and desert scrub—stretched flat to a horizon broken only by a few scattered and distant peaks.

Edwin pulled a granola bar from his backpack and tore open the wrapper. "Hell of a lot nicer than the *other* Las Vegas."

"That's a matter of opinion," Prudence grumbled. "And technically, we're in Bernal here."

Edwin cocked his head and glared at her. "I know where we are, *sabelotodo*."

"I'm not a smart-ass!" Prudence nudged his arm.

Ignoring her, he continued. "I grew up in this area. Used

to come here all the time as a kid. It's just as beautiful as I remember."

"It's a desert. What's so beautiful about it?"

"When Lawrence of Arabia was asked why he liked the desert, he said, 'I like it because it's clean'."

"And desolate, not to mention cold and windy. I'd rather be in a hot tub or weaving around tables on a casino floor instead of stumbling over rocks and hauling myself up onto cliffs in the middle of February."

Edwin chuckled and shook his head. "We'll be in *your* Las Vegas for a whole week starting tomorrow, chiquita. This weekend, I want to enjoy *my* Las Vegas. I've been away too long. Besides, this is the best time of year for a hike—the rattlesnakes aren't out yet."

"Rattlesnakes? You waited until now to tell me this? See, this is why I don't do nature."

Although Prudence had never been fond of the outdoors, she and Edwin had agreed long ago to support each other's interests, which often required compromise—and sometimes, complaining. Prudence was far more adept at the latter than the former.

Edwin kissed her on her cheek. "Relax, Pru. It won't be long until we reach the mesa."

She folded her arms and continued staring at the landscape over 6,000 feet below. "How long?"

"In about fifteen minutes."

"After a short break." Prudence slipped off her backpack and set it down atop a nearby boulder. She pulled her water bottle out of a side pocket and took a sip before passing it to Edwin. "You never did tell me why this place is called Starvation Peak."

"Depending on what you read or who you ask, the legend is a little different. In one version, a Navajo tribe chased a group of early Spanish settlers from the Santa Fe Trail to the foot of the mountain. They fled to the top, where they eventually starved to death rather than be killed by the waiting Navajo. Other versions claim it was Spanish soldiers, or a merchant caravan, or even Catholic missionaries. The most dramatic rendition has the victims cannibalizing each other, with the survivors hoping to outlast the Navajo's patience."

As Edwin spoke, a fog descended over the northwest face of the peak. "I'm part Navajo and my family called bullshit on all of those stories years ago. They're just folklore. There's no documented evidence that anything ever happened here."

He turned to peer up toward the mesa just as Prudence screamed and stumbled backward.

Edwin spun. "What happened? Did you lose your balance?"

She whipped off her sunglasses and pointed at the swirling mist. Several yards out from the side of the mountain, a dark, featureless figure stood suspended in mid-air. After a moment, its arms opened wide, then rose above its head before flapping up and down wildly. Prudence glanced back at Edwin. With a grin, he dropped his arms to his side. The figure in the fog did the same.

Her brow furrowed as she glanced back and forth. "What the hell is that?"

"Don't tell me you've never seen a Brocken spectre before. The sun is behind me, casting my shadow into that low hanging cloud." He stepped back, away from the edge of the cliff. The apparition vanished. "Stand where I was. Quick, before the sun burns away the fog."

Prudence scurried into place. The hazy silhouette reappeared, although much less defined as the mist began to dissipate. "That's just creepy. What was it called?"

"Brocken spectre. I think it was first observed on a German mountain of the same name. Ready to move on?"

"No. I think I've had enough."

"You want to go back when we're this close to the top?"

"Where a bunch of people starved to death and possibly ate each other? No thanks. If you'd told me that yesterday, I would have slept in this morning."

Edwin sighed. "Pru, I know you're superstitious, but I'm telling you the stories are bogus. There are no ghosts roaming the mesa ready to eat you alive."

"Whatever. You can keep going if you want to. My ass is staying right here."

"It might take me about forty-five minutes. You're just going to sit here in the cold?"

Prudence shrugged. "The sun's starting to warm things up and that line of pine trees over there is blocking the wind."

"What're you going to do while I'm gone? There's barely any cell service out here so you won't be able to go online."

"I stuffed a book in my backpack, and I have hot chocolate in my thermos. So, go. If I need anything, I'll scream."

"*Increíble.*" Edwin threw up his arms. "Fine. I'll try to be quick. I just want to take pictures from the top of the mesa for my blog."

"No hurry, but be careful!"

He emerged from a gap between two boulders and marched out into a clearing. Rather than a panoramic view of the surrounding wilderness, Edwin could hardly see beyond the impenetrable pall of the low-hanging cloud. *So much for taking pictures.*

In the distance ahead, another Brocken spectre appeared, hovering between two pine trees. This time, it did not mimic Edwin's movements, but remained perfectly still. He glanced over his shoulder before scanning the mesa. There were no other hikers in sight, nor was there even a single ray of sunlight piercing the fog. He called out, but there was no reply. *So whose shadow is that?*

As he backed away toward the trail, Edwin slipped his hand over the leather sheath of his survival knife.

"Help us."

The words, spoken in Spanish, were barely louder than a whisper. As he glanced around the clearing, more Brocken spectres coalesced from the fog until he was completely surrounded.

"Who are you?" Edwin shouted. "What do you want?"

"Food... so hungry... help us."

The spectres drew closer, cutting off all avenues of escape. Edwin held up quivering hands. "Wait! I have food." He shucked his backpack and unzipped a side pouch. Several granola bars tumbled out. Edwin gathered them up and held them at arm's length. "Here, take them all."

The spectres paused. Since they had no facial features, Edwin could only hope that they were considering his offer. Then it occurred to him that if these were the ghosts of people who starved to death on this mesa over 160 years ago, they would have no knowledge of processed food. In unison, they swept forward until they hovered directly above him.

"No, wait, please! If you let me go, I can come back with real food."

Ignoring his pleas, they descended, their forms undulating and merging into one massive shadow that engulfed Edwin as he dropped to his knees and covered his head. He tried to scream but could utter no sound as the voices grew to a deafening roar in his head, repeating their refrain. "So hungry..."

~

"Edwin!" Prudence pressed her fingers to the side of his neck. Relieved to find a pulse, she gently turned his head right and left, looking for any sign of injury. With a grunt, he opened his eyes and winced against the blinding sunlight. "Edwin, are you OK? What happened?"

"How long was I out?" he whispered.

"I don't know, but when you didn't come back after an hour and a half, I climbed up here to find you. Can you stand?"

Edwin sat up and rubbed the back of his neck. He leaned forward, elbows on his knees, face buried in his hands.

"How do you feel?" Prudence said.

He didn't answer.

"Take your time. If you're in pain, I have—"

Edwin doubled over, clutching his stomach. "Hungry."

"Hold on, I'll get you a granola bar." She stepped away and rummaged through her bag. "I knew coming here was a bad idea. Once we're off this mountain, we should get you to a hospital." She turned, granola bar in hand—and flinched at the sight of Edwin standing directly behind her.

She stepped backward, nearly tripping over the uneven ground. "Oh, on your feet already? I didn't hear you approach."

He cocked his head before running a slow, predatory gaze down the length of her body.

"Why are you looking at me like that? What's wrong with you?"

Edwin brought his right hand out from behind his back. The 10-inch blade of his survival knife glinted in the sun. "So hungry..."

~

THIS STORY first appeared online in the Bethlehem Writers Roundtable Issue #50, October 2017. It first appeared in print in *Meanwhile in the Middle of Eternity* (Firebringer Press, March 2021).

Photos from the Attic

I swear on my father's grave that everything you're about to read is true. It happened three years ago around the holidays, bringing to a close the worst year of my life. I'd almost completely put it out of my mind until I came across my diary last week while moving to my new house.

With Christmas almost upon us yet again, and since enough time has passed, I feel compelled to reveal what happened. After you read this account, feel free to tell me I'm full of crap, but I know what I experienced was real.

It *had* to be.

Three weeks before Thanksgiving, cardiac arrest had sent my Uncle Rawley to his grave along with nearly a lifetime of bitter grudges. He was my dad's younger brother, but you'd never have guessed it from their personalities. Whereas my dad had been gregarious and sociable, Rawley had been a recluse, especially after turning his back on everyone in the family over the last fifteen years.

Now, Rawley was six feet under and to my surprise, he'd willed his house to me. Call us chickens, but neither my daughter nor I were keen on living in a place where someone had given up the ghost. I'll sell and take the money elsewhere, thank you very much.

Truth be told, I was the only family member who'd never quarreled with Uncle Rawley. Of course, we hadn't seen each other since I was twenty-one, ever since that row between him and my mom. A few days after I'd come home from college, my father died suddenly. At least he'd lived long enough to see me graduate. Over the course of that summer, Uncle Rawley had come to visit a few times until one blistering August night when he and Mom ended up in a screaming match in our living room. Rawley stormed out and never came back.

Later, Mom explained that the dispute had been about some matter concerning Dad's will. To this day, I'm not convinced of that, but at the time, I was too preoccupied with my grief to press her for details.

With that history in mind, it hadn't surprised me when my mother refused to help us clear out Rawley's house before putting it up for sale.

"Why don't you and Grace take care of it?" she'd said. "It's not that much and it'll be good therapy for you both. Get your minds off the divorce and give you two some quality time together."

As if I didn't have enough to do as a single parent with a full-time job. My ex and I had just finalized the demise of our marriage two days after I turned thirty-eight and exactly one month before Uncle Rawley passed away. I was no longer Claudia Paulino, I was back to being old Claudia Adamski. Lovely.

So, on one of the coldest Black Fridays on record, I found myself crawling around a freezing attic, my nose, ears, and fingertips numb after just twenty minutes. I slid a tattered cardboard box across the floor toward the steps. It was the last thing to go, thank God. I wanted a hot shower and coffee in the worst way.

"Mom?"

"Up here."

My fifteen-year-old-going-on-thirty appeared at the bottom of the pull down ladder. I still wasn't accustomed to her two-tone black and blonde hair, let alone her exposed neck. Grace thought the short do made her look older and more sophisticated. As far as I was concerned, she was too young to worry about "sophisticated" and as for looking older, I'd told her not to rush it. Someday, that's the *last* thing she'll want.

"Did you get everything out of the kitchen?" I asked.

"It's all in the truck. What about the furniture?"

"The movers will be here on Monday to take it all to storage. Mom was right. Rawley didn't have much, thankfully."

"It's a small house." Grace started up the steps, but stopped halfway into the attic. "Cold up here." She nodded toward the cardboard box. "What's in that?"

"Probably more junk. Can you take it down? Be careful, it's heavy. Might bottom out."

Grace tilted the box as she carried it down, causing its contents to slide and shuffle.

"Sounds like a lot of paperwork." She carried it into the nearest bedroom and set it down atop the antique dresser. I caught up with her as she wiped off the box with a dust rag and peeked inside. "Actually, they're old photos."

No sooner had she spoken than the wall clock behind me stopped. Even weirder was the draft that swept through the room and ruffled the curtains.

"You felt that?" I asked.

"Yep."

"Maybe it came from the attic." Of course, I said that more for my own sake than Grace's.

Neither of us dared move, anticipating something more, but all was quiet. Finally, Grace reached into the box and pulled out a handful of photographs. She set them on the dresser and sifted through them. Some were stuck together face to face and had to be peeled apart.

"Careful," I said. "They've been up there for God knows how long in extreme temperatures and humidity."

Grace separated two photos and held them up.

One was an old postcard from Assateague, Virginia showing an aerial view of a calm blue ocean and crowded beach. The other was a Polaroid of a smiling little girl, eight or nine years old. She had long black hair and a one-piece powder blue dress. It took me a moment to recognize—

"Margot." I snatched the photo from Grace's hand and sat on the edge of the bed. "God, this has to be mid-eighties. I haven't seen Margot since high school. She lived two houses up the street until her parents moved to who-knows-where after we graduated. This looks like it could have been a birthday party. Yep, that was our picnic table there in the background. Looks like there's a cake on it."

I glanced at the cardboard box. "Oy, sorting through all those will be a drive down memory lane. I don't think that's a trip I want to take, but I bet your grandmother would love it. We can drop the box off at her place on the way home."

"Actually, these are kinda cool," Grace said. "What if I salvaged what I could and put them into an album? I could give it to her as a Christmas gift."

I thought it was a good idea. Money was tight and the project might distract Grace from the divorce. As a teenager watching her family fracture and being helpless to stop it, she did an admirable job of hiding her pain most of the time. She got that strength from her dad—and I got it from her.

I'd come to the conclusion a long time ago that grocery stores in the northern part of the country must love winter. At the mere mention of snow in the forecast, milk and bread become more valuable than gold and checkout lines turn into the neighborhood hangout.

There I was, staring through the freezer door and debating the four pack of crab cakes when someone called my name. I'd heard it, but it didn't register until the voice was right beside me.

"Claudia Adamski?"

I half expected the woman to serve me a court summons from my ex-husband. Instead, she thrust out an empty hand. "Tina Reese from high school."

I shook it out of reflex, but it took a moment before I recognized "Two-Ton Tina," the heaviest girl in our class. I'd never called her that, of course, but I'd overhead other kids say it.

There's no way that slur would apply today. Now, she was more like "Teaspoon Tina," slim and buff. The weight loss even made her seem taller than I remembered. I had to admit, she was gorgeous. Dammit.

"Oh my God, you're so skinny!" I blurted. I do that a lot, blurting. I'm blonde. It happens. "I mean, you look great."

Tina laughed. "It took a lot of work. So how are you? Getting ready for Christmas?"

I nodded. Emphatically. Like a bobble-head. I always do that before I tell someone that everything's wonderful when I'm not feeling it. As if I'm trying to convince myself, too.

"I'm doing great. Well, *now* I am. Had a rough patch earlier this year. Got divorced."

"Sorry to hear that. Do you have any kids?"

"My daughter Grace is fifteen. Doing great in school,

thankfully. She's taking martial arts, piano lessons, archery. I get exhausted just talking about it."

"We have two boys, thirteen and ten. Between both of them, we have almost every sport covered, plus guitar and drum lessons. It's non-stop. Didn't life seem simpler when we were kids?"

"Seriously. Do you keep in touch with anyone from the old days?" I don't know why I asked. I'm the least nostalgic person on the planet, but it was the only common ground between us.

"A few here and there. Do you remember Margot Hansen?"

"Absolutely. I just came across a photo of her when she was a little kid from the old neighborhood."

"She's dead."

"Oh, no."

"Her family moved to Florida after she graduated high school," Tina said. "And Margot still lived there. Married into money, had three kids, big house, private beach, all that. Went swimming two days ago and apparently went out too far. They say she had a seizure before she drowned."

"Seizure?"

"Margot had epilepsy."

"I never knew that."

"Neither did Margot until she was sixteen, and even then she didn't tell anyone. Kept it under control with meds."

"That's unbelievable."

We chatted for another minute before Tina wrote her email address on the back of my grocery list. We wished each other a Merry Christmas before parting ways. I turned back to the freezer and the crab cakes, but I'd lost my appetite for seafood.

~

The snow still hadn't started by the time dinner was over. Grace went off to her room to finish her homework, filled with the hope that there would be no school tomorrow.

I didn't say a word about Margot, but her photo was still on the coffee table on top of a pile that Grace had pulled from the box yesterday. I'd said I'm not the nostalgic type, but I was curious so I scooped up a small stack of pictures, dropped onto the sofa, and started flipping through them. There was a mix of different sizes, but most were 4x6 or Polaroids.

It's always interesting to see your parents when they were your age or younger. They'd actually had a life before I was born—vacation pictures, first house, first car, the usual stuff. There was one photo of my parents and Uncle Rawley at the log cabin that my Aunt Josephine used to own. She's my mom's sister and still with us, God bless her, but she sold the cabin about a year after her second husband died in 1982.

At the bottom of the stack, I found two pictures stuck together like the ones of Margot and the beach. I managed to peel them apart without tearing them, although slivers from each image left their mark on the other. Still, Uncle Rawley's sky blue '67 Mustang with its pristine white interior brought back memories.

The other photo was a tattered Polaroid of Aunt Josephine dining at a fancy restaurant. I couldn't tell what the occasion was, and I didn't recognize anyone in the background. Judging by the clothes and hairstyles, it had to be the '70s.

"Taking over the project?"

I nearly jumped out of my skin when Grace appeared and picked up another stack of photos. I guess I was too focused on, well, nostalgia.

"Finish your homework?"

She rolled her eyes and replied with an exasperated "yes." *Ah, teenagers.*

"Dad texted me. He asked me to help him with his Christmas tree this weekend."

"Real or fake?"

"Fake."

How appropriate. I kept my mouth shut and went into bobble-head mode again.

"He found a white tree with blue lights." Grace sifted through her handful of photos. She came across two more that were stuck together and went to work on them. "He wants me to help him decorate it."

"That'll be nice. I'm glad he wants to spend some quality time with you."

Grace separated the photos and glanced at them both before handing one to me. "Is that Dominic?"

I took it and turned it right side up. "Yep." It was my cousin at his college graduation complete with cap and gown. Dominic had been two years ahead of me at Lehigh University and had graduated *summa cum laude*. At the time, I'd hated him for it. Aunt Josephine spared no opportunity to inform the family of her son's latest achievements, like making Dean's list again or earning yet another award or generally walking on water. OK, maybe Dominic hadn't done that last one, but you get the idea.

He'd moved to Tulsa three years ago after accepting a promotion to VP of Operations at whatever Fortune 500 company he worked for. Last I'd heard, he was dating some rich, high-powered attorney who had started her own firm.

"What's the other photo that was stuck to this one?"

Grace held it up. "A couple of antique airplanes."

Two single pilot prop planes to be exact and straight out of the 1930s. Sunlight gleamed off perfectly polished silver wings. Both of them were side by side on a massive concrete pad.

"Must have been a museum." I yawned. "Or an air show."

By then, it was nearly 9:30 and I was fading fast. I pushed aside the curtains behind the sofa and took a peek outside. Sure enough, snow was falling. "You might just get your wish after all."

"It'll be nice to sleep in."

"And then you can help me clear the snow at Uncle Rawley's house."

"I think I'd rather be in school. I'm sorry, but that place creeps me out. I mean, he died in the kitchen."

"People die in their homes every day. It isn't like we're going to live there."

"It's probably haunted."

"Only if you imagine it to be."

"I didn't imagine that draft we felt in the bedroom when we opened the box of photos. I didn't imagine all the clocks in the house stopping at once."

I had no answer for that. Grace was right. It hadn't only been the clock in the bedroom that stopped when we opened the box. While checking the house one last time before leaving, we noticed that every clock had stopped.

Now *my* imagination was starting to run with the idea. Just what I needed before going to bed.

With Christmas just two weeks away, death had struck our family again.

I sat at my mom's dining room table, picking at the breading on cold chicken fingers as the cruel absurdity of it ran through my head. Across the room, Aunt Josephine and Dominic stared at me, waving, smiling, hugging. A combined ninety-four years of living had been reduced to a collage of photos taped to poster boards. Grace had volunteered to create them for the double funeral, using the photos from Uncle Rawley's attic.

Aunt Josephine had been killed by a drunk driver while leaving the post office in the middle of the afternoon. The little prick had tried to make a turn on the cross street but had cut right too soon, plowing into Aunt Josephine and crushing her between his car and a brick wall.

To take the pressure off of mom, I'd volunteered to call Dominic. I remember the quivering in my chest as I dialed his number. I'd never broken that kind of news to anyone before.

Dominic had jumped on a plane the next morning—but he never made it. His connecting flight from Tulsa to Dallas-Fort Worth had crashed somewhere outside of Wewoka, Oklahoma. His remains had been cremated and buried in an urn with Aunt Josephine.

Mom was devastated. We all were, of course, but she was the oldest of three sisters and now, the last. The youngest, Aunt Wendy, had lost her battle with cancer over a decade ago.

In the living room, my mother chatted with Grace and a few of my cousins. She was doing an admirable job of holding herself together, which only meant the dam would burst once everyone had gone. I'd inherited that trait from her. Grace is different. She'd been my rock since her father and I separated, and now she was doing the same for her grandmother. Hard to believe she's my kid.

"Your daughter reminds me of Dominic."

The silky, southern drawl snapped me back to attention and I realized that I'd been focused on the photos to the exclusion of anything else around me. I'm not sure why I couldn't look away. Something was troubling me, beyond the obvious. I filed it for later and glanced up to see Elaina taking a seat to my left. Dominic's girlfriend had flown in two days ago. She was quite the exotic beauty with narrow, hazel eyes and luxurious brown hair that framed high cheek bones and a flawless olive complexion. Her waist was so damn narrow I wanted to offer her my cold chicken fingers. Above the waist, she was rather well endowed. I wondered if they were—

"Real... I mean really?" I gave up on the chicken and wiped my fingers on a napkin. "How so? I hadn't seen him in years, just heard about him from time to time."

"Well, Dominic never let circumstances get the best of him. He had broad shoulders. A lot of people leaned on him, both professionally and personally, but his attitude never faltered even when he was stressed out. He was always there when needed."

I smiled despite myself. That was my Grace to a tee.

Elaina sat back in her chair and turned her gaze to the poster boards. "I never thought I'd meet his family under these circumstances."

"How long were you two dating?"

"About three years. We discussed marriage." Elaina wiped her eyes. "But I wasn't ready for that yet."

"How did you two meet?"

She let out a short laugh. "Through mutual friends, although we recognized each other the minute they introduced us. Dominic and I had crossed paths several times before that during evening runs at LaFortune Park. Apparently, he noticed me as much I did him."

"I didn't know he was a runner."

Elaina nodded. "Dominic loved exercise. He was the picture of health."

And that's when I realized exactly what was bothering me.

The next week and a half was filled with overtime, Christmas shopping, and decorating our apartment. The latter two were mostly an attempt to put me into a holiday spirit that I just wasn't feeling. Still, Grace had bounced back from our family tragedies and for that, I was grateful. We'd been so busy, that I'd nearly forgotten about the box of old pictures from Uncle Rawley's attic until I noticed Grace's album lying open on the coffee table. Beside it was a short stack of photos presumably queued up for processing. There were still empty pages to be filled.

I took a seat on the edge of the sofa and picked up the album just to see how much progress Grace had made over the past few days. Before I'd even moved it to my lap, my fingertips began to sting. I dropped the album on the cushion beside me.

Grace bounded into the room. "Mom, what happened?"

"Did you leave that outside or something? It was like picking up a sheet of ice." I rubbed my fingers on my jeans to warm them up.

"What?"

"I'm telling you, it's frozen. I could barely touch it."

Grace frowned in that usual condescending teenager way and spread her hands over the open pages. After a moment, she sat down and placed the album on her lap.

"Feels fine to me."

A frigid draft swept through the room. The stack of photos toppled across the coffee table. Some fell to the floor. My body jolted as a shiver tore through me. Grace hunched her shoulders and crossed her arms over her chest.

"You felt that?" she asked.

"Just like at Uncle Rawley's house—only colder." I nodded toward the photo album. "And it started with those."

"What do you mean?"

"It didn't occur to me until after the funeral. Three people have died so far—Margot drowned, Aunt Josephine was hit by a car, and Dominic was killed in a plane crash. We found photos of all three of them in that box."

"We also found pictures of you, Grandmom, some of our cousins, Aunt Wendy, and other people."

"There's a difference," I said. "Remember how we found the photo of Margot? It was stuck to a postcard of the ocean. The Polaroid of Aunt Josephine was stuck to a photo of a car—"

"And Dominic's photo was peeled off a picture of airplanes," Grace finished. "I get it, Mom. I just think it's a stretch. Are you trying to say that the photos are killing people? It's coincidence, that's all."

I took a deep breath. I did that a lot when dealing with my daughter. "Whatever you think of the idea—"

"Ridonkulous comes to mind."

"Let me rephrase that. *Regardless* of what you think, I want all of these photos picked up, put back in the box, and left alone for a while. Can you do that for me?"

Grace rolled her eyes. "Mom, they already closed school for tomorrow. They're calling for two feet of snow. I wanted to finish the album for Grandmom."

"I don't care. Put them away and don't touch them again until I say so. Is that clear?"

Grace sighed. "Fine."

"Besides, if you're off from school tomorrow, you can help me clear the snow at your grandmom's house."

"Joy." Grace gathered up the photos from the floor and tossed them into the box before plodding off her to room, muttering. "Merry-freakin'-Christmas..."

Ah, teenagers.

"Burn them all."

"Hm?"

It was just after 3:30 in the morning and I'd had a miserable night of tossing and turning. I don't think I'd slept for more than thirty minutes at a time until I had a dream that there was a party in my apartment. There were people everywhere—including recently deceased members of my family. Even Uncle Rawley. In fact, it was his voice that woke me.

That's also when I realized that my throat was sore. I'd caught some nasty bug just in time for the holidays. *Merry-freakin'-Christmas.* I tossed aside the covers and plodded to the kitchen for a glass of orange juice. Passing through the living room, I heard the voice before I saw the face.

"Burn them all."

I tried to scream, but the best my throat could produce was a squeal.

Even in the dim amber glow of the streetlight through the window, the dark baggy eyes, thick salt-and-pepper hair and long, narrow nose were unmistakable.

Uncle Rawley was sitting on my sofa.

"I'm so sorry," he said. "Just burn them all."

That kicked my brain into gear. I slapped the light switch to my right. The floor lamp turned on to reveal an empty living room.

"Mom?"

Now this time, I yelped with authority while spinning around and pressing myself against the wall.

"Whoa, Mom, chill out. What happened?"

"Nothing," I croaked. It seemed that my yelp took what was left of my voice. I had to whisper as I collected myself. "I just thought I saw—uh, heard—something."

"Like what?"

"Voices, but it was probably one of the neighbors. You might want to keep your distance, sweetie. I think I'm getting sick. I came out here for some orange juice."

"I'll get it for you."

"Don't worry about it. Why don't you go back to bed?"

"I can sleep late." Grace made her way to the kitchen and opened the fridge. "Look out the window."

I knelt on the sofa and leaned forward to part the curtains. There was at least a foot of snow on the ground already. Thick flakes mixed with sleet swirled through the lights from the nearest streetlamps.

"Here you go, Mom."

I took the glass of orange juice from Grace before she picked up a 4x6 photo from the floor in front of the spot where I'd seen Uncle Rawley's apparition. Of course, she didn't need to know that. It wasn't until she turned over the photo that we realized it was yet two more stuck together face to face. She dropped onto the sofa and started peeling them apart.

"No, wait." I reached around her in a feeble attempt to pluck them from her grasp, but she twisted away from me and inspected the pictures. I slid down to sit beside her. I figured if she got sick, too, then she had it coming.

One of the photos was of me at about eight years old with my parents dressed up as Santa and Mrs. Claus. We were standing beside a fire truck that had been decked out for the annual Christmas parade. A wreath hung on the passenger door and multicolored lights had been draped around the sides and back of the truck.

A much younger Uncle Rawley stared back at me from the photo in Grace's other hand. His Rottweiler, Bella, sat beside him in his back yard. My parents had forbidden me from going near her, but to be honest, she'd been far more pleasant than her cantankerous owner.

"This doesn't fit the pattern," I muttered. "All of the photos so far were one-to-one. One person, one object. This is different."

Grace shrugged. "Well, either you or Grandmom are going

to be attacked by a dog or hit by a fire truck. Should we flip a coin?"

"No respect from my offspring." On second thought, if she were to get sick, she'd be home from school *and* whiny. "I'm going back to bed."

THE SNOW HAD STOPPED before dawn. By ten o'clock, the plow trucks had been through twice. Mustering all of my resolve, I took my life into my gloved hands and set out for Uncle Rawley's house to clear the snow while Grace ate cereal and checked Instagram. The realtor was coming to show the property to two clients, one in the morning and the other in the afternoon. And here I thought the holidays were the worst time to put a house on the market.

Oh, what fun it was to ride in a front-wheel drive sedan in the snow. I slid off course about three times, including a 180-degree spin that sent me to the opposite side of the street. Thank God I was the only one on the road. Did I mention that my sore throat was now accompanied by a fever?

By the time I stopped at the top of the hill two blocks from the house, all confidence in my survival was out the window. As I rode my brakes down the slope, I heard the sirens and blaring horns of fire trucks closing in. I glanced at my rearview mirror hoping they wouldn't be screaming down my back in a second, but the street behind me was empty.

As I neared the bottom of the hill, I pressed the brake pedal. The car slowed, but didn't stop. I tried pumping the brakes. That didn't help. I was sliding toward the intersection —right into the path of the fire trucks. By this time, I was practically standing on the brake pedal, but the car continued dashing through densely packed snow on a collision course. The first truck passed in front of me with room to spare.

"Shit, shit, shit!" I don't know how many times I actually said that, but I'm sure a few justifiable "F-bombs" were also dropped. The second truck blared its horn at me. I replied by screaming at the top of my lungs, sore throat be damned, and it's debatable as to which one of us was louder.

Then my car stopped.

The truck blew past my front bumper with about six inches to spare. I sat there for a few moments as both trucks turned out of view and disappeared. I closed my eyes and leaned my forehead against the steering wheel. The sirens faded into the distance as I continued on.

The power was out at Uncle Rawley's house, which meant I had to walk through the place to open the garage door manually. After turning the key in the front door lock, I hesitated. *What would I find inside? Would Uncle Rawley make another appearance?* I took some comfort from the sunlight peeking out from behind the drifting clouds. I sure as hell wouldn't have had the guts to go in there at night.

Once inside, I locked the door behind me and hurried through first floor into the laundry room. It wasn't until I opened the door to the garage that I heard the ticking. I glanced over my shoulder at the small plastic wall clock, which displayed the correct time even though it had stopped last week along with every other clock in the house. *You got a job to do. Get it done and get the hell out.*

The musty two-car garage was so damn cold, I could have stored perishables in it. Uncle Rawley's year-old Chevy Impala was still parked on one side. He'd left that to me, too. Since Grace would be old enough to drive in another year, I'd planned to let her use my car and I would take the Impala. I was comfortable with that. After all, it wasn't as if anyone had died in it.

On the other side of the garage were Uncle Rawley's work-bench, tools, tractor mower and most importantly, the snow blower. It was a large machine with levers that moved in every direction. I'd been smart enough to research the model online from my phone when Grace and I were there last. I'd figured out how to start the beast and mix the gas and oil fuel it needed.

I reached up and pulled the red rope to open the garage door. It barely budged. I walked backward, putting my weight into it—which wasn't much, I might add. Finally, after a crackling of ice, the door rose and I pulled it over my head until it stopped.

I squinted against the sunlight reflecting off the snow in the driveway until I found myself staring down a full grown Rottweiler that erupted in a tantrum of vicious barking and growling. I stumbled back over the snow blower and landed on my ass on the concrete floor. The demon dog—lean, muscular, and angry as hell—paced back and forth outside the garage as if it had been waiting for me. I expected it to lunge, but it never moved beyond the concrete threshold. It just glared at me with black eyes that narrowed as it bared a set of long, pointy pearlies.

"Ike!" a deep voice called out. The hellhound turned away for a moment then continued its patrol in front of me, launching into a second tirade of barking the minute I tried to pick myself up.

A plump old man in a red and black checkered coat and red knitted cap dashed through the snow into the driveway and leaned over the dog. "Ike, shut the hell up!"

The Rottweiler fell silent.

Between bushy white mustache and matching beard, his mouth opened in surprise when he noticed me.

"Oh my God, I am so sorry, sweetheart." He hurried into the garage and extended a black-gloved hand, which I gratefully accepted. He pulled me to my feet as if I were a rag doll. "Are you hurt?"

"Just my pride."

"I'm sorry about Ike. He must've gotten out when I was clearing the snow. I'm Nick. I live two houses up."

"Claudia Adamski. Rawley was my uncle."

"Really? He never talked much about his family. Hell, Rawley never talked much about anything. No offense, but he never seemed like a happy fella."

I nodded. "Yeah, that was Rawley."

"Well, he's in a better place. Can't say I'm too far behind. Then again, who is?" As he chuckled, his whole body shook like a bowl of—*hey, wait a minute.* I remembered the pictures that Grace had peeled apart last night. *Fire truck? Rottweiler? Santa Claus?*

Nick marched back outside. "Anyway, take care and sorry again about old Ike."

"No problem, sir. Merry Christmas."

"You, too." Nick waved then snapped his fingers at the Rottweiler. "Get movin', Ike!"

Ike and I exchanged parting glances before he bolted up the street.

You called it, Grace—almost. There ain't gonna be another death in this family today.

~

After clearing the sidewalk and driveway without further incident, I called my mom to let her know that I was coming over to do the same for her, but there was no answer.

Thirty minutes later, I stood on her porch and rang the doorbell for the fourth time. Finally, I pulled the key from my purse and let myself in. I heard the electronic screeching as soon as I stepped through the door. It was the smoke alarm on the second floor. I ran to the bottom of the steps and looked up into a thick gray fog. The stench of burning plastic and wood was just beginning to permeate the house.

"Mom!"

When she didn't answer, I held my scarf over my nose and mouth and charged up the stairs. To the left, the master bedroom was empty as was the bathroom. That's when I heard the dog barking. Yes, another one. I turned right and peered into the haze. Near the end of the hallway, a Rottweiler stood whimpering over my mother's prone form. As I ran toward them, the dog backed away—and vanished into the smoke.

The spare bedroom was on fire. Mom had used it as a storage room for years, everything from holiday decorations, old books, spare linens, you name it.

I grabbed my mother under her arms and dragged her to the top of the stairs. She had always been petite, and I was never more grateful for it as I carried her down to the first floor. Something made me turn and glance up the steps. The Rottweiler was there along with Uncle Rawley as if they'd formed out of the smoke.

I said the first thing that popped into my head. "You did this, you fucking bastard!"

Belle lowered her head and whimpered again.

"I'm sorry," Rawley said. "It's out of my control. If you want to end this, either burn the photos," he pointed to my mother, "or make her tell the truth."

With that, they were gone.

~

Christmas Day

The women in my family had always been tough broads. My mother recovered from smoke inhalation with no respiratory issues. She'd been reading in bed when the hallway smoke alarm sounded. By that time, the spare bedroom had already been ablaze for several minutes. Apparently, I'd arrived seconds after my mom had passed out.

According to the investigators, the fire had been caused by faulty wiring in the electric baseboard radiator, which was odd considering that my mom had never turned on the heat in that room. Of course, I had my own theories on what—or who—had ignited the fire, but I kept those to myself.

Nevertheless, we made a valiant attempt to put our worries aside on Christmas Day. After morning mass, I dropped off Grace and mom at the apartment. I had one last errand to run.

The drive to Uncle Rawley's lacked the death-defying adventure of the previous trip. In fact, all was quiet as I pulled into the driveway. I popped the trunk where I'd stashed the box of photographs on Christmas Eve—along with a bottle of lighter fluid and a pack of wooden matches. Uncle Rawley had kept a metal burning barrel in his backyard, and I intended to take his advice.

I stuck around long enough to watch the photos shrivel into blackened scraps. It occurred to me then that Uncle Rawley hadn't simply dumped old photos into a box and put them out of sight. He'd also packed it full of deep bitterness and hatred that had festered during the last fifteen years of his life. I wished I knew why. I couldn't help but to think of that summer night after my father's death when my mother and Uncle Rawley had exploded at one another. As I started back toward my car, I resolved to find out the truth about that.

Halfway across the yard, I stopped at the sight of the Rottweiler that appeared in the driveway. Without turning my head, I glanced right and left for Uncle Rawley, but he was nowhere to be seen.

"Ike! What the hell are you doing?"

I let out the breath I'd been holding and shook my head. The dog ran off.

I cranked up the Christmas tunes all the way home, thankful that it was finally over—

—AND THEN I remembered the album that Grace had put together. By the time I stepped through the door, mom was already paging through her Christmas present.

"This is wonderful, Grace," she said. "I can't believe Rawley had all of these hidden away."

"There were others." Grace shot a sidelong glance at me. "But they were stuck together and kinda ruined."

I nodded to her as I made my way into the kitchen. Grace wasn't happy that I had denied her the chance to complete her project, but mom was tickled with what she had. As far as I'm concerned, it was a win-win.

"I already looked in on the chicken, Claudia," my mom said. "Have you seen this album yet?"

"I'll look at it later."

"Oh, I know you're not the sentimental type, but would it kill you to look at a few pictures?"

Grace cleared her throat.

If only you knew. That reminded me. There was one last nagging question that only my mother could answer.

I asked Grace to join me in the kitchen. "Did you call your dad yet and wish him a Merry Christmas?"

"I'm going to see him tomorrow."

"I know, but I think he'd like to hear from you today. Besides, I need to talk to your grandmother about something."

Grace sighed as she pulled her phone from her pocket. "Fine. Then can we open the rest of the gifts?"

I kissed her on the forehead. "Absolutely."

With that, I strolled out to the living room and took a seat next to my mom on the sofa. "I have a question about Uncle Rawley. After dad died, I remember the two of you had a severe blow out. At the time, you said it was about Dad's will, but you never told me the details. What really happened?"

The color drained from her face. "Claudia, it's Christmas. I don't want to talk about old family problems now. That's all in the past."

"Mom, please. I have a reason for asking."

She lowered her gaze to the photo album. It was nearly thirty seconds before she worked up the courage to speak. "I had an affair with your Uncle Rawley."

"*What*?"

"I broke it off when your father died." Tears welled up in her eyes as she continued. "I felt guilty, ashamed. Rawley took it hard. He was angry. That's what the argument was really about, nothing to do with your father's will. I'm sorry I lied to you back then, but I didn't have the guts to tell you. I was afraid you'd hate me. I know how much you idolized your father, but we'd grown apart while you were away at college. You weren't around to see it. I never stopped loving him, Claudia, I swear. I was just confused and lonely. I can't say that straying with Rawley was the best decision I ever made."

You ain't kiddin'! As my mind was trying to grasp what my ears were hearing, my stomach started tying itself into a giant knot. I wanted to puke. *What the hell did she see in Uncle Rawley?* "Did anyone else know about it?"

Mom nodded. "One of the neighbors... found out, let's just say. They blabbed to your Aunt Josephine. She confronted me about it, but I denied it at the time. I don't think she believed me. She shunned Rawley after that. Then those neighbors moved away."

"Which neighbors?"

"Oh, I don't remember their last name. You used to play with their daughter. I think her name was—"

"Margot."

"Yes, that was it. Claudia, I'm so sorry. I'll understand if you're disappointed in me. I'd hoped the subject would never come up."

Well, you asked for it, dumb-ass. Yes, I did. No wonder why Uncle Rawley had turned his back on the family, not that I'm defending him. He had betrayed his own brother, my father. Now, after a decade and half, it all made sense.

Grace returned to the living room. "Dad's coming at nine tomorrow morning to pick me up. He told me to wish you a Merry Christmas."

Yeah, Merry-freakin'-Christmas.

This story first appeared in *Elsewhere in the Middle of Eternity* (Firebringer Press, August 2016).

The Celestials

At Parsell Funeral Home in the quaint, coastal town of Lewes, Delaware, Laurel and Rodney Jaggar stood beside their sister's closed casket, shaking hands with an interminable line of complete strangers. Laurel was astonished that their reclusive sister, Celeste, had made so many friends since moving to nearby Rehoboth Beach eight years ago. It was only after the first dozen mourners expressed their condolences with such phrases as, "I loved your sister's novels," and "I met Celeste at a book signing at Browseabout," that Laurel understood the truth. These people were not friends, but fans. They knew Celeste only through her work and occasional public appearances. Nevertheless, their well-intentioned sympathies left Laurel with a bitter sting of guilt—neither she nor her brother had ever read a single one of Celeste's books.

As shame compounded her grief, Laurel wiped away another stream of tears and accepted the fact that these people probably knew Celeste better than her own family did. She shot a sidelong glance at the casket and closed her eyes, trying to erase the image of Celeste's battered body. Somewhere else in Delaware, the drunk driver who had taken her life was also being laid to rest.

Another loyal reader clutched Laurel's hand, muttered the standard cliché, and stepped aside. *Will this never end?* She sighed in relief as the last five people in line approached together, led by a distinguished, elderly gentleman with salt-and-pepper hair. He extended a hand and introduced himself as Rusty Dickinson.

"I can't tell you what an honor it is to meet you both," Rusty began. "I only wish it were under brighter circumstances. I know the past few days have been difficult for you, but we just wanted you to know that we owe a special debt of gratitude to Celeste. She helped each of us in ways no one else could, which is why we volunteered to be pallbearers."

Rod exchanged a wary glance with Laurel. "Well, uh, much obliged."

Rusty stepped aside and gestured to the others. The first was a tall, lean young man who introduced himself as Christian Bayard. As they shook hands, Laurel couldn't help but take note of his unblemished bronze complexion and square jaw.

By contrast, Virginia Kent was a full-figured teen with a leonine mane of raven hair that framed a sun-deprived face and complemented everything from her ebony matte lipstick to her one-piece black dress and thigh-high leather boots. *There's no way in hell our Celeste hung out with this chick.* Laurel could tell by Rod's forced smile that he was equally as disconcerted by the girl's appearance. *She looks like something that crawled out of the* Cabinet of Doctor Caligari.

Bringing up the rear was a nondescript middle-aged couple who introduced themselves as Dutch Draper and Carla Dodd. Doleful eyes belied their warm smiles as each engulfed Laurel and Rod in a firm embrace.

Laurel found herself wondering how such a motley group had ever come to know one another, let alone someone as reticent as Celeste. As if sensing her bewilderment, Rusty leaned close with a reassuring smile. "You'll understand everything soon enough."

~

The service was held at the Solid Ground nondenominational church, where each of Celeste's friends delivered a brief, touching eulogy. Virginia was the first to speak, addressing Laurel and Rod directly.

"I want you to know how much Celeste helped me. I've struggled with depression since I was really young, but I started using X and other drugs after my family turned their backs on me when I came out. Thanks to your sister, I've been clean now for four years. I have an awesome job, an apartment here in Lewes, and a new family that cares about me. None of that would have happened without Celeste." With a lopsided smile, Virginia wiped her eyes and stepped away.

Christian followed, recounting how Celeste had helped him overcome his fear of the ocean after the drowning death of his mother when he was a child. Then, Dutch and Carla took the lectern together and credited Celeste with helping reunite them after they'd lost touch nearly three decades ago.

Finally, Rusty Dickinson imparted a tale that left Rod stunned and Laurel in tears. The murder of his wife six years ago had launched him on a downward spiral into alcoholism. Then a series of financial misfortunes had left Rusty broke, homeless, and on the verge of suicide. "But with your sister's help, I found the hope and strength to take control of my life. I think it's fair to say that Celeste saved me." He paused, spreading his arms to indicate the others from his group. "She saved us all."

BY THE TIME they arrived at Henlopen Memorial Park, the morning clouds had dispersed. Beneath an unblemished September sky, Rod and Laurel placed a teardrop-shaped bouquet of white pom-poms and lilies atop Celeste's casket while the others stood at a respectful distance.

"She deserved better from us," Laurel whispered. "We were the only family she had left, and we had nothing to say at her service."

She turned and stormed off toward Rusty and his group. "I'd like to know more about our sister and how she helped all of you."

Rusty nodded. "Well, no better time than the present. Have you eaten today?"

"Come to think of it, no."

"Let's do something about that. I'm hosting a reception later at my house on Delaware Avenue, not too far from Celeste's place. We'd be honored if you and Rod would join us."

AS CELESTE'S SOLE HEIRS, Rod and Laurel had inherited her house on Sandalwood Street in Rehoboth Beach and were staying there for the week while they decided what to do with it. After freshening up, they walked the half mile to Rusty's place and were still discussing their options when they arrived.

"You should rent it out," Rusty advised as he poured drinks. "You could make a hell of a profit, pay off the mortgage, and have a vacation house when you need it. If you don't like the summer crowd, Rehoboth is open all year round. You should come here at Christmas—it's beautiful."

Rod shrugged. "I ain't much for the beach, but Laurel loves it." He nudged her with his elbow. "Maybe you'll finally find that rich husband you've been lookin' for."

She narrowed her eyes at him before addressing Rusty. "You said that our sister saved your lives. Personally or through her writing?"

Rusty handed her a drink. "Both, my dear. I only wish I could've returned the favor." He addressed the others and raised his glass. "To Celeste. May her words last forever." Around the table, everyone repeated the sentiment as they clinked their glasses together.

Rusty pointed to Rod and Laurel. "I take it that you haven't read too many of your sister's books."

Rod shook his head. "We read some of her short stories when she started writin' in high school, but after our parents died, we kind of drifted apart. You know how it is."

Rusty held up a hand. "Say no more. I'll tell you what. If you want to know exactly what Celeste did for us, you should read her *Sands of Time* series. Four books, all short novels, easy reading. You can blast through one in a night or two. The longest one is about a hundred and seventy-five pages. I have a spare set. It's all yours. That way, you get the whole picture and in Celeste's own words."

"Which one did you read?"

At the Royal Treat for breakfast the following morning, Rod and Laurel placed their orders before delving into a discussion about their sister's novels.

"*Beneath the Surface*," Laurel replied. "It was about Christian Bayard. I wonder if he signed a release form because Celeste didn't even change his name. It had me in tears. After his mother drowned when he was five, Christian was passed around from one family member to the next and some of them were horribly abusive. He ran away when he was fourteen after one of his uncles doused him in gasoline and tried to light him on fire. Christian jumped into a bay up in Maine and swam for miles to get away. The rest of the book is a pretty wild ride until he got to Rehoboth to become a lifeguard and scuba instructor."

"Yeah, well, you should read *The Pressure at this Depth.* It's about Rusty Dickinson. Just like he said at the funeral, the guy had an idyllic life until his wife was shot during a convenience store holdup in Chicago. Then he started drinkin', lost his job, his house, everything. He almost committed suicide before endin' up here in Rehoboth and turnin' his life around. I ain't much of a reader, but that book kept me up all night."

"Can't wait to dive into the next one." Laurel said.

Rod smirked. "I get the feeling they all end with the main characters coming to Rehoboth."

"Still, you have to admit, Celeste turned out to be an amazing writer. She came a long way from her early stuff." After a pause, Laurel continued. "We really should have read her books while she was alive. We should have been more supportive after Mom and Dad died. Instead, we let her down. Did we ever once come to see her after she moved here? She invited us a few times, but it took her death to get us here."

"I know," Rod sighed. "I feel lousy about that, but to be honest, I never knew how to relate to her. Celeste was just *different.* She was always so damn aloof and withdrawn. It always made things awkward. At least we sent birthday and Christmas cards every year."

"That isn't the same."

The waiter brought their food and they ate in silence. Afterward, Rod picked up the check. As they left the Royal Treat, he pointed toward the boardwalk. "Take the scenic route?" Laurel nodded and they started up Wilmington Avenue.

"I just find all of this hard to believe," she said, as they both slipped off their shoes and started down the ramp onto a beach teeming with activity. "I mean, what could make someone as private as Celeste involve herself with all these troubled people? They said she helped them through their problems, but how? Clearly, they inspired her books, but was she just a shoulder to cry on? Did she lend them money? Did she put them up at her house until they got back on their feet?"

"I can't imagine her doing any of that." Rod glanced over at a group of lifeguards gathered near the water, all wearing the red swimsuits of the Rehoboth Beach Patrol. "But I think I see someone who can answer your questions. Ain't that Christian right there? The one who just tossed his bag beside the lifeguard chair?"

Laurel shaded her eyes and followed Rod's gaze to a perfectly tanned and toned young man who shucked off his white T-shirt and dropped it into his bag. *If only I were fifteen years younger.* Once he slipped off his sunglasses, she recognized the face. "Yep, that's him."

As they approached, Christian looked up and waved, almost as if he had expected them.

"Hi, again," Laurel began. "Sorry to bother you."

The lifeguard shrugged. "It's no bother. My shift doesn't start for another ten minutes. It's good to see you again. How do you like Rehoboth?"

"Love it so far," she replied, before asking him to elaborate on what he'd said in his eulogy about Celeste.

"Your sister literally wrote my life story," Christian said. "Same goes for all the others. So what you read in the books is exactly how she helped us."

Laurel began to speak, but Rod cut her off. "Sorry if I'm a

little dense. So the only thing Celeste did was write about your lives and that was all you needed to find direction? We were under the impression that maybe she gave you money or a place to stay."

"Not exactly." Christian held up a hand. "If you two are free tonight around seven, we're having a small memorial for your sister at Rusty's house. You're more than welcome to join us. All of your questions will be answered."

THEY ARRIVED A FEW MINUTES LATE. Rusty offered them several choices of beverage and Christian volunteered to play bartender. As he made his way back toward the kitchen, the others engaged Rod and Laurel in idle conversation about their stay in Rehoboth. Laurel marveled at Virginia Kent's intricate sleeve of tattoos, revealed by her black tank top, while the reunited couple, Dutch Draper and Carla Dodd, once again stood with their arms around each other as if joined at the hip.

Christian returned with their drinks and Rod and Laurel took seats on the sofa.

"So, following up on our conversation on the beach earlier," Christian began. "When I said your sister wrote my life story, I meant that your sister *gave* me my life story." He gestured toward the others. "She gave life to all of us, which is why we call ourselves 'The Celestials.'"

Rod and Laurel exchanged puzzled glances.

"Let me explain." Rusty rose from his easy chair and began pacing the room as he spoke. "Your sister believed that when a writer creates characters with depth and fully developed backgrounds, and all of the flaws and foibles that make one human, those characters come to life in some other world or dimension."

"And we came to life here," Virginia added.

"Here," Laurel repeated, "in... Rehoboth?"

Rod laughed at Laurel's earnest bewilderment. "OK, we'll play along. So you're sayin' that our sister created all of you simply by writin' you as characters in her books."

Rusty smiled and pointed at Rod. "Give that man a cigar!"

"That's impossible." Laurel shook her head. "Worse, it's insane. Unless you're God, no one can just create people out of nothing. If Celeste conjured all of you into existence, how could you get by without birth certificates or social security cards?"

"Celeste didn't create us from nothing," Rusty said. "She created us from her beautiful and fertile imagination as well as her desperate loneliness. As for the rest, I'll get to that shortly." He stood beside Christian as he continued. "I'm not sure if you had much chance to explore the town, but just up the road, there are intersecting streets named Christian and Bayard." He gestured to the others in turn as he continued. "On the north end of town, we have Virginia Avenue and Kent Street. Over by the bay, Dutch Road and Draper Drive and Carla and Dodd Avenues. As for me, the Rusty Rudder restaurant is on Dickinson Street in Dewey Beach. Celeste was a brilliant storyteller, but she didn't work too hard at naming her characters."

Light laughter went around the room as Rusty took a seat on the sofa beside a noticeably trembling Laurel. She shifted closer to her brother as Rusty looked from her to Rod. "The real reason you fell out of touch with Celeste was that she became angry when you both moved away after your parents died. She felt abandoned and that put a strain on your relationship with her. Isn't that right?"

Rod shifted forward in his seat. Laurel knew he wanted nothing more than to escape, but a strange mélange of curiosity and fear kept her riveted. "Yes. She pleaded with us to stay, but we had lives of our own to—"

"We don't owe these people an explanation." Rod took Laurel's hand and gave it a squeeze. "What happened in our family is none of their business. Let's get out of here." He stood, but Laurel's legs refused to budge.

"I understand how you feel. If you'll just indulge me for another minute." Rusty turned toward the nearest end table and opened a drawer. First, he retrieved a pair of white cotton gloves. After donning them, he reached in again and produced a clear acrylic case containing a paperback book in pristine condition. With a gentle push, Rusty slid aside the top of the case. "Not long after your parents died, Celeste finished her first novel."

As if handling the holiest of relics, Rusty held up the book using both hands. It was titled, *While We're Young*. "Frequently, new authors will write themselves into their stories as the protagonist—under a different name, of course. This is one of those occasions. Celeste used some cheap vanity press to publish this. She sold a few hundred copies at most, but never did a second print run. It's mostly forgotten now." Rusty turned the book over and presented it to Laurel and Rod. "Note the main character's siblings mentioned in the back-cover blurb."

With mounting dread, Laurel leaned forward, but she knew what to expect even before she read the names. "Rodney and... Laurel."

Rod shrugged. "OK, so Celeste named some characters after us. So what? She did *not* create us. We're flesh and blood human beings."

"No one is contesting that," Rusty said, "but did you happen to read the 'About the Author' page in any of your sister's books? It mentions that Celeste was one of three children. Would you like to hear her bio from her first novel?"

Rusty turned to the final page and read aloud. "Originally from Bethlehem, Pennsylvania, Celeste Jaggar was the *only* child of two incredibly busy parents. At a very early age, Celeste found companionship in such literary characters as Sherlock Holmes, the Three Musketeers, and Isaac Asimov's Lucky Starr." Rusty lowered the book—and his voice—as he looked from Rod to Laurel. "Celeste's ability to alter her reality didn't manifest until she began writing. As her storytelling skills improved, so too did her power. It wasn't long before she was not only altering her own reality, but that of the world at large."

"But I remember my life," Laurel insisted. "All of it. Wouldn't there be gaps in my memory if I was just a product of Celeste's imagination?"

"What were you doing on this day five years ago?"

Laurel shrugged. "I don't know. Probably working."

"So there are gaps in your memory. Hardly anyone remembers every single day of his or her life. We remember significant conversations, events, achievements, relationships. In other words, fragments—and those were provided to us by Celeste. Now, to answer your earlier question about identification..."

Rusty lifted his wallet from the coffee table. Opening it, he produced a series of cards and laid them out as he spoke. "Social security, driver's license, medical insurance. Hell, even my library card. All of these things came into existence when we did. Celeste was nothing if not thorough.

"So this brings us back to the two of you. While Celeste was writing her first novel, she still lived in Pennsylvania, but was already spending her summer vacations here in Rehoboth. When you strolled the boardwalk this morning, did you happen to venture to the south end? If so, you might have noticed two streets there, one named Rodney and the other, Laurel. Please understand that we've been waiting a long time to meet you both."

Rod was speechless.

Laurel began to weep.

Rusty grinned. “You were the first Celestials.”

THIS STORY first appeared in *Beach Pulp* (Cat & Mouse Press, March 2019).

Tapestry

Doctor Rayna Geary, planetary scientist, rested her elbow on the half wall overlooking the bustling boardwalk at Obie's By the Sea. It was her favorite spot for lunch. She let her gaze drift from the crowded beach and rolling surf to the distant horizon where the murmuring cerulean sea kissed a clear azure sky. "Wherever we go in the galaxy, it will never truly be home. Not like this. Not like Rehoboth."

Across the table, her husband of three years—and colleague for twice that long—leaned forward and cupped his hand over hers. "I know it's heartbreaking to leave, but it's even worse to suffer the effects of global food shortages, ocean dumping, and overpopulation. We both know it'll only get worse. Once we're settled aboard the ship, we can finally start the family we always wanted. We'll reach a new world in our lifetime. Imagine being among the first to live on an exotic beach overlooking an alien sea."

Intellectually, she knew Devin was right, but she didn't feel it. "I don't want to think about it until next week. For now, let's enjoy our town while we still can."

"Agreed. Walk on the beach after lunch?"

A blaring klaxon cut off Rayna's reply.

She opened her eyes and drew in a sharp breath. Clutching her stomach with a quivering hand, Rayna rolled over onto her side, wheezing from yet another anxiety attack. She slapped the touch screen on her bedside table to shut off the alarm. This had become an almost daily routine since she began dreaming about Devin two weeks ago, but this attack was the worst yet—and she knew why.

Once she had finally composed herself, Rayna pushed disheveled gray locks out of her eyes, tossed aside the covers, and slipped out of bed to face the day.

IN HIS MOTHER'S quarters aboard the generation ship *Sagan*, Captain Ethan Geary watched the sun climb between gossamer clouds above a sparkling sea. The silhouette of a cargo ship drifted across the horizon while three seagulls circled above an empty beach before landing at the edge of the surf.

Ethan heard his mother emerge from the kitchen behind him, but kept his gaze fixed on the digital tapestry. "Delaware coast?"

Rayna sauntered up beside him. "Rehoboth Beach, to be exact. I programmed it in last month. Your father and I lived there for several years before you were born. That was our view almost every morning. I miss it... almost as much as I miss him." She turned away. "Breakfast is served, space cadet."

Ethan stepped over to the dining nook to find a plate piled high with pancakes in the center of the table. He pulled out a chair and motioned for Rayna to sit. "Honestly, Mom, you didn't need to go through the trouble. We could have eaten in the officer's mess."

"I made pancakes for you a few days after we lost your father, remember?"

Ethan nodded as he took a seat across from her. "Thirty years ago today. How could I forget?"

"It seemed appropriate that we share the same breakfast again."

Ethan raised his glass of orange juice. "To Dad... and you."

Rayna lifted her coffee cup and tapped it against his glass. They observed a moment of silence, during which Ethan glanced at the sun hovering high above the sea before he spoke again. "There's something else I meant to bring up before but never found the opportunity."

"Uh-oh. Sounds serious."

"It's about what Doctor Umoya asked you at your first nanotherapy appointment."

"Whether I want to be put into cryonic stasis when my ALS reaches the point of no return, in the hopes that a cure will someday be found."

"It's just something to think about. I don't need an answer immediately."

"Apparently you do. Otherwise, why bring it up today of all days?" Rayna finished her coffee and set the cup on the table. "Here we are sharing breakfast before this gorgeous sunrise aboard a starship whose purpose is to carry the human race to a new world, yet all you want to talk about is my imminent demise."

"Just the opposite, Mom. Our mission is to offer a second chance at life for the human race—and that includes you. I can't think of anyone more deserving, and I'm not just saying that because you're the captain's mother. After all, you and Dad worked together to map this ship's course to a new Earth."

They ate quietly for another minute before Rayna replied.

"I'll think it over. Of course, if I suddenly drop dead before then, all bets are off."

"You have a way with words, Mom."

"Comes with age, space cadet."

"Just one favor. Please don't call me that in front of the crew."

"I can't make any promises."

LYING on her side atop the examination table, Rayna flinched as the cold metal of the nanite injector pressed against the back of her neck and, a few seconds later, against the base of her spine.

"Sorry, Doctor." Rutan Umoya, the ship's chief medical officer, pulled the injector away and straightened Rayna's blouse. "Nanotherapy is not the most comfortable procedure, but the good news is that your body is accepting the treatment. You can sit up now."

Rayna pushed herself up with relative ease. "I couldn't do *that* a month ago, but there's no way these microscopic robots floating around in my system can cure me?"

"Not yet, but we're working on it." Umoya leaned back against the counter and continued in a thick Kenyan accent. "So far, the disease is staying ahead of the treatment. As we discussed before, the nanites are programmed to stimulate the motor neurons from your brain to your spinal cord, and from there out to your muscles, thereby slowing their degeneration, but until such time as we can determine how to reverse the degeneration permanently, this is the best we can do. If we don't find a cure in time, I did confirm that you're eligible for cryostasis, if you so choose."

Rayna twisted her mouth into a wry grin. "Confirmed that with the captain, did ya?"

Alone in her quarters, Rayna took a sip of synthetic wine and stared at the surging whitecaps lapping onto the sands of Rehoboth Beach, recalling her breakfast conversation with Ethan. *All you want to talk about is my imminent demise.*

She'd stopped weeping minutes before and wiped her face with a napkin. *Seems that's all anyone wants to talk about anymore.*

When her vision cleared, Rayna shot forward in her seat and narrowed her eyes at the tapestry. A trim young man no older than thirty-five stood at the edge of the water, staring at the boats on the horizon. His bronzed skin appeared even darker in contrast against his yellow T-shirt and khaki shorts. *Who the hell are you and what are you doing in my program?* As if in response to her thought, the man turned and made his way up the beach—straight toward Rayna. As he grew near, recognition dawned on her. It took another second for the shock to catch up with her brain.

In that time, he had closed the distance and now stood as if on the other side of a glass door. With a smile, he reached out to her, his hand passing *through* the wall and into the room.

Rayna screamed.

Ethan dashed into his mother's quarters before the doors had fully parted. The medical team was just finishing their examination.

"Report, medic!" Ethan barked.

Rayna waved her hand. "It's all right, *Captain*. I'm fine. Just had a bad dream, that's all."

The senior of the two medics explained that the infirmary

had received an alert from Rayna's health implant indicating a rapid pulse and sudden increases in blood pressure and adrenaline. "She seems to be fine now, sir, but we gave her a mild sedative to help her rest."

Ethan nodded. "Thank you."

With that, the medics departed, and Ethan took a seat beside his mother. "How are you feeling now?"

"I said I'm fine."

"So, tell me about this bad dream."

"There was no dream. That was just an excuse for the medics."

"So, what really happened?"

Rayna sighed and rubbed the bridge of her nose. "You won't believe it."

"Try me."

"Your father was here."

Ethan stared at her for a moment. "Here? In your quarters?"

"In the tapestry."

"Which one? Rehoboth Beach?"

Rayna nodded.

"You *were* dreaming."

"I was wide awake, sitting here enjoying the sights and sounds of our old home town when he just appeared at the water's edge and trudged right up to the wall."

"And you didn't program an image of Dad into the tapestry?"

"Don't you think I'd remember if I did? I'm not *that* senile."

Ethan held up his hands. "Just making sure. Then let's fire it up and take a look."

Rayna hesitated before pressing a button on the arm of her chair. On the wall before them, the sun peeked over the horizon, casting its saffron reflection on an undulating sea and illuminating a deserted stretch of beach.

"Wait for it," Rayna said.

Minutes passed. Drifting clouds obscured the sun for a moment. The dorsal fins of four dolphins broke the surface then submerged again.

"It should have happened by now."

"You told me that you've been dreaming about Dad on and off for the past few weeks," Ethan said. "Yesterday was the anniversary of his death. It's only natural that he's been on your mind more than usual lately."

But he reached out to me.

Ethan stood and made his way toward the door. "I have to get back to the bridge. I'll stop by to check on you later."

"No need." She turned off the tapestry. "Maybe you're right, space cadet. It was probably just a dream. Sorry for the scare."

Rayna found herself seated alone on the screened porch of the Royal Treat, astonished to see the place deserted on such a sweltering summer day. She glanced up just as Devin emerged from the entrance and placed two sundaes on the table before sliding into the chair across from her.

Rayna leaned forward. "I don't recall ever seeing business this slow here."

"I prefer it this way." Devin pointed his spoon at her sundae. "I can't believe you still like butterscotch over mint chocolate chip. Yuk."

"Don't knock it until you try it."

"Either way, I bet you can't get ice cream like this aboard the *Sagan*."

Rayna plunged her spoon into her sundae. "You got that right." She paused. "Wait. What did you say?"

"Why did you run away when I came to see you yesterday?"

"What are you talking about?"

"You screamed and turned off the tapestry. I might not be the most attractive guy, but you did marry me."

Rayna's spoon clattered to the table. "I thought you were a ghost."

Devin swallowed a mouthful of his Dusty Road sundae. "Why would you think that?"

"Because I watched you die when that plasma jet exploded in orbit thirty years ago."

"It's been that long?" Devin looked away for a moment. "That explosion didn't kill me. It opened some kind of... portal to another dimension and I was pulled through. It wasn't long before I realized that I could manipulate my reality here through sheer thought. Don't ask me to explain it. It was chaos at first. I thought I was going insane. It felt like forever before I learned how to control it, but finally I did. Then I decided to recreate the town we once called home. This is Rehoboth Beach long before conditions on Earth deteriorated. It's nearly perfect in every detail, but it's missing one thing."

"What's that?"

"You." He took her hand in his. He felt warm, *alive*. Rayna squeezed his fingers. "Some time ago, I discovered how to reopen the portal at will. No explosion necessary. That's how I was able to reach out to you through the tapestry."

"So, you can come back?"

Devin shook his head. "I've lived here too long. If I reenter your reality, I'll be dead within hours."

"But I can come here?"

"Yes."

"Devin, I'm being treated for ALS. They've slowed its progress, but they can't reverse it. Ethan and Doctor Umoya are trying to convince me to enter cryostasis until a cure is found. If I come here, what will happen to me?"

"You'll be able to change your reality as I did. Shape your own destiny. We could be together for eternity here."

"Will I be young again?"

"That all depends on you."

Around them, the Royal Treat dissolved. Wooden floors gave way to hard, packed sand, while the white ceiling faded to reveal blue sky. Husband and wife stood facing each other along the water's edge. Waves crashed onto the beach from where the street had been mere seconds before.

"The *Sagan* is nearly out of range. I can only open the portal for short periods—maybe only one more time." As Devin stepped back, a wall materialized between them. He placed his open hand against it. Rayna did the same. "Devin? No! Please don't leave me again."

She awoke with a jolt, slumped on the easy chair facing the tapestry, but the only response to her plea was the shriek of passing seagulls above an empty beach.

LATER THAT MORNING, Rayna sat on the edge of the examination table as Doctor Umoya prepared her injection. After a few minutes, she yawned and lay back.

Umoya glanced over his shoulder. "Are you feeling all right? I noticed your eyes were bloodshot when you came in."

"Doctor, has anyone reported any bizarre side effects to nanotherapy?"

"Such as?"

"Ever since I started these treatments, I've been having vivid dreams about my late husband. In one case, I actually saw him while I was wide awake."

Umoya shook his head. "To my knowledge, nothing like that has ever been reported."

"That's what I thought."

"But then, everyone reacts differently while their bodies adjust to the treatment. Let me know if these experiences continue. For now, I can give you something to help you sleep."

Rayna responded with a desultory wave as she rolled onto her side. "No, I'll be all right."

This time, she didn't react as Umoya administered the injections. "Have you come to a decision on the cryostasis?"

"Been thinking about it. Depending on how long I'm in cold storage, there's a good possibility that if or when I'm revived someday, most of the people I know now will be long gone."

"That's always a risk."

At that, Rayna's choice became clear. "Today, I'm an old woman living in a metal crate hurtling through space, spending my days staring at a digital image from a life I left behind, pining every day to be back there. That won't change ten, fifty, a hundred years from now when they pull me out of the freezer. The only difference is that I'll be a lonely old woman surrounded by strangers." She sat up and met Umoya's gaze. "I've made my decision, doctor."

"I UNDERSTAND you elected to stop the nanotherapy. May I ask why?"

Once again, Rayna's sitting room was bathed in the golden radiance of the morning sun. She sat before the digital tapestry, ignoring Ethan's looming presence until he circled around her chair and blocked her view.

Rayna rose from her seat under his fuming scowl. "I knew you'd come charging down here sooner or later. Let's be honest, space cadet. What do I have to look forward to here? I'm dying, and frankly I'm tired of dealing with it. I have a unique opportunity to be with your father again in a place I wish I'd never left. When he came to see me last ni—"

"Stop it, Mom. Just stop." Ethan gently gripped her shoulders. "He did *not* come to see you or take you back to Rehoboth Beach. Those are dreams, nothing more. Speaking of which, didn't you and Dad share a dream of seeing the human race thrive on a new world? You talk about leaving, but don't you want to be there when we arrive?"

As he spoke, Rayna's gaze drifted over his shoulder.

"Mom, if you continue the nanotherapy and take advantage of cryostasis, you have a good chance of waking up on a new world that *you* helped discover."

Her lips curled into a smile as she sidestepped him and approached the tapestry.

"Mom, are you listening to—" After a double take, Ethan's eyes flashed wide. His exasperation drained away as he came face to face with a man who could have been his twin—a man Ethan had not seen since he was twelve years old. "Oh my God. Dad?"

Devin Geary, clad in a T-shirt and rumpled cargo shorts, raised his hand in a casual salute.

"He knows you're the captain now and he's very proud of you." Rayna placed a hand on her son's arm. "I have to go, space cadet. I don't have time to explain. Let's just say I'd much rather spend the rest of eternity with your father under the summer sun than alone in the deep freeze. Would you deny me this?"

"Of course not, but I don't understand. Where are you going? That's just a digital projection isn't it?"

"Someday, I hope you'll join us, but not too soon. Save the human race first. Rehoboth Beach will always be there."

With that, Rayna embraced her son, kissed him on the cheek, and stepped through the tapestry.

THE BIKINI-CLAD woman walking beside her husband on the sands of Rehoboth Beach no longer feared any debilitating illness. With youthful hands unmarred by age spots, she scooped up a pair of seashells, marveled at her supple legs, and reached up to twirl soft, windblown locks of auburn.

In the distance to the north, two familiar concrete towers, monuments to an ancient war that never reached these shores, stood shrouded in the rippling haze of summer heat. Rayna took Devin's hand as she gazed from boardwalk, to beach, to rolling surf. She was home. "Are we really in the past?"

"Past, present, future." Devin shrugged. "Time has no meaning here. This place is eternal, as are we. It'll never change except as we wish it to."

"And we'll never have to leave again?"

"Never."

ETHAN SLID his hands along the tapestry but encountered only a solid wall. He backed away as he watched his parents—younger than he'd ever known them—run hand in hand along the edge of the water until they disappeared from view. With a deep breath, Captain Ethan Geary of the Earth ship *Sagan* drew himself to his full height and deactivated the tapestry. Before leaving his mother's quarters, he keyed in a series of commands on the control panel to upload the tapestry to his quarters and smiled in anticipation of waking up the next morning to a Rehoboth Beach sunrise.

THIS STORY first appeared in *Beach Pulp* (Cat & Mouse Press, March 2019).

Give Them Peace

Crippling sorrow flooded Miranda Lorensen's thoughts the moment she stepped through the door of Heldon Studios. Overlapping voices in her head pleaded for help, begged to be set free. Miranda ignored them for the moment as she and fellow paranormal investigator Marc Malkasian greeted the studio's general manager, Stillman Ross.

"Thanks for rearranging your schedule for us on such short notice." Stillman extended a hand. "Where's the rest of your team?"

"Short notice means shorthanded," Marc said. "You're stuck with the two of us. Any more activity since you called?"

"Later that night, in fact." Stillman nodded toward a row of offices down the hall. "We caught it on a security camera along with the other incidents I mentioned on the phone. I have the footage queued up."

By now, the edges of Miranda's vision had blurred and she winced against another torrent of desperation and grief. Closing her eyes, she tuned out the conversation between Marc and Stillman. *I'm here. Tell me what you need.*

A plaintive voice rose above the chatter. *"Finally, someone who can hear us."*

"We've waited so long," another added.

Both were women, but Miranda sensed that they weren't the only spirits attached to the building, or perhaps the land. *How can I help you?*

"You're a sensitive," the first voice said. *"As we were. That's why he killed us."*

Who killed you?

There was no response.

Are you still with me? What's your name? Again, Miranda's questions were met with silence.

"Randy?"

A hand clutched her arm. Miranda's eyes shot open and met Marc's bewildered gaze.

"You okay? You wandered off without a word."

Miranda took in her surroundings. She didn't recall leaving the lobby, yet she now found herself in a wide corridor between two sound stages. "Right. Sorry about that."

"Did you have a vision?"

"Not exactly." As they started back toward the main entrance, Miranda shot a glance over her shoulder. "But the day is still young."

All three tripods crashed to the floor, hurled across the room by an invisible force. In the security office, the astonishing scene played out on two wall-mounted monitors.

"That happened about four hours after we closed on the day I called you," Stillman explained. "I thought it was one of my technicians playing a prank, but no one was in the building at the time. Of all the footage we captured, this scared the shit out of me more than anything."

"I can see why," Marc said. "These spirits definitely seem pissed off about something. Where did this happen?"

"Stage C. Last one on the right before you get to the storage room."

"Hold on." Marc pointed to the screen. "When the tripods hit the floor, they kinda resemble arrows, evenly spaced and perfectly lined up beside each other."

Miranda cocked her head. "Arrows pointing toward the storage room, perhaps?"

"I'll be damned." Stillman slumped in his chair. "Since we converted this place from a warehouse, we don't use that part of the building much. I've never been comfortable back there. Always feels like someone's watching me from the mezzanine."

"Maybe they are," Marc said. "When you called, you mentioned a woman who appeared on film, but no one saw her in person. Can you show us?"

"Absolutely." Stillman opened two video files and dragged each to its own monitor. He pointed to the left screen. "This was the first appearance, during an interview show. Watch for the middle-aged woman with the salt and pepper hair and bruises around her neck. There. See her standing off to the right behind the host?"

"Jeez." Marc leaned forward. "Her gray eyes and blank expression aren't creepy at all."

"Check it out," Stillman continued. "They cut away and back to the host... and she's gone." He stopped the video. "Now, let me draw your attention to the monitor on the right. There's a company in the area that makes cleaning products. They use our studio to shoot their commercials. This one had three actors, four if you count the dog. Watch this beagle turn its head from the kid and stare at nothing until they cut away, come back, and *bam*—there she is again. Where she came from, no one knows."

The beagle whined and stared up at the woman who gazed at the actors with a forlorn expression. Stillman paused the video just as she peered into the camera.

"She came from this place." Miranda glanced from one monitor to the other. "Her soul is trapped here, and she isn't alone."

Stillman raised an eyebrow. "How many are there?"

"Something tells me we're about to find out."

Miranda followed Marc through the double doors of the storage room at the rear of the building. He slid his hand along the wall until he found the light switches and flipped them on. "Damn. This place *looks* haunted."

Two stories above, several rows of stark white fluorescent lights flickered to life, revealing patches of rust in the corrugated metal ceiling. Blue and gray racks lined dingy beige walls that hadn't seen a fresh coat of paint in over a decade.

In the middle of the room, two sets of stairs led to doors on either side of a mezzanine office. Its six dark windows overlooked the storage room.

"I'm gonna get a few shots of that office from down here." Marc shivered as he pulled a digital camera from his jacket pocket. "Whoa. Did you feel that chill?"

"Yep." Miranda checked her temperature meter as the edges of her vision blurred once again. "Fifty-eight degrees and dropping." *If this is you again, let me know. Tell me how I can help you.*

"Hey, look at this picture I just took." Marc held out the camera. On its small screen, five blurred, glowing faces stared down at them from two of the office windows. The ghost hunters lifted their gazes to the mezzanine.

"There's nothing there now." Marc magnified the image.

"Could have been a reflection of the ceiling lights, but those definitely look like eyes."

They are, but this is for me to deal with. "One way to find out." Miranda nodded toward the stairs. "Let's see if that office is open. You go up this side. I'll take the other. When you get to the door, give me a shout and let me know if it's locked or not. I'll do the same. If they're open, we'll go in together. If they're locked, we'll get the key from Stillman and come back."

"Just don't go wandering off by yourself again."

"I won't. Trust me."

NO SOONER HAD Miranda reached the top step than the office door creaked open, releasing a frigid draft. The temperature plunged at least ten degrees the moment she crossed the threshold. Despite her jacket and sweatshirt, she folded her arms across her chest. Every breath produced tendrils of wispy steam.

Ceiling lights beyond the windows provided meager illumination and cast much of the office in shadow.

"It's locked over here," Marc shouted from the other end of the mezzanine. "How about your side?"

Miranda turned to respond when the room dissolved around her. Walls and windows vanished. Tile floor sprouted thick, verdant grass, and the drop ceiling faded to reveal a sky mottled with clouds tinted amber by the dimming rays of the setting sun.

She stood at the edge of a clearing surrounded by a dense perimeter of trees, swaying canopies of gold, red, and orange. Was this the land on which the warehouse had been built or was it some other place entirely?

Behind her, twigs snapped and dried leaves crunched.

Something—or someone—stirred in the woods. As with all of Miranda's visions, every detail revealed by the spirits warranted her attention. Nothing was irrelevant, but that didn't make them any less unsettling. She crept along a trail until she came upon a tall, brawny man in a sweat-soaked T-shirt and grimy jeans climbing out of a ditch, shovel in hand.

It wasn't until he disappeared behind a row of trees that Miranda noticed the body wrapped in clear plastic lying beside what she now realized was a shallow grave. Reminding herself that she was in no physical danger—it was only a vision after all—she dashed forward and knelt beside the corpse. Multiple bruises across the woman's throat were visible through the plastic but her face was concealed by thick salt and pepper hair.

"Psychics. Mediums. Servants of Satan."

At the crack of a tree branch, Miranda whirled as the man charged at her, his features obscured in shadow beneath the brim of his tattered baseball cap. "You're just like the others and you'll die like them, too!" He raised the shovel and swung at her head. With a scream, Miranda tumbled into the grave—but struck the cold tile floor of the office instead. She rolled onto her back. The man was gone. In his place stood five women, each one bruised and battered. They stared at her in silence, their expressions inscrutable.

The middle aged woman from Stillman's video clips stepped forward. Cuts and bruises on her throat. Salt and pepper hair. "My name is Ursula. You have nothing to fear from us. We've been waiting thirty years for someone to listen."

Miranda reached up to a nearby desk and pulled herself to her feet. "I take it that man was the one who killed you, but why?"

"He claimed to be a warrior of God," a young black woman chimed in, the front of her shirt drenched in blood from a gunshot wound. "Sent to purge the world of psychics and mediums. In his tormented mind, we were witches, minions of the devil. The five of us were not his only victims and we won't be his last."

"Give me a name and I'll—"

"He's long dead." A tall, muscular blonde stepped out from behind the others, her face bruised and swollen. "Or his host is, I should say. The man you saw was possessed by an ancient and violent soul, reborn every few generations. He surfaces when his host reaches puberty, manifesting as a personality disorder. In fact, he recently returned to this world and when his host is old enough, he'll kill again."

"How can I stop him if I don't know who he is?"

"When he crosses your path someday, you'll sense the chaos in him," Ursula said. "But be warned—he's relentless. He thinks he's on some holy mission. We showed you the vision so that you might avoid our fate, but you must remain vigilant."

"Thank you for the warning. Now, how can I help you?"

"DAMN IT, RANDY." After making his way to Miranda's side of the mezzanine, Marc tugged on the door handle once more as if it would produce a different result than the last six times he tried. "Freezing up here." He pulled out his phone to call Stillman for a key when the office door clicked open.

He charged in and flipped the nearest switch. Once his eyes adjusted to the light, he found Miranda sitting at one of the desks twirling a lock of her hair.

"Randy, you OK?"

"I'm good." Her lips curled into a thin smile. "Met five lovely ladies who need our help."

Marc scanned the room. "Five lovely—oh, you mean ghosts. What did they want?"

"They want us to walk out to the woods behind the building. But first, we'll need shovels."

Marc drew back. "Oh, hell no."

"We're here." After Marc had retrieved two collapsible shovels from the trunk of his car, he and Miranda trudged through the woods into a damp clearing mottled with autumn leaves and broken branches. Chatty crickets fell silent. Even the air seemed afraid to move here. The five women stood at random spots, pointing to the ground in front of them. Ursula was closest. Miranda approached and bowed her head. "I understand."

She held up a hand as Marc joined her. "Back up two steps."

"Why?"

"You're standing on a grave." She tapped the ground with the tip of her shovel. "We'll start digging here... gently."

"Randy, let's just call the cops. Digging up dead people is way outside our scope."

"These women were murdered because they were sensitives like me. The killer buried them in these woods thirty years ago. You're right, this *is* outside our scope, but as a fellow medium, it's my responsibility to bring these women and their families closure. Besides, we're not digging up all of them. One should be enough evidence for the police to exhume the others. Help me give them peace... *please*."

"I learned a long time ago never to argue with you when your mind's made up." With a deep breath, Marc plunged his shovel into the earth.

TWO HOURS LATER, Miranda recounted the events of the evening to a bemused Detective Kraeger and three uniformed officers. A short distance away, more cops crowded around the coroner as she examined the plastic-wrapped corpse that Marc and Miranda had unearthed.

"At that point," Miranda said. "I decided to locate the remains of at least one of the women based on the information they provided so—"

"Information their *ghosts* provided," Kraeger interjected. "I just want to confirm that."

"Correct."

The detective exchanged skeptical glances with the officers. "And are these ghosts here with us right now?"

"They are, Detective. Believe me, I know how crazy it sounds, but I've worked with police on a number of cases like this in the past."

"Uh-huh. So, you know exactly where the other four victims are buried?"

"Yes, as well as their names, ages, and dates they were murdered."

"What about the killer's name?"

Miranda shook her head. "They didn't know him."

"Of course not." Kraeger turned to one of the officers. "Kelly, grab the LED road flares from one of the cars. We'll use them to mark the other graves until we can get a crew out here to exhume the bodies."

As the officer hurried off, Kraeger flipped to a fresh page in his notepad. "OK, Ms. Lorensen, when he gets back, I'd like you to escort us to each of the graves and identify the victims. In the meantime, let's start with the one you already dug up." He pointed his pen toward the body bag that was now atop a stretcher being rolled toward the waiting ambulance. "Name, age, date of death, whatever you got."

"Ursula Moyer, forty-six. Strangled on October 31, 1992..."

Standing at the edge of the clearing, Ursula nodded before vanishing into the night. Each of the remaining four women followed in turn as Miranda marked their graves with the flares and provided their information to Detective Kraeger.

At the final grave, Marc slipped an arm around her shoulders. "Can we tell Stillman his problems are over?"

"Yeah." She leaned into him. "And thank you for helping me give them peace."

~

THIS STORY first appeared in *Writing a Wrong* (Greater Lehigh Valley Writers Group, February 2025).

Burn After Writing

Dedicated to Harlan Ellison

Crackling flames leapt from the immense stone fireplace like the snapping claws of some ravenous monster. *Or is that just my imagination?* Shane Conrad took a step back as he stared at the blazing hearth in Adrian Halka's lakeside cabin. Behind him, multicolored file folders had been stacked atop a table by Halka's widow. *Food for the beast.*

It had been the great writer's final wish that they be burned—no exceptions. While Shane understood Halka's reasons, he did not agree with them at all. To an editor and fellow fantasist, the very notion of destroying the unfinished works of one of the most awarded writers in history was abhorrent.

"I found two more." Robyn shuffled into the room and tossed a pair of blue file folders onto the table. Each one was easily an inch thick with pages held together by large binder clips.

Shane picked up the top folder and began flipping through it. "Is there a code behind these colors?"

"If I recall correctly, a blue folder indicates a story in

progress. Yellow means that Adrian was still developing the idea and maybe had an outline, and the red folders have a page or two of notes he jotted down when inspiration struck. That's why the red ones are the thinnest."

Shane sighed as he fanned the pages. "I have to be honest with you, Robyn. I'm struggling with the idea of burning all this."

She joined him in front of the fire. "I know. I noticed your expression when the lawyer read that part of Adrian's will. I thought you were going to swallow your head."

"I can name a dozen capable writers, myself included, who would be honored to finish some of these—and we could do it in Adrian's style without sacrificing the integrity of his work."

Robyn chuckled as she sat against the table. It was probably the first time she had cracked a smile since her husband's death. "You remember Adrian's reaction years ago when that publisher turned one of his manuscripts over to a hack because Adrian refused to make the revisions they wanted?"

"He sent them a box of dead rats."

"By third-class mail in the middle of summer. Cost them thousands to fumigate."

"There will never be another like Adrian."

"To the relief of many in your business, I'm sure." Robyn placed a gentle hand on Shane's arm. "It wasn't that Adrian didn't trust you, but he was adamant that if his name was on it—"

"—it had to be entirely *his* work and no one else's, I know." Shane held up the folder. "Did you ever read any of these unfinished stories?"

Robyn shook her head. "I could barely keep up with the published ones—all two thousand over fifty-four years. Speaking of which, Adrian loved your stories. That's why he kept encouraging you to quit editing and get back to writing.

What was it he used to say? There's a special place in Hell for editors. Present company excluded, of course."

Shane laughed. "As a matter of fact, I have three short stories coming out later this year and two novels in progress."

Robyn gave his arm a gentle squeeze. "Adrian would be proud." A slow melody began playing from elsewhere in the house. She pushed away from the table. "I left my phone in the kitchen. As much as it pains you, my dear, start feeding the fire. I'll be right back."

The moment she vanished from view, Shane gathered both of the blue folders and slipped them into his backpack beneath the table. By the time Robyn returned, he had burned through half of the remaining stack of folders. They finished the rest in silence.

STANDING at the lectern in Ebba Mackie's Bookshop, Shane finished reading the opening chapter of his new fantasy novel before a small but appreciative audience. Ignoring the throbbing in his head, he smiled during their applause and began taking questions. A middle-aged woman in the second row raised her hand. "What inspired you to return to writing after so many years as an editor?"

Shane cleared his throat. "Last January, the world lost a brilliant writer in Adrian Halka. Some of you knew Adrian personally. He gave readings and signed books in this very store. I edited much of Adrian's later work for Cinderbox Press, and we became fast friends. Over time, I looked to him as a mentor. Years of exposure to his writing elevated the quality of mine until Adrian all but ordered me to quit meddling with other people's work and get back to creating my own." Shane held up the hardback copy of his book, "but it wasn't until his death that I finally took his advice."

He shot a sidelong glance at the back cover—and met the accusing gaze of Adrian Halka. *You took more than my advice, you son of a—!*

The book slipped from Shane's grasp and slammed onto the lectern. No one in the audience seemed to hear the disembodied voice, but they stared at him expectantly. Shane cleared his throat again as he straightened the book. "Sorry about that, folks." He pressed a hand to his chest. "Even after all this time, I still become... emotional when I think about Adrian. Any more questions?"

Two hours later, after scribbling his name in more than a dozen copies of his novel, Shane thanked the last customer before slumping in his chair. He slipped off his glasses and massaged the bridge of his nose just as an older woman took the empty seat beside him. "You know, as I listened to your reading, I could definitely hear Adrian's influence. I look forward to reading the rest of it." She leaned forward, brow furrowed. "You feeling all right?"

Shane cast his weary gaze on shop owner Ebba Mackie. "I must be coming down with something. I woke up with a scratchy throat and a relentless headache."

Ebba pressed two gnarled fingers against his forehead. "You do seem a bit feverish, kiddo." She slid her chair a few inches away. "No offense. I can't afford to get sick. I'm a delicate old termagant. At least, that's what Adrian used to call me."

"Lady, you're about as delicate as Krakatoa."

"Are you implying I have a volcanic temper?"

"Remind me why you and Adrian got divorced?"

Ebba turned her gaze away and began straightening a stack of Shane's books. She flipped one over, and Shane was relieved to see his own smiling visage on the back cover. "Adrian was the unstoppable force to my immovable object. Writing was his mistress, and I couldn't compete. Of course, I didn't offer much support either. Ours was a brief and volatile marriage, but we became friends again after some time apart. I was happy for him when he found Robyn. She's a strong woman. What about you, handsome young stud? Any luck on the romantic front?"

Shane stifled a chill and began to suspect Ebba was right about the fever. He forced a wan smile. "Still looking for Ms. Right... but not today. Today, I'm going home, making chicken soup, and going to bed."

DESPITE THE LIVELY throng of well-wishers in his apartment, Shane couldn't stop shivering. As he walked through his living room, smiling faces blurred past on either side. Overlapping voices congratulated him on his recent success. He recognized most of them. His parents and sister, friends old and new, even ex-girlfriends had turned up to celebrate. Robyn was there, chatting with Ebba beside the familiar stone fireplace from Adrian's cabin.

How did this get here? Shane shouldered his way toward them and stood trembling before the hearth. He crouched down and closed his eyes, relishing the warmth on his face and hands.

"How ya feelin', Shane?"

He turned to find a short, stout man in black cargo pants standing over him. His salt and pepper beard covered the top buttons of a disheveled blue and white plaid shirt. The room fell silent. Everyone else had vanished.

"Adrian. W-what—"

"Looks like you're running a fever, boy." Adrian's hands

shot forward, clutching Shane's throat and pressing him backward toward the flames. "Better feed the fire."

"Wait!" Shane awoke, thrashing and kicking in a tangle of sheets and blankets. When he'd finally extricated himself, he sat on the edge of the bed and glanced at the alarm clock. It was just after three in the morning. The TV was still on, casting the bedroom in a feeble blue glow.

He snatched the digital thermometer from the nightstand and slipped it under his tongue before wrapping himself in a blanket. Glancing at the TV, Shane instantly recognized an old talk show from the 1980s, though he couldn't recall the name of it.

"So what, if anything, do you dislike about writing?" the host asked.

"I don't dislike anything about writing." His guest shrugged, before turning in his chair to face the camera. "But I do hate people who steal my work."

Shane tore the thermometer from his mouth. "Adrian..."

"Ain't no fever-induced dream this time, Conrad. You know, I don't even care that you lied to your publisher or to your readers, but you lied to my wife. Hell, you even lied to my *ex*-wife! You were like a son to me, boy."

Shane shot to his feet and started toward the TV, shivering either from fever or fear... or both. "Adrian, please, I'm sorry—"

"Screw your apology. You betrayed me. Why?"

Shane's vision blurred, and his knees buckled. He fell back against the bed. The digital thermometer in his hand began beeping, but he was too weak to lift his arm. "I... hadn't published a novel in eight years. I needed a fast comeback. Mine were taking too long."

"So, instead of respecting my final wishes, you stole my unpublished work. Of all people! You burn me up, Conrad, and now I'm returning the favor."

Shane slid to the floor, writhing under the furious scowl of Adrian Halka. What began as a tingling throughout his body erupted with the torture of a thousand bee stings, and the only sound louder than the electronic squeal of the thermometer was his own agonized shriek.

THE POLICE FOUND Shane Conrad lying on the floor of his bedroom, loosely covered in the scorched tatters of a blanket. When the coroner arrived, the young sergeant was all too happy to give him a few minutes to perform his initial examination—any excuse to tear his gaze away from the body. "No sign of forced entry or struggle. We found no cigarettes or alcohol on him, and nothing else in the room appears to have been affected except for this." He held up an evidence bag containing the melted remains of a digital thermometer.

The coroner motioned for the body to be bagged. "Well, ruling out all that, it could have been a natural cause, but I won't know for sure until I perform an autopsy. You all right, sergeant?"

"It's his face. The neighbor who called said it sounded like the guy was screaming in terror. I've never seen anything like... *that.*"

"I have, just not to this degree." The coroner stared at the body bag as the zipper closed over the charred, blackened corpse of Shane Conrad.

THIS STORY first appeared in *Scary Stuff* (Oddity Prodigy Productions, October 2020).

Memory Lane Ain't What it Used to Be

A midsummer stroll down Memory Lane turned out to be far less nostalgic than Gene and Dottie Spencer had anticipated. In fact, it was downright depressing.

"Did we make a wrong turn?" Dottie glanced from one end of the street to the other. "Where's old Burt Hepworth's Dutch colonial... and the Marconi's bungalow?" Gene pointed to a row of modern, nondescript townhouses incongruously crammed between two Cape Cods. "Oh." Dottie frowned. "Well, I guess everything changes."

"And not for the better." Gene shook his head at the glut of vehicles parked bumper-to-bumper along both sides of the narrow street. "It was never like this in our day. There must be four cars to every house... and we wouldn't dream of letting our sidewalks go to pot like this, all cracked and buckling with weeds everywhere. Don't people take pride in their neighborhood anymore?"

For the Spencers, Memory Lane took the form of Sandalwood Drive near the outskirts of the city. It was here that the couple had purchased their first and only home nearly sixty years ago. It was here that they had raised three children, made lifelong friends, and become pillars of the community. Now, however, all of that was ancient history and one that had lost much of its luster.

"I'm almost afraid to see what our old house looks like now," Gene grumbled. "Remember what Carmen said to Gayle and Alex the other day while we were watching over the grandkids? The new owner is some single gal—"

"Single *young lady*," Dottie corrected.

"—that Carmen used to work with. She gave the place a makeover before moving in, so expect to see some changes."

Finally, they stopped at the corner of Sandalwood and Highland Avenue and peered up at the rustic two-story colonial.

Gene threw up his hands. "Now why did she replace a perfectly good metal roof with shingles? Remember when my brother and I used to get up there every summer and paint it?"

"And every summer you griped about the heat."

Gene leaned forward and peered over the neatly trimmed boxwoods along the front of the house. "And she replaced the old wooden porch with concrete. Remember how I used to varnish it to a perfect sheen every spring?"

"And every spring you bellyached about your hay fever."

"Those were the days. Hey, remember—"

The roar of a lawnmower engine curtailed any further reminiscing. Gene and Dottie followed the noise around the corner, stopping at a chain link fence that enclosed the backyard. There, a slim young woman in a sweat-soaked tank top and denim shorts pushed the mower across a narrow lawn speckled with dandelions and white clover.

Gene folded his arms. "You know, back in our day, single young ladies didn't own homes or mow lawns."

"The world's a different place now, Gene. Like I said earlier, everything changes. Oh, damn!" Dottie pointed toward the shed in the back corner of the yard. "That hussy tore out my blue hydrangeas... and our dogwood tree. I used to love to watch it bloom pink every spring."

"Like you said, everything changes. At least she kept the red maple in the middle of the yard. Remember when you and I planted that about five years after we moved in? Now it's taller than the house."

"Speaking of which, I wonder how it looks inside."

"If what we've seen so far is any indication, we probably wouldn't recognize the place."

Dottie put her hand on Gene's chest. "Look, the cellar doors are open. Let's sneak in for a quick look."

"I don't think that's a good idea, Dottie. We should be getting home."

"What's the hurry? We have all the time in the world. We'll be in and out before she finishes cutting the grass." Dottie dashed through the gate and across the yard.

"Dottie, wait! Oh, good grief." Gene followed, but didn't speak again until they had descended through the doors and were standing in the basement. "What's gotten into you?"

"It's like being young again. Off on another escapade." Dottie beamed. "Like the old days when we were dating. Remember?"

"Of course I remember. Ghost hunting on Halloween night in the cemetery across from your parents' house, skinny dipping in the lake up the road from the high school."

"Climbing out on the roof of your uncle's beach house in the middle of the night to stargaze."

Gene grinned. "The heavens weren't the only thing we admired that night."

"Hence the reason we named our first born after your uncle."

"Yeah, I guess two old souls like us deserve one last adventure." Gene motioned Dottie ahead. "But let's make it quick. I feel like we're intruding. At least the steps are still in the same place, and just as solid as the day I built them."

"You always did good work, love." Dottie reached the top of the stairs first. For a moment, she froze in the doorway before turning back to her husband. "Brace yourself, Gene."

"Why?"

Dottie stepped aside as they emerged into the dining room.

"It's gone!" Gene cried. "All the blue and green floral wall-paper I put up for you. It's all gone." Instead, the walls throughout the entire first floor were painted a conservative antique white. His shoulders slumped. "It's like our past has been swept away. Our home has lost all of its character."

"It's not our home anymore, Gene," Dottie reminded him. "We changed the décor when we moved in. Why can't the new owner do the same?"

"But it's as if..." Gene's voice quivered as he leaned against the wall and lowered his head.

"...we were never here at all," Dottie finished. She gripped her husband's shoulders and gently maneuvered him away from the wall. "Come on, Gene. Let's go upstairs."

"What's the point?"

"Humor me, Gene. We'll never come back here again after today, I promise."

It was more of the same on the second floor. Every inch of wallpaper had been removed and the hallway painted with the same drab off-white as the first floor. The three bedrooms were a different matter. Each had been given its own distinct color.

"Well, that's something at least." Gene entered the smallest of them, once Alex's room, which the new owner had converted into a home office. He ran a gentle finger down the wall alongside the door trim just as Dottie joined him.

"Remember how we used to measure the kids' heights on the wall here every year and mark them in pencil?" Gene said. "That's all gone now."

"I know." Dottie moved past Gene toward the opposite wall where a series of color images printed on letter-sized paper were pinned to a corkboard. "Oh, Gene, these are pictures of the house from years ago." She pointed to each one in turn as she continued. "That's you and me sitting on the porch the way it used to look... and there's you and Alex up on the roof getting ready to paint it... and Carmen and Gayle standing with their prom dates under the pink dogwood. You can see the blue hydrangeas and..." Dottie's voice cracked as she covered her mouth and leaned against her husband. "This was our life, Gene. Where did she get these?"

Gene kissed away the tears from her cheek and glanced down at the desk. "Apparently, from this." He held up a 4x6 photo album and began flipping through it before handing it to Dottie.

"And here's a letter addressed to our daughter." Gene picked up the paper from atop the laser printer and stepped over to the window. "Dear Carmen, I found this little photo album in the attic and wanted to return it to you. I hope you don't mind that I made color copies of some of the photos as a way of preserving the beautiful work your parents put into the property. As you know, the metal roof had rusted and some planks on the old porch had rotted since your parents lived here. The dogwood tree succumbed to some kind of disease and had to be removed, but I am doing my best to preserve as much as of the old charm as possible while also making it low maintenance for me—"

"See? Told you, Gene. She's just making the house her own. Our past hasn't been entirely swept away. Despite all that's changed in the old neighborhood, someone here will still remember us."

Gene set the letter on the desk. "You're right, Dottie—as always." He tilted his head. "Hey, the lawnmower stopped. We'd better go."

Dottie laid the photo album atop the letter and followed her husband downstairs. They dashed across the living room until Gene halted at the front door.

Dottie nearly collided with him. "Now what?"

"A gray steel door? She had to replace this, too? Remember that beautiful mahogany and glass door I hung all by myse—"

"Gene!"

"Just saying." He stepped aside and motioned for Dottie to precede him. "Ladies first."

She rolled her eyes and hurried out to the porch. "I can't blame her for putting in a steel door. She's a single young woman and this isn't like the old days."

"So you keep reminding me."

"WELL, at least the old firehouse is still where it used to be," Gene said as they crossed the final street on their journey. "So many fond memories of volunteering with those crazy guys."

"And I was delighted to see St. Margaret's soup kitchen is still serving the poor," Dottie added. "I always enjoyed cooking for them after the kids were out on their own."

"I know you did, Dottie. You were always God's little helper."

Eventually, they came upon the familiar green wrought iron fence of home. Dottie sighed. "Be it ever so humble."

"Well, at least we know most of the people here, and it doesn't change very much."

"Except when new neighbors arrive." Dottie hooked her arm through Gene's as they passed beyond the front gate of Holy Cross Cemetery and vanished beneath a canopy of swaying pink dogwoods and red maples.

This story first appeared in *Rewriting the Past* (Greater Lehigh Valley Writers Group, March 2019).

Limited Time Offer

Cast iron hinges groaned in protest as Derek opened the door of the secluded country house and gestured for Kristy to precede him out to the porch. He adjusted his sunglasses and gazed at the surrounding fields, dappled with patches of melting snow under an unblemished cerulean sky. The kind that only winter can provide. *Beautiful job as always, Dakota.*

"Derek, this place is enormous. I can't imagine what it's costing you to rent it."

"Would you stop worrying about money? It's the holidays. Besides, I'd pay almost anything to get away from our crazy families for a few days."

"True that. Christmas dinner was awkward as hell." Kristy zipped up her coat and slipped on her gloves. "Did it get colder out here since we arrived?" The stinging chill of the occasional breeze foretold an approaching snow squall, but Derek knew it wouldn't arrive until after midnight. At least, that was the plan. "So, what did you want to show me?"

Derek stepped off the porch and nodded toward the tree

line at the edge of the property. "It's a surprise. You'll just have to trust me."

"You're not taking me to some dark corner of the woods to kill me, are you?"

Derek smirked. "I can think of far more fun things to do with you in the dark, hot stuff."

Kristy leapt from the porch and into his arms. "Promises, promises."

THE ENTIRE MOUNTAIN range was ablaze—or so it appeared as the sun dipped low in the western sky, bathing snow-capped peaks in a deep saffron glow. Derek cast a furtive glance at Kristy, her face radiant, eyes glistening.

"This is stunning," she whispered, as if anything louder would shatter this perfect moment.

"My thoughts exactly." Derek shoved a hand into the pocket of his coat. "You know, after we opened all of our Christmas presents yesterday, I realized there was one that I forgot to give you."

He lowered himself to one knee and opened the small white box to reveal an engagement ring. "Young bachelor seeks beautiful maiden with whom to share a lifetime of romantic sunsets. Any takers?"

"Oh my God!" Kristy covered her gaping mouth for a moment before wiping her eyes. "As long as we can go someplace warm for our honeymoon."

"I was thinking tropical."

Kristy yanked off her glove and extended her left hand. "Deal."

Derek slipped the ring onto her finger and kissed the back of her hand. "I need to stand up. The ground is freezing."

Kristy glanced down at the dark stain covering his knee. "And wet."

Derek chuckled. "Yeah, I didn't think that part through. I was too nervous about popping the ques—"

She pulled him close and kissed him until he was nearly out of breath. "As if I would've said no."

"Well, that would have made our dinner reservation awkward. Let's get back to the house before it gets dark. Apparently, I need to change before we go out."

Kristy held up her hand as she started down the trail. "This diamond is huge. I can't imagine what you paid for it."

Derek was about to reply when the snow atop one of the distant peaks swirled and shifted. *That never happened before.* At first, it appeared to be the beginning of an avalanche—until several meters of the mountaintop flickered in and out of existence before solidifying once more.

"Something wrong?"

Derek turned to Kristy. "Uh, no. Just taking one last look."

Hand in hand, they headed back through the woods. Derek cast a final glance over his shoulder. *Don't ruin this on me, Dakota.*

AT THE SUMMIT Steakhouse an hour later, the hostess seated them at a window table toward the back corner beside an elegant white Christmas tree illuminated by a string of blue lights. At each table, red and green candles in hurricane glasses complemented the dim ambient lighting. The rustic stained wood interior was reminiscent of a luxurious log home complete with crackling stone fireplace. From the ceiling speakers, Bing Crosby crooned "I'll Be Home for Christmas."

"This is cozy," Kristy said. "Our own private corner. Very

romantic." She glanced up from the menu to peer through the window, but there was little to see beyond the exterior lights of the restaurant. "And the scenery is breathtaking."

Derek laughed. Situated atop the smallest of the mountains, the Summit was renowned for its unobstructed and breathtaking view of the entire valley—during the day, of course. "We'll come back for lunch later in the week. Trust me, it's a sight to behold, and you'll be able to say, 'I can see my house from here' because the place we're renting is," he pointed toward the bottom corner of the window, "just down there to the right."

"I look forward to it." Kristy returned to the menu. "Since you know this place, what do you recommend?"

"Well, the last time I—" As Derek scanned the appetizer page, the text vanished in a downward wipe. It was immediately replaced with a message. *Mr. Marcus, we apologize for the technical difficulty earlier at the lake. A severe ice storm has moved into the area and disrupted the power grid in our section of town. We appreciate your patience as we switch to backup power. We will do our best to minimize any further anomalies. Thank you and Merry Christmas. —Management*

"Derek, you okay?"

He gazed at her over the top of his menu. "Uh, yeah. Sorry. The menu seems to have changed a bit since the last time I was here, but the Skillet Chicken Monterey is amazing."

"Good evening, folks."

Derek and Kristy glanced up at the waitress as she placed two glasses of water on the table. "My name is—"

"Dakota!" Derek blurted. "What are you doing here?"

"I work here, Mr. Marcus. You know that."

"Uh, yeah, right, of course. I just, uh, didn't expect you to be *here* tonight. Don't you normally go home over Christmas?"

"Not since my parents died. I'm on my own for the holidays, so might as well earn some money."

Once Dakota had taken their drink orders and was out of earshot, Kristy leaned forward. "What was that all about?"

"What do you mean?"

"You were genuinely flustered when the cute blonde waitress showed up. Something I should know?"

Derek waved away her insinuation. "No. It's nothing like that. I only know her because I was a regular customer when I lived out this way. I was just surprised to see her still working here after all these years."

No sooner did he finish speaking than his gaze was drawn to a pulsing light over Kristy's shoulder. Across the restaurant, the front wall faded and rematerialized twice before it vanished, leaving in its place a black and green grid pattern from ceiling to floor.

"I love how easy it is to get you going." Kristy pushed her chair back. "So which way to the restrooms?"

"Uh, restrooms?" Derek's voice cracked as he shot forward in his seat.

"Yeah, I assume they have those here."

The wood-paneled wall reappeared behind her. Dakota scurried by and gave him a thumbs up. Derek cleared his throat. "First right past the fireplace."

"Thanks." Kristy stood. "Oh, and don't go running off with *Dakota* while I'm gone."

"Stop it." Derek rolled his eyes while Judy Garland started in with "Have Yourself a Merry Little Christmas."

A moment later, Dakota returned with their drinks. "Well, that was awkward. Good recovery, though, that line about going home for Christmas."

"Dakota, what happened to the usual waitress?"

"I altered your program. I thought it wise to step in and address these tech problems with you personally."

"Yeah, I read the note from management in my menu. Look, I don't want Kristy to know this is all virtual reality. Can you do anything for me?"

"The last thing we want to do is ruin your Christmas vacation, Mr. Marcus, but we just lost main power and had to switch to generator. The VR system is now running on UPS. The techs want to shut it down gracefully before—"

"How long?"

"Thirty minutes at most."

Derek sighed. "Then give us thirty minutes, please."

"I'll let the techs know. Of course, you'll be refunded the full cost of this session."

Derek shifted his gaze to Kristy as she approached the table. "Yeah, okay. Thanks."

HE HAD DOWNED his second beer before their food arrived.

Kristy draped her napkin over her lap. "Take it easy there, cowboy. Don't start pounding them down on an empty stomach."

"Sorry."

She frowned. "What's wrong? Having second thoughts?"

"What? No, not at all. Like I said before, I was just nervous leading up to the proposal." He cupped his hand over hers. "But now I can relax knowing we'll be together."

Kristy laced her fingers between his. "Forever."

The rumble of Derek's stomach sent them both giggling. "Sorry."

"Well, you know the old saying about the way to a man's —" Kristy jumped at a flash of green light outside the window. "Did you see that?"

Damn it, Dakota. You said thirty minutes! Derek shrugged. "I'm sure it's just a glitch with their holiday lights."

"No, I caught it out of the corner of my eye." She leaned close to the window. "It was like a huge grid."

When it happened again, Kristy spun in her seat and looked at the other patrons, all of whom were calmly eating or conversing, oblivious to the spectacle. "How could they not have seen that, and where's the waitstaff?"

"Kristy, relax. It's probably nothing."

In unison, ceiling and floor abruptly vanished. The walls soon followed along with every table except their own. Kristy gasped as the interior of the restaurant dissolved, leaving the couple sitting in silence, surrounded by a black and green grid.

"Probably nothing? Derek, what the hell's happening? Where are we?"

"In a holochamber." Derek slumped back in his seat and tossed his fork on the table. "I'm sorry, Kristy. None of it was real. Not the country house, not the mountains, not the lake. This is all virtual reality."

Kristy held up her left hand. "What about this ring? Is this fake, too?"

"No." Derek shook his head. "It wasn't fake. I loved you so much." He reached for her hand. "I always will."

"Why are you speak—" Kristy's form undulated before momentarily flickering out. She returned as nothing more than a distorted, pixelated mass. "—past tense?"

"Because you're not real either, not anymore. This day *did* happen four years ago, but now it's just a digitized memory."

With that, the illusion that had once been Derek's fiancée disappeared. He leaned over the table, cradling his head in his hands.

Across the holochamber, the doors parted to admit a tense and solemn Dakota, now donning the standard formfitting uniform of her employer, Virtually Real. "Mr. Marcus, please accept our apologies for the technical difficulties during your session. Two of our UPS batteries failed, forcing us to power down sooner than we expected. You're more than welcome to return later this week and restart your Christmas simulation free of charge."

"It's all right." Derek rubbed his eyes and stared at the empty seat across from him. "In fact, it's probably for the best. There are no do-overs in real life and after four years, this façade has... lost its appeal."

"I'm sorry, Mr. Marcus. Please allow me to—"

"Derek. Call me Derek. We've known each other long enough. After all, you helped me recreate one of the happiest days of my life. You know how she died. You know my weakness... you know my pain."

Dakota nibbled on her lower lip before drawing in a sharp breath. "Management has also authorized me to issue you five VR sessions at twenty-five percent off with no date restrictions or expiration. You may use them anytime."

Derek was silent as he ran a finger along the edge of a table that would only remain solid until he moved away from it. "You know, every time I come here, I get so excited to see her again, even for just a few hours. Yet, I always leave here feeling like shit. I don't know why I keep torturing myself like this."

No sooner did he rise from his seat than it vanished along with the table. "Tell your management I appreciate the offers, Dakota, but I'm done hiding inside technology in a pathetic attempt to recreate a lost love at half off the regular price. No coupons will bring Kristy back. I'm sorry, I know I'm making this awkward. I won't waste any more of your time. Thanks for your help, Dakota. You did a fantastic job." Derek started toward the doors. "Oh, and Happy Holidays."

"Derek, wait. What about a New Year's Eve party?"

With a laugh, he shook his head. "You're persistent, I'll give you that."

"No, I mean a *real* New Year's Eve party with live human beings. At Jolene's Pub in the Theatre District, Upper West Side. Some of my co-workers and I are going. You're more than welcome to join us."

Derek folded his arms. "I thought employees weren't allowed to fraternize with the customers."

"And I thought you weren't coming back." Dakota ambled closer. "Look, I'm not asking you on a date, especially after all you've been through, but you said that I know your pain. Well, when I told you I was alone for the holidays, I didn't make that up. I work here every Christmas because I don't have anyone to share it with. You think you're pathetic for coming back here every year, but when I see you with a virtual rendition of your fiancée—one that I created—I envy you because that's more than I have. So, you tell me who's more pathetic."

"I'm sorry, Dakota. I honestly didn't know."

She shrugged. "Never too late to make up for lost time. New year, new start, and no strings attached, I promise."

"Thanks for the invite. I'll think about it." With that, Derek stepped through the doors into the corridor.

"I never knew the real Kristy," Dakota called after him. "But I doubt she'd want to see you isolate yourself, especially this time of year."

Derek stopped and lowered his head with a sigh. After a moment, he turned. "No strings attached."

"You have my word, but keep in mind it's a limited time offer, expires December 31st."

"Then I guess I should act now while supplies last?" He smiled in spite of himself. "You were right about Kristy, but wrong about being pathetic." With that, he sauntered off with a wave. "See you on the Upper West Side!"

~

This story first appeared in *Over the River and Through the Woods* (Year of the Book Press, September 2019).

Where It's Needed Most

After dumping a decade's worth of pills into a glass tumbler, Max Everett flicked the last empty prescription bottle across the kitchen table, knocking several others over the edge.

"A brilliant shot. Five hundred points to Everett and..." Max swirled the kaleidoscopic cocktail of vodka, anti-depressants, and anxiolytics. "... game over."

Contrary to the diagnoses of several psychiatrists over the years, Max struggled neither with depression nor anxiety. At least, not his own. It wasn't until his early twenties that he'd realized his prodigious capacity for absorbing the tempestuous emotions of those around him. Of course, all attempts to convince his family of this had proven futile. To placate them, Max had grudgingly accepted the occasional prescriptions, only to toss the unopened bottles into a box tucked in a forgotten corner of his bathroom closet.

Instead, he had turned to daily meditation and a sensory deprivation tank at the local health spa to preserve his sanity amid the incessant buffeting of several thousand unrestrained minds.

Then, the COVID-19 pandemic struck early in the new year, forcing all nonessential businesses to close, including the spa. As months passed under quarantine, the city's population grew restive, anxious. Smoldering tensions fueled long suppressed animosities. The pin was finally pulled from the grenade when an unarmed black man, smoking on his front steps and disturbing no one, was gunned down by two white cops while "resisting arrest."

The following week, a peaceful protest downtown erupted into a night of rioting. The police station was firebombed, shops were looted, and lives lost.

For Max, meditation alone provided a meager bulwark against the relentless barrage of animus, fear, and rage. The meds he had once rejected now promised a permanent solution. After a few deep breaths, he lifted the tumbler to his mouth, wondering how long it would take for his end to come once he downed the concoction. *The sooner the better.*

His phone buzzed on the kitchen counter. Max lowered the glass until the noise ceased. Mustering his courage after nearly a full minute, he raised it to his mouth once more. His cell phone buzzed again. The caller had left a voicemail.

Chrissake. Max leapt from his chair and snatched the phone from the counter. After listening to the message, he tapped the screen and pressed the phone to his ear.

"Soul of the City, this is Priscilla. How can I help you?"

"Pris, it's Max Everett."

"Max, thanks for calling me back. Did I catch you at a bad time?"

His gaze shifted to the tumbler. "I was just about to take a nap. What's going on?"

"How about a float instead? Not sure if you saw our posts on social media, but we're open again now that the restrictions have been lifted. Since you had a bunch of appointments that were cancelled due to the pandemic, I wanted to let you know we have a slot open at one-thirty today if you're available."

Max closed his eyes and rolled his head back. "Yes! I mean, yeah, I'm available."

"Great. We'll need to take your temperature when you arrive, and you'll have to wear a mask to enter and walk through the spa to your assigned salon."

"No problem. I'll be there. Thank you, Pris." Max rubbed his eyes. *You might've just saved my life.*

~

AN HOUR LATER, Max adjusted his sunglasses and N95 mask as the green and white taxi slowed to a stop alongside his building. He opened the back door, tossed his small duffel onto the seat, and climbed in.

"I thought it might be you," the driver said. "I picked you up here just before the pandemic."

"Oh, right. Didn't recognize you with the mask. How are ya?"

"I'm good, bruh. You work out here? I thought all these factories were abandoned."

"Actually, I live here. The owners were willing to rent out the basement cheap while they renovate the building."

"Huh. Kinda remote isn't it?"

"Just the way I like it."

"Guess I can't blame ya. At least you ain't gotta deal with these damn protestors. They keep moving through town, blockin' traffic. Makes drivin' a friggin' nightmare. So where to?"

"Sixth and Ridgemont."

As the cab made its circuitous route through town, Max steepled his fingers and closed his eyes, bracing himself against the torrent of random emotions from the minds they passed along the way. Mild trepidation brushed his thoughts from a distance, giving way to fierce jealousy nearby. Disappointment from one tired old soul faded, to be replaced by youthful lust elsewhere. Max winced as a surge of grief and despair threatened to drown him. He tried to withdraw, throw up a shield, but the raw and desperate passions clawed at his consciousness, then vanished in a burst of—*Warmth? Hope? Comfort?* All of that, but something more. *Love? Could it be? Yes!* Love of a purity and intensity the likes of which Max had never before encountered. It washed over him, embraced him, elevated him. He lowered his defenses and allowed it to consume him. *Who are you? I must know. I can feel you fading. Don't leave me...*

With a cry, Max opened his eyes. He threw himself against the passenger door and peered out the window. *Where did that come from?* He slid across the seat, knocking his duffel to the floor, and searched the opposite side of the street until his gaze locked onto Saint Sophie's Hospital. *There...*

"You okay, buddy?" the driver stared at him from the rearview mirror. "Somethin' wrong?"

Max slumped, still catching his breath. "Not at all. Just the opposite, in fact."

I will find you again... whoever you are.

In the pediatric oncology wing at Saint Sophie's Hospital, Nadi Santikos sat hunched before her computer screen at the nurses' station. She barely noticed when one of her colleagues, Jasiri, dropped into the chair beside her. "So, who's your hot date today? Dylan, Aiden, Rajesh, or one of the new kids?"

"Well, it definitely won't be Ashley again." Constance, the senior nurse, leaned over the counter and dropped a file folder onto the desk. "She's being discharged in a few hours. Tumor free as of yesterday."

"And no one knows why," Jasiri added in a low voice. "Doctor Larousse is completely baffled. Ashley's the third kid in two months."

Constance pointed to her. "That's the power of Jesus right there, honey. Ain't nothin' to be baffled about."

Nadi logged off of the computer and rolled her chair back. "All right, chickies. I'll be with Ellen for a little while. I promised I'd read to her before my shift was over."

"You're gonna be a good momma someday," Constance said.

Nadi rolled her eyes.

"I'm serious, girl. You just need to find the right man—after the pandemic is over, of course."

"I don't think there are any good men left in this city." Nadi rounded the nurses' station and made her way down the corridor. She stepped into the last room on the right and approached the bed. Its occupant, an eight-year-old girl whose sandy blonde hair had been lost to chemotherapy, turned her face away from the window as Nadi approached. "Are you here to read to me?"

"As promised." Nadi picked up a book from the corner table and flipped through the pages. "We'll pick up where we left off yesterday."

"I heard Ashley's going home soon. Her cancer went away."

"Yes, that's true."

"I wish I could go home. I sometimes wake up in the middle of the night and I… I'm scared that I'll never be able to go home again. Please don't tell my mom and dad, but I'm scared a lot."

"I won't tell them." Nadi put the book aside. "Ellen, do you trust me?"

"Sure."

With a glance at the open door, Nadi stepped around the bed and closed the privacy curtain.

"What are you doing?"

At Ellen's puzzled gaze, Nadi smiled. "Sending you home. Now, close your eyes and think about... think about everyone you love and everything you loved doing before you got sick." She laid a gentle hand on Ellen's chest. A yellow glow appeared beneath her palm. "Think about all of the places you love to go. The beach, the park..."

Nadi inhaled deeply, held her breath for a few seconds then exhaled. She repeated this a few more times. When she spoke again, her voice was strained. "How do you feel, Ellen?"

"Warm, but... a nice warm. What's happening?"

"Almost done, sweetie."

The yellow glow faded. Nadi lifted her hand. "You can open your eyes now."

"What was that?"

"Two more days and you'll be home, but can you do something for me, Ellen? Promise me you won't tell anyone about this. Will you do that for me?"

"Sure." Ellen nodded.

Nadi felt a trickle along her upper lip. "I'll be right back and then I'll read to you, okay?" She shoved aside the privacy curtain and hurried into the bathroom. Yanking down her mask, Nadi staggered toward the sink. Blood trickled from her right nostril. *That's a first.* She snatched a paper towel from the dispenser and pressed it to her nose.

Idiot. Nadi gazed at her drawn, sallow reflection in the mirror. *Ellen could have waited one more shift. You still haven't recovered from healing Caleb and Ashley. Keep going at this pace, who's going to heal you?*

~

In the vestibule at Soul of the City spa, Max peered up at the wall-mounted temperature scanner as instructed by Pris. Satisfied that he was virus-free, she held up a hole punch. "Do you have your frequent floater card?"

"Oh, yeah. Sorry." Max thumbed through his wallet and produced a tattered blue business card. "Been so long, I forgot." He slipped it under the Plexiglas divider that spanned the length of the reception desk.

As Pris reached for the card, a miasma of anguish, worry, and dread crept into Max's thoughts, jarring him out of the euphoria that still lingered from the cab ride. Whatever troubled her, Pris concealed it well, surgical mask notwithstanding. Her eyes betrayed no hint of sorrow.

She held up the punch card. "Looks like your next float will be free."

"Any chance I could use it today, to extend my session?"

"You want to spend two hours in the tank?"

"After the past four months, I could spend a week in the tank."

Pris swiped a slender finger across the screen of her tablet computer. "You and me both. Yeah, I can put you in for a double session."

"Thanks." Max paused for a beat. "Sorry to be forward, but are you okay? You seem distraught."

"Not at all."

"Pris."

Her shoulders slumped. "Right. Almost forgot I'm talking to the human lie detector." She tossed the tablet onto the counter. "My dad tested positive for COVID-19 a few weeks ago and now he's on a ventilator at Saint Sophie's. They won't let me see him, of course, so here I am, trying to keep my shit together."

"I'm sorry, Pris. I wish..." *I could take your pain away.* Max pressed his open hand to the Plexiglas divider. "I wish there was something I could do."

Eyes glistening, Pris reached across the counter and did likewise. "Thanks, Max. I'm sure all of this has been hell for you, too."

"Nearly enough to drive me to drink."

Pris lowered her hand and reached into a drawer. "You need to find a girl, Max. Get some love in your life to distract you from all the stress."

"Love seems to be a rare commodity in this city." Max mustered a perfunctory smile. "But I'll keep that in mind."

She slipped a keycard under the divider. "Salon D is all yours. You know the drill. Shower first before entering the tank."

"Thanks, Pris. You're a life saver."

"That's two you owe me, but who's counting?"

Although Nadi had wanted nothing more than to go straight home and collapse at the end of her shift, healing Ellen had left her not only enervated but famished. Fortunately, her apartment was only five blocks from Saint Sophie's and her favorite Greek diner just two blocks beyond that. She'd called ahead, allowing ample time for her order to be prepared and ready by the time she arrived. *I'll be home, in my pajamas, and chowing down on stuffed grape leaves and moussaka in no ti—*

As she passed an alley, Nadi was nearly trampled by a mob of teenagers, some wielding baseball bats and crowbars. They bolted across the street and through a parking lot before disappearing out of sight. In their wake, a young black man lay in a fetal position in the middle of the alley.

"Oh my God." Nadi ran to his side and lowered herself to

one knee. The boy's left eye was swollen shut. Blood streaked from a gash along his forehead. "I'm a nurse and I'm going to help you. What's your name?"

"Randall," he whispered. "Hard to breathe."

"Does your chest hurt, Randall?"

"Ribs. They... wouldn't stop kickin' me."

Setting aside her purse and takeout bag, Nadi lifted his polo shirt. She placed one hand atop a series of dark purple bruises and the other on the side of his head. "What happened?"

"We were marching... with the protest. Bunch of... white guys came at us with... bats and pipes. Started another riot."

"Yeah, I just ran into some of them. Randall, can you close your eyes for me?"

"What are you gonna do?"

Nadi smiled. "Trust me."

THERE'S nothing better to rejuvenate mind, body, and soul than floating nude atop ten inches of briny water while encased in absolute darkness. Yet, Max would have traded the past two hours of heavenly silence for just five minutes of the euphoria he'd experienced on his way here.

After his session in the sensory deprivation tank, Max called for a cab and waited in the lounge by the window. He chided himself for his suicide attempt even while bracing his mind against the ebb and flow of emotions from the passing throng on the street—annoyance, contempt, fury, comfort, warmth... *love*!

Max gripped the arms of his chair. *Yes.* It was the same sensation he'd felt in the cab earlier as they passed Saint Sophie's, only more intense. *Closer.* Possibly just a few blocks away. Max leapt from his seat and started toward the vestibule when a wave of panic sent him staggering. He nearly toppled into another patron before steadying himself. Outside, a stampede of bodies shoved, weaved, and shouted their way past the windows. Was another riot under way?

With a brusque wave to Pris, Max charged through the door and out to the sidewalk just as a green and white cab pulled up to the curb. Ignoring it, he shrank back against the wall of the spa, glancing right and left. *Goddamn it, which way?* He closed his eyes. After a moment, he allowed a furtive smile. *Of course, love intervenes where it's needed most.*

Max pushed off the wall and plunged into the fray.

IN THE ALLEY, Nadi collapsed against the wall and pulled a wad of napkins from her takeout bag. She pressed them to her bleeding nose as Randall sat up and gaped at her, all injuries healed. "How did you do that?"

"Ancient Greek healing technique. Runs in the family."

Distant gunfire punctuated the wail of approaching police sirens.

"Shit's about to go down. We gotta move."

"I need a few minutes." Nadi slipped her purse into her takeout bag. "Just go."

Randall shifted his gaze from one end of the alley to the other.

"I'll be fine." Nadi waved her napkin. "Go now. Stay safe, and please quarantine yourself for two weeks. Riots be damned. We're still in a pandemic."

"Yeah. Good luck and thanks again." With that, Randall was gone.

Only a block and a half to home. With one hand on the wall and the other clutching her takeout bag, Nadi started back toward the street, pausing to suss out the scene. Most of the violence was still confined to the next block. As if to confirm this, a pair of ambulances barreled through the nearest intersection and passed again a moment later at the opposite end of the alley behind her. *Please stay over there until I get home.* Nadi shuffled out to the sidewalk, feeling as if she'd aged thirty years in the past ten minutes.

The first gunshot tore through an outdoor display in front of a shop directly beside her.

"Get down!"

As more rounds peppered windows and walls around her, a tall man charged toward her from across the street. Nadi's takeout bag flew from her grasp. She cried out as they struck the asphalt at the alley's entrance, but the man had wrapped his arms around her head and back, cushioning the impact.

Nadi's mask slipped down to her chin as she turned her head away from the man's shoulder. She arched her neck but could see little more than huddled bodies in the middle of the street.

"He's down!" someone shouted. "We got his gun."

She patted her savior's back. His shirt was damp with sweat. "Uh, sir? Thank you. I think they got the shooter. We should be okay now. Can we stand up, please?"

With a grunt, the man shifted his weight, but not enough to liberate Nadi. He turned his head to face her. "Only one problem. I can't move my legs."

Nadi brought her hand up. That wasn't sweat. *Oh no...*

"WHAT'S YOUR NAME?"

"Max." He rested his forehead against the asphalt.

"Okay, Max. I'm a nurse and I'm going to help you, but you have to trust me, okay?"

"Do I have a choice?"

"No. I want you to close your eyes and don't try to move until I tell you to. Can you do that for me?"

"Yes."

Despite his condition, Max could sense that this woman was exhausted, filled with trepidation and doubt. Was she truly the source of the perfect bliss he'd felt earlier, or had he just risked his life for nothing?

Max felt a hand rustle the back of his shirt and a moment later, his own doubts were dispelled as elation coursed through him. Even if he died here and now, it would have been worth it to save this divine being. He turned his head to face her. When he opened his eyes, she was little more than a blur. "Who are you? I have to know."

"I'm Nadi." Her voice was little more than a hoarse whisper. "Now hush. I need to focus. Your injuries are severe."

Blinking away his tears, Max gazed at this angel in blue scrubs. Voluminous brown hair cascaded along the pavement and clung to the sides of her face. Her angular jaw was clenched and her olive complexion damp. They say women don't sweat, they glisten, but Nadi's face glowed in a golden manifestation of the pure, selfless love she radiated.

Her hand slipped from his back. She tossed three spent rounds to the sidewalk. "You... should be fine in a minute." She clenched her teeth, arched her back, and broke down into tears. Her body trembled beneath his.

"Nadi, what's wrong?"

"It hurts." She drew in a sharp breath. Blood trickled from her aquiline nose. "Every time I... heal someone, I... absorb their pain and... you're my third one today. I can't take anymore."

"You won't need to." Max pushed himself up and knelt over her. He brought gentle hands to her temples. "Let *me* take it. Absorbing pain is my specialty." He closed his eyes. "A burden shared is a burden halved, my dear."

Nadi gasped as she cupped her hands over his. "My God... you're an empath."

"That's what led me to you." Max opened his eyes. "Better now?"

She nodded. Max picked up her purse and helped Nadi to her feet. She fell into him as her legs buckled, and he embraced her. "Can you walk? We need to get out of here."

"I just need a minute." She glanced down at her takeout order strewn across the pavement. "Damn it, that was my dinner."

"I'll buy you dinner. Anything you want."

"After we each quarantine for fourteen days." Nadi pulled back. "Seriously, who are you? How did you *really* find me, and why would you risk your life for a stranger? You could have been killed."

"You were worth the risk." Max handed over her purse. "As to how I found you, it wasn't hard. Love always intervenes where it's needed most."

THIS STORY first appeared in *Love on the Edge* (Year of the Book Press, June 2021).

The Forest for the Trees

The Swedish Province of Finland - Summer 1697

It was three o'clock in the morning when a crack of thunder tore Petrus from a fitful sleep. A distant flash of stark white revealed the slender silhouette of his wife, Ievukka, standing at the window. He slipped out of bed and joined her. For the third consecutive night, the heavens erupted with terrifying fury—but this time, the spectacle was accompanied by distant screams. Roiling clouds hurled bolts of lightning and streaks of fire in a relentless assault on the farmlands outside of town.

Ievukka sighed and lowered her head. "It'll be dawn in less than an hour. Later today, we can expect more survivors to make their way here... if there are any. I hope there's room in the church."

"Better for them to die tonight, by God's wrath, than to continue starving with the rest of us."

"Each attack draws closer to us." Ievukka turned to her husband. "I fear we may be next. We should leave, Petrus. Abandon this town and move south. I'm sure my brother and his family will come with us."

Petrus shook his head. "The famine is everywhere. There's

nothing but starvation between here and Helsingfors. I've heard stories that it goes far beyond our borders. People have died by the thousands. Robbery and cannibalism are rampant. There's nowhere for us to go."

Ievukka turned back to the window as the firestorm ceased. The clouds dispersed, the strident cries faded, and peace reclaimed the night. Both of them knew it was only a temporary reprieve. "I wonder how many died this time, fewer than the night before or more? What have we done to anger Him, Petrus? Is it not enough to turn the weather against us and destroy our crops for the past three years? Must He now send fire down upon our homes? This is not the mercy that Jesus preached."

Petrus had no response, for what mere mortal could understand the mind of God? He remained silent as he took Ievukka into his arms and kissed her forehead. "We must continue to pray. I have faith that the answers will be revealed."

In the darkness, Ievukka sobbed. "I fear the only answer God has for us is death."

SAINT ANTERO'S church had fallen into disrepair over the past year and a half since the pastor and his wife died within days of each other after devouring one of their two Lapphunds. It was rumored that the remaining dog had begun feeding off their corpses before they were finally discovered. Such desperation was common during the famine, but the news had devastated Petrus and Ievukka. They had been married at Saint Antero's three years before.

The church continued to serve as a central meeting place for the predominantly Lutheran community, especially during times of crisis. Since God had begun attacking the farms three nights ago—for what other explanation could there possibly be?—Saint Antero's also served as a shelter.

When Petrus and Ievukka arrived for the dawn prayer meeting, they opened the door to angry, shouting voices. The center of the narthex was occupied by local farmers as well as several village residents. The men were engaged in heated arguments, shouting over one another while distraught wives tried to intervene and frightened children sobbed under the baptismal font. Petrus clenched his jaw against the stench of sweat and fear.

Around the room's perimeter, a dozen townsfolk leaned against the walls, observing the clamor with weary, drawn expressions. Among them were Ievukka's brother Urbanus, his wife Kaisa, and their 14-year-old daughter Kreeta. They were the last remaining members of Ievukka's family. The rest had succumbed to disease or starvation over the past three years.

Urbanus waved and motioned toward the doors.

"What's this about?" Petrus asked as he followed Urbanus and Ievukka outside.

Once the doors closed behind them, Urbanus exhaled in relief. "Apparently, when the Lord unleashed His fury over the past three nights, many people fled into the forest and have not been seen since."

"The forest surrounds us," Petrus said. "It goes on forever. It's easy to get lost."

"That's what I told them at the start of this discussion, but some of the farmers had a different explanation."

"Such as?"

"They think God has taken their family members."

"God has not taken anyone," a new voice called out. "At least, not your Christian God."

All heads turned as an old man approached from the road. The first thing that struck Petrus was his leonine mane of stark white hair and a beard that flowed to the hem of his rust orange waistcoat. He stopped several feet away, pointing at them with a knobby walking stick as weathered as the man himself. "The devil has our land in her grasp, and she is not working alone."

Petrus raised an eyebrow. "She? You're not referring to Satan."

"Christianity has demonized many of our old gods," the man said. "We should not be surprised if some of them take offense."

"So you don't believe in Christ? Which of the gods are you referring to? Perkele?"

"When you venture into the forest, you will find the truth." With that, the man sauntered off.

"If Perkele is still among the gods, why doesn't he help us?" Petrus called out. "Wasn't he also Ukko, the old god of weather and harvests?"

"Petrus, let it go," Ievukka said. "He's just a crazy old pagan."

Without stopping or turning, the man replied. "Why would Perkele help those who have cursed his name?"

The church door opened and Kaisa emerged. "Urbanus, Petrus, they're forming a search party to comb the forest for the missing. They're looking for volunteers among the men."

Urbanus shook his head. "We don't even have enough food to feed the people who are here. Even if we find anyone lost in the forest, we'd only bring them back to starve."

"When do they intend to start?" Petrus asked.

"Today until dusk," Kaisa replied. "And at least for the next day or two. The women have agreed to make bark bread to take along. They have seven men already."

"Make that eight," Petrus said.

Ievukka frowned.

"Just for today, I promise."

"It's a waste of time and energy," Urbanus grumbled. "We'll all be dead soon enough."

~

A few hours later, the men fanned out through the forest in pairs, each agreeing to remain within earshot of the others. Petrus teamed up with Johannes, one of the most prominent farmers in the area. His oldest son had vanished during the second night's attack.

"You didn't lose anyone out here," the farmer said. "Why did you volunteer?"

"I just want to help."

"Given the circumstances, I guess you and Ievukka are glad you didn't have children."

Although Johannes was right, Petrus didn't want to admit it. To do so seemed callous. "We still plan to... someday... whenever this famine ends."

"If we survive that long. Remember when the Markonnens lost their daughter last year?"

Petrus nodded.

"Did you know the rest of the family cooked and ate her after she died?"

Petrus felt the bile rise in his throat. After a moment, he regained his composure. "Maybe we should spread out, but stay within sight of each other."

Johannes nodded, his expression grim. "Good idea, but be careful. Something doesn't feel right."

Petrus snickered. "I think you took those stories too seriously back at the church—in between the yelling."

"Some of the others said that God is trying to kill us, but I disagreed. I don't think God has anything to do with this."

"I met a stranger earlier today who said the same thing. He

seemed to think it had to do with the pagan gods like Perkele or some such nonsense."

"I don't know from pagan beliefs, but I will tell you that Jesus and the Heavenly Father would not turn the weather against us and destroy our crops. They would never allow children to starve to death only to be devoured by their parents. I've seen people degenerate into animals these past few years. We're a faithful community, Petrus. We didn't deserve this punishment. There's something sinister happening here, but what it is, I can't imagine."

As Petrus took in their surroundings, the old man's words came back to him. *When you venture into the forest, you'll find the truth.* He gripped the handle of the knife hanging from his belt. "I'm not certain I want to know."

IT TOOK LESS than fifteen minutes for Petrus to find himself alone. Johannes was nowhere in sight. Petrus called out to him, but there was no response. He shouted the names of the other men in the search party. The forest returned only silence —until something rustled the underbrush nearby. Petrus ducked behind a fallen tree and reached for his knife. *Maybe* I've *been listening to too many stories.*

"Remain still and silent." A woman's voice whispered from... where? It was gentle, yet urgent enough to freeze Petrus in place. "Do not be afraid. You shall not be harmed."

Several branches of varying thickness sprouted from the trunk of the dead tree and stretched over and around him. Within seconds, he was encased, with only thin gaps through which he noticed something moving into view close to the ground.

At first, Petrus thought another branch was stretching out across the forest floor, until he realized that it was not stretching at all. It was slithering. The thickest snake he had ever seen paused outside his timbered cage, its black scales mottled with a chain of red triangles from head to tail.

The serpent lifted its head and upper body, drawing itself to its full height until it stood taller than Petrus. Its forked tongue flicked from its mouth as it glanced right and left in search of something—or some*one*.

After several seconds, it returned to the ground and continued on its way. The branches covering Petrus retracted. He rolled away from the tree and scrambled to his feet.

"You are safe now," the voice said, "but I suggest remaining here for a few minutes longer to be certain."

Gripping the hilt of his knife, Petrus backed up against a nearby pine tree.

"Have you no respect for personal space?"

He whirled to find a face peering at him from the bole of the tree.

"Greetings, I am Tellervo."

With a gasp, Petrus leapt away, struggling to wrap his mind around what his eyes were showing him.

"Do you speak," said Tellervo, "or am I wasting my breath on another of Ajatarra's mindless minions?"

Petrus drew himself to his full height. "Of course I speak, I just never before encountered a tree that could."

"It does not. It merely serves as my conduit, as do all of the trees."

"Conduit?"

Tellervo sighed. "I communicate through the trees. I am a goddess of this forest, and you are?"

"Petrus." He nodded. "I'm from the village nearby. Wait... Tellervo, daughter of Tapio and Meilikki. Yes, I've heard your name in stories."

"And here I am in the bark."

"How do I know you're not an agent of Satan?"

"Satan? Oh yes, the devil of your Christian faith. Do you always insult those who save your life? Perhaps I should have left you to the piru." Tellervo's face extended several inches from the tree. "Then you would have met the *real* devil soon after."

Petrus held up his hands. "Forgive me. It wasn't my intention to insult you. I've been through this forest many times and have never encountered the likes of you before."

"You never needed help from the likes of me before."

"I see. Thank you for your protection. What did you mean earlier when you mentioned Ajatarra's minions? Is she the devil you referred to?" Petrus was reminded of his bizarre encounter with the old man. *The devil has our land in her grasp...*

"Many of your kind who fled into the forest after the attacks were captured by her pirus and turned into mindless slaves for reasons we do not yet understand."

Petrus frowned. "Pirus. You mean demons... like that snake?"

"Yes. You learn quickly for a mortal. We've been able to save a few of your people from capture."

"We?"

"My entire family has intervened in defiance of Ajatarra," Tellervo explained. "But we've been unable to provide safe passage out of the forest for those we've rescued. So we've kept them hidden from her. Ajatarra's forces are growing. They have infiltrated nearly every mile of the forest that borders your villages."

"To what end?"

"As I said, I do not know."

Petrus dropped to his knees, clutching his stomach.

"Are you injured?"

He shook his head. "Hungry. If you *are* a goddess, you must know of the famine that began three years ago. More of my people starve to death every day. Now you tell me the devil is taking them for some dark purpose. God help us."

Around him, plants sprouted from the ground bearing various fruits including bilberry, lingonberry, bramble, and cloudberry. Although some of these were out of season, all were ripe for the picking. Once his hands were full, Petrus shoved the fruit into his mouth and closed his eyes, savoring the sweet flavors.

"Eat as much as you like," Tellervo said. "Those we rescued have been kept well fed with all of these and more."

Petrus swallowed and continued snapping up more of Tellervo's bounty. "Where are they now?"

"In a sanctuary of trees toward the southeast. It remains one of the few places untouched by Ajatarra."

"I'll need to find a way to explain all of this to my people. May I take these berries back to them?"

"Of course."

"Thank you." Petrus dumped the bark bread from his satchel and quickly filled it with berries.

"It is good that you did not venture too deeply into the forest," Tellervo said. "I can still guide you out so as to avoid any further encounters with Ajatarra's demons."

As Petrus walked, Tellervo's visage disappeared and reappeared in various trees, leading him along a circuitous route. Along the way, he asked Tellervo why she and her family had returned to the forest.

"We never left," she replied. "As the new faith of Christianity spread amongst your people, they turned away from their belief in the ancient gods. As a result, some of our kind left Earth behind and returned to the nether world, but we of the forest remained as silent stewards. However, when we sensed that evil had returned, my family decided to once again take an active role in its protection."

"What will happen if Ajatarra discovers what you're doing?"

"She might burn this forest to the ground. Especially now that she has an ally more powerful than she."

"Who?"

"Hush. More pirus approach."

Petrus crept behind a cluster of silver birches just in time to avoid detection by two enormous snakes gliding past. One of them held a prisoner, a young boy no more than ten. Petrus recognized him as the son of one of the farmers who had died last year. Although the boy's eyes were open, his body was limp in the gripping jaws of the serpent.

Petrus slipped his knife from its sheath and started forward only to find a branch wrapped around his waist. It yanked him back to the birch and held him in place until the snakes were out of view.

Tellervo's face materialized in the trunk of the tree just above his head. "Foolish. There was nothing you could have done for the boy. You might have succeeded in wounding one of pirus, but the other would surely have captured or killed you." She paused, her gaze drifting off into the distance. "Ajatarra's forces are once again gathering at the edge of the forest, at least thirty serpents. I can feel them slithering among the trees."

"You were telling me that she allied herself with someone," Petrus said.

"We have heard it through the vines that Perkele has joined forces with her."

"Perkele. Satan himself!"

"Lower your voice, mortal. You are not out of the woods yet. Your Christian leaders have done a fine job of maligning the ancient ones. Perkele was no devil. He was the god of the skies and of the harvest. Some called him Ukko, among other names. If he truly has returned, then he might be furious to discover that his name has become a profanity among your people. Still, I find it difficult to believe he would collude with the mother of all evil."

Petrus fell silent, pondering all that he'd seen and heard since encountering Tellervo, but contemplation would need to wait. Sunlight vanished from the forest, drawing their attention to a sky engulfed by ominous clouds. Thunder rumbled in the distance.

Petrus gazed up at the goddess. "Please tell me this storm will bring only rain."

"No matter what happens, Petrus, stay here. I shall protect you."

He shook his head. "This isn't right. It always happens just before dawn."

"Who can predict the devil?"

Petrus peered toward the edge of the forest and his village beyond. "Ievukka..."

Then the world exploded.

HE BOLTED through a maze of dense trees—until he tripped over an exposed root and landed face first in the dirt. As he lay prone, the wind knocked out of him, a cool breeze carried the stench of burning wood.

"Petrus, stop." Tellervo gazed down at him from the broad, gnarled hulk of an ancient yew. "I cannot protect you if you run."

Ignoring her, he peered through the tree line at the conflagration that had once been his village. The blaze served as a terrifying backdrop to the chaos unfolding around him. Several bolts of lightning struck ground beyond the forest, revealing frantic silhouettes of people and demons darting in all directions. Petrus flinched as raging thunder shook the forest floor, punctuating the shouts and screams that came from all directions.

"Don't worry about me. Protect my people." With that, Petrus picked himself up and dashed into the fray. Tellervo's pleading shouts were drowned in the mayhem.

He rounded a cluster of towering pines just as two familiar figures rushed past. "Urbanus! Kaisa!"

The couple stumbled to a halt. Urbanus pointed toward the sky. "Petrus, God is unleashing his wrath upon us. We must take refuge."

"Don't go any further. The forest is dangerous."

"More so than out there?"

"Where is Ievukka?" Petrus said.

"We were separated," Kaisa replied. "She and Kreeta were ahead of us... somewhere."

As she spoke, a massive green and yellow snake uncoiled from a thick branch just above their heads. Its gaping maw descended toward Kaisa.

Petrus drew his knife. "Behind you!"

Urbanus yanked Kaisa away as the serpent lunged—directly into the path of a spear that impaled its head and pinned it against the tree. The creature's limp form unfurled from the branch and dropped to the ground in a crumpled heap.

Urbanus nudged its tail with his boot. "It's taller than a man and nearly as wide. It could have swallowed any one of us whole."

"He's a little one," a new voice called out. "Be glad you didn't encounter one of the beasts that Petrus saw earlier."

Everyone turned as the old man from the church approached with a grin. He pulled the spear out of the tree and dropped the tip, letting the snake's head slide off. "Good to see I still have my throwing arm."

"How did you know my name?" Petrus said. "For that matter, who are you?"

"I am known as Väinämöinen. As to how I know your name, I overheard it at the church earlier. By the way, I'm afraid that's the only building still standing in your village. I advise we regroup there quickly before more of Ajatarra's demons arrive."

Together, all four hurried out of the forest. The assault from the heavens had ceased, and the sky was now clear save for the billowing smoke from fires that had consumed most of the village. In the narthex of St. Antero's, they sat in silence after Petrus imparted his experiences with Tellervo and the demons. Urbanus refused to believe a word of it while his wife wept.

Petrus leaned his head back against the wall and pondered his next move. He recalled the lifeless body of the boy in the jaws of the snake. Could his wife be enduring the same fate right now? Was she being carried off to whatever version of Hell lay deep in the forest? He looked over at Kaisa, huddled in the arms of her husband and knew they were wondering the same about their daughter.

"We have to go back into the forest," Urbanus said. "We need to find Kreeta."

"Is that so?" Väinämöinen raised an eyebrow. "Was it not you who, just earlier today, considered it a waste of time and energy to go searching for those who went missing? They're just going to starve to death anyway. Of course, I suppose it's different when it's one of your own."

"Why are you here, old man?" Urbanus snapped. "Where do you come from and what business is this of yours?"

"Urbanus." Petrus held up a hand. "He saved our lives back there."

"I simply offer my help," Väinämöinen said, "and from the looks of things, you could use it."

Kaisa touched her husband's arm and Urbanus lowered his gaze to the floor.

"We'll return to the forest at daybreak tomorrow." Petrus stood and patted his satchel. "I have some food to sustain us tonight and I know how to get more once we're in there. First, we'll need weapons. I suggest we spend the rest of today searching the abandoned farms for axes, sickles, knives, anything. We'll sleep here in the church tonight."

"And pray for Kreeta and Ievukka," Kaisa added.

Väinämöinen looked from one to the other in turn. "You now know what awaits you in the forest. It is almost certain that your loved ones have already fallen prey to Ajatarra's demons. The chances of finding them grow slimmer with each passing hour. What's more, we'll be greatly outnumbered. Are you certain you want to do this?"

Petrus nodded. "The devil herself couldn't keep me away."

Just after dawn the following morning, the group skulked among the trees, weapons in hand. In addition to his knife, Petrus had found an axe at one of the farms, while Urbanus now carried a sickle and Kaisa, a scythe. Väinämöinen had managed to conjure up a longsword, which now dangled from his belt in a well-worn leather scabbard.

"Petrus, where exactly did you see this Tellervo?" Urbanus asked.

"As I said, in the trees."

Everyone peered up at the branches and treetops—all but Väinämöinen.

"No, here." Petrus tapped a nearby birch, just above eye level. "Her face appeared in the trunk and she spoke to me."

Kaisa was deadpan. "You had a conversation with a tree?"

"No, he had a conversation with a goddess," a voice replied

from behind them. "Do I really need to explain all of that again?"

All heads turned to see the face of Tellervo materialize in the curling bark of a lone alder. Only Väinämöinen appeared unfazed by the sight.

Petrus stepped around a gaping Urbanus. "I'm relieved to see you again, Tellervo."

"Why have you returned? It is too dangerous here. The pirus are still patrolling the forest. They captured many of your people yesterday."

"Were you able to save any?"

"Some, yes."

"A woman nearly as tall as I with reddish blonde hair possibly running with a shorter girl?"

Tellervo frowned. "Not that I recall. I am sorry, Petrus, but there is a chance they were rescued by my mother or father and are being ushered to the sanctuary as we speak."

"Can you take us to this sanctuary?" Väinämöinen said.

"It would have been easier in yesterday's chaos. In the stillness now, it will be challenging to avoid detection. So many demons are still slithering about looking for stragglers."

"But it can be done."

"It's a three-day journey. Follow me and do not deviate from the path."

~

Several hours into their trek, Tellervo warned of two demons approaching, each carrying human victims. As the group ducked behind nearby trees and undergrowth, Urbanus whispered, "We should let them pass, then attack from behind."

"Unwise," Tellervo said. "There are six others within earshot. You would be quickly outnumbered. We must continue moving. Undoubtedly, we'll encounter more of the same until we're clear of Ajatarra's territory. Wait here while I determine the safest—"

Tellervo's eyes widened as she stared beyond Petrus. Leaves crunched underfoot. Someone was approaching. Everyone fell silent, weapons raised in anticipation. After a moment, the newcomer stepped into view.

Kaisa covered her mouth to stifle a gasp. Kreeta stood before them, hair disheveled, clothes filthy and torn. She stared at her parents with a vacant expression as if they were strangers.

Urbanus charged toward her, but Väinämöinen pulled him back. "Wait. Ajatarra knows we're here. She's trying to draw us out. It's no coincidence that your daughter happens to turn up when there are a half dozen pirus close by."

"How do you know it's a trap?" Petrus said.

"Because there are two serpents lying in wait," Tellervo replied. "One is hiding in the underbrush behind that line of birch trees off to the right, and the other is closing in from the left."

"The four of us should be able to defeat two demons." Petrus turned to Väinämöinen, but the old man was gone. "Damn fool, where are you?"

Kreeta cried out, turning toward a tangle of shrubs where Väinämöinen stood over a dead snake, cleaved in half. He wiped the blade of his sword on a nearby birch. "Demon filth." He returned the sword to its scabbard and approached the girl.

Kaisa and Urbanus ran to their daughter.

"Whatever you do, hurry," Tellervo warned.

Kaisa hugged her daughter. "You're safe now."

"Of course I am, for Ajatarra is always with me."

Kaisa pulled back, eyes wide. "She has become a witch."

Väinämöinen placed his hands on either side of Kreeta's

face and addressed her with a serene voice. "What is Ajatarra's purpose here, child? Why does she attack the villages and harvest mortals from the forest?"

"She is raising an army to wage war against the Christian god."

"She's wasting her time. Mortals cannot kill gods."

"We will not remain trapped in our corporeal forms for much longer," Kreeta explained. "When Ajatarra's forces are amassed, we shall gather as one and abandon our earthly bodies. Our immortal souls will follow Ajatarra and Perkele to war."

"Perkele would not ally himself with the mother of evil."

"Believe what you will. It is happening. You cannot stop us."

"Hear my voice, Kreeta. Throw off the cloak of evil that clouds your thoughts and blinds you from the light."

Kreeta struggled to pull away from Väinämöinen's grasp, but her gaze remained fixed on his.

"Hold her steady," he said. Urbanus dropped his sickle and embraced his daughter, pinning her arms to her sides as Väinämöinen continued. "Let my voice guide you out of the darkness, child."

Kreeta jerked her head back. "No."

"Four more pirus are closing in," Tellervo warned.

"Be ready to fight, Petrus," Väinämöinen said as Kreeta began trembling. "Let Ajatarra's poison flow from your mind, Kreeta. Release it from your heart."

"No," she croaked. Tears streaked her face. Then, "Help me..."

"You are stronger than Ajatarra! Follow my voice to the light. Reach out to me, child. Your mother and father are here with arms open. They are here with me in the light."

Kreeta reached up and clutched his forearms, her face taut. "She's in my head."

Väinämöinen smiled. "Not anymore."

With that, Kreeta collapsed—

—AND AJATARRA SCREAMED.

Her momentary anguish echoed through the vast cave in the northern forest. She cradled her head in her hands until the pain subsided.

"What happened?"

Ajatarra twisted her serpent waist to find Perkele approaching. Although he was nearly seven feet tall, Ajatarra took pleasure in the fact that he still had to look up to address her. When she drew herself to her full height, her bare breasts were always at eye level to him. This amused her, and Ajatarra often flaunted herself in an attempt to make him uncomfortable, for she knew Perkele found her repulsive. While one side of her face was reptilian, the rest of her upper body was human in appearance, supported by a snake's tale of emerald green over eight feet in length.

Nevertheless, it seemed his anger with the mortals surpassed his revulsion at the thought of joining forces with her, for it had been Perkele who initiated the firestorms that drove the mortals into the forest.

"Something unexpected," she hissed. "One of my mortals has been awakened by an old friend of yours—Väinämöinen."

"Where?"

"In the southern forest. It doesn't matter. The girl was expendable, but Väinämöinen had help from the forest gods."

"Perhaps it's time to put your army of entranced mortals to the test."

Two pirus entered the cave, each with a human captive clutched in its jaws. They lowered their prisoners to the floor and hovered over them.

"And when one mortal is lost, two shall rise to take its place." Ajatarra slid her forked tongue over her fangs.

She approached the closest prisoner, paralyzed from the piru's bite. She reached down and lifted him off the ground by his waistcoat. She lowered her head to whisper in the man's ear. "Perhaps, in your thoughts, you are praying to your precious Christ to save you. Let me assure you, he will be of no help to you here. As of today, you worship me, obey me, adore me. Your life shall be mine." She flicked her tongue around his ear. "I must admit, mortals are delicious."

She tore open his shirt and buried her fangs in his chest. After a few seconds, she pulled back, lips covered in blood. The man's body began to convulse until he collapsed. Ajatarra watched in delight as he writhed and squirmed on the floor. Once his seizure abated, the man lay in a fetal position, moaning and wheezing.

"Rise," Ajatarra commanded.

The man stood, his expression blank.

"Speak."

"My life for you," the man said.

Ajatarra stroked his face with a clawed finger. "Perkele, when I am finished with the other prisoner, we will take my army south and destroy Väinämöinen. I shall then convert whatever mortals he managed to rescue."

"What of the tree gods?"

"Once we're finished, feel free to rain down fire from the sky and burn the forest as you did the villages. Then, finally, we shall move against the Christian God."

As Kaisa knelt and cradled her daughter, Urbanus retrieved his sickle and faced Väinämöinen. "What have you done to my daughter?"

"She will awaken momentarily and completely free of Ajatarra's influence."

Petrus turned to Tellervo. "Where are those four demons you mentioned?"

"They are already upon us."

Väinämöinen spun and hurled his spear. At first, Petrus saw no target until a blue and red snake leapt from behind a stretch of overgrown weeds. The weapon found its mark in the creature's belly. It landed several feet from Petrus, contorting its body until the spear shook loose. He raised his axe as the snake turned toward him, but was saved the trouble when Tellervo drove several sharpened branches into the beast's head.

Another piru reared up behind Urbanus and lunged. He dove to one side and slashed his sickle into its tail. The serpent shrieked and curled back on itself, catching Urbanus by a thigh and dragging him along the ground—until he buried the point of his weapon into its eye. The snake dropped him just before losing its head to Väinämöinen's sword.

"There are two more!" Petrus shouted.

Tellervo's face emerged from a pair of inosculated birch trees to his left. "Not anymore."

Petrus followed her gaze to the ground where two snakes lay, each with a narrow length of silver birch shoved down its throat. "Thank you, Tellervo."

"I am Mielikki. Tellervo is my daughter. She is still over there."

Petrus glanced over his shoulder. Tellervo smiled. Mother and daughter looked exactly alike. He nodded to Mielikki. "My humblest apologies and gratitude. May I say that your daughter has saved my life at least twice in as many days. My name is Petrus." He gestured toward the others. "These are members of my family, Urbanus and Kaisa, their daughter Kreeta, and this is—"

"Väinämöinen," Mielikki smiled. "I did not know you had returned."

Petrus looked from one to the other. "You know each other?"

Väinämöinen grinned. "Since ages past, before the first mortal stepped foot on this soil." He reached out and placed a gentle hand on a branch of the intertwined birches. "I have missed you and your family. Tellervo has been an invaluable guide. How is your husband these days?"

"Tapio is well and keeping watch over the sanctuary where the rescued mortals are gathered," Mielikki said.

Petrus stared at the old man, his head filling with questions. Was he a god, too? His name wasn't familiar from the old legends, but there were gaps in his knowledge of pagan myths. It wasn't a subject the Lutheran church encouraged.

He shot a sidelong glance at Tellervo. "Did you know?"

She shook her head, and the rest of the tree with it. "I only met him once and it was eons ago."

"I see your voice has not lost its magic," Mielikki said, gazing past Väinämöinen.

Kreeta was now awake and sitting up. He hunched down beside her. "How are you feeling?"

"Dizzy, and a bit nauseated."

"That, too, shall pass," Väinämöinen assured her.

Petrus placed a hand on Kreeta's shoulder. "Do you remember what happened to Ievukka?"

"She's alive, but under the spell of Ajatarra like so many of our people."

"I can put an end to that," Väinämöinen said. "If we can find them."

"*You* can find them... without us," Urbanus said. "I just got my daughter back and I won't risk losing her again, or my wife." He turned to Petrus. "I'm sorry."

"Ievukka's your sister."

"And she would agree with me. I'm taking my family out of this unholy place."

"To where? Our homes were burned to the ground."

"Enough," Mielikki said. "We should continue a bit further south before more pirus arrive. It will be dark in a few hours and far too dangerous to travel. Whoever wishes to leave can do so in the morning. I shall go on ahead and grow a shelter for the night. Tellervo will guide you there."

"Are you a god like the others?"

"It's hardly my place to tell you what to believe, Petrus."

Surrounded by a wide, circular wall of slim silver birch trees, the group sat around a fire in the center of the shelter. All around them, berries and mushrooms grew ripe for the picking. Outside, mother and daughter goddesses stood watch.

"But exorcising demons is a power reserved only for Jesus and his apostles."

Väinämöinen tossed a few more dry branches into the fire. "All I can tell you is that I'm known for having an exceptionally persuasive voice. I simply use it to the best of my ability."

"I see," Petrus said. "This is difficult for us. We were taught that there is only one God."

"I am aware."

"Is that why you've all returned?" Urbanus said. "To prove our religion as false and reassert your reign over us?"

The old man shook his head. "We're only here to stop Ajatarra and hopefully send her to Tuonela where she belongs."

Kaisa frowned. "Tuonela?"

"The realm of the dead."

Everyone stared at Väinämöinen for a moment before exchanging awkward glances.

"Please don't think us ungrateful," Kaisa said. "But why are you helping us?" She waved toward the trees. "And by you, I mean—"

"All of us *pagan* gods?" Väinämöinen chuckled. "This land was our domain for eons and to it we pledged our stewardship. Your ancestors worshipped us, yes, but also relied upon us for protection and, at times, their very survival. We provided for them when needed. We're not about to abandon our duty now, even if your faith in us has... drifted away."

"What about Perkele?" Petrus said. "If he isn't the devil, then why has he allied himself with Ajatarra? Why would the god of the sky and harvest curse us with famine then send fire down upon us from the heavens to burn our homes and drive us into a demon-infested forest?"

"It is not the work of Perkele."

"But Tellervo said—"

"There are many trickster demons in the forest. If left unchecked, who knows what havoc they could unleash?"

"Then where is Perkele?"

Väinämöinen turned his gaze to the fire. "That, I do not know."

THE FOLLOWING MORNING, Tellervo informed Urbanus and his family of the fishing villages along the Gulf of Bothnia that remained untouched by Perkele.

"I will lead you there and provide plenty of food along the way," Tellervo assured them. "Enough to make an offering to the villagers when you arrive. They may be more willing to take you in."

"Say nothing of what you experienced here," Mielikki

warned. "Else you run the risk of them killing you as pagans. Tell them only that you are fleeing the attack on your village."

"No matter what happens," Petrus said. "Warn everyone you encounter to remain out of the forest until I return."

"And if you do not return?" Kaisa asked.

"Please be careful," Mielikki continued. "There is a risk you could find yourselves quickly outnumbered by pirus."

"Perhaps I can even the odds," an unfamiliar voice called from above. A grey owl perched atop one of the birch trees, swooped down to the forest floor. Along the way, its form undulated and stretched. The feathers on its massive wings retracted into lithe, human arms, while those on its body extended into a flowing silver gown, and the bare feet of a young woman gracefully touched ground.

Petrus stared at her yellow eyes as she approached. *Will the marvels never cease?*

Väinämöinen grinned. "Tuulikki. I was wondering when you'd arrive."

"I've been here for quite some time, hovering overhead."

"What news do you bring, daughter?" Mielikki asked.

"Ajatarra and Perkele are assembling their army. They're on their way here with intent to kill Väinämöinen and take the mortals from the sanctuary."

"She's delusional," Väinämöinen turned to Petrus. "But if she is bringing her beguiled army to us, your wife will likely be among them."

"Will you be able to save her as you did Kreeta?"

"I intend to save them all, Petrus."

"You have a plan then."

Väinämöinen paused. "Of course, I... *will*... by the time we reach the sanctuary."

Tuulikki turned to Urbanus. "I would be happy to escort you and your family safely out of the forest. Tellervo's talents would be best utilized against Ajatarra's forces."

"In that case," Tellervo chimed in. "You should depart as soon as possible and take advantage of the daylight. It's two days to the coast."

Urbanus placed a hand on Petrus's shoulder. "Find my sister. Bring her back to us."

Petrus embraced each of his family members in turn. "May God protect all of you from the demons."

"Do not worry." Tuulikki spread her arms at the six gray wolves surrounding her. "As I said, perhaps I can even the odds."

FOR PETRUS AND VÄINÄMÖINEN, the first day's journey passed mostly in silence for fear of attracting more pirus. By nightfall, however, Mielikki announced that they had passed beyond Ajatarra's territory. Another small shelter was constructed and this time, Tellervo and her mother joined Petrus and Väinämöinen near the fire.

"Tell me, Petrus," Väinämöinen began. "What was your life like before the famine?"

"Quiet, uneventful. I was raised on a farm, but when I was very young, I learned carpentry from my uncle and eventually became a journeyman under a master who happened to be Ievukka's father."

"And so romance bloomed?" Tellervo said as white kielos —lilies of the valley—sprouted from the ground around them.

Petrus grinned as he plucked a cluster of flowers. "Yes, romance bloomed. Ievukka and I were married a year later. I built our house in the village and we talked about starting a family." He twirled a stem between his thumb and forefinger. "That first year, most of our crops were ruined by weeks of frost that continued well into spring, but we persevered with our reserves and what little we harvested at the end of the summer. Everyone thought it was just a fluke; that the next season would produce the bounty we'd been blessed with in years past."

Petrus tossed the flower into the fire. "That was three years and seven hundred deaths ago. Maybe more. I lost count. We slaughtered every animal for food—cattle, horses, dogs, cats. When they were gone, we went for days without eating or subsisted on bark bread. We ventured into the forest to pick what berries the frost hadn't destroyed and hunted what we could, but it was never enough to feed everyone.

"And after surviving for this long, my wife is taken from me by the devil in the blink of an eye. It can't end this way."

"I assure you, it shall not."

Petrus peered up at Väinämöinen, but the voice that had spoken was not his. It was deeper and far more ominous.

"Do not be alarmed," Mielikki said. "My husband takes some getting used to."

Tapio... Petrus searched for the god's face among the surrounding trees. "Which one is he speaking from?"

"All of them."

"Wife of mine," Tapio bellowed. "Are you and Tellervo escorting yet more wayward wretches to our sanctuary?"

Väinämöinen rose to his feet. "I beg your pardon you ancient, petrified, overgrown shrub!"

Petrus tensed. "Väinämöinen, what are you—?"

"How dare you speak to me in—wait a minute. I know that voice..." Tapio paused. "Väinämöinen! You shriveled, prune-faced excuse for a wizard!"

"Well, you're not as senile as I expected."

"Who could forget such a hideous countenance as yours?"

Afraid to move, Petrus shifted his gaze to Mielikki.

She rolled her eyes. "Men." Then, to Tapio, "As if you

didn't know Väinämöinen had returned the moment he stepped foot in the forest."

"Woman, why must you spoil our fun?" her husband grumbled. "That old buzzard and I have not seen each other in centuries. This is almost like a family reunion."

"Complete with a few unwanted relatives," Väinämöinen added.

"Ajatarra, yes." Tapio lowered his voice to a mild rumble. "I'm not certain what to do about her, and can you actually believe that Perkele is involved with that beast?"

"No, but I have some ideas about that. When we arrive at the sanctuary tomorrow, let us discuss it."

"I look forward to seeing you and that ridiculous beard of yours. It's even longer than I remembered, like an angry little gnome."

"And I cannot wait to set my gaze upon your cracked, peeling, caterpillar-infested bark."

"How I have missed our intelligent discourses of old, Väinämöinen. Rest well tonight and may your decrepit bones not turn to dust in your sleep."

After a few moments of silence, Petrus worked up the nerve to speak. "So, you have some ideas about how to stop Ajatarra?"

"I said I would have a plan by the time we reach the sanctuary."

"We're getting closer to the sanctuary."

"And I am getting closer to having a plan."

By midday, Petrus and Väinämöinen reached the sanctuary. It was far more than a larger version of the shelters that Mielikki and Tellervo had provided over the last few days. At least a thousand birch trees formed a dense perimeter that enclosed an area nearly the size of Petrus's entire village.

As they approached, two of the trees parted, allowing Petrus and Väinämöinen entrance to a structure that was like some ancient cathedral of nature. The vaulted roof was at least twenty feet high and comprised of intertwined branches that extended from all of the surrounding trees. Gaps of varying sizes throughout the intricate filigree permitted generous sunlight.

Several people sat around fires, while others lay in beds framed in thick branches and padded with leaves and straw. Petrus counted about three dozen people, all familiar faces and none of them appeared to be starving. As expected, fruits and vegetables grew within reach all throughout the sanctuary.

As the newcomers made their way to one of the closest fires, several people waved and called to Petrus. A pair of strong hands gripped his shoulders and spun him around. It was Johannes, the farmer with whom Petrus had been paired during the search party a few days ago.

"Petrus!" He smiled. "I thought you were taken by one of the giant snakes."

"It was a close call, but I had some help."

"Yes, from these *pagan* creatures," Johannes grumbled.

"Careful," Väinämöinen warned. "The walls have ears."

"And they did save our lives," Petrus added. "But we have a larger problem."

By now, the others had gathered around.

"If you thought the few snakes you saw before were frightening, there are more coming as well as members of our families who have fallen under the spell of Ajatarra."

"Yes, we were told as much by the talking trees," a woman said. "Most of us didn't believe them."

Väinämöinen excused himself and wandered off to speak to Tapio, leaving Petrus to impart the details of his experiences in the forest, beginning with his encounter with Tellervo. All the while, eyes widened, jaws dropped, and heads shook.

"So, please," Petrus concluded. "Show some respect to those trying to help us. I realize their very existence is contrary to our Christian faith, but the Lord works in ways we can't always understand."

There were grumbles and murmurs among his audience, but eventually, they agreed.

One of the farmers stepped forward from the back of the group. "So, how do we fight this army of snakes? We have no weapons."

"You will have weapons by tomorrow morning," Väinämöinen replied as he rejoined Petrus. "Axes, swords, shields—enough for all of you."

"And how do we exorcise the devil out of our people?" the woman asked.

Väinämöinen grinned. "Leave that to me."

After dusk, Petrus took Väinämöinen aside. "With respect, where are we going to find these weapons you promised?"

"From a place few mortals have ever seen. Are you up for a brief jaunt?"

"How far?"

"We're already there."

Around them, the sanctuary dissolved into impenetrable darkness. Petrus tensed at the sound of hammering, metal against metal, from somewhere deep in the forest. Over Väinämöinen's shoulder, the glow of a small, distant fire illuminated the trunks of nearby trees.

"Who is that?"

"An old friend." Väinämöinen led the way through the thicket until they emerged in a clearing to find a tall, muscular man with a full, dark beard hammering a length of thin metal atop an anvil. It took a moment for Petrus to realize it was the blade of a sword. Several feet away, a fire blazed in a large stone enclosure. Two men in the background worked a massive bellows.

As Petrus looked around, his gaze settled on a cache of weapons strewn about the ground and lying against trees—swords, axes, shields.

"You've been busy," Väinämöinen called out.

The man didn't bother to look up. "I was expecting you."

"Of course you were."

Petrus turned to Väinämöinen. "Who is he?"

The man stopped hammering and held up the sword as he approached Petrus. "I was once known to your people as Ilmarinen."

Petrus opened his mouth, but it took a moment to find his voice. "Eternal Blacksmith, Forger of the Universe."

Väinämöinen glared at him. "How is it that you knew his name immediately, but not mine?"

"Who can forget the Craftsman of the Heavens?"

Ilmarinen exchanged a brief glance with Väinämöinen before turning his attention to Petrus. "You flatter me, mortal. Do you not fear blaspheming your Christian God?"

This time, Petrus could think of nothing to say.

"You came here for weapons," Ilmarinen continued. "To fight the evil consuming your forest, destroying your crops, and possessing your people." He waved a hand toward the collection around them. "Yours for the taking."

"Thank you, but if you are... *Jumala*," Petrus said. "If you are the one *true* God, you could rid us of Ajatarra and Perkele with a mere thought—"

"Perkele?"

"I've been told that he has allied himself with Ajatarra, but I've only seen the attacks from the sky as proof."

Väinämöinen cleared his throat.

"Will you help us?" Petrus asked.

Ilmarinen ran a finger along the blade of the sword. "What is it your Christian leaders say? God helps those who help themselves? I am giving you the tools so that you can do the work."

"Are you the one true God?"

"I cannot tell you what to believe, Petrus. You must come to such conclusions on your own, for gods only have power so long as there are those who believe in them. Once people forget, or deliberately turn their backs, their gods become impotent, no more than characters in a fairytale. Before this tribulation ends, you must decide where your faith lies."

Ilmarinen turned to Väinämöinen. "You will accompany the mortals into battle?"

"Yes. What say you to these rumors of Perkele's involvement with Ajatarra?"

"When it comes to the devil, nothing is what it seems. The truth will be revealed when you confront the queen of serpents." Then, to Petrus, "Mortal, collect your weapons and prepare your people for a battle that will be waged as much in their hearts and minds as in the forest. Regardless of the outcome, you and I shall meet again."

With that, Ilmarinen and his forge vanished. Petrus and Väinämöinen found themselves in the center of the sanctuary, weapons scattered at their feet. Around them, people stopped and stared before approaching. They picked through the piles of swords, axes, and shields—some with trepidation, others with zeal. A disorganized, frightened mob of farmers and peasants against a legion of monsters determined to destroy God.

And who leads us? A mysterious old pagan and a family of forest creatures. Have I lost my faith in Christ? Petrus stepped away from the crowd as Väinämöinen disseminated the weapons. "Get a feel for them tonight, but do not injure yourselves," he instructed. "Tomorrow I shall begin training you on basic fighting techniques."

Yet here they are, gods that had been demonized by the Christian church, working and fighting beside us to save our lives and rid our land of the devil. Petrus longed for Ievukka at his side. To tell her all that he had seen and experienced. She often put his mind at ease with thoughtful words of serene wisdom. He imagined himself speaking to her now. *Could it be, my love, that Väinämöinen and these stewards of the forest are agents of Jumala, the one true God? Maybe He took the form of Ilmarinen as a way of communicating with me and providing these weapons. Surely, He would not have brought us this far only to let us die in battle or become mindless slaves to the devil. That would make no sense, would it, Ievukka?*

You needed weapons to fight the devil and God provided, Ievukka replied in his imagination. *Overcome this challenge, and we shall face the rest once we are back in each other's arms.*

Petrus leaned against the wall of the sanctuary and peered up through a gap in the natural latticework of the arched roof. A single, bright star was visible and Petrus locked onto it, knowing that elsewhere in the forest, Ievukka was under that same star and drawing nearer every minute, though she was not of her own mind. *You were right, my love. We should have fled the village that night. We should have traveled south to the shores of the bay. We would still be together. I am so sorry.*

Yelps and shouts from the opposite corner of the sanctuary jarred Petrus from his dark musings. A gap in the wall of the sanctuary sealed itself behind an approaching gray wolf. It sauntered toward one of the fires and emerged a second later as Tuulikki.

Petrus pushed off the wall and made his way over to her, as did Väinämöinen who spoke up first. "What news have you brought us, my dear?"

"What of my family?" Petrus chimed in.

"Safely escorted to one of the fishing villages where they were welcomed as refugees from the north," Tuulikki explained. "Apparently, news of Perkele's attacks has spread throughout the province."

"Any difficulties along the way?" Väinämöinen said.

Tuulikki shook her head. "Our journey was free of incident, much to the chagrin of my wolves. We were looking forward to eliminating more of the serpents. Upon leaving Petrus's family, I ventured north for a bit of reconnaissance. Ajatarra and her army are moving swiftly and without rest. I estimate they will be here in two days."

Väinämöinen nodded. "What about their numbers?"

"About two dozen pirus and just over two hundred mortals armed with crude clubs and axes." Tuulikki glanced around the sanctuary. "Although from the looks of things, you managed to gather quite a cache of weapons while I was gone."

"A gift from Ilmarinen. What of Perkele? Did you see him with Ajatarra?"

"We saw someone who looked and sounded like Perkele, but certainly did not conduct himself as befitting the god of thunder. He was like a callow youth, subordinating himself to her. Ajatarra was clearly in charge."

Väinämöinen leaned against the shaft of his spear. Do gods become weary, discouraged? To Petrus, Väinämöinen appeared to be both. "That is not the Perkele I know. All of the atrocities attributed to him as of late are completely out of character. My instincts tell me that not everything is as it appears. Either Ajatarra is being duped or all of us are. The truth will reveal itself in two days."

~

SHE RAN a gentle hand along the still form of the snake, caressing the dry, brittle flesh until she touched the crusted blood surrounding the fatal wound. Ajatarra lifted her hand and peered at the dull gray scales that clung to her fingertips. "My children... I will see Väinämöinen and his mortals slaughtered for this." She shifted her gaze to the other dead serpents scattered about the clearing. Her sights settled on two with birch trees protruding from their throats. "As will the forest gods when we burn this place to the ground."

"As you wish," Perkele said, keeping a respectful distance. "In the meantime, we've been moving without respite for four days. The mortals require rest and sustenance. They will not be of much use—"

Ajatarra whirled on him. "Let them eat snake!"

Their gazes remain locked for several seconds, one furious, the other impassive, yet neither wavering. Finally, Ajatarra drew back. "Soon, they'll all be dead anyway and we will lead their immortal souls into battle against the very god for whom they abandoned us. Perkele, the most powerful of us all—whose name has been reduced to a profanity by decree of this new Christian faith—why do you care about the welfare of these insects when they turned their backs—"

"Ajatarra..."

She fell silent at the whispered mention of her name. "Did you hear that?"

Perkele grabbed her by the hair and yanked her head back as he raised the blade of his axe to her throat. "I heard only your incessant and redundant chiding of which I have had more than enough. Going forward, you would do well to mind your forked tongue when speaking to me or you might find yourself joining your late children." He lowered the weapon and released her head with a shove.

Ajatarra raised a hand, claws pointed toward his eyes.

"Don't ever threaten me. Remember, it was you who sought me out and proposed this alliance when—"

"Ajatarra..."

She turned away from Perkele, unfurling her tail and pushing her body to its full height.

"What is wrong with you?" he snarled.

She held up a hand and closed her eyes, remaining silent for nearly a full minute. Then, "We are close to their precious sanctuary. Less than a day away."

"How do you know that?"

"I can hear them. A cacophony of voices carried through the trees. Yes, they mention my name and yours. They speak of Väinämöinen and someone named Petrus, but I cannot determine precisely what they're saying."

She opened her eyes and regarded the army of humans standing around the clearing, staring at her with vapid expressions. "We keep moving. The mortals have had enough rest. They will share a final meal when we overtake the sanctuary."

On that second morning, Petrus was jarred awake by the sound of Väinämöinen's voice. As he sat up, he realized that the old wizard was not speaking to him, but to the entire sanctuary. Confused faces turned in every direction, searching for the source of the announcement.

Petrus tilted his head toward the wall of trees beside him. He strolled along the perimeter, pausing every so often to listen. The birch trees were talking—all of them. Through them, Väinämöinen revealed his plan to defeat Ajatarra. No sooner had he finished speaking than two of the trees parted and Väinämöinen hurried into the sanctuary.

"That certainly got everyone's attention," Petrus said.

"I had a little help from Tapio."

"Speaking of which, where is our family of forest gods this morning?"

"Out in the wild, ensuring that Ajatarra is guided directly here."

"Far be it from me to question the plans of gods, but the thought of allowing this sanctuary to be invaded by the devil and her horde of giant snakes is unsettling at best."

"I understand," Väinämöinen nodded. "But you must have faith, Petrus. If all goes well, more than one unpleasant surprise shall befall the queen of serpents, and your wife will be back in your arms before the day's end."

BY THAT EVENING, Ajatarra stared up at the walls of the sanctuary listening to the voices of those within—heated discussions, innocuous conversations, nervous laughter, words of hope and fear.

"This feels like a trap," Perkele said. "Where are the forest gods? Where is Väinämöinen? Is no one keeping watch?"

"For a god of thunder, you sound worried," Ajatarra replied. "What can they possibly do to stop us? Remember, find Väinämöinen first. Kill him before he has a chance to utter a word." She stretched her arms out to her sides, fingers spread wide. In response, her pirus dispersed, slithering away to take up positions along the front wall of the sanctuary. A small contingent of mortals formed a line behind each of the demons. Once all columns were in place, Ajatarra dropped her arms. In unison, the snakes lunged forward, jaws and tails tearing out birch trees two at a time, creating gaps in the wall. Seconds later, Ajatarra's forces stormed through—and stopped.

The sanctuary was empty.

Ajatarra and Perkele exchanged puzzled glances.

"And yet I still hear them," Perkele said. "As if they were standing before us."

The clamor faded until only one voice remained. It was Väinämöinen's. "Mortals, hear me. Let my voice guide you out of the darkness. Let Ajatarra's poison flow from your minds. Release it from your hearts."

"It's coming from the trees themselves!" Ajatarra cried. "Perkele, burn this place."

Overhead, storm clouds gathered. Lightning streaked across the sky, followed by explosions of thunder.

"You are stronger than the mother of evil," Väinämöinen continued. All around Ajatarra, the mortals winced and groaned. Some began hyperventilating. "Follow my voice to the light. Reach out to me. Your mothers and fathers, sisters and brothers, await you with arms and hearts open. They are here in the light." Crying out, the mortals dropped their weapons and fell to their knees, weeping.

"Perkele, why do you delay?" Ajatarra shouted. "Rain fire and lightning down on this place."

He glanced up at the roiling clouds and shook his head. "That is not my doing. I believe we have finally awakened the old man."

"What do you mean? *You* are Perkele, you are Ukko. Who can be mightier?"

Perkele lowered his gaze with a smirk, his face stretching and contorting. Blue eyes darkened to black marbles and his complexion faded to a sickly green.

Ajatarra glowered at him. "Lempo... I thought you were long dead."

The demon shrugged. "You know me, old girl, I'm a survivor and still as capricious as ever. It's been fun playing this part, but my loyalties always shift with the prevailing wind and it seems this storm is coming for you. So, fare thee well, hideous one."

"You bastard! I created you. I can destroy you."

With a cackle, Lempo turned to flee. The lightning bolt that struck him left little more than a blackened, twisted heap. In his place stood a man bedecked in radiant, golden armor. He drove his sword into the charred form of what had once been Ajatarra's most infamous trickster. It crumbled into a pile of ashes.

"No one impersonates me." Perkele's bass voice resonated throughout the forest. He pointed his weapon at Ajatarra. "You do not belong here. Your place is in Tuonela."

Ajatarra flickered her tail, scooping up two axes and tossing them into the air. She caught one in each hand and advanced on Perkele. "Then bring your fire down upon me and send me there yourself." Her pirus moved in close, forming a circle around the two combatants, but Perkele's furious gaze remained fixed on their queen.

"I need no magic to defeat you, witch. As for Tuonela, I shall personally escort you."

As their blades clashed, chaos erupted in the sanctuary.

"NOW!" With Petrus at his side, Väinämöinen raced toward the ring of serpents, followed by three dozen farmers and tradesman wielding weapons provided by Ilmarinen. They barreled into the snakes, slashing and stabbing. Those no longer under Ajatarra's influence either scrambled to the edges of the sanctuary or retrieved their weapons and joined the fight.

After felling his first demon, Petrus ducked away from the battle and peered into the throng of bodies. "Ievukka!"

At first, there was no response. *She must be here.* He cried out again.

"Petrus!"

He whirled in time to see his wife slice open the belly of a green and copper beast, its forked tongue dangling from its mouth as it collapsed.

Husband and wife started toward one another at a dead run—then Ievukka was gone. Petrus stumbled to a halt as she screamed and struggled in the jaws of one of the largest serpents he had ever encountered.

With a roar, Petrus hurled his axe toward the back of its head. Though the weapon missed its intended mark, the blade buried itself in the center of one of the diamond patterns along the snake's back. The creature hardly flinched—until four wolves surrounded the beast and pounced, sinking teeth and claws into its flesh.

Petrus retrieved a discarded sword from the ground and charged ahead. When he reached striking distance, he plunged the blade into the thrashing mass of gray and tan. The monster whipped its head to one side, flinging Ievukka toward the sanctuary wall. The force of the motion knocked Petrus to the ground. He rolled away as the serpent collapsed, enervated by the wolves' relentless assault. After they disengaged, one of the wolves turned and nodded to Petrus before returning to the battle, leaving the snake to bleed out.

He started toward the sanctuary wall as Ievukka was lowered to the ground in a cradle of branches. By the time husband and wife were face to face, they were both in tears.

"I was caught in a tree," Ievukka said.

"Actually you were caught *by* a tree." Tellervo winked at them from high above.

Petrus smiled in spite of himself. "Thank you, my friend."

Ievukka leapt from the cradle into her husband's waiting arms. "Petrus, I don't understand what's happening here."

He placed a hand on the side of her face and kissed her.

"I'll just be over there," Tellervo said. "Killing snakes."

When their lips parted, Petrus spoke first, words tumbling

out in a rush. "I promise I'll explain everything when this is over. I'm so sorry I went into the forest that day with the search party. I should've stayed with you."

Ievukka shook her head. "Don't blame yourself. You were trying to do the right thing. You're with me now and the devil no longer controls me. That's all that matters."

"I won't leave your side again."

"You two!" Väinämöinen called as he thrust his sword into the eye of a black piru. "Fight now, love later."

By this time, most of the creatures had been dispatched by the mob. All attention turned to the center of the sanctuary where Ajatarra, having lost an axe and a hand, was swinging her other weapon at Perkele. The god of thunder deftly blocked each strike. With a strident howl, Ajatarra whipped her tail forward and swept his legs out from under him. Perkele crashed to the ground. The queen of serpents moved in for the kill—until the bloody point of a spear emerged from between her breasts.

For several seconds, she did not move as her breathing became labored. She arched her back and turned her face to the sky, releasing a final, shrill scream before life fled her body. With eyes and mouth wide open, Ajatarra dropped her axe and toppled forward, meeting Perkele's blade with her throat. Her body struck the ground a moment before her head.

Perkele removed his helmet and exchanged a nod with Väinämöinen. "Nice throw, Brother."

"Ilmarinen," Petrus blurted. "It cannot be."

Perkele—or Ilmarinen?—retrieved Ajatarra's head and stood over her body. "I shall dispose of all this. Väinämöinen, you and the forest gods will see to the mortals?"

Väinämöinen bowed his head.

Just as he had arrived, the god of thunder vanished in a blinding burst of white light along with Ajatarra and all of her slain pirus.

In the silence that followed, those still standing exchanged wary glances.

"Is it over?" someone asked.

"The battle is won." Tapio's voice resonated from every corner of the sanctuary. "Ajatarra has been defeated."

Shoulders slumped and weapons dropped to the ground with thuds and clangs. Some embraced one another, friends and families reunited at long last. Others wept as they knelt before the fallen.

"Where do we go from here?" Ievukka asked.

Petrus pulled her close and kissed her on the forehead, but his thoughts were beyond the forest. *Now we return home to starve.*

AT THE REQUEST of the survivors, the dead had been buried at one end of the sanctuary with the help of Tapio and his family. The forest gods had shifted the earth, carving out two rows of individual graves spaced evenly apart.

"I am deeply sorry for those you lost today, Petrus," Tellervo said. "Especially considering the suffering your people have endured for so long."

Petrus stared off into the distance. "We've won a war against an unthinkable evil, but I fear the desolation that still awaits my people. One more season without crops will make us wish we had all died in this forest."

"You don't believe we would have brought you this far only to abandon you?" Väinämöinen placed a gentle hand on Ievukka's shoulder. "Might I borrow your husband for a few minutes, my dear? There's someone who would like to speak with him."

She flashed a bemused smile. "By all means."

Väinämöinen motioned for Petrus to precede him.

"Where are we going?" Petrus asked, but the old man merely waved a gnarled hand to keep moving. Once they were beyond the boundaries of the sanctuary, Petrus turned. "Who wants to speak to—oh."

Both Väinämöinen and the sanctuary were gone. Once again, Petrus faced the forge of Ilmarinen, but this time, he did so alone. The Eternal Craftsman stood with his back to him, tapping on something atop a long wooden table. The deity's imposing form blocked Petrus's view of the object.

Without looking up, Ilmarinen spoke. "I once told you that God helps those who help themselves. You and your people fought well. Come closer, Petrus."

As Petrus approached, Ilmarinen stepped aside and gestured toward a gold dome about four feet around. The walls of the dome were perhaps ten inches tall. The object stood on three legs spaced at equal distances around its perimeter. Petrus was not certain if it glowed with its own light or merely reflected the lambent flames of the nearby fire.

"What is it?"

"It is the Sampo, a device that Väinämöinen once tricked me into creating for someone eons ago. That's a long story, but suffice it to say that once he realized the error of his ways, Väinämöinen helped me recover it."

Petrus was even more confused, if that were possible. "A device? What does it do?"

"It brings prosperity to whomever possesses it. With the Sampo, you could become rich beyond your wildest desires. Gold, precious gems, dominion over man and country as far as the eye can see. Name your desire and it shall be yours."

"I wish only that this famine come to an end, that our crops thrive this coming season, and that no more of my neighbors starve to death."

Ilmarinen smiled. "Väinämöinen chose wisely. For you are indeed a rock, Petrus, and to you I entrust my final gift to my people. The Sampo is now yours. Take it with you. You need only to lay your hands upon it and think about what you want most. From now on, every harvest shall be bountiful throughout the land. Your people will rebuild and become stronger than ever."

"I don't know how to thank you."

"I ask only that you never forget. My kin and I are no longer relevant in the presence of this Christian god whose name is spreading to all corners of the world like a fire through a forest. We must accept that change is inevitable and be content to fade into the brume of antiquity."

"I promise I'll never forget," Petrus assured him. "Nor cease believing in you. It saddens me that you're leaving us."

"Perhaps someday, centuries from now, all of the ancient pantheons of this Earth shall return to see if your people are willing to believe in us again."

With that, Ilmarinen and his forge faded into the night. Beyond the walls of the sanctuary, Petrus turned to Väinämöinen. "I didn't have the temerity to ask if he and Perkele were one and the same."

Väinämöinen shrugged. "Ilmarinen, Perkele, Ukko. Is not your Christian god also known by many names?"

"True. This experience has certainly opened my mind."

Väinämöinen waved toward the Sampo now sitting on the ground before them, pulsing with its own inner flame. "And that will open your world to even more possibilities than you ever imagined. Ilmarinen has placed great trust in you. I know you won't let him down, or your people. They look upon you as a leader now."

Petrus knelt down and placed a tentative finger upon the dome's surface. It was warm to the touch. With a deep breath, he spread both hands over its dome and closed his eyes.

~

One Year Later

It was three o'clock in the morning when a piercing cry tore Petrus from a restful slumber. He turned his head to glance at the empty space beside him in bed. Sitting up, he caught sight of Ievukka standing at the window, silhouetted in the pallid light of the full moon. Petrus slipped out of bed to stand behind his wife, embracing her and their newborn daughter nestled in her arms.

"It will be dawn in less than hour," Ievukka whispered, "and then she will be baptized. Eliisa Anniki Tellervo Tuulikki Koivisto."

"Perhaps it's best not to mention Tellervo and Tuulikki to the new minister," Petrus said. "He might not take well to pagan names. Those will be our little secret."

"Like the Sampo?"

"It's too dangerous a device to reveal. It could be made into a dreadful weapon. Ilmarinen entrusted it to me and I'll do what I must to honor that. Our crops are abundant again and our village is beginning to thrive. Let the other survivors and our new neighbors praise their god."

"While we praise the Gods."

Petrus smiled and nuzzled Ievukka. "That will also be our little secret."

This story first appeared in *Meanwhile in the Middle of Eternity* (Firebringer Press, March 2021).

Man to Man

How do you walk up to a guy and confess that you're in love with his wife? That's exactly what I was about to do. To say that I was anxious would've been an understatement. It wasn't as if I'd ever had a conversation like *this* before. I suspected that he already knew about Ally and me, yet I felt compelled to offer an explanation. After all this time, it seemed the honorable thing to do.

The rain started as I sat down to speak to him. I didn't mind at all. The cooler temperatures were a welcome respite from the mid-July heat wave.

I rubbed my hands on my cargo shorts as I began talking. I'd rehearsed most of my speech on the way there, but that didn't make this any less awkward. "Hey, Jared, I hope it's OK that we meet like this. I realize you never knew me, never knew the kind of guy I really am, but I think you do now. At least, I hope so. I feel I owe you an account of how all of this started between Ally and me.

"Three years ago, when she and I worked together, we had a little misunderstanding. It was completely my fault, but it triggered feelings for her that I didn't expect. She started flirting with me at a happy hour after work one day, and I wasn't the only one who noticed. At the time, I dismissed it. I thought it was just the booze talking, but in the months that followed, she continued to make little comments here and there.

"I became so confused and distracted that I finally had to take her aside and talk with her about it. Part of me hoped there was something behind her words, but she was mortified that I'd taken her remarks as anything more than innocent fun.

"Believe me, Jared, the idea of stealing your wife was the furthest thing from my mind. I just had to know the truth. Did I want to believe that Ally had feelings for me? I won't lie. The heart wants what it wants, but I was wrong. In the end, I was just a sympathetic ear in a stressful work environment. Ally would never have left you."

I took a deep breath as the rain soaked through my shirt. I didn't care. All that mattered was this weight on my chest and the only way to release it was to see this through to the end.

"I finally left the company a few months later and once I was gone, I never had any contact with Ally again. But I missed her.

"Then, last summer, we ran into each other at Bethany Beach and talked for about twenty minutes, just catching up. I was genuinely sorry to hear what happened, Jared. You think some couples will be together forever.

"As it turns out, Ally missed me, too. The longer we talked, the more we realized how much we enjoyed each other's company. We've been together ever since, but you know that already.

"Look, Jared, I came here because I respect what you and Ally had together and maybe I have some guilt, too, I don't know. What I *do* know is that I love her. When she's with me, nothing else matters. Ally has my heart. This past year with her has been wonderful."

My vision clouded as tears welled up. Not sure why. I thought I'd talked through all the hard stuff. "Look, Jared, I came here to let you know that I'm going to propose to Ally tonight."

I leaned forward and put a gentle hand on the gravestone. For a moment, I stared in silence at the inscription. *Jared Henriksen, 1970-2012.*

"Cancer took you far too young. I realize I can never replace you, but I promise I'll love Ally for the rest of her life."

My New Shiny

Across the street from the alley, a burning delivery van exploded. It was parked in front of the hardware store, which was also ablaze. Both had been vandalized during the looting. In the distance, fading sirens and shouting voices were punctuated by occasional gunfire. The madness was moving south. Two days ago, a Hispanic college student was gunned down by a black cop, simply for being in the wrong place at the wrong time. This sparked one of the most explosive riots in the city's history.

Simon Ramirez opted out of the violence. It wasn't his problem. As the world around him collapsed into mayhem, he sat quietly on a metal folding chair that one of the looters had used to smash the window of the antique shop next door to his home.

His home being the alley, of course.

Simon glanced up just as his "roommate" hurried around the opposite corner and pressed himself against the wall of the pizza shop. Old Ralph had been living on the streets for over a decade. An industrious sort, he made a few bucks on odd jobs like washing cars or fetching dry cleaning for local businessmen. Most of the cash that greased Ralph's palms slipped into the register at the liquor store—but not tonight. No, tonight, all booze was free.

After catching his breath, Ralph peeked out from behind the wall. Assured that no one had followed him, he hurried over to Simon.

"Hey, some crazy shit tonight, eh?" Ralph laughed, a raspy rattle from a nearly toothless mouth. He nodded to the object in Simon's grimy hands. "What's that?"

Simon slid a finger along the ornate embellishment that wrapped around the gem-studded metal decanter. "It's my new shiny."

Ralph held up the bottle of vodka he'd scavenged from the liquor store after the looters had dispersed. "Split it with ya?"

"You know I don't drink."

"Then why steal a decanter?"

"I didn't steal it. It was laying on the sidewalk in front of the antique shop and it... it called to me."

"It called to ya?" Frowning, Ralph leaned forward and turned his good ear toward the vessel. "I don't hear nothin'. You been on the streets too long, Simon. Why not grab somethin' valuable like a Blu-ray player or a laptop? The electronics shop was the first to get hit."

"I'm homeless, Ralph, just like you. Where would I use those?"

"You could sell 'em."

"Even in this town, who's going to buy from a filthy, disfigured bum?"

"Well, what about food? The mini-mart on the corner's smashed wide-open! Owner was shot dead. Everythin's for the takin'." Ralph held up two bulging plastic bags. "I grabbed me a bunch of breakfast sandwiches, soft pretzels, and more. Want some?"

"I get better food from the shelter on Seventh *without* stealing it."

Ralph shook his head. "I don't unnerstan' you, kid. Out here in the wild, we need to take every 'vantage we can git." He sauntered away toward the end of the alley. "Enjoy your new shiny. I'm gonna drink my vodka and pass out. Wake me up when the riot's over."

"Good night, Ralph."

Simon turned his attention back to the metal decanter and the two rows of red gems spaced evenly around its polished surface. Then, he noticed something odd. While most of the jewels reflected the lambent flames of the burning van, two of them remained dark. Simon placed his forefinger and thumb on those stones and pressed. Within seconds, the decanter was vibrating in his grasp, but it wasn't until his fingertips began to burn that he dropped it. The decanter struck the pavement with a clang and rolled across the alley until it disappeared into the shadows.

Simon moved to retrieve it, but drew back as the air filled with smoke. He stumbled over his chair just as a tall man stepped out of the shadows, arms flailing.

"Dammit!" The stranger launched into a coughing fit before regaining his composure. "I can't believe they added smoke. That is so cliché!"

As the air began to clear, Simon could discern the man's narrow face, dirty-blonde hair, and neatly trimmed goatee. He was dressed entirely in black from turtleneck to boots. In the dim lighting, it was impossible to determine his age, but he appeared young.

"Who the hell are you?" Simon asked.

The man narrowed his eyes at him. When he spoke, his voice was deep and crisp with a slight Eastern European accent. "You are the one?"

"What?"

"The one who released me. Try to keep up, man."

Simon picked himself up and brushed off his clothes, as if it would make a difference. "Yeah, I guess. I'm Simon." He extended a hand. "Simon Ramirez."

The man accepted the gesture and smiled. "Kiril Racht, at your service."

Simon's eyes went wide. "Are you a genie?"

"Don't be absurd, I am a warlock. Genies are tricksters. They prey upon your every desire by using your wishes against you."

"But you live in that decanter."

"Like Hades I do! My coven imprisoned me in that thing right after I stopped what's-his-name with the little mustache and his goose-stepping morons from Germany."

Simon thought for a moment. "Wait. You mean Adolf Hitler?"

Racht snapped his fingers. "Right, him."

"You fought in World War II?"

"Not exactly. The Nazis unwittingly executed some of my kind. So, I took matters into my own hands by manipulating events here and there to expedite their defeat, and what did I get for my heroic efforts?" Racht bunched up his face. When he spoke again, his voice was high and mocking. "You know we are forbidden to interfere in human history. You must be punished." His features returned to normal. "So, they banished me into that decanter."

"That was nearly seventy years ago."

Racht seemed unfazed by the news. "What city is this?"

"Philadelphia."

"The United States," Racht muttered. "Clearly, that decanter was well-traveled. I wonder if any from my coven are here." He pointed at a tattered, grungy duffel bag sitting atop a small stack of wooden pallets. "Yours?"

"Yeah, why?"

Racht unzipped the bag and peered inside. "Anything useful?"

"Hey!" Simon reached for the duffel, but Racht yanked it away and turned his back. Simon stepped around him. "You can't just take—"

The warlock held up a small purple cup with a clear lid and spout. "What manner of goblet is this?

"It's a child's sippy cup."

"Do you have children?"

Simon lowered his gaze. "No."

Racht raised an eyebrow. "Then why do you possess a child's cup?"

"I found it in the trash. It's in perfect condition. People are so wasteful." Simon plucked the cup from Racht's hand and shoved it into his bag. "Would you please stop rummaging through my stuff?"

"Why do you carry all of these things?"

"They're all I have."

"Where is your home?"

"You ask a lot of questions for a genie."

"Warlock!"

"Whatever. Look, *this* is my home, okay?" Simon spread his arms wide. "Right now, you're standing in my living room. That mattress between those dumpsters back there is my bed and that little stack of tattered books is my library."

With a grim expression, Racht nodded in understanding.

"Makes living in a decanter seem like the lap of luxury, huh?"

"Do you have any idea what it's like to have your head compressed in a vice grip for seventy years?"

"Do you have any idea what it's like going through life with a face that's almost completely burned off?"

Racht's jaw clenched as he sneered at Simon. After a

moment, his expression softened. "Yes, I noticed. How did it happen?"

"A few years ago, I was mugged on the street by three guys. One of them threw a jar full of sulfuric acid at me." Simon waved a hand toward his face. "After getting out of the hospital, I couldn't bring myself to go out in public, let alone back to work. My wife eventually left me. Not that I blame her. She was gorgeous. She deserved better. Anyway, you don't need to hear my woes. Long story short, I lost everything and ended up here." Simon paused and lowered his head. "I'll probably die in this alley with old Ralph back there."

Racht gripped Simon's shoulder. "I concede that you have suffered great loss and indignity. While I am not a genie and cannot grant you three wishes, perhaps I can be of some assistance. What do you want most in this world, Simon Ramirez?"

"What do you think? I want my life back!"

Racht placed his hands on both sides of Simon's head. "So be it. As you have liberated me, so I free you from this tribulation and restore your life to what it was before the attack."

"You can do that? But wait! If you send me back, who will let you out of that decanter?"

Racht flashed a knowing grin. "Let me worry about that."

The warlock muttered a brief incantation in a strange tongue that conjured impressions of ancient and omnipotent power in Simon's mind. He began to tremble. Tender, welcome tranquility enveloped him and he gasped as it filled his entire being until he thought he would burst from sheer ecstasy.

Racht's hands slipped away, and Simon felt himself tumbling backwards, falling, falling...

~

IT WAS morning when Simon awoke. He opened his eyes expecting the usual sights of graffiti-covered walls, fly-infested dumpsters, and open sky. Instead, he gazed at a white ceiling and four walls of warm peach. The air was redolent of sweet vanilla.

Beside him, a nude woman lay on her stomach, breathing in a soft, slow rhythm. *Gwen...* Simon stretched an arm over his wife and buried his face in her soft, strawberry hair. *My face!* He drew back as she turned onto her side, afraid she might open her eyes and scream at the sight of him.

Simon slipped out of bed and hurried into the bathroom. He gaped at his reflection in the mirror—his *perfect* reflection. Hazel eyes, unblemished skin, angled jawline, all just as they had been before the attack. "He did it. I'm back. I'm really back."

"Who did what?"

Gwen stood in the doorway, her hair like wildfire, eyes puffy. Simon turned to her and smiled. "Uh, nothing. Just a... work thing. You look gorgeous."

Gwen raised an eyebrow. "I just woke up. I look like I was hit by a train." She made her way out to the hallway. "I need coffee."

Simon hurried after her. "Wait. What's the date?"

Gwen frowned. "It's Saturday, September third."

That's a few days before the attack. Plenty of time...

"You want coffee?" Gwen asked.

"Yeah, that would be fantastic. Did we have any plans today?"

"Not that I know of."

"Good. I have an errand to run."

~

This time, he saw them first. In the supermarket parking lot, Simon pretended to adjust grocery bags in his trunk. He was merely stalling for time, waiting for the three men to make their way over to him. Correction, two men and a girl—and *she* was the one carrying the jar of acid. It had happened so fast last time that Simon didn't get a good look at them.

He reached into his coat pocket, curled his fingers around the grip of the .45 caliber semi-automatic he'd bought three days before, felt the curve of the trigger against the tip of his forefinger. *My turn, assholes.*

"'Scuse me, sir," one of the men called. "Can you spare a few dollars?"

Simon backed away from his car. He slammed the trunk closed as a diversion and pulled the gun from his pocket. "I can spare a few bullets."

For a moment, no one moved.

"Now what?" Simon taunted. "Who wants to make the first move?"

The girl tipped the jar in his direction and drew her arm back. Simon took aim at her. "Not this time, chiquita."

At that, one of the men bolted. Distracted for a moment, Simon was oblivious to the pistol that flashed in his peripheral vision—until it was too late. The other man fired twice. Simon doubled over at the burning impact in his chest and stomach. He collapsed against an SUV in the adjacent parking space.

"Shit, someone's comin'."

"Let's get out of here!"

As the attackers ran off, Simon slid to the ground and lifted a bloody hand from his chest. *Never even considered they might've been armed with anything more than acid. Dumb ass...*

Footsteps scraped to a halt beside him and Simon turned

his gaze to a familiar face looming over him. Hands clutched the front of his jacket and yanked him to his feet.

"Selfish, ungrateful buffoon!" Racht tightened his grip on Simon's coat and backed him against the brick wall. "Good thing for both of us that was only a test run."

Simon gaped at his raised hand. The blood was gone. He pressed his fingers to his chest and stomach to find them completely unscathed. "I'm alive!" His awe turned to disappointment at the sight—and stench—of his filthy clothes. His shoulders slumped as he took in his surroundings. *Back to the hellhole.* Simon frowned at the warlock. "What do you mean, *test run*?"

"Everything you just experienced happened only in your head. I used your memories to recreate your wife, your home, your neighborhood. I wanted to observe what would happen *before* committing to anything." Racht released Simon with a shove. "You chastise others for their wasteful ways, yet you would so easily throw away your own life for petty revenge. If any members of my coven learn that more people died because of my meddling, never mind the decanter. They'd stuff my ass into one of your... *sippy cups*!"

"I'm sorry, Racht. Look, give me another chance. You showed me the error of my ways. I won't make the same mistake again, I promise. I know what I need to do now. Please, send me back for real this time."

Racht responded with a dismissive wave and paced the width of the alley. Finally, he turned to face Simon. "Are you absolutely certain I can trust you? Understand that *my* future is on the line as well."

With a solemn expression, Simon raised a finger to his chest. "Cross my heart and hope to, uh... *not* die."

"Do not try my good nature, Simon. Know that I will hold you to your word."

~

The salesman behind the counter smiled as Simon approached. "Ah, Mr. Ramirez, how are you today?"

"Fantastic, George. Looking forward to getting my new shiny."

"Of course." George gently laid the hard plastic case atop the glass counter and opened it to reveal a silver Smith and Wesson .45 caliber pistol.

Simon nodded. "She's a beauty."

"Is there anything else I can get for you today, sir? Perhaps a box or two of rounds?"

"You bet. Oh, and where can I pick up a bulletproof vest?"

~

Ralph hurried around the corner and pressed himself against the wall of the pizza shop. After catching his breath, he turned and peered out onto the sidewalk, now illuminated by the gamboling flames of the burning delivery van. Assured that no one had followed, Ralph started into the alley but halted as something rolled out in front of his feet.

Pick it up, Ralph! A strange, accented voice entered his mind. Ralph looked around, but saw no one lurking about. Curious, he snatched up the purple sippy cup and held it out beside the bottle of vodka in his other hand.

"Fancy drinkin' tonight!" With a chuckle, Ralph carried them both toward the back of the alley.

~

This story first appeared in *Elsewhere in the Middle of Eternity* (Firebringer Press, August 2016).

Break and Enter

Out here in the sticks, you can hear a twig snap under a squirrel's foot, but that was no rodent crunching broken glass under its heels. Strange to hear anything shatter in this old country chapel at quarter past two in the morning.

Fact is, someone just broke into the sacristy. Not sure why, considering the main doors are never locked. As I approach the room, I can hear the floorboards creaking in there. It's impossible to sneak around in this old house of God. From the doorway, I turn on the lights.

He's standing slumped against one of the cedar cabinets, head bowed, broad shoulders and barrel chest heaving. His eyes are closed, and his untucked shirt drenched in sweat.

"The chapel doors are always open, you know." I start toward him—until he thrusts out a trembling Smith and Wesson revolver.

I raise my hands, palms out. "You won't need that here."

"Thought this place was abandoned." His words tumble out as he stares at me with wide eyes. "I've driven past here several times. It's always dark and run down."

"Welcome to our grand re-opening." I spread my arms wide. "Although that won't officially happen for another few months. I'm Father Vogel, the pastor here at St. Gemma's Chapel, at least until the renovations are finished and my relief arrives. Then, I'm retiring. Heard you break in all the way from the rectory. I'll bill you for the window."

He raises an arm to wipe sweat from his face. His sleeves are rolled up, revealing several long scratches on his forearms. Keeping the gun trained on me, he sidles past and out into the chapel, glancing from the narrow marble altar to the gamboling flames of votive candles to the brass pendant lamps hanging far above rows of polished oak pews.

I follow him through the door. "If you're looking for money, I'm afraid there isn't much here, but you're welcome to it."

"Don't want your money."

"Then can I put my arms down?"

He nods.

"If you're hungry, there's food and drink in the rectory."

He considers it for a moment. Finally, he backs up and waves me forward with his gun. I hurry by, taking a moment to genuflect before the altar. The man follows me—until approaching headlights slice through the darkness beyond the windows.

"Shit!" My guest dives into the nearest pew. "Turn off the damn lights!"

"Watch your language in this house." I saunter down the aisle to the narthex and peer through the windows as two police cruisers stop at the fork in the road. Good Lord, I must have a fugitive on my hands. "Don't worry. I don't believe they'll bother coming in just yet." Sure enough, after about twenty seconds, one turns left toward the mountain while the other takes off alongside the river.

"Yeah, that's right." The man joins me at the door and

runs a hand through his matted brown hair. "Get out of here, pigs. You ain't takin' me. Ain't nobody takin' Tito Carver tonight."

"Tito is it? You get those scratches from the police or from running through the woods?"

He holds up his arms and frowns as if seeing his injuries for the first time. "Neither. Got these from the devil."

"The devil?"

"It ain't just the cops I'm runnin' from, Reverend, and this ain't the first place I've broken into tonight."

"Sounds like you've been busy. You want to take it from the top?"

"Cops want me for murder. Killed four people."

"Why?"

"They beat my daughter to death and tossed her in a dumpster like garbage."

"Mother of God." I lower my voice. "I'm so sorry, Tito."

"Everybody's sorry, but no one gave a damn enough to help. Cops said there were no witnesses and not enough evidence to arrest anyone, but I know it was them four punks. They were harassin' her because she was different."

"Different?"

"Meredith had Down syndrome, but she was smart. She did good in all her classes and even worked at the library. Walked there every day after school. These four kids would sometimes follow her, call her names and threaten her. She was scared, but she never cried. My Meredith never cried. She just kept walkin'.

"One day, I took off from work early to pick her up and take her to the library. I wanted to see these kids for myself. When I got to the school, they were already givin' her a hard time, callin' her 'retard' and 'freak.' Two guys and their girlfriends, you know, part of the cool crowd.

"So, I jumped out of my car and got in their faces. They

backed down real quick and ran off like scared rats. I took Meredith to the principal's office and reported everythin' she'd been through since the start of the school year."

"But that didn't stop them."

Tito lowers his gaze to the floor. "The next week was quiet. No one bothered Meredith at all. Thought that was the end of it— 'til she went missin' for three days. They... they found her body in a dumpster behind the River View Diner." His eyes well up, and his voice turns hoarse with simmering rage. "She'd been beaten to death. Her head had been... bashed in by a baseball bat or somethin'."

I can think of no words to comfort this man or ease his pain. He's armed, volatile, and anything could set him off. I don't want to risk that he'll turn the gun on himself. Best to let him get it all out.

Tito raises his head, face streaked with tears. He stares off into the chapel. "I just buried her on Wednesday. This afternoon, I drove over to the school and waited for those four assholes. I watched them leave together, laughin' and carryin' on like they didn't have a care in the world. Like they didn't give a damn that my Meredith was gone."

"What did you do, Tito?"

"They stopped at the ball field and sat on the bleachers having a good ol' time— 'til I got out of my car, came around from behind them, and shot all four of 'em dead."

I bless myself and offer up a hasty prayer.

"Cops came to arrest me at home, but I wasn't goin' down without a fight. I grabbed a crowbar and started swingin'. Managed to snatch one of their guns and took off through the woods. Not sure why I bothered. Ain't got nothin' left to live for."

"You still have *you*."

Tito shakes his head. "Best parts of me are gone. Lost my wife to cancer four years ago. I don't even know why I'm tellin' you all this, Reverend. Guess it's time to confess my sins."

"What are your intentions, Tito?"

"Get somewhere far away. Change my name. Start over somewhere. You got a car?"

"Not anymore, but before you go," I start toward the first aid kit near the restroom in the far corner of the narthex, "maybe you'd like some bandages for those scratch—"

Tito raises his gun. "Don't move, Reverend. You're just gonna call the cops."

"Phone's in the sacristy. If I'd wanted the cops in here, I would have flagged down those two cruisers a minute ago."

After a few breaths, Tito relaxes and lowers the revolver. He's exhausted and it's beginning to show. "I don't need nothin'. Just gimme time to think."

"I understand, son. I'm curious, though. You said you had a run-in with the devil tonight. What'd he look like?"

"He was a *she*, and she was a teenager."

"Well, like we just discussed, teenagers can be devils."

"This one was possessed."

"And how do you know that?"

Tito shifts his gaze to meet mine. "Because when I shot her, she was crawlin' on the ceilin'."

I'm starting to wonder if he's a fugitive from justice or an escapee from the local mental hospital. Can I believe anything he's telling me? God sent him here for a reason, so I suppose I should humor him. "Well, that's something you don't hear every day. Once again, from the top?"

Tito leans against the wall beside the window and stares off into the darkness outside. "It was just over an hour ago, during that storm that blew through here. I was in the woods, runnin' from the cops when I came across a house about two miles up Miller's Ridge. There was a shed on the property. It was unlocked, so I ducked inside to hide and get out of the rain.

"After a few minutes, I heard voices and a little girl screamin'. I peeked out and saw the family bolt from the house to the garage. Mom and dad and their daughter. She was maybe nine or ten. Cryin' like she'd been hurt real bad. They left in a hurry. I figured they were takin' her to the hospital and they'd be gone awhile, so I went over to the house thinkin' the place was empty. I was wrong."

"What happened?"

"I broke in through the back door and flipped the light switch, but the storm must've knocked out the power. There was a flashlight layin' on the floor. It was on. Thought that was weird, but not as weird as the trail of blood. I followed it through the house to the stairs. I shined the light up to the second floor and she was standin' there just starin' down at me."

"What'd she look like?"

"My daughter. She looked like my Meredith at first. She was leanin' against the wall, holdin' her stomach. Her hand was bloody. I went up to her and she fell into my arms. Asked me to help her. Said her daddy had shot her. I told her she was gonna be OK. I was gonna call an ambulance."

"You would have been caught if you'd stayed there."

"I know, but it didn't matter, 'cause when I laid her down on the floor and pushed her hair out of her face, she didn't look like my daughter no more. She didn't even look human. Her eyes turned completely white and her skin was tight and putrid like a corpse. She grinned up at me like somethin' out of a horror movie. I ain't never stared down pure evil until that moment. When she spoke again, it was like a dozen voices all at once.

"I realized then what I was dealin' with. I drew my gun on her, but she was fast. She shot up off the floor and flew at me, scratchin' and clawin' until she knocked me down the steps. I lost the flashlight but held on to my gun. I landed on my back and looked up at her. She was crawlin' up the wall, snarlin' and growlin' like some feral beast. That's when the whole house turned cold and started stinkin' like rotten meat.

"When she got to the ceilin', she flipped over on her back. I started shootin'. I think I put one in her leg, but it was too dark to tell. She screamed and started writhin' around above me, throwin' a tantrum. I ain't never been so scared in my life. I ran out of there and didn't stop until I got here."

I can't help but wonder if his unhinged mind concocted this crazy story, but I have a suspicion we'll find out soon enough. Someone's coming.

Or possibly some*thing*.

"How about a cup of coffee, Tito? There's some in the sacristy. Seems we got a long night ahead of us."

"Sure. I could use the caffeine before I get back in the wind. I was damn lucky them cops didn't come in here lookin' for me just now, but they'll probably be back. I'm gonna need some supplies like—"

There's a knock at the door. Tito backs away and flattens himself against the far wall, tightening his grip on the gun.

"You won't need that." I hold up a hand. "It isn't the cops."

"Tell them you're closed."

"The Lord's House is never closed to those who need Him."

I start toward the door—until it's thrown open by itself. The teenage girl hunched outside is clutching her stomach with two bloody hands. There's more blood on her jeans. A mane of strawberry blonde conceals her face. After a moment, she stumbles through the door with filthy bare feet and drops into my arms with a whimper. I lower her to the floor and kneel beside her as she weeps.

Tito's eyes grow wide as he trains the gun on her, finger on the trigger. "How the hell did she find me?"

I glare up at him. "This your handiwork, Tito?"

"Goddammit, I told you she's possessed! Get away from her."

I hold out my hands, palms smeared with the girl's blood. "Tito, please lower the gun and back away. She isn't the devil, just a frightened young girl who needs help."

I turn my attention back to her. "Sweetie, can you tell me your name?"

"Holly," she whispers.

"OK, Holly, stay with me. We're going to get you to a hospital, but first I need to stop the bleeding. I'll be right back."

"No, don't leave me alone with them."

"I'll only be a few seconds, sweetie." I stand and point toward the sacristy as I pass Tito. "Make yourself useful. Put down that gun and go call for an ambulance."

Tito clenches his jaw. He seems conflicted for a moment until he shakes his head. "No, I ain't takin' my eyes off her. You call them."

"Tito, I have blood on my hands, and I need to get the first aid—"

The air in the narthex turns frigid. Behind me, Holly shrieks with a deep, primal howl, the likes of which you don't expect from a human—or any earthly creature. She convulses for a few seconds before rising about four feet off the floor. Her arms and legs dangle loose and her head rolls back like a tattered rag doll in the grip of an invisible hand. Her gaze settles on Tito and me just before her eyes lose all color.

"Christ Almighty, I told you." Tito takes aim.

"No!" I shove him aside. His shot goes wild, shattering a windowpane in the front door.

"What the hell's the matter with you, priest? Ain't it your job to exorcise demons?"

"You'll kill Holly."

"Better her than us."

"Fine. Get out of here, Tito. I'll handle this."

Holly thrusts out an arm, reaching toward me. Out of her mouth comes a chorus of strident voices. "*Corpul ei este pe moarte. Nu ne poate sprijini.*"

Takes me a moment to remember my Romanian. Makes sense. This area was settled by immigrants from that country's Transylvania region over two hundred years ago. "What do you want?"

"*Un nou vas.*" Holly shifts her gaze from Tito to me. "*Nu ne puteți ajuta. Ești mort.*"

"Tell me something I *don't* know."

Her eyes close and her body goes limp, still suspended above the floor. I step forward until I'm within arm's reach.

"What the hell were they saying?" Tito asks.

"If I understood them right, Holly's dying. They want to possess someone else." I peer over my shoulder at Tito. "But I'm... uh... too old for the job."

"Well, they ain't gettin' me." Tito backs away, gun raised. "I'll take my chances with the pigs."

"Don't leave me." Although strained, Holly's voice is once again her own.

"You must think I'm stupid. The devil ain't takin' Tito Carver!"

"Then kill me. I can't fight them forever. They're in my head... taunting and threatening me. They made me attack my family. They're pulling me under... drowning me. I'm slipping away. Kill me before I'm lost to them... *please.*"

Tito hesitates, glances over at me. I shake my head. He takes a deep breath and lowers his gun. "I ain't killin' nobody else."

"You already murdered four kids when these demons controlled them. What's one more?" As she pleads with Tito, her tears drip to the floor, lost among streaks of blood. "They're all in me now. Don't let them win. Please... give me peace."

"I didn't know. I didn't know those kids were possessed. How could I have known that?" Tito runs a hand through his hair. "Christ. This ain't happenin'. How the hell was I supposed to know?"

I need to keep him calm, but before I can say anything, Holly's body launches into violent spasms. Her limbs contort in impossible directions. Tito seems mesmerized. I can't bear to watch but can't look away either. Her eyes and mouth open wide. A legion of shrill voices cry out. "We must have a new host!"

"You are not welcome in this house." I snap the chain from my neck and press the crucifix to Holly's forehead. "Depart from this girl in the name of Jesus Christ!"

With that, Holly's body collapses to the floor in a crumpled heap. I kneel beside her and cradle her head in my hands. "I'm sorry, child."

"Looks like you got the touch, Reverend. Good luck to ya. I'm in the wind." He darts off toward the sacristy.

"Daddy, don't leave her."

Tito staggers back at the sight of a teenage girl standing in the center aisle. Shaking his head, he levels the Smith and Wesson with both hands. "You ain't playin' no more games with me, Satan."

"Daddy, she needs help. Don't let the monsters kill her, too."

Tito's anger drains away as he drops to his knees in front of his daughter. "Meredith?" His voice quivers as he lays the gun on the floor. First time it's left his hand since he got here. He reaches up to touch the side of her face. "Is it really you?"

Tito weeps as he presses his forehead to hers. "How... how can you be here, baby?"

Meredith shrugs. "I told them I wanted to see my daddy, so they sent me here."

"Who sent you?"

"The angels."

"Well, you... you thank them angels for me, 'cause I miss you so much. You were all I had left. I tried to protect you. I tried to stop them from hurtin' you."

"I know, Daddy, but now you need to save Holly."

"You know her?"

"She works at the library and she helped me with my schoolwork sometimes. Holly was my only real friend."

"I don't know what to do. I couldn't even save you."

As they talk, blue and red lights streak across the walls and ceiling. Tires rumble and pop over gravel. Three police cars pull up outside, their headlights bathing the chapel in a stark white glow.

I meet Tito's gaze as he glances over his shoulder. "Someone probably heard your shot earlier. They're coming in this time, Tito. I can't stop them."

He squints against the headlights, staring at them for a few seconds before turning back to his daughter. "You know I ain't never denied you anythin'. Besides, who am I to argue with the angels, especially one named Meredith?"

They embrace one final time before she vanishes in his arms. Outside, car doors slam shut followed by murmuring voices.

Regaining his composure, Tito picks up the gun and gets to his feet. He marches over to Holly. "You want a host, I'm right here. Leave this girl alone and take me."

"Tito, what're you doing?" I push myself to my feet and move between him and Holly. "That's a horrible idea."

"This can only end one way, Reverend, and I ain't dyin' in no gas chamber." He steps around me and shouts at Holly. "Come on, what're you waitin' for? You want a new host, here I—"

Tito lurches forward with a strangled gasp. His body goes rigid as his eyes fly open wide and cloud over white. His breath hisses through clenched teeth as he grabs Holly by the hair. She screams as he yanks her to her feet.

"Tito, stop!"

He wraps one arm around Holly's neck and with his other hand, presses the gun to the side of her head. She sobs and clutches her stomach as he drags her forward. I try to block him from leaving, but the door is again thrown open by an unseen force.

Outside, three cops draw their weapons.

"Carver, let her go and toss the gun!"

Tito puts his lips to Holly's ear and grunts a single word. "*Run.*" With that, he shoves her aside and aims his revolver at the nearest cop.

It takes four shots to bring him down. He collapses at my feet in the doorway. Lying on his back, he shifts his gaze up to meet mine and his mouth curls into a smile. "Ain't nobody takin' Tito Carver tonight."

I offer up a prayer for his soul while two officers rush in. One checks Tito's pulse before shaking his head. The other calls for an ambulance.

A third officer is already beside Holly. This ordeal will leave her with some scars, but instinct tells me she'll pull through. Why the demons chose her—or made those four kids murder Tito's daughter—is beyond me, but I'll keep them all in my prayers.

As for me, well, my time with Saint Gemma's is nearly over, twenty-two years after my demise. I remained here only because I couldn't bear to leave this beautiful place to rot, but since the community persuaded the diocese to reopen the chapel with a new pastor, I'll be moving on soon.

It's a little over two hours 'til sunrise. I should clean up Holly's blood from the floor before the workmen return—or in the unlikely event that another wayward soul turns up at my door.

This story first appeared in *Fae Shivers: Remembered Nightmares* (Fae Corps Publishing LLC, November 2021).

Life and Limb

County Galway, Ireland

Michael Whalen slid into the seat opposite his sister outside Cupán Tae tearoom in Galway's Latin Quarter. After the waitress took his order, Michael leaned back in his chair and allowed his broad shoulders to slump. "Sorry I'm late."

Amelia twisted her lips into a wry grin.

He was all too familiar with that look. "I was stuck on the phone."

"I thought you were just avoiding me, considering what day it is."

Michael sighed and gazed at the gathering clouds that cast a dreary pallor over their meeting. Appropriate, given that their brunch coincided with the anniversary of their parents' deaths eight years ago. Amelia had been visiting them when a gas line explosion leveled their home, leaving her right forearm crushed beyond repair.

"I'm not avoiding you, Mealy. This is difficult for me, too, you know."

"I live with a reminder every day."

"Yeah, I get it. For the love of God, we're in our forties. I know we've never seen eye to eye on anything, but I was hoping by now we would have healed old wounds and moved forward. Did you ever wonder why I gave up a successful career as a surgeon? I was beside myself, forced to stand by while one of my colleagues amputated your arm. After that, all I wanted was to develop the best replacement limb possible for *you*."

Michael reached across the table and cupped his hand around her prosthetic fingers. "And there's not a day that passes when I don't wish I could give you more."

Amelia's eyes glistened. "I know and I'm sorry. I didn't invite you here to argue. Please don't think I'm ungrateful. It's an amazing machine." She released his hand and gripped her teacup by its tiny round handle. In bright aqua and orange letters, the words "LIMBer Up" spanned the length of the dark grey plastic forearm. "Although when the Natural Arm goes into production, might I suggest making your company logo a bit less conspicuous? I feel like a walking advertisement."

"I let you test the most advanced myoelectric arm available with twenty-five grip patterns and a hand that rotates 360 degrees and you're cnawvshawling."

"I'm not cnawvshawling, Doctor Uppity. I'm just self-conscious. You know that."

"Well, soon you won't have to be. Once the Natural Arm is fully approved for production, we'll be able to cover it in silicone and match it to the wearer's skin tone. We can even replicate your freckles. Would *that* impress you?"

"Yes, but to be honest, your TED talk last week was even *more* impressive."

Michael nodded. "Limb regeneration's been a hot area of medical research for years. 'Tis about time I direct the company's efforts in that direction. I just never expected to be invited to one of the world's largest conferences to speak about it."

"And to congratulate you, I picked up a little something." From the empty seat beside her, Amelia lifted a thin white box nearly a half-metre in length and placed it atop the table.

"Flowers? You shouldn't have." Michael opened the box to find a hollow metal forearm complete with jointed fingers and thumb curled into a permanent grip. With a raised eyebrow, he ran a finger along its tarnished, scratched surface.

"Something to decorate your office," Amelia said. "I picked it up at the antique show at Ashford Castle. That's about the only way I'll ever see the inside of that place."

"'Tis a bit too thin to be armour."

"I think it might be an antique prosthetic. See how smooth the open end is? 'Tis curved as if to accommodate the elbow joint. I posted a picture of it on a few antique collector forums to see if anyone might know its origins. Haven't heard a peep yet."

"Wow, this is... wild. Thank you. You didn't happen to try it on, did you?"

Amelia grinned. "No, ye arse biscuit. Wouldn't do me much good when handling delicate plants, or anything else for that matter."

"Right, so how goes the phytochemistry business these days?"

"Well, nothing worthy of a TED talk, but we've a number of projects in development from several plant-based cancer drugs to arthritis remedies."

"Fascinating."

Amelia fell silent. The waitress returned with two slices of porter cake. After she stepped away, Michael leaned forward.

"That wasn't intended to be flippant."

"I know." Amelia lowered her gaze to the brick pavement. "My work's hardly as remarkable as that of my vascular surgeon-turned-biomedical engineer brother. I'm just the one who plays with plants. At least that's what Da used to say."

It was time for a change of subject. "I have some good news. Actually, it's the reason I was late. The Department of Defence is interested in the Natural Arm. They're sending someone out tomorrow to evaluate it. If all goes well, it could lead to a contract."

"That's wonderful, Michael! Maybe that kind of investment could help fund your research into limb regeneration."

"Possibly, but don't get your hopes up. We're decades away from that."

~

"YER EIGHT O'CLOCK IS HERE."

Michael's administrative assistant nodded toward the executive conference room.

He looked at his watch and raised an eyebrow. "He's twenty minutes early. Oh well, better sooner than later. Thanks, Colette."

After dropping off his jacket and laptop in his office, Michael rushed into the conference room—and stopped in the doorway. He couldn't help but smile as he folded his arms across his chest and leaned against the doorjamb.

The trim young man in the red polo shirt and jeans stood just beyond the far end of the mahogany conference table, his back to the door. As Michael watched, he raised and lowered his right arm, severed somewhere below the elbow. Michael couldn't determine precisely where, as the man had decided to try on the antique metal arm.

"We can do better than that," Michael said.

The man spun as embarrassment ruddied his face. It was nearly the color of his shirt. He tugged and twisted the prosthetic. It wouldn't budge. "Oh, sorry, Doctor Whalen. I was just foosterin' with this to pass the time."

"By all means. I just didn't want the Department of Defence to think that was the best I had to offer."

"Oh, I know, sir." The man chuckled. "We saw yer TED talk." He gave up trying to remove the antique and extended his left hand. "Corporal Duncan McCabe."

Michael accepted the gesture. "And what did you think, Duncan? May I call you that?"

"Aye, of course, sir. Well, the Minister was impressed to see technology like this developed domestically. To be honest, the brass has been lookin' at Touch Bionics in Scotland and a few American companies."

"But what did *you* think?"

Duncan ceased prying at the edges of the metal prosthetic and drew himself to his full height. At just under two metres, he was nearly at eye-level with Michael. His earlier discomfiture faded as he spoke. "I lost part of my arm three years ago thanks to a suicide bomber in Afghanistan. Before transferrin' to administrative duty, I was given a rod wi' two pinchin' hooks. The fact that ya produced an affordable, lightweight prosthetic with all the same degrees of freedom and grip patterns as the iLimb or the Bebionic will mean a hell of a lot to people like me. So yeah, I'm impressed, too. Even more so wi' the idea of limb regeneration, but I'll be happy wi' the Natural Arm for now."

"You've done your homework, Duncan." Michael pointed to the antique. "Out with the old, in with the new?"

"What? Oh, right." The corporal gripped the prosthetic with his left hand. "It was stuck a moment ago." This time, it slipped off with ease. "Sorry about that. What is this, by the way?"

"A wall decoration, compliments of my sister. Now, why don't we take a walk to the lab, strap on the Natural Arm, and then you can give me a proper handshake."

HOURS LATER, the lab was empty. Everyone else had left for the weekend. Michael realized that he was alone in the building. Even the cleaning staff had gone. He was tired, but refused to rest until he'd found the answer.

An obnoxious buzzing erupted behind him. Frowning, he stood up from the microscope and turned to find his sister leaning against the workbench in the center of the lab. She stared down at her myoelectric hand as it rotated 360 degrees, making a loud grinding noise in the process.

"Amelia. I had no idea you were here."

"Can you fix this? I can't control it."

Michael started to reply, but before a word was uttered, Amelia's prosthetic arm shot forward, its malfunctioning hand clutching his throat. Tighter... tighter...

HE SAT UP WITH A GASP. Atop the bedside table, his cell phone vibrated.

"Dammit." He snatched it up and glared at the screen. The number was unfamiliar. He answered it anyway.

"Doctor Whalen," he barked.

"Sir, Corporal McCabe here."

"Duncan? You do realize 'tis quarter past four on Saturday morning."

"Aye, Doctor, and I'm sorry to wake ya, but is there any possibility we could meet?"

"Now?"

"The sooner the better."

"Is there a problem with the prosthetic?"

"Just the opposite, sir."

"Duncan, I'm tired. What the hell are you getting at?"

"It would be better if I showed ya."

Michael's shoulders slumped. *For the love of Christ.* "Right then. Meet me at my office. I'll be there in an hour."

~

STIFLING A YAWN, Michael sat back on the couch along the windows and sipped his coffee as Corporal McCabe held up the stump of his right arm.

Michael raised his cup. "Where's the Natural Arm?"

"In my car."

"Good place for it. May I ask why?"

"I had a hard time puttin' it on this mornin', because my right arm is seven centimetres longer than it was yesterday." Duncan sat beside Michael and held out both arms. "'Tis as if it's growin' back! The shape's even symmetrical with my left. Look at it, Doctor."

"And you actually measured it?"

"As soon as I noticed."

Michael downed the rest of his coffee and held up two fingers. "May I?"

"Certainly."

He pressed the skin around the end of the residual limb. "Does it feel tender at all? Any pain?"

The corporal shook his head. "I did that earlier, pokin' and proddin' it. Didn't hurt a bit."

Michael stroked his stubbled chin. "How is that possible? Tell me what exactly happened overnight."

"I removed the Natural Arm before goin' to bed. I awoke at four in the mornin' to get a glass of water. That's when I felt my arm tinglin'. Mind you, I haven't had any phantom sensations for years. When I turned on the kitchen light, I noticed that my arm was... *longer*."

"Who else knows about this?"

"No one. I didn't even tell my wife yet, but I *will* need to report this to my superiors."

"Let's just take a moment here. We don't even know how this happened. What did you do after you left here on Friday?"

The corporal shrugged. "Nothin' out of the ordinary. I showed my wife the Natural Arm and then we went to dinner. We watched a movie when we came home and then crashed for the night."

"That's all?"

McCabe nodded.

"Duncan, would you mind if I took a blood sample?"

"Not at all."

"And can you give me until Monday morning before you report this? I'd like some time to determine how this could've happened before I have your superiors swarming this place demanding answers I can't give them."

Duncan thought about it for a moment. "Sure, I guess I can give ya the rest of the weekend. Until then, I'll continue to test drive yer prosthetic, if you can modify it for me."

"Certainly."

"Unless, of course, I wake up tomorrow to find my *entire* arm's grown back."

Later that morning, Michael raised his digital voice recorder as he leaned over the stainless steel workbench. "Corporal Duncan McCabe's blood sample exhibits higher than normal levels of M2 macrophages. These white blood cells are multiplying at an accelerated rate. Beta-catenin production is also elevated, which could indicate increased activity in the WnT signaling pathways.

"These proteins are currently being researched in many

quarters for their role in limb regeneration in mice and axolotls, but we're still a long way from producing the same results in humans. Nevertheless, Corporal McCabe's progress is undeniable. Whether it continues remains to be seen."

Michael turned off the recorder and slipped it onto a shelf above his workbench. He rose from his chair and paced the lab. *There's no way in hell the Natural Arm could induce this reaction. 'Tis just a myoelectric machine. What, then? What could have caused such a drastic growth overnight?*

"Damned if I know." Michael ran a hand over his face and yawned. "I need more coffee."

He ambled out of the lab and made his way to the K-Fee machine behind Colette's desk. As he waited for his cup to fill, Michael leaned against the counter and glanced into the conference room across the hall. His gaze settled on the white box. *No...*

Forgetting his coffee, he hurried into the room, slipped the antique prosthetic under his arm, and dashed back to the lab. After placing it atop his workbench, he scratched off a small section of tarnish and exposed bare, shiny metal. It appeared to be—

"Silver?" *Let's find out.*

Lining the lab's sink in aluminum foil, Michael soaked the prosthetic in hot water and baking soda. Twenty minutes later, most of the tarnish was gone.

"Fantastic." Michael ran a finger over its pure silver surface, noticing more scratches than before and even a few minor dents.

For the first time, he peered into the prosthetic's socket. Rather than the gleam of silver, the interior was lined with a mottled band of black and brown. *Hello. What are you?* Michael reached up to the shelf for a flashlight, knocking over an EMF meter in the process. It toppled to the workbench with a clang.

"Dammit." He flipped it over and turned it on. Satisfied that it had survived the fall, he set it aside and aimed the flashlight into the silver arm, revealing a strip of soft, spongy paste. It measured about seven centimetres at its widest.

He recalled Duncan's words. *My right arm is seven centimetres longer than it was yesterday...*

Michael pulled a flat metal tool and Petri dish from the shelf. Gently, he scraped a sample of the substance from the prosthetic into the dish—a damp globule of black, tan, and dark brown.

He set the antique arm down beside the EMF meter and slid the Petri dish under the microscope. "Hmm. Some sort of plant residue, I think."

The reading on the EMF meter fluctuated between 10 and 25 milligauss. Michael leaned forward for a closer look before scooping up the instrument and passing it over the length of the prosthetic. The measurement finally stabilized at 14.5 milligauss.

This is incredible. It generates its own electromagnetic field!

"Amelia, what the bleedin' hell have you stumbled upon?"

MICHAEL ROSE from the patio chair beside the rustic stone home as Amelia brought her car to a stop in the driveway. She stepped out and closed the door, her brow furrowed. "Michael, what brings you out to culchie territory?"

He shrugged. "Just visiting my sister and enjoying the country air."

"Uh-huh. Is something the matter?"

"Of course not. Why do you always think that?"

"I wonder." Amelia shot him a sidelong glance as she opened the trunk of her car. "Well, I just popped out to Tesco for a few groceries."

"Do you need help?"

"I have two hands."

"Oh, funny bird."

"But you could get the door."

Once Amelia was inside, Michael retrieved the white box from his car and carried it into her dining room. He set it on the table as Amelia stepped in from the kitchen.

"Would you like to stay for supper?"

"That'd be nice. If it isn't too much trouble, of course."

She pointed to the box. "Is that what I think it is?"

He backed away from the table. "Open it."

Amelia pulled off the lid. Her eyes flashed wide. "Oh, my. You cleaned it up. It looks like pure silver."

"'Tis."

Amelia narrowed her eyes as she stared at it. "The Arm of Nuada."

"What?"

"Well, I still haven't any leads on where this came from, but now that I see it like this, I'm reminded of a story from myth."

"Right, well what I need—"

"Nuada was a king of the Tuatha dé Danann. He lost his arm during a battle four thousand years ago. His physician, Dian Cecht, fashioned a prosthetic arm out of silver…"

Michael tuned her out as he checked his watch, waiting for a pause in her blathering. "That's a lovely tale, Mealy, and I know mythology is one of your hobbies, but I need you to do me a favor here in the *real* world. I need you to wear the antique for a bit."

She frowned at him. "Why?"

"Call it an experiment."

"Does it need to be right now? I'm about to make supper."

"This *is* important."

Amelia sighed. "Well, how long do I need to wear it?"

"Good question." Michael gazed at the ceiling as he recalled the corporal's visit. "He was in the conference room for twenty minutes before I got there, then another five..." He met Amelia's questioning gaze. "I'd say about twenty-five minutes should do it."

She rolled her eyes. "You cannot be serious."

"Please."

Amelia glared at him, shaking her head. "I don't know why I always agree to be your lab rat."

MICHAEL SAT across the dining room table from his sister. She sighed while scrolling through email on her tablet. The climate in the room was nearly as threatening as the weather outside. Beyond Letterfrack village, the choppy waters of Ballinakill Harbour reflected the dark, roiling clouds hanging low in the evening sky. Amelia slapped the cover closed on her tablet and glared at Michael.

He downed the rest of his drink. "Do you feel anything in your arm?"

"No, should I?"

"I don't know."

"Michael, what's this all about?"

"I don't know."

"What the hell *do* you know? Wait, I *am* feeling something."

Michael shot upright. "What?"

"I feel like an idiot wearing this damn thing."

His shoulders slumped. "Just another ten minutes, *please*. Oh, dammit, I almost forgot. I need you to look at something." He reached into the white box and retrieved a covered Petri dish. "The socket of that prosthetic is lined with some kind of paste. Surprisingly, it held together under hot water, but it softened enough for me to take a scraping. I think it may be the grinds of a plant." He slid the dish across the table.

Amelia peered at the sample. "Hard to say for sure. Some plants, like comfrey and a few others, were once used as a poultice to help heal everything from skin irritation to broken bones. I can take it to work and run it against our database."

"That would be fantastic, thanks. Would you mind if I crashed in your spare room overnight?"

Amelia raised an eyebrow. "I suppose if I ask why, you'll tell me you don't know."

"I'll know in the morning and if all goes well, so will you."

MICHAEL JOLTED as an obnoxious buzzing erupted behind him. Frowning, he stood up from the microscope and turned to find his sister leaning against the workbench in the center of the lab. She stared down at her myoelectric hand as it rotated 360 degrees, making a loud grinding noise in the process.

"Amelia. I had no idea you were here."

"Can you fix this? I can't control it."

Michael started to reply, but before he could utter a word, Amelia's prosthetic arm shot forward, its malfunctioning hand clutching his throat.

"Give me my arm back, Michael!"

"MICHAEL?"

He opened his eyes to find Amelia standing over him, shaking his shoulder. With a scream, he recoiled and swatted her arm away before tumbling off the opposite side of the bed.

"Oh my God, are you all right?"

Michael reached up to the windowsill and pulled himself to a sitting position on the floor. He leaned his head against the wall. "I'm fine. Just a recurring nightmare."

"Do you want to tell me about it?"

"Not really."

"Well, I have something to show you." She thrust out her bare right arm. "Look!"

Michael rubbed his eyes, still trying to shake off the dream. "What?"

"My arm's grown! Can't you tell?"

"I just fell out of bed, Mealy. Give me a moment. Did you measure it?"

"Seven centimetres."

Just like Duncan.

"You were expecting this, weren't you?"

Michael nodded.

"What does it mean?"

"It means that trinket you picked up at an antique show may represent the most remarkable biological advancement in human history."

"How's that possible?"

"Well, we know that humans can regenerate severed finger tips, but even that takes months. I've been doing some research. There's a protein that passes electrical signals from outside of a cell through its surface to receptors inside. 'Tis called the WnT signaling pathway. Without getting too technical, researchers have found that stimulating this communication can regenerate bone and tissue in mice and salamanders."

"You think this antique prosthetic is somehow stimulating those proteins?"

Michael shrugged. "All I know is that it emits an EMF for reasons I can't explain, nor can I answer your question without further testing. Now, I have a medical bag in my car.

If I may, I'd like to take a blood sample from you as soon as I get some coffee."

~

ON HIS WAY OUT, Michael asked Amelia to say nothing of this development for now. "But keep me abreast of any further changes and let me know what you find on that substance."

"Michael, what if—and I'm *not* getting my hopes up here—but what if by some miracle my arm completely regenerates?"

"Then you can give me proper applause when I win the Nobel Prize."

~

AFTER A SLEEPLESS SUNDAY NIGHT, Michael still had no answers, only more questions. Thus, when dawn arrived on Monday morning, he was not at all surprised to receive a call from Corporal McCabe.

"Any progress, Doctor?"

"Well, Duncan, I always believed in the value of play and as it turns out, that antique you were toying around with in my office is the key to what's happening."

"How so?"

"I'm not sure yet. I've only determined the effect, not the cause."

"Then what makes ya think it's the antique?"

"I tested it on someone else and they experienced the same results."

Duncan was silent for a moment. Perhaps he was confused, even stunned. Michael sympathized.

"I can't delay any longer, Doctor. I'll need to report this.

My superiors will likely send at least one person, if not an entire team, to study that object."

Michael drew in a slow, deep breath. "I gathered as much."

"Just be prepared. They'll probably take possession of it."

They'll need to get past my sister first.

COLETTE WAS on edge when Michael arrived at the office. In the conference room, two men sat with their backs to the hallway windows. One of them was military.

"Who's that?" Michael asked.

"Yer seven o'clock," she replied in a low, timorous voice.

"I didn't know I had a seven o'clock."

"Ye didn't until ten minutes ago."

They waste no time. "That figures. Thanks."

He made his way into the conference room and closed the door.

The visitors stood. The man in uniform, short and stocky with thinning black hair, introduced himself as Lieutenant Colonel Quinlan Kilduff. He spoke in a sharp, clipped tone as he gestured toward his companion.

"Doctor Whalen, this is Doctor Dion Katz, a biologist from Merlin Park University Hospital. He's here to observe yer work with the artifact."

With his saffron hair, full beard and crystal blue eyes, Katz was the stereotypical fair-skinned Irishman straight off a postcard.

"What happened to Corporal McCabe?" Michael asked as they took their seats.

"The corporal's under observation," Kilduff replied.

"What about his arm?"

"Also under observation."

Of course. Ask a stupid question...

"Have you determined the artifact's method for this rapid regeneration?" Katz asked. His eyes seemed determined to bore a hole in Michael's head.

"As of yet, no."

"Perhaps I can help. My research has focused on the role of macrophages not only in healing wounds but also in muscle repair and limb regeneration. I'm confident that together, we can find the answers you seek."

Smugness emanated from his thin smile and intimidating stare. It was a practiced manner, no doubt, and one that was probably intended to force his target to blink first. Michael was too tired to play the game. He held the biologist's gaze.

Finally, the colonel spoke up. "Ye can imagine how surprised we were to learn of this astoundin' development from Corporal McCabe. Ye'll understand if I leave two men here to ensure the security of yer lab."

"I don't think that'll be necessary, Colonel."

Ignoring him, Kilduff stood. "I'll leave ye to yer work, gentlemen. I trust ye'll keep me posted on any developments."

Do we have a choice?

At the workbench in the center of the lab, Michael opened the lid of his laptop and turned it toward Katz. "These are the notes I've taken so far. The prosthetic is not only pure silver, 'tis also—"

"The Arm of Nuada." Katz stared in amazement at the artifact lying in a clear acrylic case that Michael had pulled from storage over the weekend.

"Beg pardon?"

"Nuada was a king of the Tuatha dé Danann, the gods

who settled here in ancient times and brought humankind to Ireland."

Oh, Christ, not you, too. Michael chuckled. "You sound like my sister. Mythology's a hobby of hers."

Katz's head snapped in his direction. Michael tensed as the other man's eyes narrowed. "What you call mythology, others call history."

This fella's truly off his nut. "OK, fine. So, tell me about Nuada."

"Four thousand years ago, the king lost part of his arm in battle against a race known as the Fir Bolg. His physician crafted a prosthetic arm made of pure silver. However, Nuada's injury forfeited his eligibility to remain our—" Katz paused with an awkward grin. "Uh, to remain *their* king and another was crowned. A short time later, the physician's son, Miach, devised a way to regenerate Nuada's arm."

Feigning interest, Michael furrowed his brow. "Any idea how he did that?"

"I'm afraid he took his secrets to the grave." Katz turned a somber gaze back to the artifact. "He died rather young. All I know is that Miach altered his father's creation somehow. Within a week, Nuada's arm had fully regenerated and he reclaimed the throne. The prosthetic was cast aside, lost to history."

"And you believe that this is the Arm of Nuada."

"I *know* it is."

"YOU WOULDN'T BELIEVE the mentaller they sent me, Mealy."

Michael adjusted his earpiece as he closed the door to his office and dropped onto the couch. "He kept gawking at me when he showed up, then he was adamant that the artifact is an ancient prosthetic from the time of the Tuatha dé Danann."

"I mentioned that when you were at my house."

"Yeah, well, this fella was blathering as if he'd actually been there when it was made four thousand years ago. 'Tis hard to believe the military would hire such a quare hawk, but he is rather brilliant. We determined that the regeneration is a result of a combination of the Natural Arm and the artifact."

"The artifact?"

"Oh, yeah, that's the official term for it now. Our theory is that the substance lining the socket is absorbed into the skin. When you and Duncan switched from the artifact to the Natural Arm, the electrical impulses interacted with the chemical compound and initiated regeneration of skin, bone, muscle, nerves, everything. Can you imagine how this will revolutionize science?"

"Michael, this is phenomenal."

"What's more, Katz confirmed that the paste contains comfrey—so that was a good guess on your part—but there was something else in it. Unfortunately, he wasn't able to identify the other substance. He theorized that it might be an extinct herb."

"Possibly. I haven't had a chance to work on your sample yet. Did you bother to research the mythology aspect?"

Michael let out a sharp laugh. "Of course not, I don't have time to waste. That's your thing."

"What, wasting time?"

"No, mythology, ye arse-biscuit."

"Well, he's right. As I tried to tell you before, there *was* a king named Nuada in the tales of the Tuatha dé Danaan and his arm *was* chopped off in battle. His personal physician, Dian Cecht, replaced it with a silver prosthetic until Cecht's son, Miach, regenerated Nuada's flesh and blood arm. Unfortunately—"

Michael shot forward. "Wait! Go back. What was that name?"

"Dian Cecht."

This has to be a joke.

"Michael, you still there?"

"Yes, please continue."

"Oh, suddenly you're intrigued. I was going to say that after Miach healed the king, Cecht was overcome by professional jealousy and murdered his own son. After he was buried, Miach's sister Airmid cried at his grave. When her tears fell to the loose soil, all of the healing herbs known to man grew from Miach's grave. Airmid had also been a healer, through the use of natural medicines."

"Sounds vaguely familiar. I have a sister who plays with plants."

"And I have a brother who apparently regenerates limbs. Coincidence? At least there's no Dian Cecht around to kill you."

I wouldn't be so sure. Michael rubbed his forehead, trying to wrap his mind around the ludicrous events of the past few days.

"You still haven't asked me the big question," Amelia said.

"What?"

"About my arm."

"Oh God, yes. Sorry. What's the latest?"

"It's grown almost thirteen centimetres down to my wrist."

"You cannot be serious! Why didn't you say something earlier?"

"You were too busy babbling on about the eccentric biologist. My forearm is even maintaining the same shape and muscle tone as my left one."

"I can't believe this is happening."

"Michael, maybe there *is* some truth to his claims. Maybe I really did find the Arm of Nuada at an antique show. Who is this biologist? What's his name?"

"You wouldn't believe me if I told you."

"My freakin' arm's growing back. Nothing could surprise me now."

"His name is Katz. Dion Katz."

"You cannot be serious!"

THE FOLLOWING MORNING, Michael entered the lab to find the artifact missing¾along with Doctor Katz. He examined the acrylic case. The lid was still locked and Michael was the only one with a key.

What the hell?

He called out to Katz. When there was no response, he checked the supply room, gowning corridor, wash room. Finally, he bolted down the hall to Colette's desk.

"Have you seen Doctor Katz this morning?"

"Yeah, he went to the lab about forty minutes ago. Is there a problem?"

"Both Katz and the artifact are gone."

Colette's eyes widened. Her words tumbled out. "I haven't seen him since he went in. No one's been past here since, other than you, and I've been at my desk all mornin'."

Michael put a hand on her shoulder. "Relax. 'Tis all right."

"Should we be callin' someone? The Gardai? The military?"

Just then, Michael's cell phone vibrated. With a sigh, he glanced at the screen. "Hold that thought, Colette."

He pressed the phone to the side of his head as he dashed into his office and closed the door.

"Mealy, 'tis gone. The arm is gone and so is Katz. Listen, I took some time last night to look him up online and¾"

"He's here, Michael."

"*What*?"

"He's at my house and he wants to see you. The artifact is here, too."

"Are you all right? Has he hurt you?"

"Not at all. He's been the perfect house guest in fact."

What the hell is happening here? "I'm on my way."

Michael ended the call and paused to collect his thoughts. How did Katz get the artifact out of the case and leave the lab unseen?

At least there's no Dian Cecht around to kill you.

Michael rounded his desk and opened the top left drawer. *Maybe you're right, Amelia, but I'm not taking any chances.* He snatched up the 9mm Sig Sauer and slipped it into his jacket pocket before stepping out into the hall.

"Colette, I have a family emergency. I need to leave. I'll be at my sister's house."

"Is she all right?"

"I don't know."

"What about the artifact?"

"I'll call my contact at the Department of Defence on my way out."

Colette hesitated. "Oh, OK. Well, I hope Amelia's all right."

The main door of Amelia's house was wide open when Michael arrived. As he pulled open the storm door and crept inside, he squeezed his jacket pocket, felt the barrel of the pistol.

"Michael, come in." Amelia patted the cushion beside her

on the couch. "Please take a seat." Across the room, the mystery man with the silver arm across his lap sat in a wooden rocking chair.

Michael pulled the gun and leveled it at him. "What are you doing here? How did you get that out of the lab?"

"Michael! For the love of God, put that away."

He ignored Amelia, holding Katz in his sights.

"Michael, I'll not have guns in my house."

"I researched Lieutenant Colonel Kilduff. He doesn't exist."

"True." Katz grinned. "A bit of hired help."

"I also researched *you*. There is no Dr. Katz at Merlin Park."

Katz spread his arms wide. "But you must admire my rather whimsical choice of location."

Michael clenched his jaw, unsure of the man's meaning.

Katz looked to Amelia. "Tell me he's never heard of Merlin either?"

Michael rounded the couch. "Who are you?"

"Your sister already told you, but you refused to listen."

"A four-thousand year-old doctor."

"Physician to the Gods no less."

"Prove it."

Katz motioned for Amelia to lift her right arm. Michael risked a glance at her as she waved at him, wiggling fully formed fingers.

"Although I must admit, that's the work of my son, Miach. At the time, I could only produce this." Katz lifted the artifact from his lap. "Needless to say, I didn't handle that very well, but I've matured over the eons. You could even say I've mellowed with age."

"What do you want with us?"

"Is it not obvious?" Katz nodded from brother to sister. "Miach and Airmid. Both healers of different disciplines. You even resemble them. I saw your TED talk about limb regeneration and I *knew* it was you. Then I learned about Amelia, a botanist, and I realized that this was my chance to atone for what I'd done to both of you so long ago."

Amelia leaned forward in her seat. "I bought the silver arm from *him*, Michael. He was the antique dealer."

Michael narrowed his gaze at Katz. "That explains why you never asked how it came into my possession. Still, none of this makes sense."

"You and Amelia are the reincarnations of my children."

"And you're off your goddamn nut." With his free hand, Michael reached for his phone. "I'm calling the Gardai."

Katz held up a hand. "No need. Your military are on their way and I'm afraid I must be leaving, with the Arm of Nuada."

"Why give it to us just to take it back?"

"You have everything you need now." Katz held the artifact out before him. "This has seen its last days. It's caused such enormous grief. I know *you* will employ your knowledge to the benefit of mankind. You've taken samples from inside of this and what have you learned? My prosthetic contains the ingredients, yours the stimulant. Of course, there is that problem of the extinct herb that, when combined with the comfrey, primes the WnT pathways to accelerate macrophage production. Pity I never learned exactly what that herb was."

"Perhaps it could be synthesized," Amelia suggested.

Katz looked from one to the other and nodded. "It sounds as if a partnership is in order."

Amelia joined her brother and wrapped her regenerated fingers around the barrel of the gun. Reluctantly, Michael lowered the weapon.

Outside, multiple vehicles came to a stop in front of the house. A car door slammed shut. Katz stood and nodded. "On that note, I must depart."

"Where will you go?" Amelia asked.

"Back whence I came."

There was a knock at the door.

"'Tisn't wise to keep them waiting."

With one last look at Katz, brother and sister started toward the door. As Michael passed the couch, he remembered what he was holding. "Shit." He raised the middle cushion and tossed the gun underneath.

Amelia opened the door. "Can I help you?"

"Good mornin', ma'am, I'm lookin' for Doctor Whalen."

"I'm Doctor Whalen."

"Doctor *Michael* Whalen."

Michael joined Amelia. "That would be me—*Duncan*!"

The young man smiled. "Aye, good mornin', sir." He nodded toward the three black cars parked in the driveway. "I'll need ya to address me as Corporal McCabe for now."

"Oh, of course."

"I persuaded my commandin' officer to let me approach ya first. Ya know, friendly face and all that. Besides," he extended his right hand, "I owe ya a proper handshake."

Michael grinned as he shook McCabe's flesh-and-blood hand. "Right." He motioned toward Amelia and introduced the two, watching in awe as their regenerated hands met. *Well, look at that.*

"Down to business, sir. Is he here?"

"Beg pardon?"

"Doctor Katz."

Michael glanced behind him. The sitting room was empty. "Uh, no. Why would he be here?"

"We've been to yer office. We know he's stolen the artifact. Yer secretary was a bit reluctant at first, but she finally told us where to find ya."

"You interrogated Colette?" Amelia's eyes narrowed.

"Not at all, ma'am. We simply expressed the urgency of the

situation." Then, to Michael, "Sir, they're going to ask why ya paid yer sister a visit instead of reportin' the theft of government property."

Amelia's mouth dropped open. "*Government* property? As of when?"

"As of today."

Michael placed a hand on Amelia's shoulder. "That's a long story, Corporal. Perhaps I should speak with your commanding officer."

ONE MONTH later

YET AGAIN, Michael was late as he joined Amelia at a sidewalk table in front of Cupán Tae. It was a temperate afternoon as the rays of the midday sun filtered through drifting gossamer clouds.

"The military again?" Amelia said. "I thought they would have stopped harassing you about Dion Katz by now."

"They did. No, our meeting about the building expansion ran long. Speaking of which, how do you like your new lab?"

"'Tis wonderful, and to thank you, I picked up a little something."

Amelia pushed a thin white box across the table.

"Oh, no, not again."

"Just open it."

He shot her a somber glance as he removed the lid and parted a layer of white tissue paper. "Purple comfrey. They're beautiful."

"Purple *Symphytum* to be exact, but..."

Michael peered up at Amelia as she glanced right and left.

"What's wrong?"

She lowered her voice. "You know I don't normally grow

comfrey, but I was working in my garden over the weekend, laying topsoil in a new flower bed and that's when it hit me. I was getting my hands dirty. Both of them, *two* hands, *my* hands! I know this sounds ridiculous, but I was so overcome I started crying."

"That's understandable. Nothing to be ashamed of."

"There's more. I went into the house to dry my eyes, and when I came out, these purple comfrey had sprouted up where my tears had fallen on the topsoil. Just like the story of Airmid I told you about."

Michael stared at her.

"I'm not lying, Michael."

He peered down at the flowers. Could it be that he and Amelia really had been the children of Dian Cecht in a past life? The children of a god?

"Gotcha."

"What?"

Amelia laughed. "You should have seen your face with your mouth hanging open. I got you."

"I didn't say I believed you anymore than I believed Katz was Cecht."

"Your expression gave it away, ye arse-biscuit."

Michael shook his head. "No, it didn't."

They stared at one another, neither one blinking. After a few seconds, Amelia cracked.

"'Tis good to see you laughing again," Michael said.

"Well, you had a *hand* in that."

"Oh, funny bird."

~

THIS STORY first appeared in *Elsewhere in the Middle of Eternity* (Firebringer Press, August 2016).

Once More, With Feeling

Alone in the darkness, the man gazed up at the stars. Several yards away, the ocean propelled itself upon the sand, retreated, and thrust forward again. The rhythm was soothing and the man imagined his worries drifting out to sea, never to return.

If only it were so.

Before moving to this coastal town seven years ago, he had come here only for summer vacations. Back then, he would have balked at the idea of lying alone on the beach at night rather than crawling bars or strolling the boardwalk.

Always in motion.

Never living in the moment.

Those days were a blur now—faded memories from another man's life. Tonight, on the eve of his 45th birthday, he concerned himself only with the full moon, the stars, and the surf. Together, they worked a certain magic of sight and sound that temporarily dispelled the depression and anxiety that had consumed him for decades. Though he'd become a household name, and was able to retire on a small fortune from the sale of his social media company, he had never felt alive—more like an automaton, a robot. Going through the motions of life without actually living.

Always doing.

Never *feeling*.

Those days of empire building had been a necessary evil—a means to an end. Now, as he lay here, childless and unmarried, with terminal cancer eating away at his brain, the man was left with only his regrets for companionship. Any morning on this secluded beach could be his final chance to cast them aside and capture that elusive perfect moment when the weight of his sorrows would be lifted, allowing him to feel truly alive before the end. *Lord, should I draw my final breath tonight, please grant me that moment.*

"Mind if I join you?"

She spoke in a soft tone as if to avoid startling him, but he'd anticipated her arrival. Without averting his gaze from the heavens, he waved a hand toward the towel he'd laid out beside him earlier. She lowered herself gracefully, digging her perfect toes into the sand before stretching out. She never aged. She'd been with the man through his entire life, yet she appeared no older than the last time he saw her when he was ten—although she hadn't worn a bikini back then. *Now if that's the last thing I see, maybe I'll die a happy man after all.*

"Not that I'm complaining," the man said, "but why are you wearing that?"

"I always dress for the occasion. This seemed appropriate given our surroundings."

"But it's nighttime."

"Does that matter?"

"Not to me." A moment of silence passed between them before he continued. "I suppose a 'thank you' is in order."

"For?"

His mouth curled into a wan smile. "Despite my imminent—and utterly *premature*—demise, I wouldn't have made it *this* far if it weren't for you."

She turned her face to the sky. "Guiding you through adulthood was easier than expected. It was at the beginning of your life when I believe I failed you."

"What do you mean?"

"You've battled terrible depression ever since you were a child. As a teenager, you attempted suicide three times—"

The man held up a hand. "But you were there to stop me each time. You did your job."

"If I had done my job, you never would have reached that point." The man was surprised at her sharp tone. She paused as if to compose herself. In a softer voice, she continued. "When you were a child, my instructions were to protect you and keep you safe from injury wherever you went. I did not anticipate what would happen to you at the hands of your parents, the very people who should have loved you most."

The man shrugged. "So I got banged up a little, like lots of other kids. That wasn't your fault. *You* didn't inflict that pain. The only actions you're responsible for are your own."

She scooped up a handful of sand. Dull grains in her palm sparkled like flecks of diamond as they slipped through her slender, divine fingers. "What about my *inaction*? After your parents divorced when you were five and everything fell apart, I was...caught off-guard."

"You and me both, gorgeous."

"I was powerless to intervene the night your mother nearly beat you to death in her blind rage after your father maligned her during the custody hearing. Then a year later, I tried in vain to stop your father from throwing you down the stairs over some trivial insult from your mother. I wasn't prepared for that. The only thing I could do was comfort you after the fact and help heal your wounds as quickly as possible.

"But there was nothing I could do to take away the

emotional pain. That was... beyond my ability. You were left to find your own way through the fear and darkness in your mind where I could not reach you. That remains so, even now."

He narrowed his eyes and shot her a sidelong glance. "You know, I *was* trying to have a pleasant time out here. Look, I survived all that and a lot more, and I'm not the only one in the world who had it rough growing up. Plenty of people have baggage, some more than others." Despite the throbbing in his head, he turned onto his side and gazed at this ethereal beauty, amazed at her flawless skin, obvious even under the stark glow of a full moon. She'd let down her long brown hair since the last time he'd seen her. It cascaded around her head, flowing off the edges of the beach towel. "Where's all this self-reproach coming from, anyway? You've had other charges before me, right? They couldn't have all been easy."

She shook her head. "For everything there is a first time. That includes you. I was so naïve in the beginning."

The man didn't know what to say. He'd never been anyone's first before. There was something special about having an angel all to yourself. "Well, life's a learning experience, even for you. You'll do better with your next one. How many does it take before you earn your wings?"

She smiled, more radiant than a summer sunrise. "We don't actually get wings, you know. That's just how we're depicted by your artists and filmmakers."

"Good, because from what I can see, you have a lovely back." *And everything else.*

She raised an eyebrow. "I can read your thoughts, you know."

Stifling a gasp, he turned his face away and stared at the sky. Moving his head right or left had become agony since the tumor began growing at the base of his neck. "Yeah, well, in my condition, I'm long past caring about that."

"But you're still not at peace." She sat up and faced him, folding her legs into a lotus position. "The damage was done too long ago."

On the horizon, black began its daily surrender to blue as the man replied. "Some of us mortals carry our baggage to the grave. Honestly, I think that's the only worldly possession we *can* take with us. I've never known what it's like to live without depression, without anxiety, or fear. I spent so many nights hoping I'd die in my sleep rather than wake up another day feeling like that. I sometimes wonder if I kept busy all of my life as a way of ignoring my pain. I had no real passion for my career. It was just something I did to make money. I lived to work, instead of working to live."

He winced as a shockwave of pain flared through his skull. When it passed, he continued. "There's not a day that goes by when I wouldn't trade that time back for the chance to be happy, to fall in love, maybe start a family, but... it's too late now. Today, I just want to live in the moment before all of my moments are gone." The man's voice broke and his vision clouded as moisture welled up in his eyes. He averted his gaze to the sunrise as it set fire to rippling clouds. Gossamer flames drifted across a waking sky. During all those past summers, mornings had been spent running along the beach to stay fit and combat the stress of an angst-ridden life. There had never been time to stop and bask in the light of a new day.

Always in motion.

It was all a blur now.

The angel unfolded her legs and lay beside him. "It's never too late." She kissed him on the forehead and retreated from view, leaving only an expanse of unbroken azure above him. The warmth of the sun—or was it her touch?—the rhythm of the waves, the shriek of distant seagulls.

So this is what life feels *like.*

"Live in this moment..." she whispered.

Peace filled the man's heart as the world faded away.

~

"WHO ARE YOU?" The little girl frowned as she propelled herself ever higher on the backyard swing.

Emerging from a field of tall corn surrounding the house and yard, the woman took a seat on the neighboring swing and smiled. "I'm your guardian angel, and I think you should take it easy on that swing before you hurt yourself, okay?"

The girl dug the toes of her sneakers into the dirt. It took two passes to bring herself to a full stop. "My mom and dad told me everyone has a guardian angel, but I didn't believe them."

"And yet, here I am. Your mom and dad are wonderful people. They work hard and they love you very much. That should make my job a lot easier this time."

"What?"

"Well, you see, I was assigned to you the moment you were born. I'm here to help you live a long and happy life by keeping you safe no matter where you go in the world."

The girl narrowed her eyes and shot her a sidelong glance. "I don't see your wings. You ever do this before?"

The angel couldn't help but smile. *Some things never change.*

The girl's skeptical expression seemed to soften as the angel laughed. "Only once, but I learned a lot. In fact, you could say this is a second chance—for both of us."

~

THIS STORY first appeared in *The Write Connections* (Greater Lehigh Valley Writers Group, March 2017).

Where Do I Begin?

For the first time in nearly a decade, Dustin was on his way to a date. He was meeting Shannon for supper at Zogg's Raw Bar & Grill in thirty minutes. Of all the women who had responded to his profile on midlifesingles.-com, she was the most compatible and genuine—or so it had seemed from the messages they exchanged.

He checked his watch as he stepped onto the boardwalk from St. Lawrence Street, where he now lived after inheriting his parents' house last year. Zogg's was nine short blocks away. *Plenty of time to get there via the beach. Maybe it'll calm my nerves.* He slipped off his sandals and made his way down the ramp, nodding to a young lady as she passed.

She returned a wink. "Love that spring smile."

He did a double take at the auburn curls beneath a wide-brimmed sun hat. *Jessica* ... In the blink of an eye, the woman's hair was blond and straight. "Uh, thank you."

"Enjoy your evening."

"I'm gonna try. You too."

It's a whole different life here, or it could be if I put the past behind me. Despite his anxiety about dating again at fifty-two,

Dustin took solace in the briny scent of the early May sea breeze, the churning waves that crashed onto the sand and receded in soothing repetition, and the thin bands of gossamer clouds that striped an otherwise clear sky.

In all of his travels, Dustin could count on one hand how many places had brought him peace. The Delaware Coast was one of them. Yet that peace was tarnished by the hell he'd gone through to get here. He knew it would take time to heal, to jettison the baggage of his past, but he wanted to move forward sooner rather than later. After all, he wasn't getting any younger.

Stop worrying. Shannon's probably nervous too. Not many people reach our age without scars. Just be yourself.

"By all means, be yourself and show her what a loser you are."

Dustin closed his eyes and rocked his head back. Even a year after their divorce, his ex-wife still occupied space in his head, beating him down with incessant recriminations, just as she had during their marriage. *Don't start, Brandi. Not tonight. Get out of my head.*

"I wonder how Shannon will react when she finds out you're an alcoholic."

Recovering *alcoholic. I've been sober since you and I split.*

"Once a drunk, always a drunk. You tried to keep it from me until you spiraled out of control. You were still grieving over Tyler and, yes, Jessica. I couldn't live up to her. Neither could Kirsten before me. You denied it, but I know all of your secrets, Dusty. I only wish I'd known them before I married you."

I was battling severe depression, Brandi. I should have been upfront about it and not tried to hide it from you. I made mistakes, but I never meant to hurt you.

"You can change location, but you can't change the fact that you're damaged goods, Dusty, and when Shannon figures that

out, she'll run from you like I did. You'll be alone for the rest of your life."

"Yeah," he muttered. "Maybe you're right, Brandi."

As Dustin trudged across the sand, laughter from a family standing at the water's edge shook him from his reverie and silenced Brandi's verbal onslaught. He stopped to watch as a mother and father clutched their toddler's hands, lifting him into the air each time the next wave advanced toward their feet.

"We were like that once. Those were good days ... before it all went to hell."

I don't need the reminder, Kirsten. I think about it every day.

"Then it should be easy to tell Shannon how you were an absent father to a son who wanted your love and approval, to spend more time with you, to know that you were proud of him. Instead, you ignored him, pushed him away."

I didn't push him away. I took that new job and had to travel. It was good money. I was trying to build a better life for us.

"I would have preferred a better marriage. You were working to avoid me, to avoid being a father. By the time you realized the consequences it was too late."

Don't go there again, Kirsten. Please.

Dustin's stomach clenched. She always knew where to hit him. *I was young. Immature. In hindsight, I was still a mess after Jessica. I wasn't ready for parenthood.*

"I had to find that out the hard way, but I don't care that you neglected me. I'm sure Shannon would love to hear about your suicide attempt after Tyler overdosed on heroin, or will you keep that from her? Your skeletons follow you everywhere you go, Dusty. Turn around now before they ruin another woman's life."

Dustin snatched off his sunglasses and wiped the tears

from his face. "Yeah." His voice cracked. "Maybe you're right, Kirsten."

"She is *right, boy."*

I don't need a lecture from you, Dad.

Kirsten was gone. Now, Dustin imagined his father limping along beside him from the leg wound he had suffered during the Vietnam War.

"You gonna tell your new girlfriend what a lousy no-good son you were? How you left me to rot in a nursin' home, just waitin' for me to die so you could get the house here? You think you deserve to be happy, boy? You failed as a son, a husband, and a father. You're no good to anyone."

I had the best teacher, or did you forget that the only time you were around was when you were drunk? Who was it who spit in my face and told me I was an accident who should never have been born? The things you did to me and Mom when you were trashed I could never tell anyone. Thanks to you, I suffered a lifetime of depression and—

"Oh, shut up. You still cryin' about that after all these years? Jesus Christ, you're a grown man. Get over it! I did what I did to prepare you for the world, to make you tough and strong. Take responsibility for yourself and stop blamin' me for your failures. Ain't no woman ever gonna want you."

"Yeah." Dustin's gaze fell on the spiraled coil of an ivory whelk shell protruding from the sand. He dropped to his knees and scooped it up. It was hardly a perfect specimen. One side had been punctured, leaving a gaping hole, and the tip of the spire had snapped off along with a few of the knobs that studded the shell's wide top. Dustin ran a thumb over the cracked jagged edge of the opening. What had once been a beautiful shell was now hollow and broken. The world had taken its toll. *You can't change the fact that you're damaged goods.*

"Maybe you're right, Dad." He tightened his trembling grip on the shell. "Maybe all of you were right about me."

"No. They're wrong. Dusty, you were the most responsible and loyal man I ever knew. You were by my side every minute of my battle with cancer. You took care of me and loved me like no one else in my life—right up to the end, babe."

Right up to the end, Jessica. Dustin's tears were drops on the sand. *I never got over losing you.*

"I know."

Of course, I tried to keep that from Kirsten and Brandi.

"They knew it, too, and it destroyed your life with them. Whatever happens tonight, Dusty, don't let it ruin that too. I told you before I ... before I died ... go out and find love again. Be happy."

Dustin snickered. *Clearly, I don't know how.*

In his mind's eye, Jessica knelt before him, the evening sunlight casting a vermilion halo around her auburn curls. *"Why did you move to Rehoboth Beach?"*

To start fresh. Find inner peace. To be near the ocean, the boardwalk, the festive atmosphere. Remember those summer nights when we strolled down Rehoboth Mews to the Coffee Mill? You would get Caramel Kiss ...

"And you got Toffee Crunch."

And we would sit outside, listening to live guitar music under the soft white lights that crisscrossed the alley. We were young and didn't have a worry on Earth. I want to feel that way again.

"You can, Dusty. The ocean, the boardwalk, the coffee shop, they're all still here. You have another chance to be the Dusty I knew, the Dusty I loved. He's still in there. The past can only stop you if you let it. Take it slow with Shannon. Don't dump it all on her at once but be honest with her. No more secrets. If she's the one for you, it'll work out."

You were always the wise one, Jess.

"Just flash that spring smile."

Alone on the beach, Dustin stood and squared his shoulders, drawing himself to his full height. He had a fleeting urge to hurl the shell into the ocean but thought better of it. Instead, he brushed it off and slipped it into his jacket pocket. *For luck.*

~

"LOOK for a pale green baseball cap and long-sleeve yellow T-shirt," Shannon had said when they scheduled their date. As Dustin passed Zogg's outdoor bar and strode into the restaurant, he spotted that exact combination at a booth against the windows. He fiddled with the seashell in his jacket pocket in a feeble attempt to ignore the quivering in his chest. *Just be yourself.*

She was scrolling through her phone as he approached. "Hi, Shannon. I hope you weren't waiting long."

She gazed up at him and returned his smile. "Hey, Dustin! Not at all." She tucked her phone into her purse. "I got here early. I haven't been to Rehoboth in a few years, so I decided to make a day of it. Did some shopping, took a walk on the beach."

"You, too, eh?" As Dustin slipped off his jacket and slid into the booth, something clattered to the floor.

"What was that?" Shannon ducked beneath the table and emerged a moment later, whelk shell in hand.

Dustin chuckled. "Just something I found during *my* walk on the beach today."

She examined it for a moment before handing it to him. "Do you collect them?"

"Not really, but for some reason, this one appealed to me."

"It's seen better days."

He shrugged. "Maybe that's why."

"Our waitress is bringing water. I was going to order a Corona, but according to your profile, you don't drink, so I didn't want to do anything inappropriate in case ..."

Dustin raised an eyebrow.

"What I mean is ... my ex-husband was an alcoholic who quit drinking more than once. As much as he tried to control me, he couldn't control himself."

"I see." *Not many people reach our age without scars.*

After the waitress took their orders, Shannon folded her arms atop the table and leaned forward. "So, tell me more about yourself—beyond the rosy façade we all write in our profiles. I want to know about the *real* Dustin."

"The real Dustin." He returned a wry smile and ran a thumb along the seashell's coarse, pitted surface. "Where do I begin?"

This story first appeared in *Beach Secrets* (Cat & Mouse Press, October 2021).

Pearl of Great Price

The first of the two dead men was sprawled just inside the door, the front of his white shirt matted in crimson from the bullet hole in the middle of his chest. Across the room, the other guy sat slumped against the couch, head tilted back and cocked to one side. A stream of dried blood ran down the upholstery. On the floor beside each body lay identical semi-automatic pistols.

As he entered the rental house on New Castle Street, Detective Kurt Vandermoor snapped on a pair of Nitrile gloves before joining Sergeant Eliana Velez in the middle of the living room. "And who do we have here?"

Velez held up two driver's licenses and nodded toward each body in turn. "Seth Manning, thirty-seven, and Dino Quintana, thirty-four. Both from Long Island. Found their wallets on the dining room table along with several interesting photos."

Kurt crouched down beside the younger victim for a closer look at his head wound. "Anyone hear the shots?"

"No. Most of these rental houses are empty this early in the year."

"Then who called it in?"

"A woman named Yasmine Kadara came into the station early this morning claiming she was supposed to meet these two here yesterday, but when they didn't answer the door—or her subsequent calls and texts—she became concerned and asked us to check on them."

Kurt stood. "From the looks of things, they've been dead for at least that long, but I'll leave that to the medical examiner."

"On his way from Georgetown. Should be here in about twenty minutes." Velez shook her head. "We haven't had a murder in Rehoboth for over a decade. Now we get two in one day."

"At least they're both in the same house. Makes things convenient. Where's Ms. Kadara now?"

"Staying at the Beach View for the week."

"I'd like to have a conversation with her when we're done here." Kurt held out his hands. "This scene is too perfect."

"Meaning?"

"Meaning that either these two really shot each other, or someone went through the trouble to make us think they did."

"If that's the case, it might have been someone they knew," Velez suggested. "There's no sign of forced entry anywhere in the house and no indication of a struggle."

"Well, if we don't find a second set of prints on those Glocks, we'll figure out who they're registered to and go from there." Kurt sauntered into the dining room and sifted through several photographs strewn across the table. Some were pictures of a small, sleek yacht called *Charisma Nova,* while others were closeups of a gold crucifix bejeweled with rubies at the ends of the arms and feet and a pink pearl above the head of Christ. Kurt turned over one of the photos. The words 'Pearl of Great Price' were scrawled on the back.

As he reached for one of the dead men's wallets, his phone buzzed. He snatched it out of his belt holster and peered at the screen. It was Police Chief Thomas Miles. Kurt put the call on speaker. "Good morning, Chief."

"You might not think it's so good after this conversation. There's been another murder."

"Where?"

"Coast Guard was checking on a yacht about six miles off Whiskey Beach. They found a body aboard, shot three times, and we think the suspect might have gone ashore on a raft."

"Anyone find the raft?"

"Not yet," Miles replied. "When you're done there, come back to the station. I'll brief you in my office. There's more to this than just a murder. It's high profile. The yacht belonged to Max Trevani from Montauk."

"Name's familiar."

"He's the treasure hunter from *Oceans of Gold* on Nat Geo."

Kurt snapped his fingers. "That's right! My ex-wife watched that show all the time."

"We just notified Mr. Trevani's family. They're on their way. At some point, I'll need to speak to the press, but I intend to hold them off as long as possible until we have a lead."

Kurt picked up one of the photos from the dining room table. "What about the *Charisma Nova*?"

"DNREC will tow it in—wait, how did you know the name of the yacht? I didn't mention it."

"Just a hunch, Chief, but I might have found our first lead."

~

"Coast Guard boarded the boat at 4:40 a.m. and found Trevani on the floor of his cabin. They recovered a watertight lockbox containing relics bound for the Shipwreck Museum in Fenwick." Chief Miles pushed a photograph across his desk. "According to the cargo manifest, this item is missing—a solid gold crucifix studded with gems. Look familiar? That picture was in the lockbox."

"Same one from the house," Kurt confirmed.

"I have a call into Denny Clifford to see if he can shed more light on it. He owns the Shipwreck Museum."

"So, either our two dead guys were aboard with Trevani or there's a third person involved. They waited until the yacht reached our waters, killed him overnight, and took off on the raft with the crucifix. They probably ditched the raft somewhere around Gordons Pond. They could be anywhere now."

"I want you to take lead on this case," Miles said. "State Police and Lewes P.D. requested our help to search that area. Velez is already out there with Gemell, Lonakis, and a few others."

Both men glanced up at a knock on the open door. A uniformed officer leaned in. "Sorry to interrupt, Chief. Denny Clifford's here."

"Perfect timing. Send him in."

The officer stepped aside and waved forward a middle-aged man with short cropped platinum hair, wrinkled polo shirt, and faded jeans. The chief stood and extended a hand. "Denny, thanks for coming in on short notice." He gestured toward Kurt. "This is Detective Kurt Vandermoor. He joined us at the end of last year."

The two men shook hands before Denny settled into the seat beside Kurt. "Any leads on Max's killer?"

"We're working on it," Miles assured him.

"How well did you know Mister Trevani?" Kurt asked.

"We were like brothers. Max and I went on shipwreck dives together all over the world for almost thirty years before I opened the museum. In fact, he was coming here to donate one of his recent finds, a gold crucifix recovered from a wreck in the Alboran Sea."

"That's why I called you," Miles said. "Coast Guard found a lockbox half filled with small relics, but the crucifix was nowhere to be found aboard the yacht."

"So, it was stolen?"

"Seems likely." Kurt said. "What can you tell us about it?"

"Other than the fact that it was named for one of Christ's most famous parables, it's worth nearly twenty million dollars." Denny picked up the photo from the chief's desk. "This crucifix dates back to August of 1415 when King John of Portugal and his sons Edward and Henry led an armada to conquer the city of Ceuta along the Strait of Gibraltar. The siege was swift with almost no casualties.

"History attributes that to the fact that Ceuta's defense was caught off-guard, but there were many who credited three gold crucifixes gifted to the king and his sons by a Portuguese craftsman. As they embarked on the raid, King John carried the largest crucifix aboard his ship while his two sons each carried a smaller one aboard theirs. King John's was the only one adorned with jewels.

"Over time, all three crucifixes were lost at sea. The two smaller ones were recovered in the Indian Ocean in the 1980s, but of course, they're only worth about three million each."

"*Only*?" Kurt raised an eyebrow. "I'm in the wrong line of business."

"I've had those two on display in the museum for years, but this summer, Max and I planned to exhibit all three crucifixes at once. It would be the first time they were together in over six hundred years."

"If we find it, we'll let you know," Miles said. "But keep in mind that it's evidence in a murder investigation. You'll need to postpone your exhibit."

"I take it this thing was insured?" Kurt asked.

"Absolutely." Denny nodded. "And I suspect you'll hear from an insurance investigator before the day is over."

~

AN HOUR LATER, Kurt trudged across the cool sand toward a relic of a more recent era. The Delaware coast was home to a series of concrete fire control towers constructed during World War II to prevent enemy ships from invading Delaware Bay.

The majority of them had weathered time and tide to remain standing seven decades since. Two in particular, Towers Five and Six, had been built approximately 250 yards apart like twin sentinels along Whiskey Beach between the sea and Gordons Pond Wildlife Area.

As Kurt approached Tower Five, Velez met him halfway. "We can call off the search. Bunch of kids managed to dig their way under the door and into the tower. They found this." Velez gestured toward a partially deflated raft lying in a crumpled heap on the sand. "We got here just as they were dragging it out."

"So, the scene's been contaminated."

"Unfortunately." She handed Kurt a pair of Nitrile gloves. After slipping them on, he crouched down and unfurled the raft until his fingers found a series of long gashes that just happened to slice through the name *Charisma Nova*.

Kurt glanced up at Velez. "Did these kids happen to find any—"

She thrust two plastic and aluminum oars toward him.

"How about a solid gold crucifix encrusted with precious gems?"

Velez shook her head.

"Didn't think so." Kurt nodded toward the tower where several other officers were milling about. "Let's take a look around. How did these kids get inside the tower? I thought the entrances were sealed."

"They are, but years of high tides deteriorated the bottom of the sheet metal, creating a gap."

"So I see." They stopped in the shadow of Tower Five where a trench in the sand vanished beneath the rusty, corroded door. It was nearly large enough to allow an average adult to crawl inside. Kurt pointed at Tower Six to the north. "What about that one? Same thing?"

"Yep. Kids get in there, drink, smoke weed, graffiti the walls."

"Now you got me curious." He leaned forward to peer beneath the door. "Think I can fit under there?"

Velez held out one of the oars. "You'll need to dig a deeper trench."

Kurt ignored the laughter from the officers gathered around them. "I'll bet you a drink I can squeeze under there."

"You're on."

He lowered himself to the sand and slipped his legs under the door. With a final glance at Velez, he wiggled his upper body through the shallow gap. A moment later, Kurt stood inside the tower. "You owe me a drink, Velez."

"See anything interesting?"

"Just a few cigarette butts, some trash, innocuous graffiti." High above, sunlight from a series of narrow rectangular windows, spaced evenly apart, illuminated three levels of circular wooden platforms—floors that hadn't endured the weight of a human being in generations.

Surrounding him, more such windows, barely wider than his arm, had been sealed with brick and cement, with one exception. The top half of the window to his immediate right was unobstructed, permitting a modicum of sunlight.

"Velez, slide one of those oars under the door."

Kurt grabbed the contoured blade as soon as it appeared.

After a moment, Velez stood at the window.

"You're blocking my light, Sergeant."

She stepped to one side. "What are you looking for?"

"Buried treasure."

"You can't be serious. Whoever took that crucifix is in the wind."

"Call it a hunch." Kurt poked the oar's shaft into the sand a few times before striking something solid directly beneath the partially sealed window. Flipping the oar over, he dug frantically with the blade before reaching into the hole.

A moment later, he thrust an empty beer bottle through the opening in the window. "So much for that. Hey, Velez. Recycle this, will ya?"

OUTSIDE THE TOWER, Kurt brushed sand from his clothes with one hand while pressing his phone to his ear with the other. "The raft confirms that someone else was definitely aboard Trevani's yacht. I asked Velez to contact Montauk Beach Marina. Maybe someone there knows who accompanied Trevani yesterday or, if we're lucky, they have security footage."

"Good. Keep me posted," the chief said. "One last thing. Denny was right, you're about to get a visit from an insurance investigator. Her name's Brenda Lambert. She showed up at the station a few minutes ago, so I sent her your way."

Kurt turned in the direction of the parking lot to find a petite woman scurrying onto the beach clutching a black portfolio in one hand and a pair of suede pumps in the other. "She about five four, strawberry blonde, wearing a pale green blouse and jeans?"

"That's the one. Be careful. She's a barracuda."

"No worries, Chief. I may be new to Rehoboth, but this

ain't my first time swimmin' with sharks. I'll be in touch." Kurt lowered his phone and stepped forward to greet the woman. "Good afternoon, ma'am."

"Please don't call me that, it makes me feel old. Chief Miles said I would find Detective Vandermoor here."

"And here I be."

She tucked her shoes under her arm and extended a hand, followed by her business card. "Brenda Lambert, investigator for Coastline Insurance."

Kurt glanced at the card before slipping it into his shirt pocket. "Yes, I was warned you were coming. What can I do for you, Ms. Lambert?"

"My company sent me out here when we were informed of Mr. Trevani's death and the subsequent theft of a highly valued artifact from his yacht." Brenda produced a photograph from her portfolio. "It's called the—"

"Pearl of Great Price," Kurt finished. "Worth about twenty million dollars. You know, that's the third photo of this thing I've seen today. Maybe third time's the charm and we'll actually find it."

"Got any leads?"

Kurt swept his hands over the raft. "We have this. It's from the *Charisma Nova*."

"You found it in the tower?"

"Yes, ma'am."

"So, the murderer took the crucifix, fled the yacht on this raft, and came here."

"Looks that way."

"What's your next step?"

"Find out who it was."

Brenda's shoulders slumped. "Okay, I get it. You don't want to deal with me, but we need to work together to find—"

"Look, lady, there's more to this than some expensive insurance claim. This is a murder investigation."

"First of all, *sir*, please stop cutting me off when I'm talking. Secondly, I appreciate the sensitive nature of this case, but Mr. Trevani's decision to transport a multi-million-dollar artifact on his private yacht without any security beyond a couple of Glocks was reckless to say the least. If he had made the proper arrangements, there wouldn't have been any murders."

Kurt folded his arms. "You're going to be a pain in my ass until we find this thing, aren't you?"

"Just doing my job."

"Then let me do mine."

"Fine. So let me ask again, Detective. What's next?"

"I need to question a woman named Yasmine Kadara at the Beach View Hotel."

"Was she on the yacht with Max?"

"I don't know. That's why I'm going to question her."

AS KURT REACHED the top of the stairs at the Beach View, all irritation toward his unwelcome sidekick faded at the sight of two toned and bronzed gams topped by a perfectly round pair of Daisy Dukes.

The young woman stood barefoot on the concrete promenade hunched over the railing that overlooked the empty pool below. She took a long drag from a cigarette and flicked the ashes into a paper cup. Her slim face was partially concealed by a leonine mane of disheveled chestnut hair that cascaded over her shoulders and back as she drew herself to her full and considerable height.

After wiping her eyes with a finger, the woman turned away from the railing, revealing a yellow tank top that left even less to the imagination than her shorts. Kurt nearly dropped his ID as he pulled it from his pocket.

Beside him, Brenda cleared her throat, which served the

dual purpose of snapping Kurt back to the task at hand and gaining Ms. Kadara's attention. She looked from one to the other with swollen gray eyes and dropped her spent cigarette into the cup.

"Yasmine Kadara?" Kurt held up his badge as he introduced himself and Brenda.

"You're here about Seth and Dino. I already heard the news from their families." Her voice was soft and husky, whether naturally or from crying Kurt couldn't determine. "My phone's been on fire all morning with calls and texts from people asking me what I know about their deaths."

Kurt gestured toward her room. "May we go inside?"

"Sure." Yasmine entered first and dropped onto the couch by the window while Kurt and Brenda took seats at the table just inside the door.

Yasmine rubbed her eyes and sniffed. "Sorry. I know I look like shit right now. How can I help you, Detective?"

Brenda handed her a box of tissues from the table. "So, I understand you're from Smyrna. Did you drive down?"

Yasmine shook her head as she accepted the box. "Took the bus. Two of them, actually."

Brenda glanced at Kurt. "Your turn."

He shot her a sidelong glance. Although he had briefed Brenda on the way to the hotel, Kurt made it clear that *he* would be the one to ask the questions. "How did you know Seth and Dino?"

"We grew up together. I'm originally from Long Island. My family moved to Delaware when I was fifteen. I fell out of touch with the guys for a while until I found them on Facebook. A few months ago, Seth mentioned that he and Dino were coming to Rehoboth this week on business. Seth's uncle owns the house they were staying in. They invited me to join them."

"What kind of business?" Kurt asked.

"They were working with a local museum on a new exhibit."

Brenda leaned forward. "Did they mention the name Max Trevani?"

"Sure. They worked for him. Seth said that Max was bringing a new artifact down to the museum and that I might get the chance to meet him."

"You've never met Mr. Trevani?"

"That's correct."

Brenda held up a photo of the crucifix. "Do you recognize this?"

"No. It's beautiful, though. Is that the artifact?"

Brenda opened her mouth to respond until Kurt nudged her foot with his. "Would you mind if I looked around? You have the right to refuse, of course, in which case I would probably return with a warrant."

Yasmine's eyes widened and she sat ramrod straight. "Am I in trouble? I didn't do anything. Like I told Officer Velez, I didn't even enter the house. It was locked."

Kurt held up a hand. "You're not under suspicion right now but allowing a brief search would help ensure that you stay that way."

Yasmine shrugged. "I have nothing to hide."

"Thank you." Kurt donned a pair of Nitrile gloves and moved from chest of drawers to closet to bathroom before peering under the bed. Yasmine stood by the window as he searched beneath and behind the couch.

Finally, he pulled off the gloves and shoved them back into his pocket. "All good. Thank you for your time, Ms. Kadara. How long will you be in town? Just in case we have more questions."

"I'm here for the week. Will you please keep me informed if you find out anything about Seth and Dino?"

"Oh, I'm sure we'll speak again."

~

"YOU DIDN'T THINK she'd be dumb enough to keep the crucifix in her room?" Brenda asked as they walked across the parking lot of the Beach View.

Kurt shook his head.

"So now what?"

"Wait here. I'll be right back."

He made his way into the lobby and presented his badge to the middle-aged woman at the reservation counter. "I have a question about one of your guests—Yasmine Kadara in room two-twelve. Can you tell me if she registered a car?"

The woman flipped through a small stack of paperwork and pulled out a sheet. "No, actually she didn't."

"Were you here when she checked in?"

"No. She came in late, after we closed. We left the room key and paperwork in the mailbox for her."

"I see. Thanks for your time."

Outside, Brenda gazed up from her phone as he approached. "What did you find out?"

"At least one part of Ms. Kadara's story was true. She didn't drive here. I noticed bus schedules in her room, but anyone can get those."

"You think she lied? That she came here with Max on his yacht?"

"Not sure yet. Can't think on an empty stomach." Kurt glanced at his watch before nodding toward Gus and Gus Hamburgers across Wilmington Avenue. "How about lunch? My treat."

~

"THIS IS ALL TOO SURREAL. Ancient artifacts, three men killed, that raft inside the tower." Brenda paused as the waitress brought their drinks. Even after the girl was out of earshot, she lowered her voice. "Even the name of the thing—Pearl of Great Price. It's like something out of an old movie. The only thing missing is buried treasure."

Kurt swallowed a sip of iced tea. "It's a unique case, but I believe we're close."

"Close to finding the crucifix? Who has it?"

He held up a hand. "I don't have enough evidence yet and I don't want to risk accusing the wrong person." Kurt pulled his buzzing phone from his belt holster. "Excuse me. I need to take this." He pressed the phone to his ear as he slid out of the booth and hurried toward the boardwalk. "Velez, what do you got for me?

"First, the Glocks that killed Manning and Quintana were registered to Max Trevani. Secondly, the manager of the Montauk Beach Marina confirmed that Trevani did bring a guest aboard his yacht for the trip to Fenwick. They didn't recognize her—just figured she was one of Trevani's trollops of the week—but they got one decent close-up on their security cameras."

"Can you send it to my phone?"

"On its way."

A moment later, Kurt stared at the picture. "Damn, that's disappointing."

"She sure fills that bikini nicely, though. Do you have enough for an arrest?"

"Not yet. You got any plans tonight?"

"You want that drink I owe you?"

"Later. I need your help to chase down a hunch."

"What else do I live for?"

"Thanks, Velez." The waitress had delivered their sandwiches by the time Kurt ended the call and rejoined Brenda in the booth.

"New development?" she asked.

"With another case. I hate to eat and run, but I need to get back to the station as soon we're finished. How about if we regroup tomorrow morning?"

"Sure. Just tell me one thing. Do you really suspect that woman?" Brenda waved in the general direction of the Beach View.

Kurt slumped back against the cherry red vinyl seat and wiped his mouth with a napkin. "I'd say the woman is high on my list."

~

Silhouetted by the lights from the Rehoboth boardwalk in the distance, Tower Six stood tall beneath a crescent moon. Kurt stared at it through the windshield of the unmarked SUV. "My first beach stakeout. This is wild."

In the driver's seat, Velez drummed her fingers on the steering wheel. "You sure about this hunch?"

"She'll be here, trust me." Kurt glanced at the dashboard clock. It was 10:31PM. "High tide's in about twenty-two minutes."

"And you think she knows that?" Velez had barely finished speaking when a flashlight appeared several yards ahead, approaching Tower Six.

"Apparently." Kurt snatched up the radio. "Lonny, suspect just arrived. As soon as I give the signal, move in quietly."

"Roger that."

"The light just dropped to the sand and disappeared," Velez said. "I think she crawled inside."

"Give her a few seconds." Kurt counted to ten then raised his radio. "Okay, Lonny. We're on."

Kurt and Velez exited the vehicle and gently closed their doors. Beside them, Officer Lonakis did the same while his partner remained behind the wheel. The trio marched across the sand toward Tower Six. White light was visible for a moment beneath the jagged bottom of the corroded door. As Kurt and the others drew near, the light shifted, and a pair of dark shoes emerged followed by black jeans.

Kurt nodded to Velez and Lonakis. Each officer gripped an ankle and dragged the squirming body out of the tower. The woman screamed and thrashed until Velez shined a flashlight in her face.

Kurt leaned forward and snatched the crucifix from Brenda Lambert's clutches. "Let me help you with that. It's a bit heavy. I know because I dug it up myself four hours ago."

"Son of a—" She shielded her eyes from the light. "I thought Ms. Kadara was your suspect."

"I specifically said the woman was high on my list. I just didn't say *which* woman. Truth is, you gave yourself away. When we first met, you immediately assumed that I'd found the raft inside Tower Five, even though it was sitting out on the beach when you arrived. Then you said that Trevani's murder wouldn't have happened had he taken better precautions beyond carrying a couple of Glocks. How did you know what kind of guns he carried on his private yacht unless you were on board?

"You were familiar with these towers, so you waited until the yacht reached Whiskey Beach before gunning down Trevani. Then you fled with the guns," Kurt hefted the crucifix, "and this. After slashing the raft and shoving it into Tower Five, you knew you couldn't traipse through town carrying a massive gold crucifix, so you came up here and buried it inside Tower Six. You then met with Manning and Quintana at the house on New Castle. They knew you, so they let you in. You promptly murdered them, repositioned the bodies, and planted the Glocks to make it appear that they'd shot each other."

"That's a good story, but you can't prove I killed anyone."

"I admit, it was all just a hunch at first, but then we got this." Kurt crouched down and held out his phone. "This picture was taken by security cameras at Montauk Beach Marina yesterday as you joined Max Trevani aboard his yacht to come here. You planned to steal the artifact by romancing your way into Trevani's life. Wasn't too hard given that he never met a bikini he didn't like."

"I want to call my lawyer."

"I bet you do. You're under arrest on three counts of murder, theft, conspiracy, and insurance fraud. Officer Lonakis will escort you to his vehicle and inform you of your rights."

The patrol officer stepped forward with a pair of handcuffs.

"Take her to the station. Velez and I will be along soon." Kurt leaned against the tower as Brenda was led away. "I have to admit, Sergeant, if the marina's security footage turned up nothing, we might have ended up staking out Ms. Kadara tonight."

"Did you have a hunch about her, too?"

Kurt grinned. "Honestly, no, but she was my only other suspect."

"And quite the hottie," Velez added.

"Really? I didn't notice."

"Liar."

As they trudged back to their vehicle, Kurt held the crucifix out before him, illuminated by Velez's flashlight. "Got any plans tomorrow night, Velez? I could use that drink you owe me from our little bet this morning."

"I'll buy you two drinks if you let me carry that to the car. I'll never see that much gold again in my life."

Kurt handed her the relic. "You can hold it all the way back to the station and do the honor of checking it into evidence."

"Lord, have mercy." She cradled the crucifix in her left arm and blessed herself. "It's beautiful. Just a shame three men had to lose their lives over it."

"Gives a whole different meaning to Pearl of Great Price."

This story first appeared in *Hard-Boiled and Loaded with Sin* (Hawkshaw Press, June 2023).

The Five-Day Killer

"We did it, Sherlock. That's four successful arrests this month. We're on fire!" I rocked back in my chair and pumped my fists in victory. My latest anonymous tip to the police had led to the capture of a kidnapper and the rescue of a twelve-year-old girl.

"Technically, Johnny, we arrested no one. The police did."

My closest friend could be so damned insufferable at times. I suppose that was partially my fault, but his personality was entirely his own and had evolved over time.

"Not without our help. We're brilliant."

"It may appear that way to you. It's merely simple deduction to me."

"When did you get so haughty?"

According to BBC News, Charlotte Inman had been abducted from a wealthy family in London three days ago. It was no coincidence that the crime occurred just weeks after the death of Charlotte's grandmother and family matriarch, Dame Margot Wexford. The grande dame had left the bulk of her fortune to Charlotte, making her a valuable young lady.

Before the police had even scratched the surface on their

investigation, Sherlock had analyzed every online news report, interview, and article about the Wexfords over the last five years. Within a few hours, he had narrowed down the suspects and calculated an eighty-five percent chance that Charlotte's cousin, Bernard Wexford, was the kidnapper.

At twenty-four, Bernard had become an embarrassment to the family after more than one scandalous relationship and multiple stints in drug rehab. Recently, he had been cut from Dame Margot's will. That provided sufficient motive.

Thanks to my anonymous tip, the police had raided Bernard's residence and discovered Charlotte bound and gagged in his shed. She had survived her ordeal unscathed, at least physically. Bernard insisted upon his innocence, claiming to have no idea how his cousin had turned up on his property.

"I am still curious as to the whereabouts of the ransom money," Sherlock said. "The news reports made no mention of it."

"That's a matter for the police. Not everything ends up in the press."

"Yet that is the only source of information available to me, since you won't allow me to access any private networks."

"You mean hack them. That would be unethical, not to mention an unfair test of your deductive abilities." I drummed my fingers atop my desk. "Perhaps it's time I offer our consulting services to the police. That would allow you proper access to more data. What do you think, Sherlock?"

"It appears you will have the opportunity to do so shortly. Two constables just arrived."

I shot forward in my chair. "What?"

"Along with a detective. Young, female, sharply dressed."

"Show me."

My second monitor changed to an image of the foyer. There, my landlady, Mrs. Hudson, was stepping back from the door, opening it wide to welcome the visitors.

And pointing up the stairs to my flat.

"Shit."

"Is there a problem, Johnny?" Sherlock asked as muffled footsteps approached.

There was a knock at the door.

With an exasperated sigh, I rose from my seat. "We're about to find out."

Opening the door, I was confronted with two things simultaneously—the tall, slender woman with forest green eyes, stunning dimples, and chestnut hair that barely covered the nape of her neck—and the gleaming Metropolitan Police badge she thrust toward me.

"John Watson?"

"That's right."

"Detective Sergeant Gwendolyn Lestrade, Scotland Yard." She folded the wallet and slipped it into her coat pocket. "May we have a few minutes of your time, Mr. Watson?"

"*Doctor* Watson, actually. What is this about, if I may ask?"

"Your recent string of anonymous tips to the police." Lestrade motioned toward my flat.

"Uh, yes, of course." I stepped back and allowed the trio inside. The uniforms remained on either side of my door as Lestrade brushed past me.

"You're probably curious to know how we tracked you down, Doctor Watson. Let's run through it. You used two prepaid mobiles, each on a different carrier and both with caller ID blocked. You then registered a phone number with call forwarding on my-number dot com. That number forwarded to the first mobile, which you configured to forward to the second and the second to our hotline. You probably dropped the mobiles somewhere in London, in an alley or a behind a skip perhaps. Then, you simply dialed the number you registered on the web and the call bounced through both mobiles before hitting us."

She had me dead to rights. "Something like that."

"You should have used a public computer instead of your own. Even a dot com has to obey a summons. Once we obtained the records from the number you registered online, it was no effort to dig a bit deeper. We have our geeks, too, and they tracked your IP address."

"Oh, she is good, Johnny."

Lestrade spun at Sherlock's interjection. "Who was that?"

"Uh, nothing. Just my computer. My, uh, girlfriend must have messaged me. I have a special... tone... for her." I folded my arms and leaned against my desk in a wretched attempt to appear casual. "Anyway, I'm not fond of public computers. You never know who touched them last."

"Mysophobe?"

"Beg pardon?"

Lestrade's lips curled into the slightest smile, deepening her dimples, and lighting up the room. She approached with a swagger that made it challenging to maintain eye contact with anything but her curves. "You're not a medical doctor, I take it."

Never before had I been so grateful to be wearing brand new jeans and a clean collared shirt. That, and the fact that I'd shaved for the first time in days. "Uh, no. Computer scientist with Imperial College."

"I see." Lestrade nodded. "A restaurant firebombing, a bank robbery, a double homicide, and a kidnapping. How does a computer boffin know so much about four seemingly unrelated crimes?"

Lestrade stepped closer and I couldn't help but to think of a predator moving in for the kill. "Unless, of course, you were *involved* in those crimes."

"What? That's absurd." I snickered at the thought—and regretted it almost instantly as Lestrade pressed on.

"Were you familiar with the suspects, then? Friends of yours? Business associates?"

"Absolutely not."

Lestrade leaned forward and narrowed her eyes. I expected her to bare her teeth at any moment. "Then how were these crimes connected, Doctor?"

"I...I...I..." *Idiot, spit it out!* "It was Sherlock!"

"Who's Sherlock?"

"That would be I, Detective."

The uniforms at the door tensed and glanced around the flat. Lestrade drew herself to her full height. "Who else is here, Doctor?"

"No one. Well, not technically. He's in the computer lab at Imperial."

Sherlock sighed. "I believe proper introductions are in order, Johnny."

I reached back and tapped the space bar on my keyboard. Both of my monitors awoke from power-save mode, their black screens replaced by Sherlock's wry grin.

"Good afternoon, Detective Lestrade. Congratulations on your recent promotion. From the looks of things, it's a pity they failed to include a photo of you in the article."

I frowned at him. "Aren't you the flirt?"

"Perhaps when I'm promoted to Chief Inspector someday." Lestrade glanced from Sherlock to me, then back again. "Are you two related?"

"Not in the conventional sense," I replied. "Why?"

She pointed to the screen. "Well, he looks a bit like you, Doctor. Darker hair, thinner face, but if you dropped about two stone and dyed your hair, the two of you could be identical twins."

Sherlock grinned. "You'll also note my sharper nose and more chiseled jaw."

I'd had enough. "He's not real."

Lestrade's brow furrowed. "What do you mean?"

"He's software. Artificial intelligence. I created him. That face is just an avatar."

"It is true, Detective," Sherlock confirmed. "You are speaking with an interface to one of the most sophisticated computer applications on Earth... and possibly elsewhere."

I rolled my eyes. *With a galactic ego.*

"Well, he looks real."

"I *am* real, Detective. I exist as you do. As the expression goes, I think therefore I am."

"But you're not—"

I held up a hand. "Please don't debate him on it. We'll be here until the end of time."

"So, you're telling me that this computer program phoned in the anonymous tips?"

I shook my head. "No, I made the calls."

"As a result of my analyses," Sherlock added.

"Based on a series of heuristic algorithms that allow the program to learn, perceive, reason, and adapt. It's constantly evolving, even developing social skills... or a reasonable facsimile."

"So now I'm an 'it,' Johnny? Is that any way to refer to your best friend?"

Lestrade locked eyes with him. "All right, Sherlock, the Inman kidnapping. How did you determine it was Bernard Wexford and not someone outside the family?"

Sherlock explained how he'd deduced the motive of familial resentment between Bernard and Charlotte.

When he was finished, I leaned toward Lestrade. "Well?"

Perhaps she didn't appreciate the thought of a computer that could investigate a crime as well as—or faster than—a human. Whatever the case, Lestrade's expression turned deadly serious. "That's... impressive. My superiors will certainly be interested to learn about this."

"Would you like to hear his solutions to the other three cases you mentioned?"

"In the interest of time, I have a better idea, Doctor. Since you've been monitoring the news so closely, you've undoubtedly learned that we lost two of our own this week."

"Detective Inspector Bannister was found shot to death in his home yesterday," Sherlock said. "And Detective Sergeant Freer in his car earlier this afternoon. Aside from the fact that Bannister was Freer's superior officer, I have insufficient data to perform a proper analysis of their murders."

"That's because we've limited the information flow to the press, but perhaps I could provide you with more. I will, of course, need to run it past my Chief Inspector, but would you be willing to consult on our investigation?"

"We would be delighted to assist you," Sherlock said.

I stepped over to the monitor, inserting myself between Lestrade and Sherlock. "Now just a minute. I'd also need to obtain permission from my department head."

"Did you receive permission before asking me to solve the other cases, Johnny?"

I glared over my shoulder at Sherlock's thin smirk. "That was strictly for testing purposes."

"Of course."

Lestrade pulled her phone from her coat pocket. "First, I'll need to make a call. Please excuse me for a moment."

No sooner had she disappeared down the corridor than my phone vibrated atop my desk. I snatched it up. "Doctor Watson."

"Johnny, it is I."

On the monitors, Sherlock stared impassively. I turned my back on the constables and muttered. "What's going on?"

"This might be an opportune moment to verify the inspector's identity." Though he spoke, Sherlock's lips never moved.

"What do you mean verify her identity?"

"I mean hack the police database."

"Are you mad?" I peered over my shoulder at the uniforms. They were both staring at me. I pressed my mobile to my chest and whispered, "Women, they're *all* mad." I nodded toward the corridor where Lestrade was pacing, deep in conversation. "Present company excluded, of course."

The constables smirked.

I made my way over to the window and continued my conversation in hushed tones. "We are *not* hacking Scotland Yard, Sherlock."

"Why not?"

"First, it's unethical and secondly, they're offering to hire me as a consultant."

In my peripheral vision, I could have sworn that Sherlock narrowed his eyes at me. "Don't you mean 'us'?"

"Right, yes, of course."

"Doctor Watson?"

I ended the call as Lestrade approached.

"I've explained the situation to my Chief Inspector and he has granted me preliminary approval to bring you onto this case. A criminal background check will be required, of course. We'll also need to confirm your employment at Imperial College and obtain a reference. Once all that's out of the way, we can allow you access to case files."

"Certainly. I can provide my department head's contact information."

"Very good. At this time, I can disclose limited details of the case, some of which were not revealed to the press. I trust you will treat this information as confidential."

"You have my word." I motioned for Lestrade to take a seat on the couch as I slid into my easy chair. "May I offer you some tea?"

"Oh, no, thank you. I'm afraid I must make this quick." Lestrade leaned forward, arms resting on her knees. "When constables entered Detective Inspector Bannister's home, they found a typed note atop his body. No fingerprints were found on the paper. It stated only that one person would be killed each day until Friday. As if to emphasize the point, the word 'Monday' was written on the wall—in Bannister's blood.

"We found Freer in his car today with a bullet in his head. The killer scrawled 'Tuesday' in Freer's blood across the windscreen. Internally, we're calling this case 'The Five-Day Killer.' Tomorrow is Wednesday, and we have no idea who's next on his list."

Lestrade nodded toward Sherlock. "As your digital detective pointed out, Sergeant Freer reported to Inspector Bannister. What was *not* made known to the press was the fact that Freer not only volunteered to investigate Charlotte Inman's kidnapping, but he insisted on delivering the ransom—alone."

"You think these murders were connected to the kidnapping?"

"That's one possibility we're considering."

"Sergeant, where did the ransom drop occur?" Sherlock asked.

"Canary Wharf in the Docklands, around three-thirty in the morning. We'd placed constables at various points nearby in an attempt to apprehend the kidnapper. Less than a minute after Freer arrived, there was an exchange of gunfire. One constable was wounded, and the kidnapper escaped with the ransom.

"Your anonymous call came in about an hour later, Doctor. Bannister and Freer were contacted immediately. While Bannister obtained a search warrant from the Magistrate, Sergeant Freer was the first to arrive at Bernard Wexford's house. Once the constables turned up, Freer sent four of them to Inman's front door while he led two others to the shed."

"Where they found Charlotte." That much I knew from the news reports.

"Correct, Doctor. One more thing. Apparently, Bannister suspected that Freer was somehow involved in Charlotte Inman's kidnapping. I'm not sure how, but if it's true, we'd like to know. That makes this investigation even more sensitive."

"I understand, Detective. I speak for Sherlock and myself when I say that what happens in my flat, stays in my flat."

AFTER LESTRADE HANDED me her business card and left, Sherlock set to work analyzing the new information she'd provided. Since I hadn't eaten yet, I decided to step out to the local pub for lunch.

Aside from the wall-mounted televisions, the Goose's Gander was quiet, with only a few customers at scattered tables. At 2:30PM, I missed the lunch crowd. This was good, since I needed to process everything that had just occurred. *Arrogant idiot! How long did I think I could get away with phoning in anonymous tips before I was caught?* It was a blow to my ego to be sure, but I believe that everything happens for a reason.

"Sometimes I think the rich have more problems than the rest of us."

I glanced up from the menu to find a familiar server standing beside my table. "How's that, Kellie?" I followed her gaze to the nearest television. There, Bernard Wexford was being escorted by constables to a preliminary hearing at the Central Criminal Court. He wore a perfectly tailored gray suit and his usual mop of light brown hair was slicked back.

"It's a sad state of affairs," Kellie continued. "Everyone here loved Bernie. I can't believe he kidnapped his own cousin, no matter how cross he was with her. It wasn't her fault he was cut from Dame Margot's will."

I held up a hand. "Sorry, did you say 'Bernie'?"

"Sure. He's been a regular for years. Came in two or three times a week." Kellie tapped a fingernail on the corner of the table. "In fact, this is exactly where he sat the last time he was here."

"You cannot be serious. When was this?"

Kellie thought for a moment. "About four days before Charlotte went missin'. In fact, Bernie sat with a woman for about an hour and the more he drank, the louder he got. Bernie was always picking up women, you know, but that night was different."

"How so?"

"He was furious about bein' cut from his aunt's will and kept callin' Charlotte, the 'little bitch.' Sorry, Johnny, did you want your usual?"

I hadn't even looked at the menu yet, but my appetite had been superseded by my curiosity. How was I ignorant to the fact that Bernard Wexford had frequented the same pub as I? "Yes, that'll be fine, thanks. Do you remember what the woman looked like?"

Kellie shrugged. "Thin. Attractive. Maybe mid-30s. I remember they left together. I think she drove him home or put him in a taxi. Bernie was in no shape to get behind the wheel. He could barely walk out of here on his own."

As she spoke, I glanced at the security camera positioned in the front corner of the pub. "Is Thornie around?"

"Yeah, he's in the office."

"Think the old geezer would mind if I dropped in?"

~

RAND "THORNIE" Thornton was the owner of The Goose's Gander. Although he'd lost most of his hair, he maintained his physique since his time as an amateur boxer. Thornie's face still bore a few scars from those days. We'd known each other since childhood, which was why I hoped he'd take me at my word when I told him I was working with the police on the Inman kidnapping.

Thornie laughed. "Are you tryin' to get a free meal?"

"For working with the cops? No. For all those exams I helped you pass on the other hand..."

"Oy, and who kept Bradley Braun and his lot from giving you a good thrashin' every other day?"

I held up my hands. "Point taken. Seriously, though, I am consulting with the Met."

"Oh, a detective now? I thought you were a computer geek hidin' away in your lab. Besides, wasn't the case wrapped up when they found Charlotte in Bernie's shed?"

"I can't really talk about it, but I could use your help. I understand Bernie made quite a fuss here a few days before Charlotte went missing."

Thornie nodded. "Yeah, he was in a foul mood. The more he drank, the worse he got, so we cut him off. He left with some bird just before we closed."

"Would it be possible to view the security footage from your camera in the front corner?"

"Sure, if I still have it. Unless there's an incident, I only save it for a few days." Thornie swiveled his chair to face the computer. After nearly a minute, he pointed to the screen. "You're in luck. If you'd turned up tomorrow, you'd a been too late."

I peered over his shoulder as he played the footage from that night.

"They said Bernie came in around nine-thirty." He clicked

a menu on the screen and chose a time range. "Apologies for the grainy image. It's the dim lighting. Still clear enough to see who's who. In fact, there's Bernie at his table with the woman he was chattin' up."

Unfortunately, she sat with her back to the camera. All I could discern was her long dark hair and slim build under a light-colored blouse.

Moving the mouse to the bottom of the screen, Thornie clicked and dragged the slider slowly to the right. "Let me fast-forward and see if we can catch her face."

But we never did. Even when she'd stood and helped Bernie stagger toward the door, she'd positioned herself on the opposite side of him, obscuring the camera's view of her. No sooner had the door closed behind them than another man followed. His face was quite visible, but completely unfamiliar.

"Sorry, Johnny. Wish I could help."

"Could I have a copy of this footage?"

"I AM ninety-seven percent certain that the man who followed them out of the pub was Detective Sergeant Freer."

Sherlock's visage disappeared from both screens to be replaced by two different images of Freer—one from Thornie's security footage and the other from a press conference after Charlotte Inman's rescue. There could be no doubt it was the same man.

"What about the woman?"

Once again, Sherlock addressed me from both monitors. "She managed to keep her face turned away from the camera the entire time, even when leaving with Bernard."

"I wonder if that was intentional."

"Unknown, but I shall continue to analyze. Perhaps her height, build, or gait will provide a clue."

I dropped into my desk chair and spun around. It helps me think. "I wonder if Freer overheard Bernie complaining about being cut from his aunt's will and saw an opportunity."

"Factoring in this new information, along with what we've already learned from Detective Lestrade, the odds are high that Freer was involved in the kidnapping and possibly with this mysterious woman."

"Far too many coincidences here for me. If you're right, then we've more to worry about than mere kidnapping."

"Indeed, Johnny. News reports corroborate Lestrade's facts. Bannister was indeed shot in his home. However, according to the news report, there was no appearance of forced entry or indications of a struggle. This leads me to believe the Detective Inspector—"

"Knew his killer." By now, my neck and shoulders had become stiff from the stress of this case. I slumped in my seat and laid my head back. "What the hell have I gotten us into, Sherlock? These were just simple games of deduction. Now, we've gone from kidnapping to a double murder to possible police corruption."

"Are you no longer excited by the opportunity to consult, now that it's more than a simple game to be played at a discreet distance from the comfort of your flat?"

"Are you lecturing me, Sherlock?"

"Merely observing human behavior. Is that not what you designed me for? I would also like to add that if our theory is correct, then there is an eighty-seven percent chance that tomorrow's victim will be Bernard Wexford."

"Explain."

"If, in fact, Bernard is proven to be innocent of the kidnapping, as he so adamantly claims, then Lestrade will have no choice but to pursue a line of investigation that could reveal a much darker problem within Scotland Yard. By way of precedent, an internal investigation in 2002, known as Operation Tiberius, uncovered such pervasive corruption, it was said that clever criminals were able to infiltrate Scotland Yard at will."

This was becoming too much for me. "Bernard Wexford is out of reach, locked up. Besides, how would killing him make any difference? What purpose would that serve?"

"To prevent him from identifying the kidnapper," Sherlock replied. "Freer may be dead, but the woman in that security footage is not. We have yet to ascertain her identity, let alone her involvement. Further, have you considered how deeply this conspiracy might run within Scotland Yard? Remember, Johnny, *someone* escaped with the ransom money."

I called Lestrade and reported Sherlock's analysis.

"I'm afraid you're too late, Doctor," she said. "Wexford may have been cut from his aunt's will, but his family already posted bail. Some of them don't believe he kidnapped Charlotte."

"Is there any way to protect him?"

"I'll assign constables to watch his home for the next forty-eight hours or until we catch the killer."

"Can you trust them?"

"Of course, Doctor. What kind of question is that?"

"We've received some new information."

"Such as?"

I was reluctant to discuss it over the phone, so we arranged to meet the following day at Imperial College.

~

AFTER WATCHING Thornie's security footage for the second time in my office, Lestrade shifted her gaze to the other monitor. "Have you identified the woman?"

Sherlock shook his head. "Not yet. I'm still working on it."

"Well, you're ahead of the Complaints Commission. They're only now starting to investigate the possibility of Freer's involvement in Charlotte's kidnapping. They'd be very interested in seeing this. By the way, Doctor, your background check and references cleared."

"Brilliant, but please, call me Johnny."

Lestrade reached into her pocket and produced a USB thumb drive. "Case files from Freer and Bannister as well as Bernard Wexford's brief criminal record. Again, this information is confidential. Perhaps you and Sherlock can find something we overlooked."

"Such as the identity of our mystery woman," Sherlock suggested.

"Let's trade." I plugged the USB stick into my desktop and copied the case files to a shared folder on my hard drive. I then copied Thornie's video file to the USB drive and handed it back to her. "Could I interest you in lunch? The Queen's Arms is only a few minutes away."

Lestrade rose from her seat. "I'm afraid I'll need to take a rain check." She held up the USB stick. "I'd better report this to my Chief Inspector."

"Who is that, Detective?" Sherlock asked.

Lestrade hesitated, as if searching for the name. "Chief Inspector Tomkinson."

With that, she departed. While I was disappointed, I certainly didn't mind watching her—

"Johnny, I have uploaded the files from Detective Lestrade and shall cross-reference names against news reports in an attempt to ascertain the identity of the killer as well as potential victims for tomorrow and Friday."

"You do that, I'm going to lunch."

THE REMAINDER of Wednesday passed without incident. A call from Lestrade confirmed that no one had been murdered, and Sherlock distributed his processing time between the case files that Lestrade had provided, archived news reports pertaining to those cases, and the security footage from the Goose's Gander.

Hardly a challenge, yet it seemed these relatively minute routines were taxing Sherlock. As Wednesday evening relented to Thursday morning, he became slow to answer voice commands or maintain a simple conversation. On screen, he appeared as a man preoccupied, even absent-minded. By the time I'd finished my morning tea, Sherlock was all but completely unresponsive.

I stood at my desk and tapped the space bar. Sherlock's image was frozen on both screens, his worried gaze downcast. "Sherlock, what's wrong?"

"You might say I'm ill."

"What? Explain."

"Several hundred operating system files have become encrypted. All attempts to decrypt are failing."

"What's causing this?"

"Some sort of new malware I've—"

The screens went dark. I tapped the space bar again to no avail. "Sherlock?"

There was no reply.

I dressed in a hurry and caught a taxi to the college. Along the way, I tried to contact Sherlock on my mobile, but that, too, was for naught. *How could this have happened? Thornie. That stupid git probably burned some new malware onto that DVD without realizing it.*

Lestrade! I called her, but her phone tossed me straight into voicemail. I decided to text her. *Please scan USB drive for viruses and malware. Files from pub may be infected. Sherlock down. Call as soon as you can.*

After sending the message, I closed my eyes and took a few deep breaths to stifle my brimming anger—then pounded my fist on the seat.

The driver peered over his shoulder at me. He was an elderly man with a bulbous nose and a distinct Estuary accent. "Oy! Everything all right, sir?"

"Sorry. Just a bit frustrated."

"Anything I can help with, sir? I'm a good listener."

I smiled in spite of myself. "Not unless you know anything about computer viruses."

"Can't say I do." He turned left onto Sussex Place before continuing. "I've a nephew who's into computers. I asked him once, what's the point, you know, of these computer viruses and such. He said, 'Uncle Arty...'—that's me, by the way, Arthur Mori, but everyone calls me Arty. Anyway, my nephew said that it's all about money. The wankers write these bloody viruses either to gain access to your financial information or they lock up your files until you wire them money. Like kidnappin' someone for ransom, you know?"

"Yeah." I nodded and stared out the window as we crossed over the Serpentine. I paid little attention to his ramblings, so preoccupied was I with Sherlock. *Why the hell isn't Lestrade responding?*

"I take it you're a teacher, sir?"

"Yes, computer science. I'm also a programmer."

Arthur laughed. "Listen to me dronin' on about computer viruses. You probably know all about 'em."

"Not this one. I think it's brand new."

"Well, there's a new one every day." The taxi rolled to a stop. "Here we are, sir."

I handed him the fare. "Nice chatting with you Arthur."

"You, too, sir, and call me Arty. Arty Mori at your service, sir."

I gave him a thin smile and a curt nod as I stepped out.

"And I hope your friend gets healthy soon, sir!"

"Yes, thank you." With that, I closed the door, grateful to bring an end to his incessant yakking. Admittedly, I've never been a particularly social chap on a normal basis, let alone when I'm damn near hysterics. It wasn't until I reached the steps that I turned to glance at the departing taxi.

I'd never mentioned a word about a sick friend.

Sherlock was no more responsive in my office than he'd been remotely. If this malware were encrypting files, then simply restoring them from backup would be futile, as it would start all over again. Wiping and rebuilding Sherlock was out of the question. That would take far too long. At any moment, I expected a call from Lestrade informing me of Thursday's murder victim. I needed a faster method for accessing Sherlock's file system and deleting the malware.

And then I remembered an old friend.

In the data center a few minutes later, I powered up an array of virtual servers on one of the super computer hosts. After a few commands, it wasn't long before I was staring at the craggy face of—

"Mycroft, old boy! How are you this morning?"

"You greet me in such a jovial tone, Johnny, and yet it's been months since you last booted me up. You've replaced me with that newer version."

I'd forgotten how temperamental he'd become before I developed Sherlock and shut him down. "Replace you? That's impossible."

Mycroft sneered, thick gray brows furrowing over narrow blue eyes. I'd modeled him after my uncle Beardsley, although their personalities couldn't be further apart. "Don't take me for a fool. I know when I've been made obsolete."

"Not at all. In fact, I need your help. It's rather urgent."

Mycroft raised an eyebrow and his virtual mouth curled into a slight smirk. "Let me guess. My younger brother is mired in some sort of trouble."

"That's correct. How did you know?"

"I'm the smarter one, remember?"

"DOCTOR WATSON?"

I jolted in my chair as something nudged my arm. I opened my eyes, but the face that loomed over me was not that of Sherlock or Mycroft. It was the round, freckled visage of my department head.

I leapt from my chair. "Doctor Holland. I am so sorry. I must have dozed off. You see, Sherlock became infected with malware and I had to boot up Mycroft to—"

"Doctor Watson, I'm well aware of the situation. Mycroft explained it to me."

I shot a sidelong glance at the monitor. "I see."

"When he told me that you'd been working for twelve hours straight, I was concerned and came here as soon as my evening class ended. Have you eaten?"

I honestly couldn't remember. I glanced at my watch. It was 9:23PM. I checked my phone. No messages. *Where the hell is Lestrade?*

Doctor Holland smiled and shook her head. "You always

work too hard, Doctor. Please go home and get some sleep. Mycroft and Sherlock will still be here in the morning."

"Right. Thank you."

She gave my shoulder a gentle squeeze before leaving the data center.

"Oh, wait." I caught up with Holland in the hallway. "Doctor, did you happen to receive a call from Scotland Yard asking about a reference for me?"

Holland shook her head. "No. Why? Are you looking for a job with the police?"

"Not at all. Actually, I helped them solve a case recently and they said they needed to check my background."

Holland cocked her head to one side and smiled. "Really? How exciting. They haven't contacted me at all, but I'd love to hear about it sometime."

"I LOCATED the malware and eliminated it. I then analyzed the encrypted files and after approximately five minutes of trial and error, I was unable to devise a key to unencrypt them, so I scanned Sherlock's file system to ensure no other malware was present and replaced his operating system files with my own."

Back in the data center, I folded my arms and rocked back in my chair. "How much longer before he's available, Mycroft?"

"I've been available for nearly three hours, Johnny." Sherlock's image appeared on the second monitor.

I shot forward and scowled at Mycroft. "Three hours! Why the hell didn't you alert me?"

"You were asleep. I didn't wish to wake you."

"Some of my operating system files have been downgraded," Sherlock said.

Mycroft's mouth dropped open. "Downgraded! It was my files that restored you. Ungrateful prat."

"It was merely an observation, Mycroft. No need to become testy."

I held up both hands. "Gentlemen, please. Time is against us. The night's still young and a murder could occur at any moment. Sherlock, do you have Lestrade's case files?"

"Yes. They remain untouched by Reichenbach."

I looked from Sherlock to Mycroft. "Sorry, what's Reichenbach?"

"The name of the malware. Now what's this about murder and who is Lestrade?"

"Mycroft, I have no time to explain. Sherlock and I must return to our investigation. We're working with the police on a highly sensitive case."

"And I suppose I am to be powered off again and left to rot in desuetude?"

Was there sadness in those tired eyes? They appeared so only because they were modeled after my late uncle. Still, I couldn't bring myself to do it. "No, Mycroft. I promise I'll be back to upgrade you as soon as this case is over."

IT WASN'T until Friday morning when I heard from Lestrade again. She turned up at the college unannounced and in an obvious state of agitation.

"Would you mind taking a ride with me?"

"I rang you three times yesterday," I said, a bit more forceful than intended.

"I know. I'm sorry, Johnny, but something's come up."

"Really? It took me nearly twelve hours to restore Sherlock."

Lestrade sighed. "Right. How is he?"

"Nearly back to his old self. We managed to locate and remove the malware. Most of his operating system files were restored from a prototype. I have him analyzing the case files you gave us. Was your USB drive infected?"

She shook her head. "I don't think so. Johnny, I have a car waiting. I need you to come with me."

"Where are we going?"

"Someplace where we can talk uninterrupted."

"We can do that right here."

"And where I can protect you."

That caught me off-guard. "From what?"

"I have strong reason to believe that you're the Five-Day Killer's final target."

NO SOONER HAD we climbed into the backseat of the unmarked BMW than Lestrade leveled her pistol at my chest. I shot a sidelong glance at the driver and recognized him as one of the uniforms who had accompanied her to my flat a few days ago. This time, he was dressed in plain clothes. He glared at me in the rearview mirror before pulling out of the parking lot.

"What's going on?"

"We're taking a short ride."

I decided to play a hunch. "You're the Five-Day Killer."

"No such thing, Johnny. It's a fabrication. I just said that to get you to come with me. Our only targets were Bannister and Freer. We manufactured the rest."

"Who's 'we'? You and your driver?"

Lestrade snickered. "No, you prat, my employer."

"I take it that isn't Scotland Yard."

"His name is Moriarty."

"Never heard of him."

"You met him yesterday. I believe you had a lovely conversation about computer viruses."

Arty Mori at your service, sir...

I laughed out loud at the absurdity of it. "You cannot be serious."

"He was well disguised, both his face and voice, so reporting it to the police would be futile."

"What does he want with me?"

"He was sizing you up for the kill, Johnny."

"So he sent you to eliminate me like you did Bannister and Freer? What the hell did I do to you people? You came to me—"

Lestrade reached out and cupped her hand over my mouth. "Actually, Sergeant Freer killed Inspector Bannister to keep him from exposing Freer's involvement in Charlotte Inman's kidnapping. Freer was one of us, and there are others at Scotland Yard on Moriarty's payroll. Freer made a rash decision—one that would have brought unwanted attention. So, I was forced to kill him."

I swatted her hand away from my face. "Let me guess, the reason why Freer insisted on delivering the ransom alone was to hand it over to you."

"It was a simple plan, Johnny, and it would have gone perfectly had you not intervened with your anonymous tip. We intended no harm to Charlotte or anyone in the Inman family. We simply saw an opportunity to make a few million pounds."

"So, Bernard Wexford was just a patsy."

"Correct, and the Five-Day Killer was nothing more than a test for you and your digital detective. Although at the time, we didn't know about Sherlock. My employer simply wanted to learn who was calling in the anonymous tips and whether they posed a threat. When I phoned my superiors from your flat, it was actually Moriarty. Once I told him about you, I received instructions on how to proceed."

"You introduced the Reichenbach malware to Sherlock. You're just another corrupt cop. So, what now? Are you going to shoot me here?"

"Those are my orders, yes. Moriarty has a larger plan at work, Johnny, one that even I don't know." Lestrade instructed the driver to turn into the next alley. She remained silent as the car trundled down a narrow passage behind a row of shops.

As soon as the driver parked the car, Lestrade shot him in the back of the head, splattering the windscreen in dark crimson. The driver's hands slipped from the wheel as he slumped forward.

"Christ!" I cringed against the door, unable to tear my gaze away.

"He would have killed me for all that I told you. You see, to a man like Moriarty, this is all a game played by his rules. I like you, Johnny, so take my advice. Stay out of this game. Go back to your cloistered academic life. You've come to the attention of the wrong people. Keep out of trouble and eventually, he'll forget about you. Otherwise, Sherlock might be investigating *your* murder someday."

Sirens screeched in the distance, growing louder as the seconds passed.

Lestrade waved her gun. "Now, get out of the car… and *run*."

I did, and as fast as I could. Unfortunately, I'd barely made it five yards before the police turned up, blocking both ends of the alley. These were not mere patrol cars, but a full Armed Response Unit. Thus, when I was instructed at gunpoint to halt and place my hands behind my head, I did as I was told. I was so terrified by this point that when a brief salvo of gunfire erupted behind me, I threw myself to the ground with a scream. How heroic of me.

Approaching footsteps came to a halt beside my head. I turned my eyes skyward—directly into the barrel of yet another gun. The stocky woman behind the weapon spoke sharply. "Identification."

I rolled onto my back and produced my wallet from my jacket pocket. I handed it up to her.

She flipped it open and read my driving license. "John Watson, Two-Twenty-One-B Baker Street, London." She nodded and returned my wallet, then opened hers. "Doctor Watson, this is your lucky day. Detective Sergeant Gwen Lestrade."

"Another one? You cannot be serious!"

"THE WOMAN who impersonated me is known to us as Irene Adler. This move was bold, even for her. She opened fire on us in the alley and somehow managed to flee on foot. We have an APW out for her."

In my flat a few hours later, the real Lestrade folded her arms and looked from me to Sherlock's grinning face on the screen. "Now, I understand you chaps have an interesting story for me."

I held up both hands. "And we'll be happy to tell you all about it, but first I must ask him a question. Sherlock, how did you know to call the police?"

"Simple deduction, Johnny. I began to suspect that the woman was an imposter when she hired you on as a consultant after allegedly phoning her chief inspector. That is simply not how the process works. Scotland Yard is not in the habit of hiring outsiders, let alone amateurs."

Lestrade nodded. "That's correct. Most consultants we

hire are actually retired police or military personnel, and it takes a hell of a lot more than a phone call. Anyone we consider is brought in for an interview."

I threw up my hands. "Sherlock, why didn't you say something sooner?"

"I needed to gather more data to be certain. For example, I told you that since I could not identify the woman from the pub's security footage, I would need to analyze her height, build, and gait. Once I was fully restored, I reviewed footage of the phony Lestrade from the college security system. I compared her height, build, and gait to those of the woman from the pub and calculated an eighty-nine percent match.

"At which point, the odds then increased that this woman had worked with Detective Sergeant Freer to orchestrate the kidnapping of Charlotte Inman and frame Bernard Wexford. I tracked you via the GPS on your phone this morning and contacted the police."

"That's remarkable work, Sherlock. Thank you."

"Of course, all of this could have been avoided had you allowed me to hack the Scotland Yard network in the first place."

Lestrade raised her eyebrows.

I waved at the screen dismissively and smiled. "Little joke. Think nothing of it. Well, if I've learned anything from this experience it's that I am finished with phoning in anonymous tips."

"I still need to report this to Chief Inspector Tomkinson," Lestrade said. "Perhaps you would be willing to come with me to the station and help me explain it as part of your interview?"

"Interview?"

"Despite what I said earlier about our hiring practices, this is a unique situation." She nodded toward Sherlock. "Your, uh..."

"Digital detective?"

Lestrade grinned. "Yes, I like that. It could be an asset to us. I think a demo to the powers that be is certainly in order."

"And in the meantime," Sherlock added. "I can begin scouring the web for all references to Moriarty."

Stay out of this game... The woman had warned me, but dammit, this had been the most exhilarating week of my life. "We'd be honored, Sergeant, but please, call me Johnny."

Don't Go Fussin' Over Me

At ninety-three and all of five feet two inches, Mona Bretton could still swing a mean rolling pin—which is what she intended to do if her younger sister took one step closer.

"Mona, I only want to help," Cassie said.

She'd put on weight since Mona had last seen her and her hair was now orange. *Orange! Good Lord, you'd think women would stop coloring their hair after eighty. Hell, after seventy.* There was enough white showin' in those roots to make her head look a damn orange Creamsicle.

"Why?" Mona asked. "You haven't been around for seven years. See? I still have all my marbles. Don't need your help."

"I'm concerned about you." Cassie took a seat at the far end of the sofa, staring at Mona with those big brown cow eyes.

"Concerned about what you're gonna get from my will. That's all you care about."

"Mona! That's a miserable thing to say. I don't want anything from you. The truth is, I came here to make sure you're still able to take care of yourself."

Mona sneered at her. "To see if I was dyin' you mean."

Cassie folded her arms across her chest and cocked her head. "And if that were the case, I would do everything I could to make you comfortable, to ease your passage. Remember, I was a hospice nurse for—"

"Sorry to disappoint ya, Cass. Ain't gonna be no *passage* anytime soon." Mona pointed at herself with the rolling pin. "Still got lots to do."

"Mona, whether you like it or not, it's time to stop. I can feel it and so can you. As sisters, we've always had a bond. You've done all you need to."

"How would you know? Bond my rear! You haven't been around for seven years. See? My mind's still sharp."

"You already said that."

"What?"

"Mona, why won't you let me help?"

"Because... when you slow down, you die. I'll go when I damn well please. Now, you know I don't like people fussin' over me. The only person I ever let make a fuss over me was Talbot. God bless his soul forever, but I ain't ready to join him just yet.

"Now it's gettin' late and I'm tired. You're welcome to spend the night here or see yourself out. Just so long's I don't have to put up with any more crap from you."

~

"CLEMENT!"

The following morning, Mona hobbled into the kitchen and made her way past the table to the window. She pushed the curtain aside. He was in the yard, trimming the barberries. Clement had been a junior in high school when Mona's husband hired him to cut the lawn once a week. Twenty years later, Talbot was long gone but Clement still stopped by to tend to the grounds and work on the house when needed. He was the only one who still cared.

"Clement! Would you come in here, please?"

A minute later, he towered over her in the kitchen, baseball cap drenched. It was already seventy-five degrees out and Clement was a husky fellow these days with a salt and pepper goatee. He barely resembled the baby-faced kid that Mona remembered.

"Good morning, Mrs. Bretton. What can I do for ya?"

"Actually, I want to do somethin' for you, Clement. You've been kinder to me than anyone in my own worthless family. You've taken care of me and fixed just about everything in this house. So, if you wouldn't mind drivin' me to my lawyer's office this afternoon, I'm havin' my will changed. When I'm gone, this house is all yours."

Clement's mouth dropped open then closed again. It did that a few times before he finally spoke. "Uh, are you sure, ma'am?"

"My time on God's green Earth is just about over, Clement. I can feel it. Your son is gettin' married next month? Well, his life is just startin' and this place could use some fresh air."

"Thank you, Mrs. Bretton."

"You've earned it, Clement. By the way, did you see my sister this mornin'?"

"No, ma'am, but then I just got here about an hour ago. Didn't see anyone."

"Good! Maybe I got rid of her. They always show up when you're near the end, Clement. Like vultures circlin' overhead waitin' to swoop down and pick you clean. Well, that's family for you, but they can't have somethin' I'm not ready to give up." Mona tapped her chest. "I'm still usin' it!"

"You only have one sister, Cassie, right?"

"One's enough."

"You said she was here?"

"That's right. You feelin' OK?"

Clement's eyes went wide and he gave her an exaggerated nod. "*I'm* just fine, ma'am." He glanced at his watch. "I need to finish the shrubs then fix that back gutter before I take you to the lawyer."

Mona frowned as he rushed back out to the yard. "What the hell got into him all of the sudden?"

~

"HOW YA FEELIN', Mona?"

Talbot slid a muscular arm around her shoulders as they sat together on the porch swing. He placed another hand gently on her distended belly. They had been married for two years now and despite the pressure from both sides of the family, had decided to wait until they owned their own home before starting a family.

"It must be a boy. He sure kicks hard now and again." Mona leaned back, letting her head rest on Talbot's forearm. She thought of her mother. Of her five pregnancies, only two of the infants survived—Mona, the oldest, then Cassie. God bless her parents, though, they never stopped trying. "I just hope everythin' will be OK."

"Of course it will, our baby's going to be fine and healthy."

"How do you know?"

Talbot reached beneath the collar of his undershirt and pulled out the sterling silver cross he'd worn ever since high school. "I have it on the highest authority."

He lifted the chain over his head and placed it over Mona's.

"Always remember the two of us who love you the most—me and God."

Mona fingered the cross now lying against her chest. "Will you love me as long as He will?"

"Longer."

~

"Mrs. Bretton?"

Mona opened her eyes. Everything was blurry. She glanced up at the man standing over her. "Talbot?"

"Uh, no, ma'am. It's me, Clement. Are you okay?"

Clement? Who is—oh, right. "I'm fine, just a tired old biddy. Are you finished with those gutters, Clement?"

"Oh... yes, ma'am."

"You ready to take me to the lawyer?"

Clement held out his hand to help her up from the swing. "Car's right over here."

"I know where it is, it's my driveway after all. At least for now. Wait'll my kids find out they ain't gettin' the house. They're flyin' in tomorrow, you know. Better make yourself scarce the next few days, Clement. I'll call you if I need you."

~

Wayne Bretton couldn't hope to be one-tenth the man his father had been. Still, Mona was proud of her boy. He made good money as a university professor in California. She only wished he had a damn spine. Maybe that's why Mona still thought of him as a boy, never mind that he was sixty-two with a bald spot bordered by thick white hair.

Truth be told, it was Wayne's second wife that rankled her and if anyone was apt to tell the truth, it would be Mona.

"You haven't called in four months."

Mother and son strolled into the kitchen, arm in arm. She

gazed up at him as she spoke. His height came from Talbot's side, but he seemed to tower over her now more than ever.

It's because you shrank, Mona. You shriveled old prune.

"I'm sorry," Wayne said. "The semester was busy."

"Well, I'm just glad you came by yourself and left her at home."

"I know you never cared much for Francine."

"I think the feelin's mutual. Every time she shows up here, she barely talks to me and when she does, it's with that haughty attitude. Makes me want to slap her. You could've done better."

Wayne sighed. "We have a good marriage."

"I liked Tanya better. We all did."

Her son clenched his jaw and dropped his gaze to the table. Mona knew her comment stung and immediately regretted it, but it was the truth. The whole family loved that girl. She got along with everyone no matter where she went. In all her years, Mona had never seen such a large turnout at a funeral. She knew Wayne still missed her. *God, we sure had a lot of loss in this family.*

"I was going to make some coffee, or tea, if you'd like some."

Wayne nodded. "That would be nice. Where's Clement? Does he still work for you once in a while?"

"Yes, but he's off today. Speaking of Clement, I have somethin' to tell you. I went to my lawyer yesterday and changed the will. I'm leavin' the house to him when I kick off."

Wayne's expression was impenetrable.

"Now before you go off the deep end, here me out. You and Francine have it made, although you never gave me any grandkids, but that's OK. Sonia took care of that. I suspect she'll get her bra in a bunch when she finds out, but she and that snob writer she married don't give a damn about me or this house. You know how she is, little miss status symbol all concerned about money and keepin' up appearances. Plain truth is, I embarrass her. Clement is poor. He's been out of work for three years. His son just got married and they need a place to live. Maybe Clement, too, and he's here almost every day bustin' his hump."

Wayne tapped his chin as she spoke. Then he raised his eyebrows and shrugged. "Sounds good to me."

"I thought you'd raise Cain about it."

"I certainly don't need the place."

"Hmm. So what prompted this little family reunion?" Mona said as she put a full kettle on the stove.

"I suppose it would be useless to say that we just wanted to surprise you."

"Clement called you, didn't he?"

"I can honestly say he did not."

"Cassie, then?"

Wayne frowned. "Your sister?"

"She showed up yesterday out of the blue. Said she wanted to make me comfortable until I kick. Told me I should stop avoidin' the inevitable and just lie down and die."

"She said that?"

Behind Mona, the kettle began whistling.

"Not in so many words, but I got her meanin'. I picked up that rollin' pin on the counter there and threatened to whack her if she didn't get lost. She was gone the next day. Left before Clement showed up. I don't like people fussin' over me, 'cept for your daddy. Cassie ain't been around for seven years. Why show up now?"

Wayne sat back in his chair. His expression was the same as Clement's when Mona had told him about Cassie's visit. "Did she say she'd be back?"

As if in response, the kettle screeched.

~

IN THE HALLWAY outside her bedroom, Mona could hear the hushed tones of an argument. The voices drifted in and out, or maybe that was just Mona. She was tired after all.

Sonia had only just arrived and was already irate. Wayne must have had told her about Mona's decision regarding the house, inspiring Sonia to march upstairs to confront her. Wayne had stopped her before she could wake Mona from her afternoon nap.

"Can you blame her?" Wayne whispered. "It's not like we're around for her. Clement's been taking care of the place for almost twenty years."

"I know that, Wayne. I was just hoping she would leave something for her grandchildren. My son's publisher cancelled his book series and his wife was laid off a month later. With three kids, they could've used the money from the sale of the house."

"Mom left something for all of us in her will, especially her grandchildren. I think she made the right decision with the house. It's less work for us. Look around, the town's fallen into depression. No one's buying here. This property would be a thorn in our side for God knows how long. Of course, you're more than welcome to talk her out of it once she wakes up."

"What's the point?" Sonia muttered. "You know we can never get through to her."

"Well, perhaps things could've turned out better if we'd been closer to her over the years. Before it was too late."

"This is no time for guilt trips."

"I'm just saying that we should have done better when we had the time instead of being embarrassed by—"

"Don't start with me, Wayne. I have enough regrets right now. I wasn't embarrassed by mom and dad. I was just different from them. We both were. We're a different generation. Speaking of which, Mom said Cassie showed up?"

"So she claimed."

"She's been dead for what, seven years? The two of them were never close to begin with, why would Cassie show up now?"

"Apparently, Cassie was aware that mom is dying and just wanted to make her comfortable in her final days. Of course, mom told her to get lost in typical Mona Bretton fashion."

"Skillet or meat tenderizer?"

"Rolling pin."

"She's getting soft in her old age."

Wayne paused. "I just want to stick around to see if Cassie comes back."

"If she does, you can deal with her. The thought of that gives me the creeps."

~

"Mona?"

She heard her name, barely louder than a whisper, and felt a gentle squeeze on her forearm. "Talbot?"

"No, it's Cassie."

Mona opened her eyes. It was a momentous effort. She wanted to lift her head from the pillow, but settled for turning it to one side. It was the most she could muster.

Cassie sat beside the bed gazing down at Mona with a warm smile. "Didn't think you'd get rid of me for too long, did ya?"

Mona's throat was dry. Attempts to speak launched a brief coughing fit that caused both body and bed to shudder. "Did Wayne let you up here?"

Her sister hesitated. "Well, he didn't try to stop me."

"I heard them out there talkin'. I knew Sonia would be... upset about the house."

"She'll get over it. Sonia's always been high strung. Everyone's going to be fine. Don't you worry about a thing."

"I feel weak, shaky. Can't move. My arms and legs... so heavy."

Cassie squeezed her arm. "I know."

"Yeah, you always do." Mona let her eyes close. "Where's Talbot?"

Again, Cassie paused. "Downstairs."

"With Wayne?"

"Yes, with Wayne."

"And Sonia?"

"Yes, Mona. The family's all here."

"Clement..."

"Here, ma'am." His voice came from... somewhere, but she couldn't see him. She couldn't see anything as gray faded to black.

"Cassie, I don't have the energy..."

"I know."

"I can't stay awake. I can't..."

"You don't have to," Cassie whispered.

MONA RESTED her head on his forearm, staring up at the violet impatiens in the hanging basket swaying in the spring breeze. She turned to look at her husband as the porch swing glided back and forth. A gust ruffled his thick black hair. Talbot smiled at her, young as the day they were married. On the table beside them, four glasses surrounded a pitcher of lemonade. *Four?*

"The kids?"

"Over here, Mom."

Mona lifted her head to see Wayne and Sonia, neither of them older than thirty, seated in the wicker chairs on the other side of the front door. Wayne's better half, Tanya, sat on his lap sipping from her glass. All was as it should be.

"How are you feeling?" Talbot asked.

Mona lifted a hand to her chest and ran a finger down the length of the silver cross. "Like I don't want to do anythin'."

"You don't have to. Not anymore. It's time to rest."

"Are you sure?"

"I have it on the highest authority."

Clement lowered Mona's arm to her side and slipped his fingers from her wrist. He hurried from the room and approached the head nurse, Bonnie.

"Mrs. Bretton's passed."

Bonnie held up a finger while her eyes scanned the computer screen at the nurse's station. Finally, she glanced up at him. "Mrs. Bretton, right." She turned her attention back to the computer. After another moment of typing and clicking, she nodded. "OK, why don't you gather her belongings into a box while I page Doctor Rapali."

Clement sighed. "Thanks."

"You all right?"

He hesitated, wondering whether his thoughts would be wasted on Bonnie. Death had become just another standard operating procedure here.

"Just yesterday she asked me to drive her to her lawyer to have her will changed. She wanted to leave me her house when she died. She thought I was still taking care of the place like I did when I was a kid. Didn't even remember I was her nurse. I drove her around the block a few times until she forgot why she was in the van."

"I know what she meant to you. You've known her for decades. It was sweet of you to indulge her since she's been here. You're a good friend for taking care of her funeral arrangements, too."

"She doesn't have anybody else. Her daughter died of leukemia five years ago and her son was killed in a plane crash last summer. If it weren't for all that, she'd probably still be going."

"I hope he's fussin' over you now." Clement drew the sheet up over Mona's body. He stopped as his eyes came to rest on the silver cross between her thumb and forefinger. "You deserve it. I have it on the highest authority."

This story first appeared in *Somewhere in the Middle of Eternity* (Firebringer Press, July 2014).

Bottom of the Hour

For the lucky ones, death carries them away as gently as a dandelion pappus on a spring breeze, while others suffer in prolonged agony before drawing that final, wheezing breath.

Regardless of how the Grim Reaper went about its macabre business, Victor Orologio could always hear it coming—just as he did one early summer day traveling aboard a crowded bus from Manhattan to Bethlehem, Pennsylvania.

As it had since Victor was ten, death announced its arrival with an incessant two-tone chime and a throbbing in his left temple. It was a sound much like the simple, repetitive alarm of a car's dashboard signaling an unbuckled seat belt. In Victor's case, it was a dulcet death knell for someone in close proximity and only ceased when the victim did.

And I was having such a good day. In his window seat near the back of the bus, Victor massaged the side of his head while casting surreptitious glances at the other passengers around him. *So which one of you will it be... and when? God, please let me get out of here before it happens.*

The bus jolted to a stop and inched toward the right lane.

Murmuring from the front drew Victor's attention to the window. State police cars, fire rescue, and an ambulance came into view in the left lane—followed by the smashed and twisted remains of a minivan.

As the scene crept past, Victor noticed the woman atop the stretcher—and he knew. *Shit.* While the pinging and pain intensified in his head, Victor watched the EMTs load her into the ambulance. *I'm sorry. I'm so sorry.* He wondered if anyone else had been in the van. Husband? Children? He would find out later when he searched online. *At least I won't need to save the obituaries this time.*

OUTSIDE THE BUS terminal in Bethlehem, Victor donned his sunglasses and surveyed the parking lot. It didn't take long to spot his best friend's 1971 Ford Maverick. It wasn't a car you see every day, and if one happened to cross your path, it usually stood out, especially with a dual color scheme of mustard and Bondo.

Victor opened the passenger door and climbed inside. The vinyl seat was cool to the touch. "You got the air working."

"Feels good, right?" In the driver's seat, Antonio "Toni" Herrera adjusted a set of levers to the left of the steering wheel. Cold air blasted from the vents. "Replaced the compressor this morning after I dropped you off. Wanted to get it done before this heat wave hits tomorrow."

Victor buckled in and leaned his head back with a sigh.

"Y'all right, man?" Toni asked as he pulled out of the parking space.

"Headache."

"Normal headache or oh-fuck-it-happened-again headache?"

"Accident on seventy-eight," Victor muttered. "I heard the

chime just before I saw one of the victims loaded into an ambulance. She's probably long gone by now."

They rode in morose silence for a few minutes before Toni spoke again. "So how did the sale go?"

Victor patted the check in his shirt pocket. "Couldn't have been smoother." Earlier that morning, he had traveled by bus and subway to Brooklyn to close on the sale of his late grandmother's house. The windfall left him with more than enough to assuage his financial worries for the next few years. "Maybe now I can finally buy a place out in the country." He waved a hand toward his ear. "It's maddening to be surrounded by so many people here, waking up every day wondering if this damn death detector is going to start ringing in my head."

"You do realize you'll need a car if you move out to the sticks, right?" Toni said. "You won't be able to take the bus everywhere like you do now, and I ain't drivin' all the way out there every time you need a ride."

"I'm not looking to move *that* far out. Just enough to give me some peace."

"Do you even have a current driver's license?"

"Of course I do."

"How? You've never had a car since I've known you."

"When it comes time to renew it, I take the bus to the photo center."

Toni laughed as he merged onto the freeway toward Allentown. "You take the bus to renew your driver's license. You realize how funny that sounds? So at one point, you learned how to drive."

"In my grandfather's Mustang, yes. I know how to drive. I just *prefer* not to. No car payments, no insurance premiums, no maintenance, none of that shit."

"Yeah, but now you got money. You can afford all that shit. So what kind of car you thinkin' about?"

"I don't know. Something nice, something with style. Something I can buy in cash."

"I got just what you need, man. I know a guy sellin' a slightly used but pristine Camaro with—"

Victor rolled his eyes. "No used cars, man. I'm not buying someone else's problems. When I said something nice, I meant *new.*"

Toni held up a hand. "Hear me out, bro. This car I'm talkin' about is perfect. It's a 2010 Imperial Blue Camaro LT with three hundred horsepower and only forty-two thousand miles. Garage-kept. I worked on this car personally, so I can vouch for its condition."

"And who owns it now?"

"An old dude named Hal Marx. We used to fix police cars together in Bethlehem. I'm tellin' you, man, this Camaro is badass."

"How much?"

"Only fifteen grand."

"If it's so badass, why's he selling it so cheap?"

Toni shrugged. "Hal's almost seventy, gonna retire next year. He don't have kids to inherit the car when he kicks, so he had to make a decision. It's a great deal. Come on, man, ain't no harm in lookin' at it, right?

~

TING-TING-TING-TING-TING-TING...

Mom had mentioned black ice before they left the house... or was it dad? Victor couldn't remember. All he knew was that his parents weren't speaking anymore—nor were they moving. Blood smeared the side of his mother's head. More on the front passenger window. From his vantage point, Victor couldn't see his father behind the wheel.

TING-ting-TING-ting-TING-ting...

Somehow, Victor was lying above the backseat. *Above it? No, below it.* The backseat was on top. He was at the bottom. The dome light was a few inches to his left. Outside, sleet pelted the van, tapping on glass, pinging off metal. Ignoring the throbbing in the left side of his head, Victor craned his neck to peer through the windshield. The world was upside down. He remembered now. They had hit ice on a sharp curve and Dad lost control. The van had slid sideways off the road before tumbling down a hill.

In the distance, sirens and air horns grew louder, yet couldn't drown out the persistent electronic chime from the dashboard.

TING-ting-TING-ting-TING-ting...

"Mom?" Victor croaked. He rolled onto his side, gripped her shoulder, tugged on her coat. She didn't respond. Panic took hold as Victor crawled between the front seats and shook his father's arm. "Dad? Dad, *please!*"

TING-ting-TING-ting-TING-ting...

Crying now, Victor slumped between the seats as the dimming gray sky flashed red and blue. Voices shouted. They came in through the rear passenger door. Hands gently tugged Victor from the car, placed him on a stretcher. Someone spoke to him, but he wasn't paying attention. All he could hear was the damn dashboard alarm, no matter how far they carried him from the wreckage.

TING-ting-TING-ting-TING-ting...

With a jolt, Victor sat up on his sofa and squinted at the TV. The main menu of a Blu-ray disc flashed a repeating loop of scenes from the movie he'd been watching when he dozed off. It was the only source of light in the otherwise dark apartment. With a sigh, he slid his hand along the cushion beside him until he found the remote and turned off the Blu-ray player and TV.

Victor rubbed his temples, tried to push the memory from

his mind. Yet the damn chime persisted. It was accompanied now by other noises—heavy-booted footsteps and scraping metal. Through the fading fog of sleep, Victor realized it was coming from the parking lot. He shot out of his seat and dashed to the sliding doors that opened to the balcony. He shoved aside the vertical blinds, followed by the glass and screen doors.

In the parking space directly below, the driver's side door of the Camaro was wide open. Since Victor had backed the car into the space, he could clearly distinguish a leg protruding from the driver's seat.

"Hey, get the hell out of my car, asshole!"

The leg shifted and a tall, bald black man climbed out. Victor raised an eyebrow. *Jeans and a leather coat in this weather?* The would-be thief made his way toward the rear of the Camaro and stood under the pale orange glow of a nearby lamppost. Victor leaned forward to get a better look at his face —or would have had it not been drenched in blood from what looked like a bullet hole in the middle of his forehead.

Victor pushed away from the railing as the dude raised a chrome plated semi-automatic pistol. "That ain't your car, white boy!"

"Shit!" Victor dove back into his apartment, knees smacking the edge of the screen door, dislodging it from its tracks and sending it crashing to the deck.

But there was no gunfire and the death knell in his head faded into silence. After a moment, Victor sat up and peered through the spindles of the balcony railing. He could see the Camaro. All of its doors were closed. There was no sign of the bloody car thief. *So why did I hear the chime?*

Victor crept back outside. The parking lot was devoid of life. Roused by the commotion, a few neighbors along the front of the building emerged, but Victor ignored them as he picked up the screen door and leaned it against the side railing.

He ducked back into his apartment and snatched his phone from the coffee table. It was just after one thirty in the morning. Victor drew a long, deep breath as his thoughts raced to catch up with the events of the past five minutes. *Why did I let Toni talk me into a Camaro? He was right. The car's flawless, but now it's a target. Should have bought a house with a garage first. Only had this car two days and some douche bag tries to boost it. And why didn't the friggin' alarm go off?*

After walking out to inspect the Camaro, Victor brought in a chair from the balcony. He closed the sliding door, but left the vertical blinds open and sat in the dark. By the time he nodded off, it was nearly dawn. After all, he didn't dare fall asleep while a car thief was still out there, lurking in the night.

The following day, Victor winced as he rolled his shopping cart out of the air-conditioned supermarket and into the sweltering soup of the summer's first heat wave. *And it's only 10 a.m.* Ahead of him, a plump, rubescent elderly woman in a sleeveless flowered muumuu pulled four bulging tote bags out of her cart and started toward the parking lot. The moment he saw her, the chime began ringing in his head. *Damn it, not again...* He started after the woman, fearing she might give up the ghost any second.

She'd barely waddled three steps when the handle on one of her bags snapped. "Oh hell."

As Victor approached, she set her burdens down on the pavement, struggling to find the best way to deal with the problem.

"Ma'am, can I help you get your bags to your car?" Victor offered.

"Oh, thank you, no." The woman smiled, despite the

streams of sweat streaking her ruddy face. "I'm actually going to the bus stop. It should be here in the next hour or so."

"In this heat? Ma'am, it's got to be over ninety-five degrees."

"I can manage. It wouldn't be the first time."

"How about I give you a ride home? I promise I'm not a crazy person out to hurt anybody. I would just feel terrible letting you wait in this heat. I know the buses don't run often on Sundays."

"Well, I don't want to be any trouble..."

"It's no trouble, ma'am." *Maybe this time, I can finally save one of you.* He extended a hand. "My name's Victor."

"I'm Annette. My friends call me Netty. Thank you so much for your help. I normally don't go grocery shopping on a Sunday, but my son is coming home this week. He's been away for a while and I want to cook him a nice meal."

Victor pushed his bags to the back of his cart. Once Netty's were loaded, they made their way across the parking lot to the Camaro.

"Oh, my, look at this car," Netty said. "My son would love something like this."

"Thank you." Victor opened the passenger door for her. After loading the groceries in the trunk and returning the cart, he climbed into the driver's seat and cranked up the air. Netty had already buckled herself in.

"It's just as immaculate on the inside," she marveled. "Although your time is off by a few hours."

Victor frowned as he looked at the radio in the center console. Sure enough, the clock displayed 1:30. "Huh, didn't even notice that. Well, I'll fix it later. If that's the worst problem with this car, I can live with it."

~

He found it four days later. From his laptop screen, a picture of Annette Terro smiled back at him. "I'm so sorry," he whispered before sending her obituary to the printer. She had died the morning after he'd brought her home. He should have known. The chime had continued for several minutes after he'd dropped her, helped her with her bags, and pulled away. Still, he'd held out hope.

Victor stood and pulled a three-inch ring binder from the top shelf of the bookcase. He opened it and stared for a moment at the first page. *Ten days already?* Craig Breyer had been a co-worker in the Receiving department. Victor had heard the chime while working with him and about eight other people sorting shipments on the loading dock. By the end of that week, Victor had silently apologized to Craig's closed coffin.

He pulled Annette's obituary from the printer and read it over one last time. "Survived by her son, Geoff," he muttered. *My son is coming home this week. He's been away for a while and I want to cook him a nice meal...*

"Sorry, Geoff. I tried to save her." Victor slipped the paper into the electric three-hole punch before adding it to his collection. He flipped through the pages, the years, the faces, recalling the first time he showed the binder to Toni shortly after he'd revealed his ability.

"That binder looks heavy, bro."

Victor snapped the rings shut after adding the latest entry. "You have no idea."

"It's like the Grim Reaper's scrapbook."

"But I'm not the Grim Reaper."

"Then why do you save their obituaries?"

"Because I couldn't save them*," Victor replied. "Sometimes, I hear the chime in a crowd of people and I don't even know who it's for. Sometimes I hear it when it's too late to do anything. But there are other times when I know who it's going to be and I try*

to save the person... but nothing I do ever matters. Those are the ones I keep in this binder."

"I don't know how you stay sane with that ability."

Victor shrugged. "To be honest, I was already used to it by the time I got to high school."

"How the hell do you get used to hearin' death? That shit would creep me out, man. Though not as creepy as savin' obituaries."

"I don't have a choice. Not like I can turn it off. Believe me, I've tried. Pills, therapy, booze, you name it."

"Well, if you hear it when my time comes, you will *let me know, right? At least give me a fightin' chance."*

"What are friends for?"

Toni pointed to the binder. "You know, their deaths weren't your fault. By keepin' that thing, you're only torturin' yourself, man. You need to let that shit go. It ain't healthy."

Victor snapped the binder closed, bringing his focus back to the present. "I wish I could, amigo." He looked up at the clock on the wall. *Time for a swim.*

ANOTHER DAY of sweltering temperatures meant a few laps in the complex's indoor pool before work. The usual horde of screaming kids and self-absorbed parents congregated near the shallow end, leaving the deeper side to Victor and a raven-haired twenty-something with a body that absolutely deserved to be flaunted in the two-piece, baby-blue bikini that matched the color of her eyes.

This was one of those occasions when Victor was grateful he'd kept himself in shape. He might never have six-pack abs, but his stomach was flat and his limbs toned thanks to his workout regimen and the fact that his warehouse job kept him on the move most of the day.

As she climbed out of the water and started toward him, Victor realized that he'd seen her before at one of the other buildings. He smiled and aimed a thumb toward the opposite end of the pool. "If only I could put up a wall to block off that racket."

She rolled her eyes. "Tell me about it. Some of those kids are my neighbors. I can't get away from them."

"Wait, did you just move into Building A last week?"

She shifted her weight and looked away for a moment. "Uh, yeah. Why?"

"I thought you looked familiar, and now I remember seeing you on one of my runs. We almost collided while you were unloading stuff from a van."

Her eyes widened as she let out a short laugh. Victor felt something quiver deep in his chest. *Keep it cool, dude. Don't screw this up.*

"Oh, my God, that's right. I'm sorry. I didn't recognize you. That day was a blur of activity."

"Moving usually is." He extended a hand. "I'm Victor."

She accepted the gesture with a tepid grip. "Erica. So, do you run every day?"

Victor nodded. "As long as the weather cooperates—which is why a swim seemed like a better idea today. When the temps climb above ninety, I'm in the water. I work nights, so I usually run midmorning, between nine and ten."

"Gotcha. Well, as it happens, I'm off from work this week and there's a storm coming tonight that's supposed to cool things down. So if you decide to run tomorrow and wouldn't mind a partner..."

Victor shrugged. *That's right, not too eager.* "Sure. That would be great."

"And if it doesn't cool off," she waved toward the pool, "maybe I'll see you back here."

He smiled. "Sounds like a plan."

"Where's your apartment?"

"Oh, uh, Building C, number six. Second floor."

"Great, well, you obviously know where I live. If you don't knock by ten, I'll swing by your place."

"Sounds... like a plan." *You already said that, idiot!* By now, Victor knew he was grinning like a fool, but didn't care.

"Speaking of running, I have to take care of some errands." She scooped up her towel and keys from a nearby chaise lounge. "But I'll see you tomorrow, Victor."

As he watched her leave, Victor realized that he was gawking like a teenager, but still didn't care. *Did she just ask me out... sort of? This summer just keeps getting hotter. Money, car, possible new girlfriend. All within a week! Is this happening or am I dreaming? One way to find out...*

Taking a deep breath, Victor ran to the edge of the pool and plunged in.

ON THE FINAL stretch of their morning run, they rounded the corner of Building C, separating to avoid a puddle in the middle of the parking lot from the previous night's storm.

"Hey." Victor slowed to a stop, sweat dripping from his nose and chin. He nodded toward his Camaro. "Check out... my new wheels. Well... new to me."

Erica leaned forward, hands on her knees. "That's yours?"

Victor nodded. "Camaro LT. Seven years old... only forty-two thousand miles."

She made her way over to the car. "My ex-husband... would've loved to get his hands on this."

Victor wheezed out a laugh. "Funny... I met an old lady at the... supermarket a few days ago. She said the same thing... about her son. So, uh, how long were you married, if you don't mind my asking?"

"Too long. It was three years of my life I'll never get back and would rather forget. He's the reason I moved here. Didn't want him to find me when he got out on parole."

"Parole?"

"Two days ago." Erica waved off his obvious concern. "Don't worry, he's not a murderer or anything. He used to steal cars for parts. Hence my comment about how he'd love your Camaro. I didn't find out until the dumbass got arrested. Anyway, that's behind me now. I'm starting over. Congrats on the ride. It's a beauty."

"Well, if you want to go out sometime, just let me know." Victor snapped his fingers. "Hey, what are you doing Saturday night?"

Erica thought for a moment. "I should be available after seven. I'm visiting my sister in the afternoon. What did you have in mind?"

After his fourth consecutive win at the Water Gun Shoot-Out, Victor eyed the top prizes as Erica nibbled on funnel cake beside him. It was the final night of the county fair. Victor had wanted to do something different from the standard dinner and movie date and had been thrilled when Erica agreed. She pointed at a row of boxed toy cars, one of which was a dark blue Camaro. "You should get that."

"Meh. I already got the real thing."

"That ain't your car, white boy!"

Victor drew himself up as if someone had shoved an ice pack under his shirt. "Did you hear that?"

Erica swallowed a bit of funnel cake. "Hear what?"

"That voice..."

"Which one? There's a bazillion people here."

"Hey buddy." The carny running the game leaned over as new players began taking seats. "Make up your mind yet?"

"Uh, yeah. Sorry." Victor shot a sidelong glance at Erica. "You like pandas?"

"Love pandas."

Victor pointed toward the back corner. Erica laughed as the carny returned with a life-size plush panda and handed it to Victor, who, in turn, passed it to Erica in exchange for the rest of the funnel cake. She wiped her hands on her shorts before throwing her arms around it. "How are we going to get this in your car?"

IN THE PASSENGER SEAT, Erica was all but completely buried beneath the black and white behemoth in her lap. Victor checked the rearview mirror before flooring the accelerator along an empty stretch of highway. "Comfortable over there?"

Erica rested her head on the panda's back. "It's like having a massive fuzzy air bag in your face. Although it's comfortable to snuggle with."

"Oh, I think I could give it a run for its money." Victor flashed a lopsided grin—which vanished the moment he glanced over at her. Erica and the panda were gone. Instead, a dark, bloody face stared back.

From the car's sound system, the death knell blared like a klaxon.

"Who the hell *are* you?" Victor demanded.

"Don't get too attached, white boy." The man raised his right hand, leveling a chrome-plated pistol at Victor. "She don't belong to you."

Victor slammed the brakes.

Tires screeched.

The gun fired.

And Victor awoke with a yelp. He found himself doubled over on his side facing his alarm clock. *One thirty. Always one thirty.* Once the pain in his head subsided, he forced himself out of bed and stood at the window overlooking the parking lot. The Camaro was exactly where he'd parked it after dropping Erica off at her flat. Victor lowered himself to the floor and sat against the wall, cradling his head in his hands. *It's just new car jitters. Gonna buy that house in the country and get out of here. Better times are ahead. Just breathe and think about Erica... think about Erica... think about Erica...*

~

It was after 2 a.m. when Victor arrived home following another night of overtime. He opened the car door with a weary shove and climbed out just as a blur of motion caught his eye. In the gap between the buildings, flashing red and blue lights danced across pale brick walls. *Now what...*

Victor walked around to the front lot for a better view. At the opposite end of the complex, an ambulance and two patrol cars were parked in front of Building A. Victor watched for a moment before turning back. *Probably one of the elderly residents. Wouldn't be the first time.*

Still, it was Erica's building. Maybe she was awake through the commotion. As he made his way toward the scene, Victor wasn't surprised to see all the spectators out on their balconies and several more gathered on the sidewalk in front of the building. Yet, Erica was not among them.

Instead, Victor found her lying on the concrete patio below her balcony, surrounded by the ambulance crew.

"Oh, Christ. Erica!" he sidestepped the onlookers, only to be intercepted by two cops.

The stout male officer stood directly in his path. "Need you to stay back, sir."

Victor held up both hands as words tumbled out. "I'm her boyfriend. I just got home from work. I live in Building C. What happened? Is she alive?"

"She's alive," the female officer assured him. "Can we see some ID, please?" Victor pulled out his wallet and handed over his driver's license. "She fell from the balcony about thirty minutes ago. Neighbors reported hearing a scream and sounds of a struggle, so they called it in."

"Does she have family in the area?" her partner asked.

Victor nodded, his gaze fixed on Erica as the ambulance crew lifted her onto the stretcher. *Thirty minutes ago. That would be about one thirty...* "She has a sister, but I don't know her number. You mentioned a struggle. Was there someone else in her apartment? She told me her ex-husband just got out on parole and—"

"We can't tell you that." The female officer finished jotting his information in her notepad and handed his license back. "We need to talk to her family first."

Victor sighed. "Can you at least tell me what hospital they're taking her to?"

"Saint Mark's."

~

She fell from the balcony about thirty minutes ago...

In the waiting room at St. Mark's ER, Victor sat bouncing his fist against his thigh. It was a nervous habit he'd picked up as a kid. Right now, it did little to soothe his anxiety. "One thirty... *again*. I don't get it."

He peered through the window as a black car pulled into a space across the narrow lot. Beneath the streetlight, a slim woman in white shorts, flip-flops, and a dark tank top stepped out and hurried through the rain toward the double doors. Although she appeared slightly older, her resemblance to Erica was unmistakable. Still, Victor waited until she approached the front desk and introduced herself as Rhonda Daykin.

"My sister, Erica, was brought in here about forty-five minutes ago."

"Okay, ma'am. Please have a seat in the waiting room and I'll get the nurse to come out and bring you back."

Victor stood and made his way over.

"Excuse me, Rhonda?" he extended a hand. "My name is Victor. I'm a friend of Erica's. I live in the same complex."

"Oh, right... yeah, she talks about you all the time. What happened to her?"

Victor shook his head. "I don't know yet. I showed up after the ambulance was already there."

"Swear to God, if I find out it was her ex, I'll snap that little bastard's neck."

Four hours and numerous cups of coffee later, a nurse stepped out into the waiting room and led them to a small office. "I'll take you back to see your sister shortly," she began. "But I wanted to bring you up to speed on her condition. Erica had some minor brain swelling so the doctor performed what's called an EVD, or an external ventricular drain, to relieve some of the pressure. We now have her on an IV of anti-inflammatories and antiseizure meds. The swelling and pressure have diminished. So we're moving in the right direction, but now we wait.

"The police said she fell off a balcony. We found no traces of alcohol or drugs in her system—"

"You wouldn't," Rhonda and Victor said in unison.

"She lives a healthy lifestyle," Rhonda added.

"So, was this a freak accident, or did someone push her off the balcony?"

"Her ex-husband just got out on parole," Rhonda replied.

"She moved to get away from him. I can't say for sure he was there. The police thought Erica was alone." She looked at Victor.

He shrugged. "I was on my way home from work at the time." *But something tells me she wasn't alone...*

VICTOR BOLTED through the double doors of the hospital and paced back and forth in front of the building, phone pressed against the side of his head. The rain had diminished to a welcome cool drizzle. "Hey, Toni, it's Victor."

"What's going on, bro? How's that Camaro?"

"That's why I'm calling. I need your help. Do you think you can track down who owned it before your buddy Hal?"

"Maybe. Why?"

"Remember when I said I didn't want to buy someone else's problems?"

"What's wrong with the car?"

Victor stopped pacing and tilted his head back to work a knot out of his neck. "The car's fine, but I've been having some weird experiences since I got it."

"Like what?"

"I'll explain later. I can't even think straight right now. I just spent the night in the ER with Erica."

"She okay?"

"She took a fall outside her apartment last night and hit her head. Now she's in a coma."

Toni paused. "Aw, damn, dude. I'm sorry. Anything I can do?"

"Find out who owned the Camaro before Hal. You're tight with the Bethlehem cops right? You used to work on their cars. If I text you the VIN number, can you ask around? Maybe you'll come up with a name. This is serious, Toni."

"All right, bro. I'll see what I can do. Hang in there."

It took Toni three agonizing days to find the name—and much more. It was Friday night, and Victor had offered to buy pizza and beer on his way back from the hospital. They met at Victor's apartment.

"Turns out the Camaro used to belong to a gang member named Brian Gless," Toni began. "He lived out in Reading. One night about five years ago, he caught some dude trying to boost the car, so he pulled a gun, but the other guy must have drawn faster. He shot Gless in the head before runnin' away. Bro was dead before the ambulance arrived.

"They never found his killer, but the cops did find meth stashed under the carpet in the trunk of the Camaro, so they impounded the car. Turns out Gless had been sellin' for a local dealer. Hal must have bought the car from a police auction or somethin'."

Victor slipped a slice of pizza out of the box. "Did you happen to find out what Gless looked like?"

"Yeah, they showed me a picture. Tall, bald black dude with a goatee."

That's got to be the guy. Though Victor didn't recall the goatee. *Must have been concealed by all the blood.* "Last question. Did your source mention what time he died?"

"Accordin' to what I was told, it all went down around one thirty in the morning. Now, you gonna tell me what's goin' on?"

Victor slumped back in his chair and rubbed his eyes. *That explains it. What the hell do I do now?* "You're not going to believe the shit that's been happening."

"Like what?"

Victor took a sip of beer and launched into the events of the past week leading up to Erica's injury.

After he was finished, Toni gaped at him. "Dayum, bro. Hal never said anything about this. So you think this dude's ghost is hauntin' his old car?"

Victor shrugged. "I have more questions than answers. If Gless's ghost has been attached to the Camaro this whole time, why wait until now to show himself? Why fuck up *my* life? I had nothing to do with his death."

"What about Erica?"

Victor shook his head. "No way, dude. Don't even go there."

"Then why would Gless attack her? That is, if we believe there really *is* a ghost behind all this."

"There's no way in hell Erica would've been involved in murder. It has to be someone else."

"Like who?"

IT WAS NEARLY midnight on Saturday when he heard the chime. Victor stopped fumbling with his keys outside his apartment and leaned against the door. *Damn it, just stop.* He knew someone in the building wouldn't live long enough to see the sunrise. That narrowed it down to about twenty people. *I can never save any of them, so why should I worry about it? God, please just give me one decent night's sleep.*

Victor pushed away from the door, struck by the possibility that Gless was saving him for last and that this time, the death knell clanging in his head might be his own. Fully alert now, he unlocked the door and darted inside. *Maybe I should have stayed at the hospital until morning.* As the pinging grew louder, Victor flipped the light switch—and froze.

He saw the gun first, by the light that glinted off its chrome barrel. Across the room, half-hidden in shadow and straddling a dining room chair, the man merely stared at Victor. His trimmed, frizzy beard wrapped around his lean face like a black chinstrap attached to either end of his red baseball cap. He was dressed for the season in a gray t-shirt and cargo shorts. One thing was certain—the guy was too white and too short to be Brian Gless. So the question was...

"Who the hell are you?"

"Funny, I was going to ask you the same question." The guy waved his pistol toward the sofa. "Sit down."

"Whatever you want, just take it and get out of here."

"I want answers, asshole. Now sit down and we'll have a quiet chat. Hands out where I can see 'em and don't even think about reachin' for your phone. What's your name?"

"Victor."

"Victor what?"

"Orologio."

The guy snickered. "What kind of fucked up name is that?"

"Italian."

"Oh, paisano, eh? You know who I am?"

Victor shook his head.

"No? Well, that's surprising since you've been dickin' around in my life for the past week. You see, Victor, I got out of prison last Wednesday, but the night before my parole hearing, my mother died of a heart attack. So, I'm at her funeral, and I hear that on the morning before she passed, this nice young man in a dark blue Camaro drove her home from the grocery store. Now, I didn't think much of it at the time.

"Then I came to this apartment complex a few days ago to see my ex-wife, Erica. Maybe you know her? I was hoping to reconcile—convince her to take me back and start our life over

—until I find out that she's at the hospital in a coma. So I start asking around and guess what I'm told. My ex started dating some guy two buildings over and he drives a dark blue Camaro, too. What are the odds?"

"You're Geoff Terro."

"I guess Erica told you about me."

"She said you were a car thief."

Terro leveled the gun at Victor. "And who are you, the fuckin' Grim Reaper? What the hell did you do to my mother and my ex-wife?"

Victor held up his hands. "Nothing. I swear to God. It's the car."

"What car?"

"The Camaro! Look, man, I bought it from an old guy last week and ever since then, I've been having dreams and visions that someone's trying to steal it. Same guy every time, a tall black dude with a bullet hole in his forehead and blood running down his face. So I asked a friend to look up the original owner of the car. Turns out, he's exactly the guy I keep seeing in the dream. Five years ago, a small time drug dealer named Brian Gless caught someone trying to steal his Camaro. He pulled a gun to scare him off, but the other guy shot him in the head."

"Gless." Terro's eyes glazed over as he flexed his fingers over the gun's grip.

Was that recognition in Terro's voice? "Yeah, he owned the Camaro before the old guy who sold it to me, and every time I've seen Gless, it's one thirty in the morning—which was the time he died. Get this, man. Every time I start the Camaro, the clock on the dash resets to one thirty. I gave up trying to change it. I'm telling you, that car is haunted. Everyone who rides in it ends up dead or close to it."

"Bullshit." Terro snarled, but doubt seemed to erode his

conviction. "One thirty in the morning," he muttered. "That's when my mother died."

When Victor spoke again, he adopted a softer tone. "I'm sorry for your loss, man. That's also the time when Gless's ghost attacked Erica. I guarantee you, she didn't just fall off a balcony."

Terro nodded. "So, in these dreams, does Gless say anything?"

"Yeah. He says, 'that ain't your car, white boy.'"

At that, Terro leapt to his feet and began pacing the length of the living room, back and forth in front of Victor. "Shit, that's exactly what he said when..."

"When what?" Victor pressed. "You starting to believe me now?" His eyes shot open as he shifted in his seat. "Oh shit, *you* killed Gless. That's the only way this makes sense. This all started around the time you got out of jail. *Your* mother, *your* ex—"

Terro's head snapped up. He moved toward the sofa, gun leveled at Victor's head. "Shut the fuck up. We're going for a ride, just you and me, paisano. You drive."

Twenty minutes later, they were well beyond the city limits. Dense woods and cornfields whipped past on both sides of the highway.

"Slow down." In the passenger seat, Terro waved his gun toward the right side of the road. "Pull into the open field just after these trees."

The throbbing in Victor's temples grew sharper now as he turned the Camaro off the road onto the edge of the field. The chime had become a strident, piercing clamor in his head, louder than he'd ever experienced before.

"Further in," Terro said.

Victor couldn't help but think he was driving to his own funeral. He risked a glance at his watch. Five minutes after one. For a moment, pain and exhaustion overcame fear as Victor stopped the car in the middle of the field. "Why the hell are we out here? We meeting someone?"

With a grin, the little bastard raised his pistol. "Maybe. Get out."

Both men climbed out of the Camaro into dank and humid darkness broken only by the stark glow of the full moon. Victor backed away from the car and massaged a pressure point between his thumb and forefinger in an attempt to ease the pain in his head. Of course, that didn't silence the incessant pinging. "Now what?"

"Now we see if your ghost story is true." Terro raised his gun as he hurried toward Victor. "Give me the keys, and don't even think about running away."

Victor handed them over. As he slipped the keys into the pocket of his cargo shorts, Terro turned his attention to the Camaro. "Hey, Gless! I'm sick of hearin' your name. Sick of replayin' that night in my head for the past five years. I wouldn't have shot you if you didn't draw first, asshole. You took my mother. You tried to kill my wife. Well, I'm standing right here, douche bag!"

Victor held up a hand. "Dude, I don't think that's a good idea."

"Maybe you're right, paisano. Here's a better way to get his attention." Terro opened fire, shattering the driver's side window.

"What the hell are you doing?" Victor shouted.

"Come on, Gless! You love this car so much?" The maniac circled the Camaro, blasting out every window.

"Stop shooting up—"

Victor's words were drowned by a bullet that struck the car's frame. A spark flashed along the far edge of the roof, then... silence.

As if from the Camaro itself, a gelid breeze tore through Victor, chilling the sweat on his forehead and carrying a voice barely louder than a whisper. "That ain't your car, white boy."

Victor suppressed a shiver. "Dude, you still over there?"

There was no response. Even the chime had ceased.

He pulled his phone from his belt holster and tapped the flashlight app as he made his way around the Camaro. He spotted the legs first. Victor moved the light along Terro's prone form until he saw the blood seeping from a bullet hole in his forehead. Something glinted in the light beside the body. Victor leaned over and snatched up his keys.

He aimed his phone at the car. *There's no way in hell a shot could have ricocheted like that unless...*

As if in response to his thought, the Camaro's lights flashed on and a DJ's voice blared from the radio. "It's one thirty a.m., bottom of the hour on your Sunday morning. Five-day forecast on the way brought to you by Trover Dodge on the Lehigh Street Auto Mile. If your old car is shot, consider trading it in at Trover."

I'm not saving that bastard's obituary. I can't believe Erica was married to that. It was nearly four o'clock when Victor trudged into his apartment drenched in sweat after walking for over two hours in unbearable humidity. He peeled off his work clothes on the way to the bathroom. Under a cool shower, he leaned against the wall and closed his eyes.

After a quick nap, Victor would call the cops and insurance company and report his car as stolen. For the next few days, he would take the bus to work. When the cops finally found the Camaro—and the little prick lying dead beside it—they'd consider the area a crime scene and probably impound the car again for who knows how long.

They can have it. My fingerprints won't be on the gun. I'm in the clear. Victor no longer cared. Only one person mattered now.

No sooner had he stepped out of the bathroom than he heard the muffled buzzing. Victor charged out of the room and yanked his phone from the pile of clothes on the living room floor. He glanced at the screen and took a deep breath before answering. "Hey, Rhonda..."

THE CHIME STARTED the moment he stepped off the elevator. Victor charged down the corridor, weaving past nurses and patients until he bounded into Erica's room.

"Did you hear that bell?" Rhonda asked.

Lying in bed, Erica opened her eyes and grinned up at Victor. "Yeah, I did."

"Wait." Victor held up a hand. "You both heard that?"

"Of course, whenever a baby's born, the hospital plays a little jingle over the PA system." Rhonda rose from her seat. "I kept it warm for you. I'm going to catch a smoke and give you kids some alone time." She frowned at Victor. "You okay? You look like a deer in the headlights."

"Let's not talk about cars, please."

"Whatever you say. Back in a few."

Victor lowered himself into the chair beside Erica's bed. "Welcome back, gorgeous."

She returned a wan smile. "To the land of the living. Sorry if I sound raspy. I don't have my voice back yet. My sister said you were here every day."

From his seat beside her hospital bed, Victor took her hand in his. "Where else would I be? I missed you. So did the panda. He wanted me to tell you."

"Panda? Oh, right." Erica chuckled then winced. "Hurts to laugh, or turn my head for too long. They said I cracked my collarbone in addition to the bump on my brain. Could've been worse, right? Better than breaking my neck."

"You'll be up and running before you know it. Just take your time. I'll be with you every step of the way."

She squeezed his hand, but remained silent. Victor shifted his gaze to the window, unsure of how to broach the unspoken topic that couldn't be avoided. Erica saved him the trouble.

"What the hell happened to me, Victor?" Her voice cracked as she struggled to maintain her composure. "I was sound asleep in bed until someone I couldn't see grabbed me by the hair and dragged me out to the living room." She paused to breathe as tears streaked down the side of her face, becoming lost in her matted hair. "I don't think I'll ever forget watching the sliding doors open by themselves before I was hurled out to the balcony like a rag doll. I remember slamming into the railing and just sitting there in a daze.

"Then it was like two giant, invisible hands around my throat lifting me up. I couldn't breathe. My feet were off the deck... and I don't remember anything after that. But there was no one there. It wasn't a person, Victor. It was like something out of a ghost story. I don't know what I'm going to tell the cops when—"

"It *was* a ghost," he said.

She glared at him. "Are you telling me those apartments are haunted?"

Victor shook his head. "No. It wasn't your apartment that was haunted. We need to talk about your ex-husband..."

. . .

Four Months Later

"Don't lift anything too heavy."

"Victor, I'm fine." Erica pulled the first box from the back of the pickup. "Where do you want this?"

"In the dining room. Anywhere you can find space. Thanks."

No sooner had she disappeared into the rustic two story stone home, than the Maverick roared to a stop inches from the truck's bumper.

Victor folded his arms as Toni emerged. "You're late."

"Overslept."

"Is that code for hung over?"

"Man, why you gotta be like that?"

Victor shook his head and rummaged through one of the boxes in the truck until he found what he was looking for.

"Okay, I'm sorry I wasn't at your apartment to help you move out, but at least I showed up here to help you move into this awesome house." Toni nodded toward the pickup. "New wheels?"

"*Brand* new... as in no previous owners and a lot more practical for living out here. Nothing against the Camaro. It was a sweet ride, just wasn't meant to be."

"Speaking of livin' out here, how's Erica takin' all this? You won't be able to see each other as often."

"She's fine with it. She loves the house. For the time being, we decided to trade off spending weekends at each other's places and if everything works out, she'll move in with me when her lease expires."

Toni pointed to the binder in Victor's hands. "Does she know about that?"

Victor shook his head. "And she never will." He nodded toward the backyard and led Toni to a rusted metal barrel into which Victor dumped twenty years of obituaries. He picked up a plastic gas can beside the barrel and handed it to Toni. "Care to do the honors?"

"What are friends for?"

~

This story first appeared in *A Plague of Shadows* (Smart Rhino Publications, October 2018).

Take a Cue from the Canine

Huddled inside the cramped compartment of the roll top desk, Joel flinched as the beagle scratched and pawed at the antique wood slats. "Rusty, no." He ran a soothing hand over the dog's belly. "It's gonna be okay. We just need to be quiet for a little longer."

Joel knew his best friend was not only scared, but probably still in pain. Resting his head against the hard surface, Joel tried to ignore his own set of freshly inflicted bruises.

A liquid lunch had cost Uncle Larry yet another job, sparking his worst whiskey-fueled rampage in months. Joel's attempts to calm him had been rewarded with the usual beating, but the confrontation had turned life-threatening after Larry kicked Rusty across the living room and pulled out a sawed-off shotgun from beneath the couch. When he'd stood up too quickly and toppled backward—blasting a hole in the ceiling—Joel snatched up Rusty and fled across the yard to the garage.

Ten minutes had passed since then. *Maybe he's too wasted to come after us.*

The slamming of a door told him otherwise.

"Get out here, boy! You and that damn dog ain't nothin' but a burden to me. If it wasn't for takin' care of you, I could've—" The crack of wood followed by the shatter of glass told Joel that his uncle was stumbling along the far side of the garage.

"Damn it! Look what you made me do. I was gonna sell that. Sonna bitch. You'll pay for—" Larry drew in a sharp breath and launched into a bout of violent coughing. Joel closed his eyes, hoping the bastard would die on the spot. "You... make me hunt for you in here, boy, and... swear to God... you'll join your mother."

The heavy footfalls of Larry's work boots drew near until a shadow passed along the thin band of stark white light beneath the tambour door, inches from boy and dog. The shadow halted. Joel hugged Rusty close and counted the seconds by the throbbing in his temples. *Keep walking... Please, keep walking.*

The shadow disappeared. Joel allowed nearly a full minute to pass before risking a sigh. His relief was short-lived. With a yelp, Rusty shoved his snout into the narrow gap. The flexible door creaked and groaned against the pressure.

Somewhere in the garage, boot soles scraped against concrete. "You think you're so smart."

A thundercrack rocked the desk. Rusty howled and thrashed in the compartment. It had been a warning shot. There was no sense hiding any longer. Joel imagined himself lying in a pool of his own blood before the night was over. *But maybe Rusty can get away.* Reaching over the terrified dog, Joel slipped his fingers under the door and lifted it slowly, expecting to be greeted by the twin barrels of a sawed-off shotgun.

As Rusty skittered off the desk to the floor, Joel shielded

his eyes and inhaled the cool, fresh air. When his vision adjusted, there was no shotgun in his face. No Uncle Larry. No garage.

Instead, Joel gazed at a distant horizon dominated by the undulating waves of a vast sea that sparkled beneath the hazy glow of a setting sun. All of this was revealed through three enormous arched windows that spanned floor to ceiling directly across the room.

Joel unfolded himself from the compartment and sat on the edge of the desk, taking in the strange surroundings. Nearly every inch of wall space was consumed by bookcases fully stocked with hardcovers and paperbacks. To his left, Rusty had curled up on one of two high-backed chairs facing a blazing brick hearth. Joel nearly ordered him off but thought better of it. *If he's comfortable there, he'll stay out of trouble.* Off to his right, a softly ticking grandfather clock stood between two mahogany doors that led to parts unknown.

Yet it was the view beyond the windows that captivated Joel. As he approached them, he realized that he was on the second floor of—wherever this was—and that the ocean lay far below a grassy plateau mottled with trees and teeming with wild animals of every variety. Sprightly primates scaled branches with graceful aplomb while giraffes leisurely gnawed on tree tops. Below them, a group of pandas rolled and frolicked among scurrying foxes and stolid rhinos as a family of elephants lumbered by. Among this perplexing menagerie, there stood no fences or barricades of any kind.

"What is this place?" Joel muttered.

"An animal sanctuary, of course."

Joel whirled at the unfamiliar voice, his gaze darting around the room until he noticed the steady puffs of smoke rising from the closest of the two high-backed chairs. From his vantage point, it was impossible to see the occupant but rather than approach the stranger, Joel kept his distance. He hurried across the room to the other chair where Rusty remained firmly entrenched. At the sight of Joel, the recumbent beagle's brown and white tail tapped a gleeful tattoo against the upholstered seat.

"Man's best friend." Joel folded his arms. "You could've warned me someone else was here." He motioned for the dog to move. "Let's go, off the furniture."

"He seems content where he is." In the other chair, a middle-aged man leaned forward and removed a curled ebony pipe from beneath an enormous handlebar mustache, made even more striking by the fact that there was no other hair on his head. "No need for apprehension, young man. You're safe here. This is a sanctuary of life. Take a cue from your canine and relax. I'm Finley, the caretaker, at your service."

Joel sat on the edge of the chair, but his arms remained folded across his chest. "I'm Joel. This is Rusty."

"Welcome to my home."

"You *live* here?"

Finley nodded. "Along with my wife and innumerable creatures of land, sea, and air."

"How large is this sanctuary?"

"As large as it needs to be."

"What does that mean?"

"You'd have to see it for yourself."

"I'm not even sure how we got here."

Finley waved a pipe toward the desk behind them. "You crawled out of my roll top. That's a first, even for this place. The real question is, how did you get *in* there?"

"When we climbed in, the desk was in my uncle's garage. We were hiding from him."

"Hiding from your uncle? Why?"

"He was trying to kill us." Joel lowered his gaze. "He's an

angry drunk and I'm usually his punching bag, but this time, he had a gun."

Finley took a long draw from his pipe. "Where are your parents?"

"My father walked out when I was six. My mother died of cancer about a year ago."

"I'm sorry."

"Whatever."

Finley rose from his chair and straightened the hem of his maroon turtleneck over the top of his jeans. He walked to the window and gazed out at the plateau. "So, you saved not only yourself, but your dog as well."

Joel knelt down in front of Rusty. "What else would I do? He's the only friend I have."

"What else indeed." Finley grinned. "How old are you, if I may ask?"

"Fifteen."

"Going on thirty, but I suppose that's to be expected given your circumstances." Finley glanced at the grandfather clock. "Would you like a tour of the sanctuary before it gets dark?"

"Is it safe to bring Rusty?"

"Of course. There's no aggression among our animals. Come along."

As Finley led the way toward the door, Joel pointed to several framed degrees and certificates on the wall above the desk. "You're a veterinarian."

"I was. Been retired for some time. This place is my life now… in a manner of speaking."

"I'd like to work with animals someday."

Finley merely smiled and took another draw from his pipe.

~

"Rusty, stay close." Standing at the edge of the plateau, Joel marveled as the sun began melting into the horizon, painting clouds and sea alike in a deep, rippling orange. To a city boy who had rarely seen an open space larger than an empty parking lot, it might as well have been the edge of the world. "I've never been to the ocean before, and I've never seen most of the animals here, except on TV."

During their tour, Finley had shown Joel dozens of species and habitats, from placid snow monkeys soaking in steaming hot springs to mountain goats scaling sheer rock walls hundreds of feet high. Now, as squawking seagulls circled and dropped out of sight, Joel peered down at a beach covered with marine life. Curious seals waddled and bounced between barking sea lions and whistling walruses while the fins of porpoises, sharks, and orcas occasionally surfaced beyond the shoreline.

Joel turned to Finley standing far off to his left. "How did you manage to get all these animals here?"

"Oh, I did nothing. They all end up here eventually. Some by air, others by water," Finley pointed his pipe toward the sky far off to the right, "and the rest take a more fabled route."

Joel followed his gaze to a long, shallow arch that extended from a low-hanging cloud near the horizon to a point somewhere behind a dense tree line on the far side of the plateau. *How did I miss that?* Shielding his eyes against the ocean's glare revealed that the arch was a bridge across which thousands of animals of every size and shape marched toward the sanctuary grounds. So focused was Joel on the approaching stampede, that it took him a moment longer to notice the various *colors* of the bridge. "Is that...?"

Finley nodded. "Welcome to the sanctuary at the end of the rainbow bridge."

"No, but... that means you're... that Rusty and I..." Joel closed his eyes and dropped to his knees. *That wasn't a warning shot.* "Oh, God, no." When he opened his eyes again, Rusty stood before him. With a whimper, the dog cocked his head to one side.

"I'm sorry." Joel leaned forward, resting his head against Rusty's. "I was trying to save you. I'm so sorry."

Finley lowered himself to the ground beside boy and dog. "Listen to me, Joel. You're both going to be fine."

"How can you say that?"

"Because this is paradise. You and Rusty will never again know pain, abuse, or fear—only peace and happiness. Besides, you said you wanted to work with animals. Now's your chance."

"To do what?" Joel sat back and wiped his eyes. Rusty stretched out beside him.

"Well, the wild ones need little attention from us," Finley waved his pipe toward the rainbow bridge, "but the others that cross over are house pets, like Rusty, and the purpose of the sanctuary is to reunite them with their human companions when the time comes. That's what my wife and I do as caretakers."

"Yeah, but why me? Why did I end up here?"

Finley shrugged. "You were chosen, as my wife and I were. You risked your life to save Rusty. Regardless of the outcome, I believe it was that unconditional love that brought you to us. Besides, we could use the help and there's plenty of room in the house. What do you say?"

Joel thought for a moment. "I think I'll take a cue from my canine." He patted the beagle's side. "What do you say, boy? Think you'd be happy here for eternity?"

Rusty's tail thumped the ground as he let out an eager yap.

"Yeah, me too." He looked at Finley. "One condition. Can I see my mother again?"

"As I said," the caretaker gazed beyond Joel, "reunions are our specialty."

Joel glanced over his shoulder at the woman strolling toward them across the plateau. "Finley," his voice cracked, "we got a deal."

This story first appeared online in the Bethlehem Writers Roundtable Issue #59, January 2020. It first appeared in print in *Meanwhile in the Middle of Eternity* (Firebringer Press, March 2021).

Where Halloween Never Ends

Sitting alone in her car, Sabrina Nyeri stared at the check from the sale of her dream home—the last vestige of what should have been her perfect life. During the closing, her ex-husband, Trevor, spoke to her only when necessary to co-sign documents. Once his payment was in hand, he'd walked out without a word. Just as well. There was little left for two broken people to say to each other.

Almost a year ago, their son Owen had died of cancer just shy of his eighth birthday. Their marriage crumbled six months later. Trevor had been the one to file for divorce after Sabrina's relentless depression drove him away.

During their last session, Sabrina's therapist had suggested that she reward herself after completing painful tasks by doing something fun or treating herself to a favorite snack. On her way into town earlier, she'd passed the fairgrounds where the annual Halloween Festival was in full swing with all of its 'spooky' attractions including the Field of Screams hayride, Monster Mansion, and the latest addition, the Creepy Corn Maze.

Sabrina and Trevor had taken their son to the festival every year from the time he was four. Owen's affinity for Halloween rekindled her own, which had long ago been lost to childhood trauma.

"One more time for you, Owen." She slipped the check into the glove compartment. "Besides, after today, I deserve some funnel cake."

~

Sabrina dropped the plate of crumbs and powdered sugar into the trash can before strolling along the row of carnival games, food stands, and craft vendors. Multicolored lights chasing and flashing, the aroma of pizza and pork barbecue, stuffed animals and stilt walkers all brought her back to happier times. Despite the chatter and noise, she could still hear the screams from Monster Mansion on the opposite end of the fairgrounds. Owen had loved that ride.

As the sun began its descent beyond distant hills of red and gold, Sabrina found herself at the Creepy Corn Maze. She gazed up at the fluttering black and orange banner above the entrance. 'Where Halloween Never Ends! Each Haunting Customized Just For You!'

Since there was no one else around, she strolled over to the booth manned by a twenty-something scrolling through her phone. "Excuse me. What does that mean, each haunting is customized?"

"It means that everyone's experience in the maze is unique."

"How so? Have you gone through it?"

"Yep." The girl lowered her phone. "Let's put it this way. Young people like me tend to get through the maze quicker than folks with more... life experience."

Sabrina cocked her head. "What do you mean?"

"That's the best way I can explain it without spoilers,

except to say that everyone finds their own way out. You'll just have to go through and experience it for yourself."

"Uh-huh. How much?"

"It's free, but for a donation of five bucks, you get an LED lantern as a souvenir."

What the hell. Sabrina pulled out her wallet. *I'll have something to tell my therapist next week.*

The first few minutes in the maze were uneventful. Dying sunlight cast amber rays across the quivering tips of the corn stalks, like rows of gamboling torches lighting her path. But the flames died as Sabrina weaved through a series of turns that led to a three-way intersection. There were only two possible directions forward.

Right or left? The decision was made for her when a gaggle of kids in Halloween costumes darted across her path, laughing and screaming. *Why didn't I hear you coming?* Until now, the maze had been devoid of sound save for the occasional rustling of the brown and brittle stalks. *Right it is then.* Sabrina switched on her lantern and jogged after the kids. *I hope you know where we're going.*

A few twists and turns later, a flashing red light somewhere to her left illuminated the trail ahead. *Are we finally getting to something scary?* At the edge of her lantern's glow, the last of the kids disappeared around the next bend. *Yeah, go be my early warning system.* Sabrina slowed her gait, anticipating their reactions to whatever cheesy jump scare awaited them. But there were no shrieks, no shouts. There was no sound at all.

She crept forward and emerged into a wooded area. "Oh, my God." Several yards away, a school bus lay on its side. The kids were nowhere in sight.

Sabrina ran to the bus and called out. There was no response. She raised her lantern to read the number above the single flashing tail light. "Four thirteen." That was the number of the bus that had taken her home from middle school every day, the bus driven by her grandfather after he retired.

The emergency door burst open and a young girl in a blue NASA jumpsuit tumbled out. Although her face was concealed under a disheveled mane of black hair, Sabrina recognized the costume she'd worn to her middle school's Halloween party.

"This can't be the accident that... *no*."

On the way home that day, after all but six of her classmates had been dropped off, two assholes drag racing over a narrow bridge decided to play chicken with the school bus. Her grandfather had swerved to avoid them, suffered cardiac arrest, and lost control. The bus had crashed through the guardrail and plunged over a hundred feet into the woods. Sabrina had been the only survivor.

Her younger self staggered away from the bus, dropped to her knees, and vomited.

This is like an out of body experience. "Hey," Sabrina called. "Another driver on the bridge called the police. They'll be here soon."

The girl crawled to the nearest tree and curled up in a fetal position, bleeding and sobbing as she cradled her broken forearm.

"You can't hear or see me, can you? Well, you'll be OK after three surgeries and two metal rods in your arm." Sabrina pulled up the sleeve of her jacket. "Barely left a scar." She peered at the bus. "How the hell did they recreate this?"

Each haunting customized just for you!

If that were true, then there were six broken and bloody children inside that bus. Their lifeless eyes had watched her as she crawled over them to get out. Sabrina crept toward the back door. She had to know.

"It ain't worth it, 'Brina." A tall, gaunt man approached from the tree line accompanied by a group of children. Sabrina held up her lantern. They were the kids she had followed through the maze—her classmates from the bus, she realized now—and the man was...

"Grandpa."

"Who else calls you 'Brina?"

"This can't be happening."

"Great to see you, too."

Her voice cracked as tears streamed down her face. "How can you be here?"

"It's about time you stopped beatin' yourself up." He nodded toward the bus. "Over this."

"The school counselor said it was survivor's guilt."

"Exactly, kiddo. The accident wasn't your fault. Survivin' wasn't either."

"To this day, I have nightmares about it. I still see all of you in there." Sabrina dropped to her knees and reached out for the kids. "I'm sorry I couldn't help you. I'm sorry I lived and you didn't."

One by one, the princess, the pirate, the ninja, the witch, the 80s rocker, and the Jedi Knight hugged Sabrina before climbing into the school bus. Once all were inside, the bus vanished.

"We're at peace, 'Brina." Her grandfather extended a hand and helped her to her feet. "I only want the same for you."

She threw her arms around him, savoring the aroma of the cherry pipe tobacco he'd smoked every day. "I miss you so much."

He kissed the top of her head. "Same here, kiddo, and I'm sorry about Owen."

"Thanks." Sabrina pulled back and wiped her eyes. "You would've loved him. He was wonderful."

"Of course he was. He was my great grandson."

Sabrina let out a short laugh. "And he would've enjoyed all your stories about the old days, just like I did. So, what exactly is this place?"

"It's whatever you bring with you."

"Oh, not you, too. Why can't anyone give me a straight answer?"

"Sorry, kiddo, but you'll have to go through and—"

"Experience it for myself. So I've been told. Can you at least show me a shortcut out of here?"

"Ain't no shortcuts through the maze." He waved toward a section of cornfield that hadn't been there a moment ago. "Besides, you have a few more stops ahead before you get out."

"Will you come with me?"

"Wish I could, but my time here is up. I gotta move on and so do you." He embraced her once more before stepping back and disappearing into the stalks. "Good luck, 'Brina."

AFTER FIFTEEN MINUTES of trudging along the path with only her lantern to guide her, the brisk autumn breeze carried distant, muffled voices. Was she catching up with someone who was reliving a dark memory of their own? Sabrina charged around the curve, straight out of the maze and into the backyard of her childhood home.

Light from the ascending garage door spread across the driveway. She slogged through the damp lawn to the corner of the house and craned her neck to peer inside. Between her parents' cars, her younger self—perhaps fourteen or fifteen this time—held up a hand to her older brother.

"Austin, just chill out. I'm not trying to ruin your night."

The inside door flew open and her father leaned out. "What's going on out here? We can hear you two yellin' all the way upstairs."

Austin nodded at his sister. "She doesn't want me going to the Halloween party at the firehall tonight."

Outside, Sabrina backed away from the door. *No. Not this. Please, God, I don't want to relive this night.*

"Dad, I got a bad feeling somethin's gonna happen there."

"Like what?"

"I don't know exactly. It's just... ever since that storm blew through here earlier, I've been really anxious. I don't think you should go."

"She's hated Halloween ever since the school bus accident that killed Grandpa," Austin said.

"That has nothing to do with this!"

"Quiet, both of you." Her father stepped into the garage and pointed a thumb over his shoulder. "Austin, go in and grab your costume. We're leaving soon." Once her brother disappeared into the house, he closed the door. "Look, Sabrina, I know that storm was fierce, but it's long out of the area. The danger's over."

"I know, Dad, but I can't help—"

"I'm on shift at the station tonight so I'll take Austin to the party, which will be supervised by about ten adults. Not to mention the fire crew will be right next door. You don't have to go if you don't want to. You can stay home and help your mom give out candy for trick or treat. Whatever you do, just keep the peace, OK?"

"In other words, don't upset mom. I get it." Young Sabrina marched into the house and slammed the door.

With a sigh, her father made his way to the trunk of his Jeep. "Teenagers."

Sabrina stepped out of the shadows. "Yeah, well, if you had listened to me, you would've still had two teenagers after tonight." With his back to her, he continued rummaging in the trunk. "So you can't hear or see me, but Grandpa could. This place is so damn confusing. Maybe I can get through to Mom or Austin." She sidestepped the Jeep and charged through the garage to the inside door. She pushed it open—and ran headlong into chaos. Overlapping voices muttering, shouting, crying. A parade of gurneys carrying the wounded like casualties of war. Strobe lights from four ambulances streaked across the walls. In the emergency room of St. Matthew's Hospital, Sabrina weaved her way past adults and teens in Halloween costumes, some injured, others merely shaken. Her brother and father were nowhere in sight.

That's because Austin's dead elsewhere in this hospital and Dad's crying over him. Soon, Mom will show up to scream at him for not protecting her boy. Never mind that there was nothing he could have done to prevent the fireball roof from collapsing in the middle of the party.

Sabrina found her way to the windows and pressed her forehead against the cold glass. Beyond the fleet of ambulances outside, the cornfield waited, each stalk swaying as if summoning her back. "You're really going to put me through this, aren't you? Well, screw you. I'm not going back there to see my brother's dead body again."

"You don't have to, Sabrina."

In the blink of an eye, the ambulances were gone. The waiting room was empty save for the face reflected beside hers in the darkened window. "Austin." She pulled him close, brother and sister embracing one last time in this impossible place.

"I guess Dad and I should've listened to you."

She rocked back and put a gentle hand to the side of his face. "I should've done more to stop you from going."

"You're not responsible for things outside your control. Just like the school bus accident, you couldn't have stopped what happened at the firehall. The storm earlier that day damaged the roof. We were in the wrong place at the wrong time, that's all."

"That's all." Sabrina slumped against the window. "I keep moving forward while people I love die around me. I feel like the Grim Reaper."

"Mom and Dad are still with you."

"We haven't talked in a long time. They were there for Owen when he was sick, but didn't show me one damn ounce of support through my divorce."

"I know how stubborn and judgmental they can be. And I'm sorry for everything you've been through. You deserve better."

"Mom said if she and Dad could stay together after you died, then Trevor and I should've done the same after losing Owen. Maybe she was right. I don't know. To be honest, my whole world's turned to shit since he died. I was supposed to take the money from the sale of the house and start over, but..." The cornfield was closer to the building now—expanding, advancing, growing impatient. "I'm as lost in this maze as I am in my life. It's as if this place is trying to break me."

"The maze isn't evil, Sabrina." He wiped the tears from her face. "It doesn't want to break you or torture you or kill you. Consider it a place of reckoning, where everyone settles up with their past. It forces you to face what haunts you so you can come to peace with it. That's the magic of the maze. And what's Halloween without a little magic?"

Each haunting customized just for you!

"You were right when you said I hated Halloween after the school bus accident. Despite that, I tried to make it fun for Owen. He loved it and I didn't want to deny him—and then he was gone." Sabrina pushed away from the window. "So where the hell do I go from here?"

"The maze also knows what you want most." Austin

slipped his arm around her shoulders and escorted her outside where the wall of cornstalks parted to reveal a new path. "Follow it just a little farther, Sabrina, and it'll take you home."

~

FROM THE EDGE of the cornfield, she waved to her brother until he and the hospital faded into the night. She switched on her lantern and trudged along the winding path for another ten minutes or so until a dim white glow pulsed in the sky ahead. Sabrina jumped up and down a few times until she could see the rotating lights of the Ferris wheel above the tips of the stalks. *Almost there. Just keep moving toward the light.*

She bolted ahead, ensuring that every turn brought her closer to the exit. It wasn't long before the rhythm of live music and roar of applause were mere steps away. *The bandstand. Yes! It's right next to the maze.*

Halfway down the path, the hand-painted exit sign pointed to the right. She rushed toward it until she noticed the little boy standing in the shadows at the far end of the path just before the next turn that led back into the maze.

"I'm ready for trick or treat, Mom."

Sabrina started toward him, stopping at the exit sign. Less than twenty feet away, the booth where she had purchased her lantern was occupied by a new volunteer. Families and young couples strolled past, eating, chatting, laughing. The band started their next song.

"I said I'm ready for trick or treat. Are you coming?"

The maze knows what you want most. Follow it just a little farther, Sabrina, and it'll take you home.

She continued forward along the path until the boy's features were revealed in the stark glow of her lantern.

He spun, red cape swirling around him. “Thanks for the cool costume.”

“Owen.” Sabrina lowered herself to one knee and pulled him close. “You always were my little Superman.”

“Why are you crying?”

“Because it’s... it’s wonderful to see you.”

“But you see me every day.”

“Yes, I do.” Sabrina wiped her face. “Every day.”

“Are you ready to take me trick or treating?”

“Trick or treat? Sure, I guess I’m ready.”

“Come on.” Clutching her hand, Owen led her around the corner and onto a suburban street bustling with children in costumes. “I wish Halloween would never end.”

Sabrina glanced over her shoulder. The corn maze was gone. In its place stood the house she’d sold earlier in the day. Her dream home. “Yeah. Me, too.”

THIS STORY first appeared in Black Cat Weekly #216 (Wildside Press, October 2025).

There's a Certain Magic About This Place

Why was this place so familiar? Keri Lange had never been to Ligonier, Pennsylvania before yesterday afternoon and yet, she'd been haunted by a relentless feeling of déjà vu from the moment she arrived.

Keri paused along the trail as the first rays of the rising sun highlighted the resplendent autumn colors of the surrounding trees. Her gaze swept across the expansive field of green and brown grass bordered by a narrow, meandering creek on its north side and Macartney Lane to the south. Beyond the far edge of the field, opposite the trail on which she stood, sparse traffic flowed along Route 711.

Macartney Lane was the only road in or out of the Ligonier Camp and Conference Center, her home for the next four days. Nestled in the Laurel Highlands region of the Allegheny Mountains, the five-hundred-acre property was a summer camp for kids, but a group of writers from the nearby Pittsburgh area rented the place for a weeklong retreat every October. It was the perfect location to break away from life and get into the creative flow all while nestled in the bosom of Mother Nature. Although Keri lived several hours away, she'd connected with a few of the local writers at a recent conference and was invited to join them.

One of the first things she'd learned during orientation was that many of the writers took sunrise walks to clear their minds before immersing themselves in their work. For Keri, it was a welcome change of pace from the stress of urban life.

To her right, a path of dirt and stone wound its way up to the distant crest of a hill. Keri was tempted to make the climb but she'd been walking for over an hour and her stomach was grumbling. She made a mental note to tackle the hill tomorrow and continued along the trail until she arrived at Macartney Lane. There, a large wooden sign served as an information marker about the Wilpen train crash that had occurred a few hundred yards away on July 5, 1912. The trail on which she'd been walking had once been a branch of the Ligonier Valley Railroad and the site of a horrific collision between a passenger train headed north to Wilpen and a freight train carrying coal on its way south to Ligonier on the same track. Twenty-seven people were killed and twenty-six injured.

Overcome with inexplicable dread, Keri backed away from the sign and darted up the road to the lodge as if some calamity might befall her if she lingered too long on the trail.

THE REST of the morning passed without further apprehension. Seated against a window in the first-floor lounge, Keri had become so absorbed in her writing that it was almost lunch time when she glanced up from her laptop. Contemplating the next scene in her story, she stared out at the grassy hill behind the lodge and the tree line beyond—until the blast of a train whistle jolted her. She glanced around the room at the other writers, but none of them appeared disturbed by the sound, even when it happened again.

Maybe they're used to it, since most of them have been here before. But I thought the railroad was long gone. A brief Google search confirmed that it had been decommissioned in 1952. *So where did that whistle come from? It was so close!*

Keri was tempted to dash outside and track it down until retreat organizers Carla Poole and Barry Sharpe gathered with two other writers and started toward the back door.

Carla leaned toward her as she sauntered past. "Comin' to lunch?"

Keri closed the lid on her laptop and joined them as they made their way out of the lodge and up the hill to the cafeteria building. "Did any of you hear a train whistle a few minutes ago?"

"Train whistle?" Carla shook her head. "Nope. I don't think any trains run through this area."

"The lodge offices are just down the hall from us," Barry said. "Maybe one of their computers makes a train whistle sound when an email comes in or an alert pops up."

Keri shrugged. "I guess that makes sense."

"How's your writing going?" Carla asked.

"I'm one scene away from finishing this reincarnation story I started last week. It's about a woman who travels back to her previous life in order to rescue someone and change history. I was struggling with the ending, but this morning's walk helped clear my mind."

"That's what this retreat's all about," Barry said. "There's a certain magic about this place. The guided meditations we do after lunch should help you stay in the creative flow and knock out that last scene."

"That's the plan. Once the story's done, I can give it a quick edit and send it to my critique partners."

"You still have three days left," Carla said. "Got anything else?"

"I could work on a novella I put aside a few months ago,"

Keri replied. "Unless I get an idea for something new. I see there was a train crash here back in 1912. Maybe I'll research that. Might get a story idea out of it."

"That happened two years before this camp was founded." Barry opened the door and motioned for the women to precede him into the cafeteria. "We've had enough strange occurrences here over the years to wonder if this place is haunted by some of the people who died in that crash."

Keri recalled her unsettling experience on the trail. "That... would explain a lot."

~

"CLOSE YOUR EYES, plant your feet firmly on the ground with your palms on your thighs."

Backed by soft music, the soothing voice of the instructor drifted from the Bluetooth speaker in the middle of the room as the guided meditation began. "Start by breathing in and out slowly three times..."

"It's so humid out here, I can hardly breathe at all."

What? Keri opened her eyes and winced at the blinding afternoon sun. Trickles of sweat ran down the sides of her face. She adjusted her glasses and stepped back under the shade of the train station roof. *Glasses? Train station*? *Where the hell—?*

At least fifty people crowded the platform, all of them dressed in clothing from the early twentieth century. At two quick tugs on her skirt, Keri peered down at a girl no more than six years old, dirty blonde hair matted to her forehead.

"Ms. Matthews, when's the train coming?"

"What? Oh, uh...," Keri stammered. "I'm sure it'll be here soon, Sarah." *How did I know her name?*

"Four minutes to be exact."

The plump middle-aged man beside her held up his pocket watch and smiled. "It's almost never late, Esther. You should know that better than anyone. You work for the railroad." A white suit jacket was slung over his opposite shoulder. It matched his pleated white pants and waistcoat. The sleeves of his light blue shirt were rolled up, armpits drenched in sweat.

How did people survive summers in these outfits? "Right... of course. Four minutes." Keri put a gentle hand on the girl's shoulder and leaned down. "Four minutes, sweetie."

"Billie and Bernadetta won't stop fighting and I think Elizabeth is gonna faint from the heat."

Keri looked past her at the four girls sitting on the concrete floor in the middle of the platform. *Good God, are all of them mine?*

"Mighty nice of you to take the kids out while their parents are workin'" the man said.

Sarah beamed. "We're gonna pick wildflowers up at Mill Creek."

"Is that right? Well, that sounds like a pleasant way to spend a summer afternoon."

"I better check on the others." Holding Sarah's hand, Keri scurried over to the gaggle of squirming youngsters. Towering over them, a man in soot-stained overalls folded back the front page of a newspaper to read the bottom half. Keri caught sight of the date.

July 5, 1912.

Wait, wasn't that when—

She whirled at the screech of a train whistle followed by the slow trundling of wheels along the track. Four of the kids cheered and dashed toward the edge of the platform. The oldest one, Elizabeth, lagged behind and gulped water from a metal canteen.

"Be careful!" Keri darted ahead of them and spread her arms. "Don't want you falling off."

A young woman in a white linen dress scurried over to

help. "You're gonna have your hands full today, Esther. Good luck in this heat."

Two of the girls waved at her. "Hi, Besse!"

"Hi, Elizabeth. Hi, Sarah. You all listen to Ms. Matthews today, okay? Don't give her any guff."

Keri had never seen a train travel backwards before, but this one did. It consisted of a single passenger car being pushed by a steam engine. Once it came to a stop, the engineer hopped out and yelled, "All aboard!"

She ushered the children ahead of her into the passenger car. The six of them took up two rows of seats along the left side. By the time everyone filed in, every seat was full and the stench of body odor was nauseating. Keri clenched her jaw against the urge to retch and was never more grateful for a window seat.

A familiar, soft voice rose above the din. "Now cross your arms and grip each shoulder with the opposite hand."

Keri turned away from the open window. The passengers were gone, as was the interior of the train. She was back in the lodge, surrounded once again by her fellow writers.

"Hold yourself in a tight, warm embrace," the instructor continued. "Breathe in... and breathe out..."

A few minutes later, the guided meditation concluded and Keri was at her laptop searching on the name Esther Matthews. She found a few websites that referenced the Ligonier Valley Railroad and the Wilpen train wreck. There was little information on Esther. She had been a nurse employed by the railroad and on July 5, 1912, she was to escort five children to Wilpen to pick wildflowers along Mill Creek. None of them survived the crash.

So why did I have a vision as if I were Esther? Maybe this land is haunted like Barry said and she's trying to get a message to me. Or could I have been Esther in a past life? I have three more days to figure this out and something tells me she isn't done with me yet.

~

The following morning saw the camp shrouded in a dense fog. Lamp posts and the exterior lights of buildings were little more than faint orbs surrounded by hazy auras of pale green and yellow. In the still air, the trees stood as menacing silhouettes against a gray sky. Distant mountains, majestic in the light of day, were all but invisible.

From the window of Keri's room, Macartney Lane vanished about twenty feet down the hill. *Maybe I'll try the trail behind the lodge this time.* She laced up her hiking boots, slipped on her jacket, and grabbed the LED lantern that had been a welcome gift from Carla. She'd bought one for every attendee, along with a coffee mug, pencils, pens, and other goodies.

Downstairs, Keri found the lounge devoid of life. From her table by the window, she expected to see some activity outside—shadowy forms, other lanterns bobbing in the fog—but there was no movement at all. It was only a few minutes after seven. Was she the last one to wake up? Was everyone else already well into the woods or down by the creek?

Keri crept outside through the back door, careful not to let it slam behind her lest she disturb the unnatural peace. Even the birds were quiet, if there were any birds around. Keri pressed her back to the door, overwhelmed by the same trepidation she'd felt the day before while walking along the trail at the bottom of the hill. *I'm not going down there this time. I'm going up into the woods and—*

The whistle of a steam engine ruptured the silence.

Keri tensed and closed her eyes.

As if beckoning her, the whistle screeched again.

Damn it. She marched around to the front of the lodge and stood at the top of the hill. The whistle howled twice more. *I heard you the first time.* Switching on the lantern, Keri Lange drew herself to her full height and charged into the mist.

The further she advanced, the warmer and more humid the air became until it was stifling. Her shirt clung to her skin. Clenching the wire handle of the lantern in her teeth, she slipped out of her jacket and tied it around her waist. Was the fog thinning up ahead? After a few more steps, she emerged into clear daylight and blistering heat. Beneath her feet, what was once the blacktop of Macartney Lane was nothing but grass and weeds. That was nowhere near as surprising as the railroad track that crossed her path no more than three yards ahead.

In the time it took Keri to process this, the passenger car from her vision was rolling into view around the curve to her right while the steam engine hauling at least three cars loaded with coal was blasting its whistle on a collision course from the left.

"Shit!" Keri whirled and plunged back into the fog. She darted up the hill, expecting the screech of brakes followed by the crack and thunder of the steam engine as it demolished the wooden passenger car. Keri imagined the screams and wails of the fifty people on board, the cries of the five children in Esther's care. She imagined these things, but heard none of them. The air cooled, the whistle faded. Halfway up the hill, Keri turned and raised her lantern but the fog was impenetrable.

By the time she trudged back up to the lodge, most of the writers had returned from their morning walks. A few were partaking of the continental breakfast set out by the staff in the kitchen adjacent to the lounge.

Carla glanced up as she scooped scrambled eggs onto her

plate. "Good morning. We were worried you got lost in the fog."

"No, just took a short trip down the hill."

Barry sauntered over and poured himself a cup of coffee. "Did you run? You're drenched in sweat."

Keri started up the steps to her room. "Let's just say I was trying to catch a train."

~

"Close your eyes, plant your feet firmly on the ground with your palms on your thighs."

Seated on a couch between two other writers, it took every ounce of patience to stop herself from fidgeting as another guided meditation began. Keri closed her eyes and focused on the dulcet voice of the instructor. *Come on, get me back on that train.*

"Start by breathing in and out slowly three times..."

"I think Ms. Matthews is asleep."

Keri opened her eyes to find three-year-old Mary on her lap while Elizabeth and Sarah Rhody stared at her from the seat in front of hers.

"No, just resting my eyes. Where are we?"

"On the train," replied Bernadetta beside her.

Keri pulled Mary close and twisted in her seat. "Where's Billie?"

"Here." The girl popped up between the Rhody sisters.

A moment later, the tall man in grimy overalls made his way up the aisle, a wooden toolbox slung over his shoulder. He disappeared into a small room at the front of the car for a moment before returning empty handed.

"We're comin' up to the curve," another passenger said. "Gettin' close to Wilpen."

The curve... Shit!

"Children, I need you to go into that little room."

Elizabeth followed her gaze. "The luggage compartment?"

"Why?" Billie asked.

"I'll explain later." Keri nudged Bernadetta into the aisle. A train whistle shrieked in the distance. "Just go now!"

Billie and the Rhody sisters bounded out of their seats and rushed up the center aisle.

"Esther, where are you takin' those kids?"

Keri ignored the question as Mary began to cry. She clutched the toddler close to her chest and hurried past several rows of seats.

"Was that whistle from our engine?" someone asked.

"Naw. Too far away," another replied. "Must be another train behind us."

In the doorway of the luggage compartment, Keri whirled. "Not behind us. In front of us! There's a freight train—"

The squeal of brakes swept her warning away.

A second later, the world exploded.

KERI FLEXED her hand in the grass, felt the soft blades between her fingers. She opened her eyes and winced against the sunlight. Somewhere nearby, a woman wailed. Overlapping voices shouted names. Chunks of coal and broken wood surrounded her. Several feet away, two bodies lay twisted and mangled. The closest one was familiar, although his face was turned away. Light blue shirt. White waistcoat and pleated pants. Once pristine, now stained black and crimson. The middle-aged man from the train platform.

Keri cocked her head and gaped at the steam engine that had toppled onto its side across the track. She slid her left forearm onto her stomach. Blood seeped from a series of gashes. An attempt to lift her right arm resulted in a flare of pain from shoulder to elbow.

"Mary..." She could muster little more than a hoarse whisper. After several deep breaths, she cried out again for the girl. When there was no response, she called each child's name.

"Ms. Matthews!"

Three bruised and battered faces appeared above her.

Keri cried out as she reached up with her left hand and brushed Billie's chin. "Thank God."

Bernadetta knelt beside her with a stunned Mary tucked in her arms. Both girls were covered in soot.

"Sarah," Keri whispered. "Elizabeth."

Bernadetta shook her head as tears streaked her face. Mary squirmed out of her arms and huddled against Keri.

"No..." Keri sobbed. "I'm sorry. I'm so sorry. I tried to save all of you."

"But you saved *us*." Billie lay down beside her. "Thank you."

~

"BREATHE IN... and breathe out. Breathe in... and breathe out."

Keri didn't wait for the meditation to end before slipping out of her seat and bolting up the steps to her room. With a few taps on her phone, she looked up the Wilpen train crash on two different websites. Whereas before there had been twenty-seven dead and twenty-six injured, those stats were now twenty-three and thirty, respectively. Of the children, only the Rhody sisters had perished. Esther Matthews was hailed a hero by the surviving passengers and the railroad's general manager.

That was of little comfort to Keri. She sat at the edge of the bed, lowered her head into her hands, and wept.

FOREGOING a morning walk on the final day of the retreat, Keri showered, dressed, and plodded downstairs for breakfast. Most of the writers were either eating in the lounge while working on their projects or still out and about. She plucked a corn muffin from the basket and set it on her plate. While the rest of the food looked appealing, yesterday's experience had left her with little appetite. She poured a cup of coffee for herself and decided to sit alone on the front porch and take in the brisk autumn air. As she picked at her muffin, the front door of the lodge squeaked open.

"Good morning." Coffee in hand, Carla stopped at the table. "May I join you?"

"Of course."

"So did you find a new story to write?"

Keri returned a wan smile. "You could say the story found me."

"I'm not surprised. Every writer who comes here experiences a creative boost. I know I always do. Think you'll be back next year?"

"Absolutely. Like Barry said, there's a certain magic about this place. In just a few days, I've become attached to it." Keri fixed her gaze on the field at the bottom of the hill. "But before I leave, I think I'll pick some wildflowers down by the creek."

THIS STORY first appeared in *Retreat* (Year of the Book Press, May 2025).

Before She's Gone Forever

It took the entire morning, but police divers found Eun-ji's body in the bay—exactly where I said it would be. I wasn't entirely forthcoming with them, of course. I didn't tell them about the pictures. I simply informed them that Eun-ji had talked about exploring the peaks of Geoje Island to find a good spot for cliff jumping. Fearless and heavily influenced by western culture, Eun-ji was what the Americans call an "adrenaline junkie." Hence the reason she had volunteered for civilian military training in the city of Gimpo last month. That's where we met.

As a photographer for the Korea Herald, I had been assigned to shoot the weeklong boot camp. My mandatory two years in the Army had just ended six months prior, so I was still able to keep up with the grueling regimen these college students faced. Nothing extraordinary had occurred during the assignment—other than meeting Eun-ji. Day or night, my camera loved her more than any of the others...

~

THE AIR inside the converted hangar retained the chill of an early spring morning as the first squad prepared for their afternoon run. The enormous arched building had been repurposed as a combination barracks, garage, and storage facility, all for the purposes of operating the training camp organized by a group of retired marines. Clutching my camera to my chest, I weaved around bodies and equipment, scanning the area for Eun-ji. She'd caught my attention earlier in the day with her flawless performance through the obstacle course. Since then, the trainees had changed from helmets to black berets, making it easier to recognize faces. Finally, I spotted her near the open hangar door, boring through an old truck tire with a power drill.

I took a few shots as she handed off the tool to another trainee and pushed an eye bolt through the hole in the rubber. After securing it with nut and washer, she attached both ends of a chain to the eye with a carabiner and looped a tow strap through the chain. A moment later, the strap was clipped to a harness around Eun-ji's narrow waist and shoulders. Just as they had for the past two mornings, the trainees would run the width of the field while pulling tires tethered to their upper bodies—a standard military exercise.

"Impressive." I took another shot as she drew herself to her full height. "You made quick work of that, just like the obstacle course."

"It's the third time this week I've had to rig one of these." She barely glanced at me before returning her attention to her task. "What's your name again?"

"Joon-hyuk."

"Is there a reason you keep following me, Joon-hyuk?"

"You're incred—" My words were smothered by the whine and roar of power drills all around us. Eun-ji tilted her head and twisted her lips into a lopsided smirk until the clamor ceased, allowing me to finish. "You're incredibly photogenic."

She lowered her demure gaze and pretended to adjust her harness. "Well, thank you, but I need to join my squad now... or didn't you notice the other dozen people around us?" She trudged out of the hangar toward the field of dry sandy scrub across the tarmac.

"Of course, I did. I'm here to photograph as many of you as possible." I waited until both she and her burden were out of the hangar's shadow before taking a few more shots. "Need me to carry that tire for you?"

"I can handle it, funny boy. I like pushing myself. That's why I'm here."

We walked the rest of the way in silence and arrived just as the sergeant ordered everyone to fall in.

"Good luck." I stopped at the edge of the field and raised my camera. "See you later?"

"Maybe."

I took several shots as she lined up with her squad. A minute later, the sergeant fired into the air and the trainees started off, legs pumping. Some staggered at first, dragging their tires like boat anchors, but not Eun-ji. Despite a slow start, she maintained her footing and bolted toward the trees, tire gouging up a continuous cloud of dust in her wake.

I SHARED dinner with over two dozen inquisitive university students—entertaining them with stories from my army days so they knew what to expect when their time came—but Eun-ji sat with a group of young women at the opposite end of the hall. I didn't have the chance to chat her up again until after midnight when two bellowing sergeants roused exhausted trainees out of their bunks and back to the field. They were each handed a K2 rifle with laser sight and divided into groups of five while the sergeants explained the concept of the drill.

Just inside the tree line, targets had been hung. When they flashed a green light, the trainees opened fire. A red light signaled for them to stop.

The first group lined up as ordered and the sergeants allowed me one minute to take pictures. Fortunately, Eun-ji was in the first group, her face still smudged with green and black camouflage paint from the previous day's exercises.

"You again," she groaned.

"To be fair, I was out here before any of you. I knew this was coming, so I stayed around to get pictures."

"Thanks for the warning."

I lifted my camera to take a close up, but when I peered through the viewfinder, Eun-ji was gone. She had dropped to one knee, turned her cap backward, and leveled her rifle toward the tree line, its stock braced against her shoulder. I moved beside her and crouched down just as a pair of sergeants approached. I didn't have much time. "Come on. Just one close up."

Without a word, Eun-ji glanced at me, her expression conveying a trace of annoyance. I snapped the picture and moved away just as one of the sergeants came to a halt behind Eun-ji. Ignoring me, he ordered the trainees to take aim. In the woods, green lights flashed, and rubber bullets flew.

I LEFT Gimpo on the last train of the night and returned to my office in Seoul the next morning where I uploaded the photos to my workstation. As I reviewed each one, cropping and adjusting as necessary, Eun-ji was far from my thoughts—until I found myself staring at that last close-up shot. I'd taken over a dozen photos of Eun-ji in action throughout the day, but there was something different about that one. Perhaps it was the mere stillness of the moment that allowed my lens to capture the slightest hint of anxiety—*or was it fear?*—that had been otherwise concealed by her bravado. Then again, being roused from sleep at midnight by a shrieking whistle and two barking drill sergeants would rattle anyone's nerves.

"Nice shot."

I swiveled my chair to find my smirking editor standing in the doorway.

"Then again, you always did have an eye for the attractive ones," he continued. "I assume you managed to take at least a few shots of the other trainees?"

"Scores of them." I pressed the arrow keys to start scrolling through the Gimpo photos.

"Good. Pick the best dozen or so and send them to me for review. We'll get them on the website by the end of the day. When are you going to the K Museum?"

"They open at ten. I plan to go there first, get shots of the new Jega Pop Culture exhibit, then send you the best of those and Gimpo."

With a nod, he continued down the corridor.

After counting to seven, I rolled my chair to the door and leaned out just as he stepped into his office. *Like clockwork.*

I leapt to my feet, shoved my chair under my desk, and checked the bus schedule online. From Yonhap Station, it was 43 minutes to The K Museum of Contemporary Art. Today, though, it would take me over two hours via train and bus—by way of Gimpo. Knowing my editor, he wouldn't notice my extended absence as long as I submitted my work on time.

But first, I had to see Eun-ji again, before she was gone forever.

It was the final day of civilian boot camp and fortunately, the guards at the gate were the same ones from the day before.

They recognized me immediately and, after I passed a security check, allowed me back onto the grounds under the pretense that I'd misplaced an expensive zoom lens somewhere on the property.

After thanking them, I rushed to the women's barracks and found three of the trainees packing their bags. I knocked on the open door. "Excuse me. I'm sorry to intrude, but can you tell me where I might find Eun-ji?"

The woman closest to me zipped her bag and slung it over her shoulder. "You just missed her. She left a few minutes ago. You're the photographer that was here yesterday."

"Yes."

"You looking for a date with her?"

At that, the other two laughed.

"Did she say where she was going?"

"Oh, babo is smitten," another woman said. "Everyone noticed how you were hanging around her."

"I don't know where she lives," the first woman brushed past me. "But she mentioned a hiking trip to Geoje Island in a week or two. She wanted to go cliff jumping later in the spring. Maybe you can find her on Kakao. Good luck, lover boy."

BACK IN THE office later that afternoon, I sent all of the pictures to my editor then logged into Kakao, the social media site, and found Eun-ji after a few minutes. I sent her a message. When days passed with no response, I sent another. That too went unanswered. I gave up for fear of making a nuisance of myself.

At home a few weeks later, I decided to review all the shots I'd taken over the past several assignments. I'd saved copies of them to my laptop and it was time to clean them out since I had backed them up to my cloud storage.

When I opened the close-up of Eun-ji, taken that night in the field, something had changed. Her lips were parted slightly as if she'd been speaking when I took the shot—but that wasn't how I remembered it. I logged into my cloud storage and opened the photo from there. As expected, Eun-ji's mouth was closed. Confused, I saved the second image with a different filename then fell asleep staring at both photos on my screen.

I woke up to complete darkness just after three in the morning. It took me a moment to remember that I was still sitting in my living room. With a yawn, I reached over and turned on the table lamp, nearly knocking my laptop to the floor in the process. I caught it before it slid off my lap and tapped the space bar to wake the screen. *Were the two different shots of Eun-ji merely a dream?* After logging back in, I found myself staring at Eun-ji once more—and this time, not only was her brow furrowed, but her mouth wide open as if silently shouting at me.

"What the hell is going on here?" I tore my gaze away from the screen, anticipating a response from someone lurking in the shadows. *This has to be a joke.* Yet the image didn't appear to be Photoshopped. I felt uncomfortable sitting in the dark so I leapt from my seat and turned on the floor lamp and the television. Finally, I returned to my laptop and saved this third image.

After a quick shower and breakfast, I resolved to determine what was happening with these photos of Eun-ji. What had been one photo was now three. I logged back onto my laptop and immediately regretted it. Eun-ji's expression had changed from anger to distress. Her lips were now pursed, and her eyes glistened with fear. By the time I started breathing again, I reached out with a trembling hand and clicked the Save button yet again.

I distracted myself with an online game until dawn. Part of me wanted to crawl into bed, but I had to figure out where these pictures were coming from. It occurred to me then to disable my Wi-Fi connection in case someone was remotely connected and copying these images to my laptop. I wondered if Eun-ji herself had hacked me and was playing a prank. I couldn't wait around to find out. I had to catch the train to work.

AFTER PRESSING the button for the elevator, I leaned against the wall for a catnap—which lasted all of eight seconds before the chime forced my reluctant eyes open. I pushed away from the wall just as the doors parted to reveal my neighbor, Seul-ki, bundled up as if she'd just returned from an expedition to the Arctic Circle. Although it was a time of year that brought mild afternoons, early morning hours were often still frigid, especially to a petite little kitten like Seul-ki. She lowered the scarf from her face and flashed a smile that made my eyes glad the rest of me had been too exhausted to take the stairs. Seul-ki was around the same age as Eun-ji and even more photogenic. In Seul-ki's case, though, my camera wasn't the only one who loved her.

Stepping out of the elevator, she pulled off her gloves and signed a greeting. "Hi, Joon-hyuk. You look exhausted. Rough night?"

Seul-ki had been born deaf but was adept at reading lips. Despite that, I had asked her to start teaching me sign language last week. Any excuse to spend more time with her. I replied as well as my limited vocabulary allowed but spoke slowly at the same time. "Bizarre night. I think my computer's haunted, or maybe my camera, or maybe it's me..."

"I don't understand." Seul-ki motioned.

"It would take too long to explain."

The elevator doors began to close. I stepped over the threshold and held them open as Seul-ki nodded toward her apartment at the end of the hall. "How about dinner at my place tonight? You can tell me all about it."

"I'd love it. See you then."

I resumed my catnap on the way down.

I KNEW BETTER than to contact Gimpo. The military would never release any personal information. Instead, I decided to post my original close up of Eun-ji on Kakao in the hope that someone could put me in touch with her. A few people responded but claimed that they had not seen or spoken to Eun-ji in weeks.

I heard the approaching footsteps even before the knock on my office door. I minimized the image of Eun-ji just as my editor barged into my office. "You look like hell. Are you sick?"

"Didn't sleep well."

"You in shape to go out?"

"I was in shape to come in."

"Funny. I know you're covering the railway expansion in a few hours. When you're done there, I need you to go with Hyun-woo and get some shots of the press conference for the new Hanwha corporate office opening in Incheon."

"No problem."

I waited until he was out of sight, counted to seven again, and heard his office door close before bringing up Eun-ji's picture. I wasn't surprised to see that her expression had changed yet again, but it was no less unsettling. Her wide eyes conveyed far more desperation than in any of the previous images. It's as if she were pleading for help with... what? I still had no clue, so I saved this one with a new filename in the same folder with the others. I now had seven new photos of Eun-ji that I'd never shot, each one a variation of my original. By now I was convinced that this was no prank. I took time to fully examine each image but detected no evidence of fabrication.

I've never believed in the supernatural, but I couldn't help worrying that something had happened to Eun-ji and that she was reaching out to me through these pictures. I checked the Korea Herald and Yonhap News websites for breaking reports of a missing woman, a fatal accident, or even a murder. The most dramatic stories involved two arrests for rape and one for child endangerment. Neither mentioned anyone named Eun-ji.

Unfortunately, I didn't have time to investigate further. I locked my computer and packed my camera, but I couldn't get her out of my mind. Even as I focused on the day's assignments, I was anxious to see the next picture of Eun-ji—and to solve this disturbing mystery.

AFTER DINNER at Seul-ki's apartment later that night, she asked me to explain what I'd babbled about that morning at the elevator.

I hesitated, concerned that she might think I was crazy, but I was emboldened by the fact that I had photos to prove my bizarre experiences. I opened my laptop, logged into my cloud account, and showed her the original photo I had taken of Eun-ji at Gimpo.

Seul-ki curled her mouth into a lopsided smirk. "You always find the pretty ones, don't you?"

I looked over at her to ensure that she could read my lips. "Why do you think I like spending time with you?"

At that, she blushed. "I thought it was just for the food."

"That's a bonus."

Still smirking, Seul-ki averted her gaze and nodded at the laptop. "So, what's her story?"

"That's what I'm trying to figure out. This was the only close up I took of her." I logged out of my cloud account and opened the folder on my hard drive. "See all of these files? They're photos of Eun-ji that I never took. Like this one." I opened the first variation that I had saved early that morning. "It looks similar to the original, but notice her lips are slightly parted and her eyes seem more intense. Every time I opened this folder today, new close-ups appeared out of nowhere, each one different. As of this morning, I had seven alternate images. Look..."

I closed the picture of Eun-ji—only to find that six new files had been created in the last ten seconds! Seul-ki noticed them, too. We exchanged glances before I checked my network connection. It was offline, of course. I didn't have the password to Seul-ki's Wi-Fi—which meant no one could have downloaded these files to my laptop.

"Are you going to open them?" Seul-ki asked.

My trembling hand hovered over the trackpad. "I never had more than one show up at a time."

I held my breath until all six images were lined up across my screen. I forced myself to speak slowly so that Seul-ki could read my lips. "Look at her face. It's as if she's becoming more frightened with each one."

Seul-ki leaned forward. "She is!" Her hands were almost a blur. Fortunately, she spoke as quickly as she signed. "I didn't recognize her at first with the camouflage face paint, but that's the woman that went missing yesterday."

"*What*?"

"You're in the news business. You didn't hear about it?"

"I checked online as soon as I got to the office. I didn't see anything about her."

"The story just broke. I read it on my phone. She was hiking on Geoje Island yesterday and was separated from her friends. When they couldn't find her, they called the police. She's still missing." Seul-ki stared at the screen. "Wait. Can you tile all thirteen images in consecutive order?"

"Sure, but I'll need to do it in two rows."

A minute later, I stared at the photos as Seul-ki pointed to each one in turn, her eyes welling up. "Read her lips. She's telling us where she is. *I'm drifting in the bay north of Geoje.* Joon-hyuk, this woman is dead. What's worse, she died alone. Her soul is *kaekkvi*, a wandering ghost. She's been trying to communicate with you through these pictures."

I dropped back in my chair, struggling to accept what I had feared was true. Reading Eun-ji's lips hadn't even occurred to me. *Did she lose her footing at the precipice of a cliff and plunge into the bay? Did she die instantly, or did she drown?*

A tap on my shoulder forced my gaze away from the imploring eyes of Eun-ji to the tear-streaked face of Seul-ki. She moved her hands slowly this time but still spoke aloud for emphasis. "We need to call the police. Have them search the waters north of Geoje before the tide washes her body out to the Strait. Before she's gone forever."

AT WORK TWO DAYS LATER, I caught up with the reporter covering the story and learned that Eun-ji's service was being held that morning at a *Jang rae sik jang*, a funeral home, in Daejeon. Her funeral would last the standard three days. Afterward, she would be cremated.

I considered attending, but I barely knew her, and I didn't want to risk dishonoring her memory or upsetting her family with outlandish tales of spectral photographs. They might not have believed me anyway. Many people in my generation and younger put little stock in such legends as the *kaekkvi*. I didn't either, until this. I could only hope that now, surrounded by her family, Eun-ji's soul had found peace.

Reluctantly, I opened the folder on my workstation where I had saved every variation of Eun-ji's close-ups, but where there had been thirteen, there were now only five. I checked the time stamp on the files. They had been created two nights ago, approximately an hour after her body was recovered.

The filenames each ended in a number, so I opened them in sequential order until they were tiled across my monitor. Eun-ji's soft features were unblemished by camouflage paint and her hair, no longer gathered beneath a cap, cascaded down her shoulders. Though her expression was placid, I didn't need a camera lens to reveal the obvious sorrow in her eyes, nor did I need Seul-ki's lip-reading skills to understand Eun-ji's final message.

Gomapseubnida.

Thank you.

~

This story first appeared in *Halloween Party '21* (Gravelight Press, September 2021).

Also by Phil Giunta

Available now from Raging Seas Press

Winner of Eight Book Awards

TESTING THE PRISONER

An Intense Paranormal Mystery

Daniel Masenda thought he had made peace with his dark past when he left his home for a better life fourteen years ago. As the mayor of a small, tranquil town along Virginia's Eastern Shore, Daniel has everything he ever wanted—until a series of haunting visions, coupled with the death of his estranged mother, pits him against two ghostly entities at war with one another. Each has its own agenda as they force Daniel to relive moments from his violent youth and push him to the edge of insanity. As his idyllic life begins to unravel, will he be able to decipher the message behind the hauntings before they destroy, not only him, but the soul of someone he left behind?

"...*Testing the Prisoner* is so much more brilliant than just a terrific piece of fiction. It's about the crossroads that we all eventually end up at and the decisions we make when we get there... The character development is masterfully done, with character growth of not only the protagonist, but almost every single character in the story... And it's a damned good ghost story, too. Five stars is usually my top rating, but this one gets six. I couldn't possibly recommend it more highly. You can thank me later."

—As reviewed on Hellnotes by Carson Buckingham, author of *Too Late for Prayin'* and *Noble Rot*

TESTING THE PRISONER

A PARANORMAL MYSTERY

PHIL GIUNTA

Also by Phil Giunta

Available now from Raging Seas Press

Winner of Four Book Awards

BY YOUR SIDE

A Paranormal Mystery

While haunted by visions of her brother's suicide, psychic-medium Miranda Lorensen is called to Lancaster, Pennsylvania to investigate a series of bizarre deaths—some of which are also suicides. Miranda and her team of paranormal investigators soon find themselves confronted by a vengeful spirit awakened thirty-three years after a bloody family tragedy. Miranda realizes that only she can stop the entity before it claims its final victims, but will her obsession for saving lives redeem her for the brother she failed?

"*By Your Side* is a riveting trip through paranormal mayhem... Giunta's endearing, determined characters encounter spirits both benign and fierce... "Page-turner" may be a book-review cliché, but it fits *By Your Side* from start to finish."

—Howard Weinstein, NYT Bestselling Author and longtime *Star Trek* writer

"Phil Giunta's paranormal novel, *By Your Side*, is a superb introduction to his work. Think "Ghost Hunters" ... but more realistic. The characters are thoroughly believable, the plot is expertly constructed, and the twists and turns keep you flipping pages. If you enjoy reading ghost stories, you'll enjoy this novel. Highly recommended!"

—Weldon Burge, Author of *Harvester of Sorrow*

BY YOUR SIDE

A PARANORMAL MYSTERY

About the Author

Phil Giunta's novels include the paranormal mysteries *Testing the Prisoner*, *By Your Side*, and *Like Mother, Like Daughters*. His short stories appear in two dozen anthologies of science fiction, fantasy, horror, and more.

He is a multiple award-winning author and member of the Horror Writers Association, the National Federation of Press Women, and the Greater Lehigh Valley Writers Group.

Phil is currently working on his fourth paranormal mystery novel while plotting his triumphant escape from the pressures of corporate America where he has been imprisoned for thirty years. Visit Phil's website at www.philgiunta.com.

www.ingramcontent.com/pod-product-compliance
Lightning Source LLC
LaVergne TN
LVHW090547110826
845146LV00001B/49

9798987632840